JENNIE FELTON

The Widow's Promise

HEADLINE

Copyright © 2017 Janet Tanner

The right of Jennie Felton to be identified as the Author of
the Work has been asserted by her in accordance with the
Copyright, Designs and Patents Act 1988.

First published in Great Britain in 2017 by
HEADLINE PUBLISHING GROUP

First published in paperback in 2018 by
HEADLINE PUBLISHING GROUP

1

Cataloguing in Publication Data is available from the British Library

ISBN 978 1 4722 4091 0

Typeset in Calisto by Avon DataSet Ltd, Bidford-on-Avon, Warwickshire

Printed and bound in Great Britain by Clays Ltd, St Ives plc

HEADLINE PUBLISHING GROUP
An Hachette UK Company
Carmelite House
50 Victoria Embankment
London EC4Y 0DZ

www.headline.co.uk
www.hachette.co.uk

...d to share my new Families of Fairley Terrace ...ow's Promise, with you. Whether you're new to the ...ve read the other books so far, I do hope you'll enjoy ...a's story as she rebuilds her life with her two children, Meg ...d Mattie, following the tragic loss of her beloved husband Robert. There's plenty of drama, romance and dark secrets which I hope will intrigue and entertain you!

It's truly wonderful to hear from my lovely readers, so please do visit me on Facebook www.facebook.com/JennieFeltonAuthor or follow me on Twitter @Jennie_Felton for my latest news!

Love,
Jennie x

Praise for Jennie's enthralling sagas:

'Fans of Katie Flynn will love this'
Peterborough Evening Telegraph

'Believable characters, a vivid sense of time and place,
thoroughly enjoyable' Rosie Goodwin

'Enthralling . . . Jennie Felton . . . writes her stories straight
from the heart . . . evokes time and place with compelling
authenticity, and conjures up a feisty heroine and a cast of
engaging characters' *Lancashire Evening Post*

'Has everything a family saga should have – happiness,
extreme sadness, love, death, births, etc. but above all
it was a real page turner . . . Thank you, Jennie,
for writing such a wonderful book' *Boon's Bookcase*

'If you like the style of Catherine Cookson, Josephine Cox
or Katie Flynn then you'll enjoy this'
Books With Wine And Chocolate

'A great read with a cast of believable characters'
The People's Friend

By Jennie Felton

The Families of Fairley Terrace Sagas
All The Dark Secrets
The Birthday Surprise (short story featured in the
anthology *A Mother's Joy*)
The Miner's Daughter
The Girl Below Stairs
The Widow's Promise

For my granddaughter Tabitha Jane Lazenbury.
With much love and best wishes for her first year at university.

Acknowledgements

Another year, another book, and so many people to thank!

First and foremost, my thanks go to my wonderful editor Kate Byrne, and my agent Rebecca Ritchie. It's great to have their unfailing support at every stage of the process. My thanks to you both for always being just a phone call away, and for coming to see me in Bristol last summer when I was recovering from spinal surgery. I hope you both enjoyed our lunch together as much as I did!

Behind-the-scenes at Headline, the team who have made The Families of Fairley Terrace such a success beaver away tirelessly – Katie Bradburn and the publicity team, Emily Gowers, Kate's editorial assistant, the creative team who come up with the beautiful and eye-catching covers, and the sales team who make sure the books make it to the shelves – thank you all.

I also owe a huge debt of gratitude to my daughters Terri and Suzanne, and to many friends for all their help last year when I moved from the four-bedroomed house we had lived in for thirty years to a two-bedroomed flat in lovely Leigh Woods. Sorting everything out was a massive task – I could never have done it without them!

Last but not least, thank you, my dear readers, for continuing to follow The Families of Fairley Terrace. I love to hear from you by e-mail or on my Facebook page or Twitter account, and I'm really grateful for some great reviews for the books. It's lovely to know you are enjoying sharing this journey with me, and I hope you continue to enjoy my stories.

Prologue

Bristol, 1899

The raised voices roused Robert from sleep. His mother's shrill, frightened, yet defiant. His father's belligerent, the words a little slurred. He'd been on the drink again. There had been work today at the docks; Robert had seen a couple of big cargo ships come in whilst out on his rounds as an errand boy, and when his father had not come home by the time Robert went to bed, he'd guessed Joel had stopped off at a pub while he had money in his pocket.

That would be what the row was about now. Essie, his mother, would have dared to berate him for spending the wages she desperately needed to feed the family and pay the rent; Joel would be telling her he'd do as he liked with his hard-earned cash. Robert had heard it all before, more times than he cared to remember.

The trouble was, it didn't end with angry words. More often than not, Joel would become violent. Frustrated that Essie could articulate her arguments far more fluently than he could, he would resort to the use of his fists, and sometimes his booted foot too. Next morning Essie would have a blackened eye or a cut lip, and sometimes she would wince when she moved from a pain in her ribs so sharp she could scarcely catch her breath. She would pretend everything was all right; say she'd walked into a door, or fallen down the steps leading from the street to the basement rooms that were their home. But Robert knew different, and hatred for his father would burn and bubble like acid in his gut.

Why didn't Essie have the sense to leave well alone when Joel had the drink in him, or at least know when to stop? But for all that she knew very well what challenging him would lead to, she was spirited enough to fight for the money that would put food on the table for her children and keep a roof over their heads. That was his mother's way, and Robert loved and respected her for it.

Why wasn't he big enough to be able to take on his father and stop him in his tracks? But he wasn't yet. Though by his thirteenth birthday he had grown quite tall, he was still slender in build, and no match for the big, powerful man who earned his living working on the docks. He'd tried to intervene once or twice and Joel had swatted him aside like a fly, even more maddened by what he saw as his son's daring to interfere, and Robert had realised he was only making things worse. The helplessness was galling. Until he was big enough and strong enough to take Joel on, it was best he stayed out of it.

And one day soon he would be. He'd begun going to the gym, just a few streets away, taking boxing lessons and working hard to build his muscles. He could do it, he felt sure. Though some of the men and boys there were big bruisers with shaved heads and fists the size of hams, others were not much bigger than him, except that their muscles were hard and wiry and it was clear they knew how to take care of themselves. He wasn't there yet, but it wouldn't be long before he was ready to teach his father a lesson he wouldn't forget.

For now, though, there was nothing for it but to pull the thin sheet up over his head and try to shut out the sounds of the row, which was escalating, just as he had feared. His mother's voice was shriller than ever, his father's a stentorian drunken roar, and he was glad that at least his younger sister, Sally, was not here today to hear it. He knew how it upset her when Mam and Dad fought. But Sally had gone to stay at their grandparents' farm, as she so often did during the long summer holiday. Robert had used to go too, before he left school – he loved helping out with the animals, and had even learned to milk a cow – but now he had started work as an errand boy there was no such escape, and the rows and the beatings seemed to come more often than they ever had, and be far worse.

Or perhaps it was just that he noticed it more now that he was older. When he was a little boy, they had been so much a part of the pattern of his life, he had hardly realised that every family didn't behave in this way.

Even though he knew she was frightened by the raised voices and the other, more sinister, sounds, was that how it appeared to Sally still? A normal part of family life? Or was she, at eight, beginning to understand that it wasn't normal at all? Somehow he doubted it; she still worshipped her father, and he her. There was no way Joel would lay a finger on her, thank God – or not yet, anyway. If – when – she acknowledged what was going on and took her mother's part, it might well be a different story.

A loud knocking reverberated through the basement rooms, startling Robert, though he knew what it was: Mrs McMurtry, who occupied the ground floor, banging on the floorboards with her stick. She did that when Mam and Dad were yelling at one another, though she never dared venture down to tell them to be quiet. She had more sense than to interfere.

For a brief moment there was a lull, then Robert heard Joel's voice rise to a roar that sounded for all the world like Grandpa Luke's bull when the local lads tormented him in a dangerous game of 'chicken', followed by a sickening thud that shook the wall dividing Robert's bedroom from that of his parents.

Robert sat up in bed, gripping the edge of the sheet with trembling hands balled to claws. His mother was sobbing now, awful, tearing gasps, and a scream wrenched from her throat.

'Joel . . . no . . . please!'

There were more thuds, quieter but no less sickening, and a crash that Robert imagined was a chair being overturned as his mother stumbled blindly into it. She would be on the floor now, helpless, and he turned cold as he imagined his father burying the steel toecap of his boot into her defenceless body. Though the scenario was sickeningly familiar, he knew instinctively that this was worse, much worse, than usual. This time he couldn't just lie here and wait for it to end; whether he was ready for it or not, he had to do something. If his father turned on him, then at least it might give his mother time to escape.

He thrust aside the bedclothes and swung his bare feet on to the floor. There was silence now, nothing but the ragged sound of Joel's heavy breaths drawn in through bared teeth.

Robert opened the door, and walked in on a horrific scene that would change his life for ever.

Chapter One

Meadow Farm, Dunderwick, June 1910

The motor was a Rover, sturdy and solid enough to cope with the rough track that led down to the farm from the main road, a quarter of a mile away. Robert had bought it a few months ago to replace the trap when Captain, the pony that pulled it, had become too old for the job and had to be retired. An investment, he'd said, as he pored over the books, working out a way to pay for it. Motors were the future, and it would make getting to Hillsbridge or High Compton much quicker and easier.

Old Luke Green, his grandfather, had objected at first. A waste of money, these new-fangled contraptions, he'd said, and not nearly as reliable as a horse and cart, which had served him well for fifty years and more. But in the end he'd been persuaded. Frail now, almost blind, and crippled by an accident when a bale of hay had fallen on his leg – he'd already been too old for heavy work, though he'd refused to admit it – Luke had been forced to turn the running of the farm over to Robert, and the decisions were his now.

At the time of the discussions, Carina hadn't been sure who she wanted to win the argument. Until she had married Robert,

5

she'd never been closer to a horse than summoning the courage to rub the nose of the parcel delivery man's patient old shire, but once she'd overcome her nervousness, she had enjoyed driving the trap with Captain in the shafts. The thought of getting used to another horse that might be a good deal more spirited than Captain was a daunting one, though, even more daunting than learning to drive a motor. At least a motor wouldn't have a mind of its own, she thought; once she'd got the hang of it, she'd be in control . . . wouldn't she?

And so it had proved. The lessons had been put on hold now for a week and more, as the spell of good weather had meant the hay was ready for harvesting and Robert had been out in the fields from dawn to dusk, while she was kept busy providing food and cold drinks for the casual labourers who had come in to help with the harvest. But she had really enjoyed being behind the wheel of the motor and was pleased with her progress – she was taking to it like a duck to water, Robert had said. She'd enjoyed the astonishment of the people they passed on the road, too. A motor car in itself was still enough of a rarity to attract attention, but a woman behind the wheel – quite unheard of, and possibly not quite respectable! But since the farm was two miles outside the village of Dunderwick, which boasted only a post office and general store, one public house and a tiny church, and a good five or six miles from the twin towns of Hillsbridge and High Compton, Carina needed transport of some kind. There was no way she could walk so far with two small children.

Of course, she hadn't yet been out in the motor on her own but this morning she was sorely tempted.

With extra mouths to feed, supplies were running low. Though there was still plenty of their own butter and cheese in the dairy, when she'd baked fresh bread early this morning, she had realised she was running out of flour, and the tea caddy was almost empty.

She could walk into Dunderwick, she supposed, if she got Sally, Robert's sister, in to mind the children – during harvest, Sally was only too happy to be out in the fields with the men. But enough flour to bake bread for the next few days would be heavy to carry, and already the sun was high in an almost cloudless sky; another hour and it was going to be very hot indeed. Besides which, the post office and general store in Dunderwick might not have enough stock for her to get what she needed. Much better to go into Hillsbridge, where she could be sure of buying enough supplies to last for a few days – if only she dared take the motor.

She stood looking at it, lower lip caught between her teeth. She could do it, she was sure, and there had to be a first time, so why not today? She'd never have a better excuse. She wasn't altogether sure Robert would be agreeable, but she knew he was two fields away, threshing. She could be there and back before he came in for his dinner.

She couldn't take the children with her, of course, but she knew Sally was much closer to home – Carina had seen her come in to supervise the stacking of some of the finished bales into the first of the hayricks they would build now that the barn was full.

Making up her mind, she hurried across the farmyard to where Sally was raking the remnants of a bale that had broken apart, Cymru, the farm's Welsh collie, watching her, lying with his head between his paws.

At nineteen, Sally was tall and slender, but as strong as any boy from the work she did on the farm. From behind she might almost have *been* a boy, Carina thought, her long dark hair swept up inside a man's cap, and narrow hips and long legs hidden by

7

a pair of Robert's old trousers hitched up around her slim waist with a leather belt. When Carina called to her, though, and she turned around, it was clear she was no boy, with her small straight nose, full lips that formed a natural Cupid's bow, and dark eyes fringed with long thick lashes.

Sometimes Carina envied her sister-in-law her prettiness; she felt herself almost mousy in comparison, though Robert would have told her different had he been the sort to give compliments. He had fallen in love with her soft waving hair that sometimes looked light brown and sometimes ash blond depending on the way the light fell on it, her hazel eyes and even features. Her mouth might not be as perfectly shaped as Sally's, but it smiled a lot, and he loved the dusting of freckles across the bridge of her nose and cheeks.

'Carina!' Sally dug her fork into the pile of hay and wiped that perfect face with the sleeve of her shirt – yet another of Robert's cast-offs. 'Surely it's not dinner time already!'

'Not for another hour at least,' Carina said, smiling. 'I need to go into Hillsbridge, and I've come to ask if you'd keep an eye on the children for me while I'm gone. I can't trust Grandpa Luke to do it. He can't see well enough to know what they're up to, and if they took it into their heads to run off, he'd never be able to catch them.'

'That's true enough,' Sally agreed.

At three years old, Meg was a bundle of mischief, and though Mattie, at one, had only just learned to walk, he could move like greased lightning crawling on all fours.

'But Hillsbridge, Carina! You'll be gone for ages, and I've got work to do here. Can't it wait?'

'Not if the men want bread with their cheese tomorrow,' Carina said. 'And I won't be gone that long if I take the motor.'

Sally's eyes widened.

'You're taking the motor? Does Robert know?'

'No, and you're not to tell him. I'm sure I can manage if you give me a hand getting it started.'

'He'll kill you when he finds out!' But Sally was laughing. She'd been nagging Robert to give her lessons too, but so far he'd said he didn't have the time. At least, that was his excuse. Sally suspected the chief reason was that he thought her too young and irresponsible – 'wild', he'd called her more than once, and she supposed it wasn't far from the truth. She had been only eight years old when their mother and father had died and they'd left Bristol to live with their grandparents on the farm, and she'd grown up lacking parental discipline. Though Margaret and Luke had done their best, they'd been no match for the spirited girl.

'By the time he finds out, I'll be back and no harm done,' Carina said. 'Come on, Sally, are you going to help me or not?'

Sally tossed the fork against the half-built haystack.

'I don't suppose I have any choice, do I?'

'Not really.' Carina could be every bit as determined as her sister-in-law when she put her mind to it.

On the way back to the motor, Carina made a detour into the kitchen, where she'd left the children. For a wonder, they were still playing happily together, Meg pulling Mattie around and around the big scrubbed oak table on his wooden engine, while he scooted, his plump little legs working like pistons.

When he caught sight of Carina, he stopped abruptly and the engine came to a halt.

Meg turned to him, rosy cheeks puffed with annoyance.

'You have to help, Mattie! I can't pull you if you don't help yourself.'

But Mattie had lost interest in the game.

'Ma!' It was one of the few words he could manage. 'Mama!' He held out his chubby arms, asking to be picked up.

Carina's heart twisted with love for the little boy, with his dark curls and eyes and the thick lashes that any girl would die for, a miniature version of Robert. When he lost his puppy fat, there would be no mistaking who his father was, she thought.

Meg, on the other hand, was more like her, fairer-skinned, freckled, her hair still ash blond, though it would probably darken a shade as she grew older. She had Carina's stubborn streak, too, and could be a little madam when she chose.

Now she let go of the rope attached to the front of the wooden engine, planting her hands on her hips and glaring at her brother.

'All right, don't, if you don't want to. I'll go and play with Elsie instead.' Elsie was her doll.

'Now don't start squabbling, you two,' Carina said. 'Play nicely, like you were. I have to go out for a while. Auntie Sally is going to look after you, and I want you to behave for her.'

'I'll play if he will, but he just wants you,' Meg complained, pouting. 'Can't you take him with you?'

'Not today.' The last thing Carina wanted was Mattie in the motor with her. She'd need all her concentration to drive it safely to Hillsbridge and back again. 'I'm sure Auntie Sally will find something to keep you both entertained until I get back. Just be good for her is all I ask.'

She dropped a kiss on Mattie's dark head, ignoring his outstretched arms, and ruffled Meg's curls. Then she fetched her bag and hurried out of the house.

By the time she reached the motor, Sally had cranked the engine into life and was standing, hands on trousered hips, regarding the chuntering monstrosity.

'Are you sure about this, Carina?'

For answer, Carina hitched up her skirts and climbed into the driver's seat.

'The children are in the kitchen playing. Just don't let Meg bully Mattie. You know she will if she gets the chance.'

'Don't worry, I won't let your precious son come to any harm,' Sally said, a touch acerbically. Carina favoured Mattie, and could be hard on Meg sometimes, she thought. 'Just concentrate on driving this thing and leave them to me.'

After a couple of vain attempts, Carina got the motor into the right gear, and with a jerk and a series of kangaroo hops, the motor surged forward so suddenly that Sally had to leap out of the way. Then she was off, turning on to the track that led to the main road.

Sally stood watching for a moment, Cymru at her heels, shading her eyes against the glare of the sun, then she turned and went indoors.

She only hoped Carina knew what she was doing.

By the time she reached the main road, Carina was already beginning to feel more confident. Really, there was nothing to it! The gear changes were awkward, but she loved the feel of the steering wheel beneath her hands, and the way the motor responded was exhilarating. It was so much nicer being on her own than having a watchful Robert sitting beside her, just waiting for her to make some silly mistake, which she inevitably did just because he was expecting it.

There was no other traffic on the main road apart from the horse and cart that went from farm to farm collecting the milk churns that had been left out by the roadside in readiness. She slowed as she passed it so as not to frighten the horse, and waved cheerily to the driver, who was loading a churn into the back of the cart.

He raised a hand by way of reply, but she saw the expression of astonishment on his face when he saw who was driving, and she couldn't suppress a smile of triumph.

I can't believe I'm doing this! she thought. What would Mam and Dad say if they could see me now?

But they couldn't, of course, and nor were they likely to. Daisy and George Button were far away in Pontypridd – though until Carina was nine years old, they had lived just a few miles up the road, in High Compton.

Sometimes Carina thought longingly of the rank of miners' cottages where she'd grown up with her mam and dad. She'd learned to recite the address – number 5, Fairley Terrace – as soon as she could talk. 'Just in case you get lost,' Mam had said, though why she should have thought such a thing possible, Carina didn't know. Everyone in Fairley Terrace knew everyone else, they were always in and out of one another's houses, and Carina never went further than the end of the terrace alone. Mam even walked her to school each day and collected her again in the afternoon, because by the time she was seven, and deemed grown-up enough to go with the older children in the rank, Harry, her younger brother, had started school too, and Mam didn't trust them to keep him safe.

Carina had thought it all a bit stupid, and had been rather embarrassed at always being accompanied by her mother, but now she had children of her own, she could understand it. Keeping them safe was her number one priority. Robert sometimes accused her of being overprotective, especially where Mattie was concerned, but Carina didn't care. Better safe than sorry, she thought, and the farm was a totally different kettle of fish from the friendly terrace of cottages where she'd grown up – isolated, and with dangers everywhere.

'Number five, Fairley Terrace.' She said it aloud now, though the breeze took her words and the chuntering of the engine drowned them out, and experienced a wave of familiar nostalgia for those long-gone days when in summer the sun always seemed to shine, and in winter the snow lay deep on the track and the nearby fields, where they could toboggan down the steep slopes. She thought of the children who had been her neighbours – Ted and Edie Cooper at number 1, Kitty and Lucy Day next door at number 4, the Weeks children further along the rank at number 7. The Weekses were the closest in age to her; she'd loved going with them to feed their hens and stroke the tiny balls of yellow fluff when there were chickens. The Coopers and the Days were all younger than her by several years, and most of the lads were older – scruffy Billy Donovan next door on the other side at number 6, big bruiser Charlie Oglethorpe at number 3, and his pal Frank Rogers at number 2.

What happy, carefree days they had been! And then, when she was nine years old, the terrible tragedy had occurred at Shepton Fields colliery, and nothing had ever been the same again. Frank Rogers had been killed that awful day when the hudge carrying twelve men and boys went plummeting to the depths of the earth, and three of the men from the terrace too: Paddy Donovan, Billy's father; Kitty and Lucy's daddy, John Day; and Jack Withers from the end of the rank, next door to Carina's Auntie Hester, Mam's older sister.

Mam and Dad had kept her in the dark with regard to the details, but Carina had known something terrible had happened. The drawn curtains at windows up and down the terrace, the anguished faces, the sound of weeping, the conversations in hushed voices, the instructions not to play noisy games outside all contributed to the dreadful atmosphere that had frightened Carina as much as, if not more than, if she had been told the whole truth. She crept about, round-eyed, her fertile imagination conjuring up a disaster of her own making.

She didn't see anything of the funeral at the mass grave in the parish churchyard, but she did see the mourners coming home afterwards with their black armbands. She saw Dr Blackmore's pony and trap outside the Rogers house on more than one occasion and overheard her mother saying that poor Mrs Rogers was taking Frank's death very hard, and she saw the Weeks children taking baskets of eggs to the stricken households, their faces solemn and almost as afraid as she felt.

And then, not long afterwards, she had been told they were moving away, to Wales.

'Your dad won't work here any longer,' Mam had said. 'Fairley's pits aren't fit for a dog, let alone a man.'

Carina's heart had sunk into her boots.

'But I don't want to go to Wales, Mam!' she'd cried. 'I want to stay here!'

'Well you can't,' Mam had said flatly.

'But what about school? What about my friends?'

Uncomfortable as she still was with the atmosphere of gloom and doom that hung in the air like a threatening thunderstorm, Carina was appalled by the thought of leaving all that was familiar.

'You'll soon make new friends. And there's schools in Wales, same as here,' Mam had said.

And so they had gone, their furniture and belongings loaded on to the back of a haulier's cart.

Their new home in Pontypridd was not unlike the one she'd left behind, though the terrace of miners' cottages straddled a hillside and overlooked the pithead instead of open fields, and the neighbours seemed just as ready to pop in and make them welcome. But they were strangers. The children in her class at her new school stared at her with open curiosity, and when they did speak to her, she had difficulty understanding what they said. They would get her to say something, too, just so that they could hear her Somerset burr, as foreign to them as their sing-song accent was to her. More than one night Carina cried herself to sleep in the unfamiliar room, and woke wishing it was to the crowing of the Weekses' cockerel and the comforting sound of her old neighbours knocking on one another's doors on their way to work.

To her surprise, she even missed Auntie Hester – Hester Dallimore, her mother's sister, who lived at number 9. She had used to groan inwardly when Hester called in for a cup of tea and a chat. She'd stay for ages, talking endlessly – 'gossiping', Dad called it – and Carina had always been glad when she finally left. Now she thought she'd never complain about Hester again, just as long as she could be back in Somerset.

Oddly enough, it was through Hester that she had met Robert, some nine years later.

Carina had served an apprenticeship as a seamstress and now, more often than not, worked from home, her sewing machine on the kitchen table, singing to herself as she stitched. So when Mam decided to take a week's holiday back in High Compton, staying with Hester, there had been no reason why Carina shouldn't go with her.

It had been years since Carina had been back, and she had been looking forward to revisiting her old haunts and catching up with friends. But when they arrived, though High Compton and Fairley Terrace had changed little, Carina felt strangely displaced. She no longer belonged here. Not even the sight of her old home stirred her in the way she'd expected. A different family lived there now, the door and kitchen window frame had been painted dark red rather than the brown she remembered, different curtains hung at the windows, and a stocky woman sat on the bench outside where her father had used to sit. She nodded to Carina as she passed, and her eyes followed her as she walked along the track, making her uncomfortable. The woman would know who she was – Hester would certainly have told all and sundry that her sister and niece were coming to stay – and Carina felt conspicuous somehow, and almost guilty that she knew the interior of the house as well as the woman whose home it now was.

Her old friends were no longer in evidence. The Weeks girls had left home and were in service, the Days had moved away – Annie had married again, the under manager of the glove factory in Hillsbridge, Hester told them, adding unpleasantly: 'I expect she thinks she's a cut above the rest of us now.' Even little Edie Cooper, who Carina remembered as a child pushing her dolls along the rank in a makeshift pram, had started in service at Fairley Hall. Unbelievable! Carina had thought. Where had the years gone?

On the Saturday, anxious to escape from her aunt's constant chatter, Carina had made the long walk to Hillsbridge.

'Why ever do you want to go all that way?' Hester had asked, her tone scathing. 'If you want a walk, you can come to High Compton with me.'

'It's Hillsbridge market,' Carina said. 'Dad took me once on the crossbar of his bike. It was really lively, as I remember it.'

Hester sniffed.

'A push and shove, more like. Well, suit yourself, but your mother and I won't be coming with you.'

It had been a fine day when Carina set out, and she covered the three or four miles at a brisk pace. To her delight, the market was the one thing that was just as she remembered it. The stalls selling everything from fruit and vegetables to fresh fish, broken biscuits and knick-knacks of all kinds filled the market hall and spilled on to the square outside, where the vendors who lent the market novelty value shouted their wares. There was Smasher the China Man, tossing cups and plates into the air to shatter on the paving stones in order to attract attention; there were Quilley and Rainbow, the quack doctors, promising that their pills and potions would cure all ills, Rainbow with his brightly coloured turban and bushy grey beard. And there was the dentist's wagon, and some poor soul in the chair having his teeth pulled with what looked like giant pliers in front of a cheering audience of onlookers.

So fascinated by it all was Carina that she didn't notice the dark clouds gathering until the first heavy spots of rain fell, rattling on the striped awnings and making dark splodges like spilled ink on the dusty paving stones.

She stepped back into a doorway to shelter, hoping it would be what her mother called 'just a storm and over', but the rain showed no sign of abating, falling heavier and more steadily than ever from a sky now thick with grey cloud, and water ran in a torrent in the gutters and pooled around clogged drains. She was going to be soaked before she got back to Fairley Terrace, Carina thought grimly, and she could just imagine what Aunt Hester would have to say about it. But there was nothing for it, she'd have to brave it and walk as fast as she could.

The marketplace, which had been crowded, was almost empty now but for stallholders hastily packing up their wares under awnings from which rainwater ran in steady streams and sudden cascades. Pulling her thin shawl up over her head, Carina made a dash between them. She had just reached the edge of the pavement when a pony and trap appeared, trotting briskly along the road from the farthest end of the market hall. She took a quick step backwards, but not quick enough. The wheel of the trap caught a puddle in the gutter and a wall of water was thrown up, soaking her feet and the hem of her skirt.

'Hoi!' she squealed involuntarily. 'Look where you're going, can't you?'

To her surprise, the pony and trap slowed. A young man was driving it, a young man with thick dark wavy hair, and he was looking at her with consternation.

'Sorry, love . . . Are you all right?'

'No! I'm not! I'm wet through! And I've got to get all the way back to the other side of High Compton!'

The young man huffed breath over his bottom lip.

'High Compton? You'll get soaked!'

'I already am, thanks to you!'

'Sorry . . .' His eyes, dark as his hair, were looking her up and down. 'You'd better hop up, I reckon. I'll give you a lift.'

Carina hesitated. She didn't know the young man from Adam. Really, she ought to know better than to accept a ride with him. But the thought of the long walk back to Fairley Terrace was daunting, and the young man didn't look threatening. In fact, he looked rather nice.

She made up her mind.

'All right. As long as you take me straight there.'

He raised his eyebrows, shaking his head and grinning.

'Come on then.'

Carina clambered up into the trap. There was a stack of empty crates and boxes in the back, she noticed. The young man pushed one or two aside and fished out a waterproof sheet.

'Here you are. Put this over you.'

As she tucked herself in, he flicked the reins and the pony moved off.

'High Compton, you said?' he asked.

'Yes. Fairley Terrace. Do you know it?'

He shook his head.

'I'm from Dunderwick. Well, near enough.'

'Then High Compton is well out of your way,' Carina said, frowning. Dunderwick was on the far side of Hillsbridge, in completely the opposite direction to High Compton.

'Won't take long. Captain could have won the Derby if he'd been born a racehorse. Anyway, it's the least I can do, seeing as I've soaked you through.'

Carina cast him a sidelong glance, still a little unsure of him. He'd better not get any ideas! she thought, but was surprised that she didn't find the idea altogether unappealing.

'What were you doing in Hillsbridge?' she asked to hide the disconcerting tingle she'd felt deep inside.

'It's market day, isn't it? We've got a stall. Butter, cheese, eggs, bacon . . . all stuff from the farm. My granny used to run it, but she took bad last winter. Our Sal does the serving now – that's my sister, Sally – but she's meeting a friend for a cup of tea once she's sold out, so I shall come back and fetch her later on.'

'You live on a farm?' Carina asked.

'Yeah. Me and Sal and Grampy Green. We've lived there since we lost both our parents when I was thirteen.'

'Oh!' Carina was so shocked, she was lost for words. She couldn't imagine anything more awful than being orphaned at such a young age.

'Yeah, Granny and Grampy were really good to us,' Robert went on. 'Then last winter Granny took bad. Got a cold and it went on her chest. Pneumonia, the doctor said. There was nothing he could do for her.' He shook his head. 'A proper shock, it was, her dying like that. She'd always been as strong as an ox. Never so much as a day's illness that I can remember.'

'I'm sorry,' Carina said, feeling really awkward now and not knowing how to respond to this catalogue of disaster.

'Well, that's life, isn't it?'

He sounded remarkably resigned. Perhaps that was what life on a farm did for you, Carina thought. Close to the earth, to life and death, seeing the animals give birth, watching the babies grow, then sending them off to market and somebody's dinner table . . .

They were almost home now, and the rain was at last beginning to ease.

'You can drop me here,' Carina said when they reached the track that led down to Fairley Terrace.

'Okay. Sure you'll be all right now?'

'Yes, it's just down there.' Carina had no intention of letting him take her any further and attracting the attention of Hester's neighbours, not to mention Hester herself.

She unwrapped the tarpaulin, and he took it and replaced it in the back of the trap.

'Can I see you again?' he asked suddenly and quite unexpectedly.

'Oh . . . I don't live here . . . at least, not any more, though I used to,' Carina said. 'I'm staying with my Auntie Hester.'

'Oh. Right.' He looked away from her, but not before she had seen the disappointment of rejection in those dark eyes. What he had taken to be her put-down had hurt him, and she was sorry. He had been so kind, and besides . . . Her heart did another flip.

'I'm here till next Wednesday, though,' she said.

She saw him brighten.

'I'm not doing anything tomorrow, if you're free.'

'I'll see you here then, shall I? About – what – three?'

'All right. I'm Carina, by the way.'

'And I'm Robert Talbot.'

* * *

20

That was how it had begun, their whirlwind romance. Carina thought she had fallen in love with him that first day; she was certainly in love by the time she went home again. They corresponded regularly, and he came to Wales to visit a couple of times, and she went back to stay with Aunt Hester. Just a few months after they first met, he asked her to marry him, and her parents gave them their blessing – 'I wish it didn't mean you moving so far away, but you've got a good one there,' her mother said, and her father, tears shining in his eyes, shook Robert's hand and told him to be sure he took good care of her.

Once they were engaged, Carina moved in with Aunt Hester and took a job in the big grocery store in High Compton. She hoped that when she and Robert were married, she would be able to set up as a seamstress, working from home, but for the time being she quite enjoyed serving in the shop. The wedding was in Ponty, of course, a day that swam by for Carina in a happy blur – afterwards her memories of it were like snapshots taken on a Brownie box camera, to be pored over and relished but not quite real. Afterwards she went back to Somerset with Robert and moved into the isolated farmhouse with him, his grandfather and his sister Sally. At the time, Grandpa Luke was still very much in charge, though Carina could see he was really no longer up to the hard physical work, but since the accident that had crippled him, his health had deteriorated rapidly, along with his sight, and Robert had had to take on the running of the farm. Carina's plans to take in sewing never came to fruition – she was far too busy to even think of it.

Meg had come along eleven months after the wedding, and was christened Margaret after Granny Green. When Mattie was born two years later, Carina had wondered if Robert would like him to be called after his father. She knew next to nothing about his parents and what had happened to them, and although of course she was curious, Robert always clammed up when she asked questions. 'I don't want to talk about it,' was all he would say, and as he clearly found the subject distressing, Carina didn't like to press him, or to ask Sally in case it looked as if she was going behind Robert's back.

This, though, seemed the ideal opportunity both to pay tribute to his father and to open a line of communication about him and Robert's mother, but when she suggested it to Robert, he had merely snorted in disgust, turned and walked away.

Puzzled, and a little hurt, she had mentioned it to Luke, but he too had reacted in much the same way, his mouth setting into a hard line and his failing eyes blazing hatred through the milky mist that enveloped them.

'Best not,' he said, his voice dangerously quiet.

Joel Talbot had not been the husband and father he should have been, Carina realised, and though she longed to know why both Robert and his grandfather could barely bring themselves to mention his name, she knew better than to ask. One day, perhaps, Robert would tell her about his life before he had come to live on his grandparents' farm. For the moment, the subject was clearly taboo.

Matthew was settled upon for the baby's name, though it was shortened almost immediately to Mattie. Carina smiled to herself as she thought of him now. Mattie, the apple of her eye. Her precious son . . .

As she passed the first outlying cottages, and approached the long terraces of houses interspersed with a couple of little stores that lined the road on either side, Carina came out of her reverie abruptly. Just down the hill now, and she'd be in Hillsbridge. It was time to stop daydreaming and start concentrating!

Chapter Two

The hill, like all the roads in and out of Hillsbridge, was quite steep and winding. Carina negotiated it carefully, her ankle aching from the pressure she needed to apply to the brakes in order to keep the motor from running away. She reached the bottom and huffed in relief as the road wound along the relatively flat valley floor and over the river bridge, past the church and into the town centre.

Just as she reached a narrow track that skirted the churchyard, however, disaster struck. She never even saw the wasp; the first she knew was the red-hot needle of pain shooting down her neck inside the collar of her blouse. She gasped, instinctively swatting at it, which only made things worse. Another sharp jab, this time just below her collarbone, and a third on the side of her breast. Somehow the thing had got trapped, and was stinging her again and again.

In panic, Carina tried to loosen the front of her blouse, so distracted that for a moment she could think of nothing else but the pain and the angry wasp. Then, to her horror, she saw a sporty-looking motor parked beside the narrow pavement below the churchyard wall. She braked fiercely, swinging the steering wheel hard to the right, but too late. She caught the rear offside of the parked motor with a resounding crash, and the Rover lurched to a sudden halt.

Horrified, she sat motionless for a moment, frozen with shock. The stings were burning like fire, but miraculously the wasp seemed to have escaped. When she undid the front of her blouse with hands that trembled violently, no buzzing insect flew out and there were no more sharp pinpricks of pain, but oh, dear God, the damage was done. Carina looked over her shoulder and saw the rear fender of the motor she had hit lying in the road, surrounded by other bits of debris.

An angry shout made her look up sharply.

'Hey, you!' A man had appeared on the high pavement above the road; he must have been walking along the churchyard path when the accident had happened. Now he was coming down the stone steps to road level. 'You've hit my Benz!'

He was tall, perhaps in his early thirties, broad-shouldered, moustached, dressed casually but expensively, and he walked with a pronounced limp, though of course Carina was in no state to notice any of these things. Tears of shock, panic and pain had started to her eyes.

'I'm sorry . . .'

'What in God's name were you thinking of?' His voice was cultured, with no trace of a Somerset burr.

'I was stung . . . a wasp . . .' Carina wailed.

'And what is a woman doing driving a motor?'

The incredulity and accusation in his voice roused Carina's indignation.

'I said I'm sorry,' she said defiantly.

'And so you should be!' He was in the road now, picking up the piece of fender, examining the huge dent in the rear wing. 'Just look at the damage you've caused!'

'I'll pay for it, of course.' Robert would be furious, especially since she knew money was tight; too often these days he was up late poring over the ledgers, trying to find a way to make ends meet. But what choice did she have?

The man snorted. 'You certainly will! Who are you anyway?'

'Carina Talbot. My husband is Robert Talbot. We live with his grandfather, Luke Green, at—'

'Meadow Farm.'

Carina's eyes widened.

'You know him?'

'I do,' the man said curtly. His eyes went to the Rover. 'Is your motor drivable?'

'I . . . don't know.'

He walked around to the front of the Rover. Carina climbed down on legs that threatened to give way beneath her and joined him. Amazingly, there was little damage to be seen – a smashed headlamp and a nasty dent to the front mudguard, but that was all.

'Remarkably unscathed,' the man said. 'I suggest I get you going and you go straight home before you kill someone.'

'I have to go to the shop first,' Carina said distractedly.

'Really?' His tone was sarcastic. 'I would have thought shopping would have been the last thing on your mind at the moment. What in heaven's name is your husband thinking of, allowing you to drive alone?'

'He doesn't know.' Carina instinctively defended Robert.

'Well, he's going to have to know now, isn't he? Are you able to turn round, or do you only drive in straight lines?'

The thought of driving again at all was making Carina feel sick with fright, but she stood her ground.

'I have to go to the shop before I go anywhere,' she said stubbornly. 'It's not a pleasure trip. If I don't buy some flour, there'll be no bread tomorrow.'

The man sighed, shaking his head impatiently and scowling.

'If you must you must, I suppose. I'll get your motor going and turned around while you're gone.'

Relieved, but too proud to show it, Carina retrieved her bag from the front seat and set off along the road without further argument. She was still shaking from head to foot and close to tears again, but somehow she regained control of herself as she bought flour, tea and sugar.

By the time she returned, the man had turned the Rover so that it was now facing back the way she had come, the engine chuntering, and he was once again inspecting the damage to his own motor.

Carina approached him nervously.

'Thank you.'

'Straight home, now.'

'I really am sorry,' she said humbly. 'And we will pay for the damage.'

His eyes were narrowed in a face that would have been incredibly handsome but for a long white scar running from the corner of his eye to his mouth.

'I rather think you will.'

'I . . . I don't know your name and address.'

He raised an eyebrow.

'You don't know?'

Carina shook her head.

'Melbrook,' he said. 'Dunderwick House. Your husband will know where to find me.'

He turned on his heel and walked back across the road, leaving Carina startled and even more worried about the catastrophe she had caused.

* * *

Melbrook. Dunderwick House. The words, spoken in that cultured voice, echoed and re-echoed in Carina's ears as she carefully nursed the Rover back through the winding lanes. Though she'd never had cause to so much as set eyes on him before, the name was familiar to her as it was to everyone in the locality.

Melbrook. *Lord* Melbrook.

Dunderwick House. The huge estate surrounded by low dry-stone walls that followed the main road for a mile or more, and extended most of the way down into the valley to the village that bore its name. Dunderwick House, surrounded by many acres of woodland and park. It was impossible to see the house itself from the road because of the thick mass of trees, but once Carina had taken Meg for a long walk in her perambulator along one of the tracks through the meadows that bordered the estate, and from a high point on the hillside beyond she had glimpsed the turreted roof nestling in a clearing she imagined to be gardens.

The estate extended far beyond those dry-stone walls, though. It encompassed the village of Dunderwick and almost all the surrounding farmland. Tenant farmers occupied the houses and worked the land. Once, the Greens' farm had been part of the estate, Robert had told her, but many years ago, when Grandpa Green was just a boy, his father had saved one of the Melbrook children from a maddened bull the youngsters had been tormenting, driving it off with a pitchfork and carrying the injured lad home in his arms. By way of showing his gratitude, the then Lord Melbrook had given Luke's father the freehold of his land, which had then passed to Grandpa Green and would one day be Robert's.

Carina trembled ever more violently as the enormity of what she had done ran like ice through her veins, though her face was burning with shame. Bad enough that she should have damaged Robert's precious car and someone else's into the bargain. But why, oh why, did it have to have been Lord Melbrook's? Not that they owed him anything – or hadn't, until now – but just the same . . .

And what had he been doing in Hillsbridge churchyard anyway? There was a church and graveyard in Dunderwick. Carina experienced a barb of annoyance. If he hadn't gone visiting a church outside his own domain, the accident would never have happened. She'd have been able to stop quite safely and get rid of the wretched wasp, do her shopping and come home again without any of this. As it was . . . Robert was going to be furious with her.

The stings on her neck and breast were throbbing with an intense burning pain, and quite suddenly the tears were back, stinging her eyes and aching in her throat. She gave her head a shake, blinked them away and swallowed hard. Crying would do no good. She just had to concentrate on getting the motor home in more or less one piece.

The men were still out in the fields when Carina pulled into the farmyard. She parked the Rover close to one of the outbuildings, facing inwards, hoping the damage wouldn't be immediately visible when they came in for their dinner. The last thing she wanted was for Robert to lambast her in front of them all.

Luke was sitting on the bench outside the door, snoozing in the sun with Cymru lying beside him, but even if he had been awake the old man's poor eyesight would not have allowed him to see the shattered headlight and bent wing, and for that Carina was grateful.

There was no hiding what she had done from Sally, though.

She was in the kitchen, cutting hunks of the fresh bread Carina had baked earlier in preparation for the onslaught, and the moment she saw Carina's face, she knew something was wrong.

'Oh no, what have you done?' To Carina's annoyance, she sounded almost amused.

'Well, for a start, I've been stung,' Carina retorted. 'Three or four times. A wasp got into my blouse, and it hurts like billy-o.'

She looked around, her tight-strung nerves making her anxious that some other calamity might have occurred in her absence.

'Where are the children?'

'Oh, they're fine. Mattie caught a beetle and they're looking for a matchbox to put the poor thing in . . .'

As if on cue, Meg came racing into the kitchen.

'Mummy! You're back! Did you buy something for me?'

'No, Meg, I didn't.'

Mattie had followed at a slower pace, tottering unsteadily on his plump little legs and clutching something tightly in one fist. Carina scooped him up, eager for the comfort of his chubby arms around her neck, but the pressure of his body against the places she had been stung made her gasp and wince and she quickly put him down again.

'Sorry, darling, I can't . . .'

Sally put down the bread knife.

'Let's have a look, Carina.'

Carina undid her blouse, revealing the angry red swellings, and Sally whistled softly.

'Nasty! You'd better put the blue bag on those.'

She crossed to the wooden cupboard that stood next to the big stone sink, opened it and rummaged around until she found the muslin bag containing the blue that they used for whitening the linen. She moistened it with some water and held it out to Carina.

'Here you are. This should help.'

Carina took it, rubbing it on the stings and wincing again. But she knew from past experience that the blue should take some of the heat away.

'What a day!' she muttered.

'So go on, tell me. What else went wrong?'

'Everything.' Suddenly Carina needed to confide what she'd done. 'Oh Sally, you were quite right. I should never have taken the motor. I've really done it now, and Robert is going to be furious with me.'

The words came pouring out in a garbled stream, only stopping when she realised Sally was laughing, her hand clapped over her mouth, tears of mirth streaming down her cheeks.

'It's not funny!' Carina snapped.

'No, you're quite right, it's not.' With an effort, Sally controlled herself. 'But oh, Carina – Lord Melbrook! You certainly know how to do things in style! I wish now I'd come with you! I wouldn't mind meeting him myself. I've heard he's very handsome – and a hero – and quite the most eligible bachelor in Somerset. Is he as gorgeous as they say?'

'Really, Sally, I have no idea. I was more bothered about his wretched motor than I was with him.'

A squeal from Meg interrupted her.

'Mummy! Mummy! Stop him!'

'What's wrong now?' Carina groaned.

'Mattie! He's eating the beetle!'

'Oh Mattie!' Carina dropped the blue bag on to the table and fell to her knees beside Mattie. The now empty matchbox was discarded and the little boy was indeed stuffing something into his mouth.

'Spit it out – now!' she ordered.

Mattie's dark eyes fastened on hers, full of pleading, but when she repeated the command, he did as she said, and most of the beetle dribbled down his chin. Carina forced her finger inside his mouth, running it over his tongue and gums to retrieve any remaining particles, and as she did so, she heard men's voices floating in through the open window. The casual labourers were coming in for their dinner, and Robert would be with them.

'Don't tell him, please!' she mouthed at Sally.

'He'll have to know,' she mouthed back.

'I'll tell him in my own time.'

And then the men were filling the kitchen, hungry, sweating from their exertions, and Luke was shuffling after them, leaning heavily on his stick.

As she poured beer that had been cooling in the larder into mugs and cut chunks of cheese, Carina did her best to hide her anxiety, but it gnawed away inside her all the same. Shaken and ashamed, she was dreading the moment when she would have to confess to Robert the awful thing she had done.

It was sundown before the men finished work for the day; Robert was anxious to get the harvest in before the spell of good weather broke, as it surely soon would. A thunderstorm with the accompanying downpour, and it could be days if not weeks before the hay was dry enough for baling and stacking. If there was any moisture in it, it could easily self-combust and a hayrick or even a barn could be lost to a fierce fire.

Carina had long put the children to bed in their little room under the eaves. Meg had been quite upset when Mattie's cot had been moved in – she considered the room her own, with its pink drapes and her rag dolls all neatly arranged along the shelves, and she had complained that he would disturb

31

everything. Truth to tell, Carina had been none too pleased either; she had known she would miss the baby in the cradle beside her bed. But Robert had insisted it was time: Mattie was getting to be a big boy and should begin to learn independence.

When Carina, Sally and Luke had eaten their supper of cold pork and potatoes baked in their jackets, Carina had dressed the ulcer on Luke's leg. It had started as a result of the accident that had lamed him and had never healed. Pus oozed from it constantly, and washing it in warm water, applying ointment and rebandaging it was just one of Carina's daily chores – Sally, strangely, was far too squeamish. His leg attended to, Luke had taken himself off to bed. He seemed to do little but sleep these days, but still he was ready for an early night, and it concerned Carina at times. But tonight she was quite glad of it, as her stomach was churning as she anticipated having to confess to Robert what she had done. She and Sally discussed it in low tones.

'He's going to kill me! Goodness only knows what the repairs are going to cost.'

'And Lord Melbrook will want his pound of flesh,' Sally said. Her first reaction of amusement had metamorphosed now into a serious appreciation of the consequences. 'He might be quite the charmer, as people say, and a hero to boot, but he has the reputation of being a hard man too.' A brief smile had twisted her mouth. 'Perhaps that's one of the reasons he's so attractive.'

'He wasn't very charming this morning,' Carina said ruefully. 'He was just livid. And what's this about him being a hero?'

'Oh . . . he fought in the Boer War, I understand, and won some kind of decoration,' Sally said.

'He did have a limp, and a scar,' Carina remembered. 'But how come you know so much about him?'

Sally shrugged. 'Oh – just local gossip.'

A snuffling cry followed by a loud, insistent wail coming from upstairs claimed Carina's attention. She sat forward in her chair, head cocked to one side, listening. Mattie wailed again, the agonised sound quickly followed by a series of hiccuping sobs, and Carina got up.

'I think he's teething. I'm sure I felt a lump in his gum when I got that wretched beetle out of his mouth this morning.' She crossed to the chiffonier, opening it and getting out a quarter-bottle of brandy. 'This should do the trick.'

She climbed the two flights of stairs to the attic room and lifted the wailing Mattie out of his cot, rocking him in her arms and shushing him. Luckily he hadn't woken Meg – she was a sound sleeper, but if she was disturbed, it would be ages before she could get off to sleep again.

It was hot in the attic room, which collected all the heat of the day. Carina reached up and opened the window wider, then sat down in the wicker chair beneath it.

'Does it hurt, my love?' she asked softly, unstoppering the brandy bottle and dripping some on to her finger. 'Open your mouth for Mummy.'

Mattie obediently did as she asked, and she massaged the spirit on to his gums, feeling for the lump she thought she'd noticed this morning. Yes, she'd been right. There it was, and a tiny sharp point growing out of it. His first tooth! Her heart swelled with love, even though this was probably only the start of a succession of broken nights ahead. Meg had teethed easily, but then Meg was a girl. Girls grew into women, equipped to bear pain. In many ways they were much tougher than boys, Carina thought.

She rubbed a little more brandy on to Mattie's sore gum, then rocked and sang to him softly. His cries were quietening now to the occasional hiccuping gasp, and before long his head was heavy on her shoulder and his breathing slow and even. Still Carina sat there cradling him. Up here, with her son in her arms and her daughter sleeping peacefully, she could almost forget the day's disasters, and she was reluctant to return to the world downstairs, where there was no escaping them.

At last, however, she sighed and stood up, placing Mattie in his cot. She straightened the sheet over the sleeping Meg, who had kicked it down around her legs, and dropped a kiss on the little girl's forehead, damp with perspiration. Then she left the room, softly pulling the door closed behind her.

She was on the landing above the lower flight of stairs when she heard Robert's voice, raised in anger.

'What! My motor? I don't believe this!'

She stopped short, holding tight to the banister with a hand that had begun to shake again. Robert was home at last, and Sally must have told him what had happened. There was some more yelling, Sally now as well as Robert, but the blood was pounding so loudly in Carina's ears that she couldn't make out the words. Then she heard the slam of the back door and everything went quiet.

For a few minutes longer she stood there, imagining Robert outside examining the damage to the Rover and steeling herself to face him, then she descended the last flight of stairs and went into the kitchen.

Of Sally there was no sign, but Robert had come back into the house. He was standing beside the table, where his meal was laid out ready for him, leaning on it heavily, head bent so low his chin almost rested on his chest. He didn't move as Carina entered the room.

'Robert?' she said tentatively.

He did move then, with a suddenness that startled her,

straightening, then banging his fist down on to the table so hard that the plates jumped and rattled.

'Christ!' He turned, his face suffused with anger. 'What were you thinking of, Carina?'

Carina flinched. This was every bit as bad as she'd feared. It wasn't often that Robert lost his temper so thoroughly, but when he did, the change in him was frightening, and she was not as used to his rages as Sally, who had grown up with him. But she met his furious gaze evenly, determined to hold her ground.

'I'm sorry, but we needed flour—'

'Flour! Bloody flour!'

'Yes, to make bread for the men's snap tomorrow,' she said defiantly. 'You wouldn't want them to go hungry, would you?'

'I wouldn't want my Rover involved in an accident either,' he grated between clenched teeth. 'And Lord Melbrook, into the bargain! It beggars belief. How could you be so stupid?'

'It was the wasp . . .' Carina began, but Robert was scarcely listening. He raised both hands to shoulder height, fists clenched and shaking.

'Bloody Melbrook, of all bloody people! And my bloody Rover that I've scarcely finished paying for!'

'There's not that much damage to it,' Carina said, trying to placate him. 'Just the headlamp and the mudguard.'

'And what about the damage to *his* motor? What about that? God alone knows how we'll pay for it. Christ, I know Sally's a wild one, but I never thought she'd be so stupid as to do something like this!'

'Sally?' Carina said, uncomprehending. 'What are you talking about?'

'Taking my bloody Rover into Hillsbridge, of course, when she's never had a lesson in her life! What was she thinking of? What were *you* thinking of, to let her do it?'

'But she didn't!' Carina said. 'It wasn't her.'

'Don't lie to me, Carina. She's just admitted it.'

'Oh!' For a second, Carina was so startled she was lost for words. Why would Sally say it was she her who had taken the motor? Oh, she'd known how worried Carina was about the consequences of her actions, of course, but even so . . .

'Stupid, headstrong little flibbertigibbet!' Robert exploded, bringing his fist down hard on the table again.

'Robert, really, it wasn't her!' Carina said urgently. Kind as it was of Sally, she couldn't let her take the blame, and in any case, it would come out in the end. When Lord Melbrook met Robert to demand compensation for the damage, he'd be sure to tell Robert it was his wife who had been behind the wheel, not his sister. 'It was me!'

Robert snorted.

'Don't try to cover up for her, Carina.'

'I'm not! She's the one doing the covering-up. Really, Robert, it was me!'

He glared at her for a moment in disbelief.

'She knew how worried I was about telling you. She thought you'd be easier on her than on me, I expect.'

As he took in what she had said, another wave of fury darkened his face.

'You stupid, stupid woman!'

'I'm sorry, Robert . . .'

'I should think so too! I would have credited you with more sense. You know the struggle I have to keep this place going. Put food on the table, keep a roof over our heads.' He turned angrily, sweeping the plate containing his supper across the table so that it went over the edge and crashed down on to the flagged floor, smashing to smithereens. 'You'd ruin us for a bag of bloody flour!'

Carina was close to tears now.

'I've said I'm sorry. What more can I do?'

'And what's that?' He had spotted the brandy bottle, which she was still clutching.

'Mattie has started teething. I rubbed some on his gums,'

'You did what?' His hands had balled to fists.

'Rubbed some on his gums. To dull the pain.'

He took a step towards her, his hand raised, and for an awful moment Carina thought he was going to strike her. Instead he grabbed the brandy bottle and hurled it with all his strength against the wall. The bottle shattered, brandy pooling in a huge dark stain against the floral-patterned wallpaper and dripping down to the flagstones beneath.

'You'd give him a taste for the stuff before he can even talk? What sort of a mother are you?'

'What's going on?' Luke appeared in the doorway, wearing his striped flannelette nightshirt and peering around the room with his almost sightless eyes.

'Don't you know?' Robert snarled. 'Where have you been all day?'

'What I do know, my lad, is that you'd better calm down before someone gets hurt.' Luke's voice was surprisingly authoritative, giving Carina a glimpse of the man he had once been. Holding on to the door frame, he raised his walking stick, waving it in Robert's direction. 'Control yourself, do you hear? You're no better than your father.'

For a moment Robert stood stock still, as if he had been turned into a pillar of stone. Then his face changed and his hands dropped to his sides. He looked for all the world like a prizefighter whose opponent has landed a killer blow that has not quite floored him but knocked him senseless all the same.

'Just think on that, my lad!' Luke waved his stick again. The colour was high in his sunken cheeks, his breathing ragged. Concern for him flooded through Carina, heightened by the shock and fear that had overwhelmed her when Robert had turned from her much-loved husband into a raging bull. She hurried to his side.

'It's all right, Grandpa. Nothing to worry about.'

'So you might think,' Luke grunted.

'It's not Robert's fault. It's mine,' she tried to reassure him.

The back door opened and slammed shut. Robert, going outside to cool down, Carina imagined. But Luke still gazed sightlessly over her shoulder into the now empty room.

'I don't like it, Carina. His father, all over again.'

'Come on, let's get you back to bed.' She took his arm, helping him to his room, which had once been a parlour, but which he'd moved into when he could no longer manage the stairs. He was still chuntering to himself, his voice too low for her to be able to make out the words, but once she'd got him back into bed, propping his stick against the cabinet beside it so that it was within easy reach, his gnarled fingers closed over her wrist.

'You just take care, m'dear. You're a good girl. I wouldn't want to see you hurt.'

'I'm fine, Grandpa.' She plumped the pillows behind his head. 'Don't worry about me.'

But as she left him, closing the door behind her, Carina was as shaken by his reaction to Robert's fit of rage as she had been by the altercation itself.

Luke was usually the most placid of men, a typical farmer, usually so unruffled that he could appear taciturn. This, however, had upset him dreadfully. So much so that he had raised what always seemed to be a taboo subject – Robert's dead parents. Had his father had a violent temper? From what Luke had said, it would seem so. Had it somehow resulted in their premature deaths? That would explain why Robert would never speak of it. In spite of the heat still hanging in the kitchen, Carina shivered.

She had to get to the bottom of this. Had to find out why Luke had become so upset. When the moment was right, she would ask Robert about it. But not tonight. After what had happened, certainly not tonight.

Chapter Three

The balmy air was heavy with the scent of new-mown hay. Warm as it still was, it cooled Robert's hot cheeks, and after a moment his blood was cooling too, leaving him sick with shame.

What the hell was the matter with him? A ruined dinner, a bottle of brandy smashed against the wall, and worst of all, he had come as near as dammit to striking Carina. Thank the Lord that Grampy Green had intervened when he did, or goodness only knew what he would have done.

Oh, he'd been provoked. Any man would have lost his temper given the circumstances. Bad enough that Carina had been stupid enough to think she was ready to take the motor out unsupervised and damaged it, but to have damaged Lord Melbrook's motor too . . . God alone knew how much he'd demand in compensation, and if Robert was unable to settle up . . . Robert tried in vain to try to close his mind to the possibility of a disastrous outcome – that Carina's foolishness could cost them the farm they had been proud to own since his grandfather was a boy. But that she had been weaning his son on to hard liquor before he could even walk or talk properly had been the last straw. Robert loathed and feared hard liquor – and with good reason.

None of it was any excuse for the way he'd behaved, though.

He'd always had a fierce and quick temper, but he'd thought he was learning to control it; since he'd married Carina, the moments of mad rage had come far less frequently, and not been nearly so severe. He loved her. She had made him happy. And her steadying influence had been good for him.

Tonight, however . . .

Robert shuddered, punching the rough stone wall of the farmhouse to release the last of the anger that had consumed him.

Grandpa Green was right. It was his father all over again.

Dear Lord, history must not repeat itself.

The thought that it might was his worst nightmare, and now the terrible scene from his past replayed itself before his eyes, making his stomach clench as it always did, even after all these years.

With his father, of course, it had been the drink. When he had been drinking, the smallest thing would set him off, some wrong word or imagined slight, sometimes nothing at all. Robert scarcely touched it, just a cold beer sometimes after a long day. The smell of spirits still made him sick to his stomach, and he knew it was the sight of the brandy bottle in Carina's hands and her admission that she had rubbed some on Mattie's sore gums that had proved the last straw tonight. Mattie was his son – the direct line from his own father. The last thing he wanted was for him to be given a taste for the stuff.

He leaned against the rough stone wall of the old farmhouse, massaging the back of his neck, as if by doing so he could erase the shadows of the past, but for the moment they were too vivid, too real. The best thing he could do now was go back inside and try to make up with Carina. If he should lose her, and through his own fault, he couldn't bear it.

As he straightened up, he thought he saw something move, a

shadow against the whitewashed wall of one of the outhouses. Sally, perhaps. She had flounced out when he'd yelled at her and must still be out here somewhere, waiting for the storm to pass.

He called her name, but there was no reply. More likely than not it had been just a trick of the light; some clouds were scudding across the moon, a sign perhaps that the weather was on the change. Sally was probably out in the fields, curled up in the half-built hayrick and looking up at the sky for her 'Mummy and Daddy' stars. When she was a little girl, lost, lonely and in mourning for her parents, it had been her way of finding comfort – 'They're watching over me,' she would say, and Robert had taken care not to tell her different. Now, though she was no longer a child, he thought she still did the same when she was upset.

Whatever, she'd come back when she was good and ready. He couldn't worry about Sally now. The most important thing was to make his peace with Carina.

He took one long last steadying breath and went back into the house.

Carina was alone in the kitchen. She had cleared up the spilled food, broken glass and china, and was now trying to mop the last of the brandy from the wallpaper with a big soft cloth. She looked round as he came in, still wary.

'I'm sorry, Robert, really I am.'

He crossed to her, pulling her to her feet and putting his arms around her.

'I'm the one who should be sorry. I just saw red.'

'With reason,' she said against his chest. 'I should never have taken the motor, I know, but I really thought I could manage it. I never for a moment thought—'

'I know,' he said softly into her hair.

She raised her face, looking at him.

'I'll do my best to put things right. I'll go and see Lord Melbrook and explain.'

'Much good that would do,' Robert said heavily. 'Leave Melbrook to me. I'll find the money to pay for the damage somehow.' He looked around. 'Where's Grandpa?'

'I put him back to bed. He was so upset, Robert, I thought he might be going to have a stroke.'

A wave of guilt washed over Robert.

'He's all right now, though, is he?'

'I think so. When I looked in on him just now, he was snoring peacefully.'

'And the children?'

'Not a sound from either of them. I think the drop of brandy I rubbed on Mattie's gums did the trick.'

'Please don't do it again, Carina.'

'But it works wonders. It's what Mam always did when we were teething. Where's the harm?'

Before Robert could reply, the back door burst open and Sally came rushing in.

'Robert, come quick!' she gasped, breathless. 'There's somebody creeping about round the outhouses!'

Abruptly, Robert released Carina.

'I thought I saw something just now.'

With a couple of quick strides he crossed the kitchen, wrenching open the door of the cupboard where the shotguns were kept and pulling one out of its housing.

'Whatever the bastard wants, he'll get more than he bargained for!'

'Robert!' Carina cautioned, alarmed.

Sally was reaching for another of the shotguns.

'I'll come with you.'

'No, stay here, both of you. I'll deal with this.'

Before Carina could stop him, he was out of the door. Sally followed, standing in the open doorway, the shotgun cocked and ready, for all the world as if she were a sentry on guard at Buckingham Palace. At the end of his leash outside his kennel, Cymru was barking madly.

Carina ran to the window. Her heart had begun to race again, and an awful feeling of dread was making her panic.

What now? Suppose Robert were to fire his gun at a trespasser and injure him, or even worse? He could be up on a charge of manslaughter. Or what if the intruder was armed? Poachers carried rifles, and knives too, to slit the throats of rabbits caught in their snares. Even a vagrant would have something to defend himself with like as not. Suppose hidden in the shadows an intruder saw Robert before Robert saw him?

With the sort of day she had had, nothing seemed impossible.

As Carina watched anxiously from the window, Robert crossed the farmyard to the outhouses, kicking open doors and shouting for the intruder to show himself, before vanishing inside to search by the light of the moon, which was now shining brightly again in a clear sky. Carina held her breath until he emerged again.

Nothing there, thank goodness.

Then he disappeared around the corner of the biggest shed, heading, Carina guessed, for the henhouses. The hens had been shut up for the night to keep them safe from marauding foxes, but it would be easy for a thief to snatch a couple from their roosts, wring their necks and stuff them into a sack. It wouldn't be the first time.

'Can you see anything?' she called to Sally.

There was no reply, and she realised that Sally had gone out herself, unable to bear not being part of the action. It was typical of her. Sometimes Carina thought Sally should have been a boy.

A sudden shot rang out, making her squeal in shock. She hurried to the door, peering out into the darkness. Sally was halfway across the farmyard. Carina ran to her, grabbing her arm.

'I heard a shot! What . . . ?'

Sally shook her off impatiently.

'Stop panicking, Carina. That was me. I thought I saw something.'

'For goodness' sake, Sally! You might have killed someone!'

'Well I didn't,' Sally snapped. 'Go back inside.'

'I'm staying here with you to make sure you don't do something stupid.'

'Suit yourself.'

For seemingly endless minutes they waited, Carina like a coiled spring, Sally appearing to be enjoying herself. At last Robert reappeared from the direction of the henhouses.

'Nobody there. Did you see where he went, Sally?'

Sally shook her head regretfully.

'I only saw him for a moment. He was by the barn.'

Robert lowered his gun.

'I think we're both seeing shadows.'

'I wasn't!' Sally protested. 'And Cymru was going mad too.'

'Because you were shouting, I expect. But if there was someone creeping about, he's not here now. I reckon you and Cymru scared him off between you.'

'I'm not so sure. How could you see properly in the dark?' Sally challenged. 'I'll get a lamp, and you can look again.'

'There's nobody there, Sally,' Robert reiterated. He sounded weary. 'I've had enough for one day.'

He went back inside, Carina and a reluctant Sally following.

'I'll get you something to eat,' Carina said, mindful that his dinner had been wasted on the floor. 'There's some more ham, and another baked potato in the oven.'

Actually she had recovered it from the floor, but she wasn't going to tell him that. What he didn't know wouldn't hurt him.

'I think I'm past it,' Robert said, but Carina ignored him, cutting ham and slicing the potato in half and forking butter into it.

Once he had begun, Robert ate ravenously. Carina finished the clearing-up, but Sally still hovered by the window, peering out.

'Let's have one more look round,' she said when Robert had finished eating. She lit the storm lantern and stood waiting by the door.

Robert sighed. 'All right, if it will make you happy.'

'Well I'm going to bed,' Carina said.

She was in her nightgown at the dressing table, brushing her hair, when she heard Robert and Sally coming upstairs. They exchanged a few brief words on the landing, then Robert came into the room, shutting the door behind him.

'Nothing?' she asked.

'Nothing.'

He began undressing, tossing his clothes on to the chair beside the bed, his movements slow and heavy, as if it was all too much trouble.

Carina watched him in the dressing-table mirror, delighting as she always did in the sight of his body. Hard labour had changed the skinny boy he had once been into a man whose muscles rippled in his arms, shoulders and back, and a feathering of dark hair across his chest accentuated the hard, flat stomach beneath. A sudden wave of desire tingled hot deep inside her, and all the awful events of the day made her ache for the reassurance of his arms around her, his body close to hers. He was turning back the sheet now, swinging himself beneath it, and Carina put down her hairbrush and went to her side of the bed.

As she slid beneath the sheet, she leaned over, pressing her lips against his shoulder. His skin smelled of sweat and freshly mown hay, and tasted slightly salty. Her desire ratcheted up a notch and she curled her body around his hip, feeling tingles of excitement twist within her.

'Robert?' She ran her fingers over his chest, down to the hard muscle of his stomach, before his hand covered hers, stopping her from exploring further.

'Not tonight, Carina.' He shifted away from her.

The rejection was a sharp pain where a moment ago desire had tingled.

'You're still cross with me.'

'No, just dog tired. Go to sleep, there's a good girl.'

Hurt, she rolled over, her back towards him, fighting the tears that had been threatening ever since her horrible altercation with Lord Melbrook this morning.

Stupid, she knew. He *was* exhausted. A hard day in the fields, with the prospect of another tomorrow if the good weather held. The fierce row, which must have used up what little reserves he had left. The adrenalin rush and sheer physical exertion of searching for an imagined intruder. But knowing all that was somehow of no comfort. She wanted him so badly, needed him, longed for him to hold her, tell her he loved her, as he used to do in the early years of their marriage.

The lovemaking, oh, she wanted that too, but somehow it was less important than the closeness that would precede and follow it. Truth to tell, it always was. Much as she loved him being inside her, she was always left faintly dissatisfied, as if there was something more, something she had never yet experienced. Then she would lie in his arms, feeling the beat of his heart against her own, and tell herself she was lucky – lucky, lucky. What more could she wish for in life than to be Robert's wife, the mother of his children, falling asleep in his bed, in his arms, and she would push aside the slight nagging feeling that she was being cheated in some inexplicable way.

Tonight, however, even that comfort was denied her. Robert was asleep already, his breathing deep and even, interspersed with the occasional soft snuffling snore.

Carina turned towards him again, curling herself around his sleeping form and trying to pretend the awful events of the day had never been. But it was a long while before she fell asleep, and when she did, her dreams were confused and disturbing, a crazy kaleidoscope of anxiety, frustration and apprehension.

Chapter Four

Carina was not the only one finding sleep elusive that hot June night.

Cal Melbrook had long since given up any hope of getting comfortable in the vast four-poster bed that he disliked with a ferocity bordering on hatred and that he would have consigned to the rubbish heap the moment he had come into the title and been forced to move back into the family seat had it not been for the outrage of his mother.

'It is a family heirloom, Calvert,' she had declared. 'If it was good enough for your father, your grandfather and his father before him, it's good enough for you and your sons. If ever you have the sense to marry and have heirs, which I sometimes doubt.'

And so the four-poster had remained, with its feather mattress that had seen better days and the heavy drapes that made it dark in winter and unbearably hot on summer nights such as this.

He'd rather be under a mosquito net in a tent on the South African veldt, Cal thought. Less than comfortable that might have been, but also far less claustrophobic.

Now he sat in a wicker chair in the orangery at the rear of the house, a glass and a half-empty bottle of good Scotch whisky on the low table beside him, gazing up at the starlit sky above the trees that bordered the kitchen garden.

His leg was paining him, and from time to time he stretched and rubbed it absently. He had gained the wound in the second Boer War, where he had served as a captain, and it was so much a part of him now that he scarcely noticed it any more. It was just something he had to put up with, like the four-poster bed. At least he was alive, while so many of his men, and good friends too, were dead.

As of course was his elder brother, Stafford.

Cal's mouth twisted wryly as he pondered the irony of it. Stafford, who had never faced any greater danger in his life than learning to handle a gun on a game shoot. Stafford, mollycoddled by his doting mother. Stafford, who had inherited the title and estate on the death of their father and then followed him to the grave, dead of a fever Cal suspected he had contracted at one of the less salubrious gambling or whoring houses he had frequented in town – unknown, of course, to his adoring mother. Whilst Cal, who had faced everything the Boers had thrown at the British army, had survived.

Even though it was to a lifestyle he'd never wanted nor expected, he should count his lucky stars, he told himself. Even if it had saddled him with problems that at times seemed insurmountable, at least it meant that he might be able to rescue the estate that had been the family home for generations from the disastrous consequences of Stafford's profligate stewardship, if his tenure as Lord Melbrook could be honoured with such a description.

What a mess Stafford had left things in! Cal thought, pouring himself another whisky and rolling the crystal tumbler between his hands. Nothing had been spent for years on the upkeep of the house, nor on the tenant farms. When he'd visited them after returning to Dunderwick, each and every one of the farmers had complained about some problem that had not been dealt with though they'd reported it many times – roof tiles that needed replacing, barns falling into disrepair, cesspools unemptied, crumbling door and window frames. Claud Robbins, the agent, had done nothing about any of it, simply collected the rents and ridden away and they'd not seen hide nor hair of him until the next quarter day.

The trouble was, Robbins had grown old and lazy. Once, when Cal's father had been alive, he'd done a reasonable job, but under Stafford he had let things slide, and Cal was not altogether sure he hadn't been lining his pockets with some of the profits that should have gone into the coffers of Dunderwick House. The books, frankly, had been a mess.

One of the first things he'd done when he'd taken up the reins and seen how bad things were was to dismiss Robbins, paying him off with a pension the estate could ill afford, but which was considerably less than his overgenerous salary. Once the finances were beginning to look healthier, he'd consider taking on a new agent, but for the time being he'd run things himself. How difficult could it be? He'd studied accountancy during his long recuperation from the wounds he'd sustained in South Africa; although the thought of being cooped up in an office all day had horrified him, he'd persevered – what choice did he have? His army career was over and he was equipped for nothing else, unless, as his father had suggested, he entered the ministry, and that would have been even worse. Quite unthinkable!

Salvation had come in the shape of a brother officer he'd met in the stately-home-turned-hospital where he'd been taken when he had been shipped home to England, hovering between life and death. His leg had been so badly damaged when he and his men had been ambushed in the guerrilla stage of the war that amputation had been a very real possibility. Thankfully the dreaded gangrene had not set in, however, and the leg had been saved, though it would never be the same again. But his recovery had been long and frustratingly slow, and Cal sometimes thought he would have gone mad with boredom had it not been for Aubrey O'Leary.

The young captain had also been badly wounded in South Africa, and when they were fit enough to leave their beds they had spent hours together, chatting in the conservatory that served as a day room, sharing a bottle of whisky that had been smuggled in and kept hidden from Matron, and later, when they were able to take short constitutionals in the grounds, a cigar too.

Aubrey's father bred and trained racehorses at a yard and stables in the south of Somerset. After their discharge, Cal had gone to visit him and been made welcome by his family. At the end of his stay, during which he had admitted he didn't know what he was going to do with his life now that he could no longer be a soldier, Aubrey's father had offered him a position.

At first his pride had made him refuse – he thought, probably with good reason, that the offer had been made out of pity. But the silver-tongued Irishman had eventually persuaded him that he could be of some use – he was good with horses, he'd even begun to ride again, though too long in the saddle became almost unbearably painful, and he had acquired some skill in accountancy and bookkeeping.

Cal had enjoyed his time at the yard. The fresh air had put colour back into his cheeks and the good food on the table helped him regain the weight he had lost during his time in hospital. He and Aubrey continued to enjoy one another's company, and when they went into the nearby town, there were always girls who took a shine to the two good-looking young men. Another attraction was Aubrey's sister, Rose, but Cal had the good sense not to get too involved with her. He had a feeling she wanted more than an idle flirtation, and he was far from ready for that. Though Rose was an attractive young woman, he knew she could never fill the empty place in his heart. That still belonged to the woman he had loved and lost – yet another reason why he had joined the army and built a life far away from Dunderwick and all the painful memories that lurked there. To give Rose hope was unfair on her, and if he hurt her, as he surely would, it would sour relations between him and her family too.

Perhaps in time he might have come to feel differently and things could have developed between them. But just as he was beginning to think that might not be such a bad thing after all, the news had reached him that Stafford had died and he was now Lord Melbrook. There was nothing for it but to pack his bags and go home to look after the estate, which had come to him whether he wanted it or not.

The weight of responsibility was overwhelming. How the hell was he going to square the books and make the estate solvent again? he wondered now, rolling the whisky glass between his hands. He couldn't increase the rents on the properties until he'd restored them to a decent standard, and he knew that in any case two of the four farms were so small that their profit margins would probably not support a raise. He'd already been forced to put some of the family heirlooms up for sale, much to his mother's distress, but they hadn't fetched nearly as much as he'd hoped for. He could only pray that his father's collection of Chinese porcelain would do better.

He was due to leave for France tomorrow in an effort to find a buyer for it; a wealthy collector in Avignon had expressed an interest and he hadn't been prepared to entrust it to a carrier or an agent or dealer. Carriers could be criminally careless, and his suspicions regarding Claud Robbins had made him wary of middlemen. The items were valuable, he was fairly sure – a glorious Kangxi vase in vibrant colours, finished with gold leaf, and a number of even earlier pieces, Ming jars, vases and teapots. He was not looking forward to the long journey, but he didn't feel he had any option.

Really, he thought, he should be in bed getting some rest for the day ahead, not sitting here in the early hours drinking whisky. But he refilled his glass all the same.

Damn Stafford! Damn his creditors. And damn all the repairs and maintenance he had to find the money for.

And as if all that was not bad enough, now his beloved Benz was damaged and would have to be repaired. Well, he'd make sure the Greens paid for that, at least – he still thought of Meadow Farm as belonging to the Greens, though he knew the grandson, Robert Talbot, was running it now, and it was his wife who had gone into the back of the Benz.

The thought took him full circle, back to the matter of the tenant farms.

If his grandfather had not given the tenure of Meadow Farm to the Greens, it could well have been a great asset to the Dunderwick estate. Much bigger than the two smallest farms, Low Combe and Blackberry, and set on higher ground, which was less prone to flooding, it had the potential to be far more profitable. Besides which, it sat between High Combe and Rookery, a whole swathe of prime land that did not belong to the estate.

For some reason he couldn't quite explain, this nettled Cal. Perhaps it was the reason he had come down so hard on the girl when he'd learned who she was. But then again, he would have been just as furious if it had been anyone else.

Somewhere out over the valley an owl hooted, and Cal heard

the faint distant chime of the Dunderwick church clock as it struck the hour. One . . . two . . . three.

He sighed, drained his glass and set it down. He really should go back to bed and try to get some sleep. If this damned leg of his would let him!

Chapter Five

'Mummy! Wake up!'

Carina came to with a start. Meg was beside the bed, shaking her by the arm, and Mattie's head was just appearing around the door.

As usual, her first conscious thought was for his safety. How had he managed to get out of his cot and down the steep attic stairs? He could have fallen and broken his neck! To her knowledge he'd never attempted such a thing before, but of course she was usually up with the dawn and waking the children, not the other way around. She must have overslept this morning. Early sun was streaming in through the window and the bed beside her was empty. Robert must have got up and dressed without disturbing her – unheard of!

But of course she hadn't slept well last night. Even when she had eventually dropped off, it had been a restless, troubled sleep peppered with vaguely disturbing dreams, though presumably towards dawn she'd gone off more deeply. If it hadn't been for the children, she could easily have turned over and dozed off again.

'I'm hungry, Mummy!' Meg complained. 'And so is Mattie. Why are you still asleep?'

'I must have been very tired, Meg. But I'm awake now. What

about Auntie Sally? She's already up, I expect. If you go down and ask her nicely, she'll get you something to eat, I'm sure.'

'She's not there,' Meg said. 'Only Grandpa Luke.'

'You've been downstairs already?' Carina asked.

'And Mattie.'

'Mattie went downstairs on his own?' Carina was horrified. Yet another flight of stairs where he could have taken a bad tumble.

'He wasn't on his own. He was with me. And he came back up again, didn't you, Mattie?'

Mattie was beside the bed now too, scrabbling over from all fours on to his plump little bottom and staring up at Carina with wide dark eyes and an expectant toothless smile.

'Meg, you know Mattie is supposed to be kept away from the stairs,' she scolded, hastily getting out of bed and thrusting her feet into her slippers.

'He's really good at it,' Meg objected. 'He got back up again nearly as fast as me, too.'

'He could have fallen. Just make sure he doesn't try it again while I get dressed.'

She tipped some water from the jug on the washstand into the matching bowl and swilled it over her face with a flannel, washing the sleep out of her eyes. She still felt thick and muzzy, though, and a headache was niggling in her temple.

Trying to ignore it, she got dressed in the same clothes she'd worn yesterday, and tugged a comb through her hair.

'Right. Come on then, you two.'

Mattie began crawling at a fast pace across the landing, eager to practise his new-found skills, but Carina picked him up, balancing him on her hip. No way was she going to allow him to attempt it unless there was someone below to catch him if he fell.

As Meg had said, only Luke was in the kitchen. The clock on the dresser showed past seven; Sally was probably rounding up the cows for milking, and Robert was either helping her or getting ready for another long day in the fields. But the kettle was singing on the hob and porridge was bubbling in a pan. Either Sally had put it on before going out, or Luke had managed to do it himself.

'I'm so sorry, Grandpa,' Carina said, putting Mattie down. 'I don't know how I came to sleep so late.'

'After last night, it's no wonder,' Luke said. 'Are you all right?' His cloudy eyes peered at her anxiously.

'Yes, fine.' It wasn't true, but she wasn't going to say so. 'Would you like a cup of tea?'

'Don't worry about me. Sally made me one before she went off to do the milking. You see to the children.'

'If you're sure.'

She stirred the porridge. It seemed to be ready and she dolloped some into bowls. Meg was already sitting up at the table. Carina set one bowl in front of her, lifted Mattie into his high chair and placed the other, and a spoon, in front of him. He'd probably make a terrible mess, but she was encouraging him to learn to feed himself, and porridge was reasonably easy for him to manage.

'Did you want porridge, Grandpa, or would you rather have a cooked breakfast?' she asked.

'That's what I were hoping you'd say, m'dear.'

Frail as he might have become, Luke's appetite was still as good as it had ever been.

Carina fetched bacon from the cold slab in the pantry, melted some lard in the big cast-iron frying pan and filled it with as many rashers as it would take. Sally and Robert would both be hungry when they came in and would need a good breakfast to sustain them for another long day in the fields.

As it sizzled, Luke sniffed appreciatively.

'You're a good girl, Carina,' he said. 'Our Robert ought to know when he's well off.'

'And he's a good man.' Carina sprang to Robert's defence. 'I'm the lucky one.'

But Luke was intent on sticking to his theme.

'Takes after his father, that's the trouble,' he said heavily. 'That temper of his . . . I don't like it, and that's the truth.'

It was almost unheard of for Luke to so much as mention his dead daughter's husband, but it was plain both from his words now and his outburst last night that he had had no time for him. Curious as Carina had been for a long time as to why he was usually a taboo subject, this seemed an ideal opportunity to probe. Perhaps Luke would open up where Robert would not.

'He had a temper then?' She made a great show of turning a rasher of bacon in an effort to pretend it was a casual question.

'You can say that again,' Luke said with quiet emphasis. 'Not that he ever showed it in front of Margaret and me. Too canny for that. But what our poor Essie had to put up with . . . oh, it fair breaks my heart.'

He fell silent, tears filling his rheumy eyes, and fished in his pocket for his handkerchief, a square of khaki torn from the tail of an old shirt.

Carina thought this was probably an end to the conversation, but after a few minutes he went on reflectively, 'She were such a lovely girl, too. Kind-hearted, pretty as a picture, and she could always make you smile. I tell you, she'd have been as proud as Punch of your little 'uns, if only she'd lived to see them. She'd have spoiled them rotten, if I know anything about it. But there you are, she's gone, and that's an end to it.'

'That's so sad,' Carina said.

'It's life, m'dear. Full of ups and downs and not a darned thing we can do about it.'

Luke seemed to have become his usual pragmatic self, and Carina wondered if she dared ask the question that had been bothering her ever since she had met Robert. Deciding it was now or never, she moved the rashers of bacon into a neat pile and cracked an egg deftly on the side of the pan before sliding it in. Then she took a deep breath and turned back to Luke.

'How did she and Robert's father die, Grandpa?'

Luke's cloudy eyes met hers; he looked both puzzled and uncomfortable.

'You don't know? Hasn't Robert ever told you?'

'No. He won't talk about them. All I know is that they died when he was thirteen and he and Sally came here to live with you and Grandma Margaret.' She flicked hot fat on to the egg so that the yolk began to cream over, then turned back to Luke. 'Please, Grandpa,' she urged him. 'I'd really like to know.'

For a long moment Luke was silent again, then he shook his head slowly.

'It's not my place, m'dear. It's for Robert to tell you.'

'But he won't,' Carina reiterated. Suddenly it seemed more important than ever that she learn the truth. What could it be that neither Robert nor Luke would talk about it? And it wasn't just a matter of curiosity any more. Luke had said that Robert had inherited his father's temper, and intimated that that was behind whatever had happened. Well, Mattie was Robert's son – and the spitting image of him; he was Joel's grandson. Was there something she should look out for? Something that could be passed down from generation to generation?

'Grandpa Luke,' she implored. 'If there's something I should know—'

A sudden crash interrupted her. Mattie had pushed his bowl over the side of the high chair tray, splattering porridge across the floor. A good deal of it was smeared on his face and hands too, and in his hair, so that it stuck up in sticky tufts.

'Oh Mattie!' Carina groaned.

She slid Luke's bacon and egg on to a plate she'd put to warm and took it to the table along with a knife and fork and the bread plate with the remains of yesterday's loaf.

'Here you are, Grandpa.'

Then she turned her attention to cleaning up Mattie and the mess he'd made. The time for confidences had come and gone and she was still none the wiser.

Luke had finished his bacon and egg and was tucking into a thick slice of bread and jam when Sally came in.

'Something smells good!' she said as she headed for the big stone sink to wash her hands.

'I've cooked plenty of bacon for you and Robert,' Carina said. 'I'll put an egg in the pan now you're here. I would have thought Robert would be in by now too. Have you seen him anywhere?'

'No.' Sally grabbed the kitchen towel from its hook, drying her hands roughly. 'He'll have to get a move on if he wants some breakfast, though. The men will be here soon.'

As if on cue, Wally Scrivens, one of the casual labourers, ambled past the window with his son, Joey. By rights Joey should be in school, Carina thought, but he was a strapping lad, big for his age, and Robert had said he was worth two of his father. Thinking she'd better keep them sweet, she went to the door.

'Robert's out somewhere on the farm,' she said. 'Would you and Joey like a cup of tea while you're waiting?'

'Ah, I wouldn't say no.' Wally was retrieving a half-smoked cigarette from behind his ear and looking for a match to light it. 'D'you want one, our Joey?'

'Yeah, all right.'

Carina went back in and poured tea into two mugs, adding milk and generous spoonfuls of sugar.

'I don't know where Robert's got to,' she said, handing them to the men. 'If he's not back when you've drunk your tea, perhaps you could go and have a look for him, make sure he doesn't need help with whatever it is he's doing.'

For some reason she couldn't quite explain, she was beginning to feel anxious. It wasn't like Robert to be late for breakfast, late to start a long day in the field while the good weather held.

Two of the other casual labourers arrived, and she took them mugs of tea too, but there was still no sign of Robert.

'All right, missus, I'll go and have a look for him.' Wally stubbed out what had been a fresh cigarette and tucked it behind his ear. 'Are you coming, our Joey?'

'Can do.' Joey, it seemed, was a lad of few words.

Carina went back into the kitchen. Sally had finished her breakfast and was stacking dishes in the sink; Grandpa Luke had retreated to his favourite chair and was cleaning out his pipe into the coal scuttle prior to lighting it, and Cymru, attracted no doubt by the smell of bacon frying, had crept in unnoticed and was sitting expectantly beside the stove.

'Come on then, you two,' Carina said to the children. 'Let's get you washed and dressed.'

She drew a stool up to the stone sink for Meg to stand on and lifted Mattie up to sit on the oilcloth-covered cupboard that stood beside it. As she washed Meg's face and hands she saw Mattie reaching over in the direction of Grandpa Luke's cut-throat razor, hanging on its leather strop under the window, and quickly moved him away. She was going to have to ask Grandpa to find somewhere else to hang it well out of Mattie's reach. She'd never had this trouble with Meg.

As she rinsed the flannel clean, movement outside the window caught her eye. Joey was sprinting across the farmyard towards the house as if all the demons in hell were after him, but as he neared it he came to a dead halt, looking back over his shoulder to his father, who was emerging into view around the corner of the barn. Wally was hurrying too, moving more quickly than she had ever seen him move before, but it was the expression on his weathered face, a mixture of shock and horror, that made her go cold with alarm. Stopping only to lift Mattie from his seat on the cupboard, she hurried to the door with him in her arms.

'Wally? What's wrong?' she asked.

He came towards her, more slowly now, though Joey still hung back.

'I think you'd better go in and sit down, missus.'

'What is it? What's wrong?'

Wally passed a hand across his mouth. Carina saw that it was shaking. Realised too that the labourer was lost for words.

'Wally – tell me. Is it Robert?' Her voice was rising, shrill and panicky. Sally, alerted by the commotion, was in the doorway behind her.

'What's the matter, Wally?'

Wally looked from one to the other of them and somehow found his voice.

'There's bin a terrible accident. Oh missus, oh Miss Sally . . . he's in the stable . . .'

Carina stared at him blankly for a moment. An accident? In the stable? What was he talking about?

'You mean something's happened to Captain?' Captain was the old carthorse who had been hard at work these last days drawing the wagon to bring in the harvest. Carina's mind instantly flew to the suspected intruder of the previous evening; had he done some harm to the horse?

'No, missus, not Captain . . .'

'What then? You don't mean . . . ?'

'The boss.' Wally wiped his hand across his mouth again. 'Looks like he's been kicked . . .'

'Oh no!' Carina had begun to tremble violently. She turned to her sister-in-law. 'Take Mattie, Sally. I must go to him . . .'

She thrust the little boy into Sally's arms and made to hurry out. But to her surprise, Wally seemed to come out of his trance, spreading his arms wide to obstruct her.

'Missus, no!'

'Get out of my way!'

She pushed past the man, past a frightened-looking Joey, who appeared to be rooted to the spot, and ran across the farmyard in the direction of the stables. The other two casual hands were standing outside, peering into the shadowed interior, apparently as shocked as Wally and Joey. When they saw Carina and realised where she was headed, one of them moved towards her as if to ward her off as Wally had done. She evaded him, making for the stable door, which was fully open.

The stable was dim; after the glare of the bright sunshine outside, Carina could see nothing but Captain's solid form in the far corner. He began to lumber towards her, and for a fleeting second Carina thought they had all gone mad. Robert was not here; he must be behind the outbuildings, checking the threshing machine or something similar. Whatever Wally thought he'd seen, it hadn't been Robert. Then her foot encountered something soft but solid, and she looked down and saw the dark shape at her feet. Dear God, she had almost trodden on him!

'Robert!' She dropped to her knees beside him, feeling for his hand. 'Robert, my love, whatever has happened?'

There was no reply, but his hand was warm in hers.

She lifted his head, laying it in her lap and brushing the dark curls off his face.

'It's all right, Robert, we'll send for the doctor. Just lie still now . . .'

'Missus . . .' One of the casual labourers appeared in the doorway, bent over her, urging her away.

'Leave me alone!' she snapped angrily.

Only then did she realise that her fingers were sticky, and that something warm and wet was oozing through her skirt on to her bare legs. Her eyes were becoming more accustomed now to the light. She looked down, at her hand, at her skirt, at a large dark patch spreading across the pink and white flowered cotton, and realised to her horror that it was blood.

Her whole body electrified with shock, Carina gasped, once, twice, before her breath came out all at once on what was midway between a sob and a scream.

Chapter Six

In the hours, days and weeks to come, when she looked back on that terrible day, it was the heart-stopping moment when she realised that Robert was beyond help that stood out most clearly to Carina. It was imprinted indelibly on her memory, and the horror of it haunted her dreams. Everything else was shrouded in a fog of unreality. She had felt as if she was floundering in a murky morass, and the summer sunshine took on a macabre corona of darkness, somehow making everything seem even more nightmarish.

Sometimes she wondered just how she had carried on that day, doing what she had to do while her mind raced in circles of panic, shock and grief, her limbs trembled uncontrollably and her mouth was so dry she could barely swallow.

How, for instance, had she been able to tell the casual labourers to carry on with the day's work? Yet she had. When they'd collected their coats and their flasks, preparing to leave, she'd said no, the harvest had to be got in, it was what Robert would have wanted.

How had she been able to stand by while Dr Blackmore from High Compton examined Robert's bloodied body and pronounced him dead, and then, while they waited for Sergeant Love to arrive from Hillsbridge police station, make a pot of tea and put out biscuits on a plate, for all the world as if the doctor and policeman were making a social visit?

And when the policeman had given the word, how had she been able to bear the sight of her beloved husband being carried into the house, where he would lie on the parlour floor until Seward Moody, the undertaker, was able to get a coffin made? But somehow she had, following the little procession on legs that seemed not to belong to her, hands clasped tightly together to keep them from shaking, all the muscles of her face clenched to stop the threatening tears. Sally had taken the children out on the pretext of feeding the hens so they wouldn't witness what was going on, but even though they were safely out of the way, Carina was too proud to let the others see her cry.

Most of the discussion between the two men as to whether a post-mortem would be required had gone over her head. The decision would be up to the coroner, she gathered, but both Sergeant Love and Dr Blackmore, who had been a police surgeon in his younger days, seemed satisfied that somehow Robert had been kicked in the head by Captain. Either he had been checking the horse's hooves, or perhaps he had fallen and startled the animal. No one would ever know for sure, but one thing was certain: Robert's head had been caved in, no post-mortem would find anything different, and the coroner wouldn't want to waste time and money investigating what was clearly a tragic accident.

Carina had hoped desperately that that would be the case – the thought of Robert's body being further desecrated on a cold mortuary slab was more than she could bear – and she didn't question their explanation of what had happened. It was Sally, who had brought the children back into the kitchen when the coast was clear, who had expressed her doubts that everything was as simple as it seemed.

'Did that intruder we were chasing last night have anything to do with it?' she demanded when the doctor and the policeman had left. 'That's what I'd like to know!'

Carina stared at her blankly. She'd forgotten all about the supposed intruder.

'But there wasn't anybody . . .'

'We didn't catch anybody, but that doesn't mean there was nobody there. Was he still hanging about this morning? Did he bed down overnight in the stable? Was there a fight? Is that what frightened Captain?' Sally's cheeks were flushed, her eyes bright with tears and her tone vehement.

'Don't talk silly, my girl.' Luke worked his gnarled hands back and forth over the knees of his trousers, the only visible sign of the grief and distress he was feeling.

'What's silly about it?' Sally flared. 'You know Captain! He's the quietest, gentlest horse imaginable! And Robert would never do anything to cause him to kick out. He knows better.' She caught herself, blinking hard, so that one of the tears escaped and rolled down her cheek. '*Knew* better . . .'

'Even a quiet horse can get spooked,' Luke argued. 'There's no point going over and over it. That won't get you nowhere. And it won't bring Robert back.'

'Oh, I dare say you're right. What does anybody care about justice for people like us?' Sally said viciously. 'I'm going to help with the harvest.'

'They can manage without you, Sally,' Carina said.

'Maybe, but it might just keep me sane.' Sally headed for the door, Cymru, who had picked up on their distress, following her like a shadow, ears flat, tail between his legs.

Scooping up Mattie, changing what smelled like a filthy nappy, setting what biscuits Dr Blackmore and Sergeant Love hadn't eaten on the table for Meg, Carina knew what she meant.

Routine was the only thing that would keep her sane, too. Routine – and caring for her beloved children. Mattie, at least, was too young to understand what was going on, but Meg knew all right that something terrible had happened. Though Sally had done her best to keep her out of the way, she'd heard and seen enough to frighten her, and now she was clinging to Carina's skirts with a timidity that was quite unlike her. Leaving Mattie to play with the coloured building bricks that were scattered all over the floor, Carina sat down in one of the easy chairs and lifted the little girl on to her lap.

'Everything is going to be all right,' she said into Meg's soft fair hair.

'But . . . my daddy . . .' Meg turned her head to look at her, her blue eyes huge and solemn in her pale face.

'Daddy has had to go away,' Carina said.

'When will he be coming back?'

Carina blinked against the threatening tears and managed to control the muscles that were making her chin wobble.

'He won't, my darling,' she said quietly. 'Daddy has had to go and live with the angels. But he'll still look down and look after you. Don't worry. Everything is going to be all right.'

Those blue eyes regarded her earnestly and with pleading.

'Promise?'

It was a word Meg often used. 'You can have a biscuit if you are a good girl.' 'Promise?' 'If you let Mattie play with your spinning top I'll make sure he gives it back to you.' 'Promise?' Usually Carina replied quickly and without much thought. 'I promise.'

But this was different. This wasn't some silly childish request. This was about the terrible way her children's safe and happy lives had been torn apart, about their whole future. *Would* everything be all right? At this moment nothing had seemed less certain to Carina. But the most important thing now was for her to make sure that it was. How she would do it she didn't know. But somehow she would find a way.

She smoothed a stray curl away from Meg's forehead and cupped the little girl's face in her hands, holding the tearful gaze.

'I promise,' she said with emphasis. And it seemed to her that it was more a solemn vow, made not only to Meg and Mattie, but to Robert too.

The resolve with which Sally had set out ebbed from her as she left the farmhouse behind. On the horizon she could see the men working in the farthest field and the big old wagon with Captain in the shafts silhouetted against the clear clean blue of the sky, and suddenly the tears she had fought so hard against were coursing down her cheeks. Robert should be with them but he wasn't. Never would be again. She'd fully intended to lose herself in hard work and some semblance of normality, to make sure the casual hands weren't slacking as she suspected they would without supervision, but for the moment she simply couldn't do it. Grief was welling up in her in a flood tide and she was no longer able to contain it.

She turned, cutting across the stubbly field that had been mown just yesterday, when everything had been as usual and none of them had realised how their world would be turned upside down in the space of a few short hours. To the right of it lay a meadow sloping down to a stream that formed the boundary with the neighbouring farm. It was too steep for easy harvesting, and in summer the cows were turned out here to graze to their hearts' content. She could see them now, moving slowly but purposefully as they cropped the sweet grass. Later, when the sun was high, they would move to the shade of the trees that fringed the stream, even paddle in the shallows, churning it up to thick brown mud.

Sally headed for the stream, stumbling on the uneven tussocks, crying as she went and repeating her brother's name over and over like a mantra. *Oh Robert! Robert . . . Robert . . . Robert . . .* She couldn't take in the reality that he was gone for ever, yet at the same time she knew it was true and she didn't think she could bear it.

Since their parents had died, Robert had been her rock, her protector, her saviour, her friend. Oh, Grandma Margaret and Grandpa Luke had been there for her too, but it was Robert she had clung to in those early days when she had felt so lost and frightened; Robert whose bed she had clambered into when the nightmares came or when she couldn't sleep because she was missing Mam and Daddy so; Robert who had listened to her, comforted her as best he could, looked out for her in every way. It had been Robert, she remembered, who had sorted out the bullies who were tormenting her as a new girl at the village school, waylaying them as they walked home and putting the fear of God into them. After that they'd left her alone, even treated her with kindness and let her into their circles. It was a long time now since she'd needed him to stand up for her; these days she was well able to defend herself. But then, when she had been young and vulnerable, he'd been there, daring anyone to hurt her, and she'd known he always would be if the need arose.

Quite simply, she worshipped him, and he was one of the reasons why she'd never been able to bring herself to care much about any of the boys who tried to capture her interest. Not that she knew many – living on an isolated farm didn't afford much opportunity for meeting them – but those she did come across at village fetes and dances, or when she went into Hillsbridge on a

Saturday to sell butter, cheese and bacon on their market stall, just didn't measure up. David Perkins, whose father farmed High Combe, was the only one who had come close to being a sweetheart, but going for walks, dancing with him at Christmas parties or summer events and sharing a fumbling kiss was about the limit of their relationship, though she knew David wanted more. As a child, she'd adored her father, and when he was gone, she'd put Robert in his place. He was so like Joel, and had grown even more like him as the years went by. His appearance, his voice, the way he made her feel safe, made her feel she could do anything she wanted, be anyone she chose. He had even inherited Daddy's temper.

Sally smiled through her tears as she thought of it. Everyone had been so frightened of Daddy. Even Mam. Even Robert, and he was a boy. Everyone except her. She'd been so used to his ranting and raving, it had just been a part of who he was. The father who would take her down to the docks to look at the ships – they'd lived in Bristol then – and if she was tired carry her home on his shoulders or, when she was too big for that, 'piggyback' her, as he called it. The father whose handkerchief she liked to keep under her pillow when she was unwell because it smelled of him – tobacco, lighter fuel and the unmistakable smell of the docks. The father who had called her 'my little queen', and given her bullseyes out of his pocket, and entertained her with tricks like 'find the lady' – she could never tell which of the three cards he laid down in front of her was the queen, even though she'd watched so carefully she was sure that this time she had got it right. Then there was a trick with a match that he'd put into the corner seam of a handkerchief, snap in two and tell her to feel to make sure it was broken, then miraculously make it whole again. She'd eventually realised how it was done – a second match hidden in another corner of the handkerchief hem – but when she was little she'd been convinced Daddy really could work magic.

Sally's faint nostalgic smile faded again as she recalled how her blissful world had fallen apart, the grief and loss she had felt then resurrected and intensified fresh and new and totally bound up with this new loss. The two men she adored, both gone. And of course her mother too.

She hadn't been there when her parents died. It had been in the school Easter holiday and she had been staying with Grandpa Luke and Grandma Margaret.

In springtime, the farm was an exciting place. There were chicks, little balls of yellow fluff that fitted into the palm of her hand. There were lambs skipping in the fields, not at Meadow Farm – Grandpa Luke didn't keep sheep – but on some of the neighbouring farms, especially those where the land sloped as steeply as the meadow she was crossing now. And there were the calves, tottering on spindly legs, fiercely protected by their mothers. Another calf had been due to be born at any time; Sally had been looking forward to it eagerly, hoping against hope that it made its appearance before it was time for her to go home and even – guiltily – that for some reason it would have to be bottle-fed.

She shouldn't hope that, she knew; it would mean that something had gone wrong with the birth, and besides, Grandma Margaret would have sleepless nights sitting up in the rocking chair in the kitchen so as to be able to tend to it. But oh, she did so love it when she was allowed to help, holding the bottle at just the right angle, hearing the soft slurping sound as the calf fed, laying her cheek against its rough yet silky coat.

Well, she had got her wish, but at what a price! Not only had she been at Meadow Farm to see the calf born, she had never gone home again.

When Grandma Margaret and Grandpa Luke had explained to her that from now on she and Robert would be living with them, Sally had wondered if it was all her fault that something terrible had happened to Mam and Daddy. Had it been because she had wished so hard to stay on at the farm? I didn't mean it! she'd thought, frightened and remorseful. I didn't mean I wanted to stay for ever, just long enough to see the calf born. And I'm sorry . . . I'm sorry . . . I'll never wish for anything ever again, just as long as I can have Mam and Daddy back . . .

They hadn't told her, of course, how her parents had died. They simply said it had been a terrible accident.

'Just try and forget about it, my love,' Grandma Margaret had said, and though Sally had questioned him, Robert wouldn't explain either. Somehow she'd known she shouldn't press them. They were on a knife edge, all of them. She'd even seen tears in Grandpa Luke's eyes before he wiped them away with one of the rags he used for a handkerchief, and she'd heard Grandma Margaret crying in the night. As for Robert, he was morose and moody. Altogether the atmosphere in the farmhouse was as heavy as if a thunderstorm was brewing, and if she asked questions it only grew heavier.

Sometimes Grandma and Grandpa would talk together in low voices. She tried to overhear what they were saying but could not, though she did hear Grandpa Luke swear once. 'That bloody bastard!' he had said, his voice full of bitterness, and she had wondered if he might be talking about Daddy, though she couldn't understand why he should say such a thing. And once, when she had crept into his bed for comfort, Robert had been threshing about like a madman and talking – no, shouting – in his sleep, but she couldn't make any sense out of that either, and in the end she gave up trying.

Mam and Daddy were dead. Nothing else really mattered.

It was years before she'd been any the wiser, putting together the bits and pieces she'd gleaned over time with memories of things that back then she had been too young to make sense of.

As a child she had accepted the fights between Mam and Daddy as normal. She'd never witnessed them, only heard the commotion, and it had never occurred to her that the bruises and cuts Mam sometimes had were connected to the rows in any way. She'd accepted without question Mam's explanations of walking into a door, or tripping over a loose board. After all, as a fairly adventurous child, she was always in the wars herself. Once she'd cut her head open when she tried to 'fly' from the top of a wall, convinced that if the birds could do it, so could she. She bore the scar to this day, though it was mostly hidden by her hair. On another occasion she had tripped over her own feet when she caught them in her skipping rope and ended up with a bloody nose and two black eyes that had gone through all the colours of the rainbow before the ugly marks had faded. To her, there had been nothing sinister about being covered in scrapes and bruises; they were just a part of normal everyday life.

Later, however, she had realised the truth – that Mam's injuries had probably been inflicted by Daddy. Yet still she had made excuses for him. Her daddy would never have meant to hurt anyone. He just lost his temper sometimes and didn't know his own strength. He liked a drink, and everyone knew how that could make people not responsible for their actions. And even when she began to reluctantly acknowledge that perhaps one day things had gone too far, she still adjusted her version of what might have happened into something more acceptable.

Perhaps Daddy had struck out blindly and Mam had fallen and hit her head. Perhaps when he realised what he'd done, he had ended his own life in a fit of terrible remorse.

Sally no longer asked questions. She didn't think she wanted to know the answers. Better by far to keep her precious memories intact.

Now, even if she wanted to learn the truth, it was too late. Robert should have told her, she thought. She had a right to know the truth, and whether the dark suspicions that sometimes nagged at her were real or just a figment of her imagination. She should have been brave enough to try to pursue it while she had the chance. Now it was too late. Robert was dead, and she wouldn't upset Grandpa Luke by bringing up the subject, especially when he was grieving for his grandson. When you were old, as Grandpa was, you had a right to expect that you would go before your children, never mind your grandchildren. But really, what did it matter? She couldn't think about it now, overwhelmed as she was with grief for her beloved brother.

And far more important than wondering about the past was trying to work out how Robert had met his death. She still couldn't imagine he could have been careless enough to spook Captain, or how he had ended up in a position that the horse could kick him to death. But perhaps she was just looking for someone to blame. She couldn't accept that it had been no more than a tragic accident, but maybe that was exactly what it had been. Whatever had happened, Robert was gone.

Sally sat down on the grassy bank above the stream, buried her face in her hands and cried until she could cry no more.

Chapter Seven

'For as much as it has pleased Almighty God in his great mercy to take to himself the soul of our dear brother here departed, we therefore commit his body to the ground . . .'

Though Carina had never before attended a funeral, the words were somehow oddly familiar, as if she had heard them a thousand times before. They seemed to come from a long way off, even though she was standing just a few feet away from Rector Clarke, the ageing cleric who had been the incumbent of the tiny church of St Mary's, Dunderwick, for as long as anyone could remember.

She clasped her hands together tightly in the folds of her skirt, watching as if in a dream as the simple oak coffin was lowered into the ground by four sturdy local men attired in ill-fitting black jackets and trousers. Beads of perspiration rolled down their faces and perhaps their hands were slippery with sweat too, for one corner of the coffin suddenly jerked downwards, hanging at a crazy angle before the man got a hold on the strap once more and steadied it.

'Earth to earth, ashes to ashes, dust to dust . . .'

A handful of dirt pattered down on to the brass nameplate: *Robert James Talbot. 1886–1910. RIP.* It seemed as unreal and unbelievable as everything else. It couldn't be Robert in that coffin. There must be some terrible mistake. But it wasn't . . .

You can't do this! Carina wanted to cry. *You can't! I won't let you!*

But of course she remained silent.

A light touch on her arm: Seward Moody, the undertaker, urging her to follow suit and toss a handful of earth on to the coffin. She answered him with a brief shake of her head. She couldn't be part of this ritual. She wouldn't help to cover him forever. Sally stepped forward, a small bunch of moon daisies in her hand. They fluttered down as she dropped them, and Carina wished she had thought to pick some as Sally had on their way to the church along the lanes, following the farm cart that served as a hearse, drawn by Captain. It had somehow seemed right and fitting, even if he had been the cause of his master's death, that he should take him to his last resting place. Just as wild flowers seemed right, while dirt seemed all wrong. But it was too late now. Sally's flowers would have to suffice.

Besides Carina and Sally, just a handful of mourners stood around the grave. Martin Harvey, from Rookery Farm, had brought Grandpa Luke in his horse and trap, and he now stood beside the old man, who was leaning heavily on his stick, ready to support him if the committal became too much for him. George Button, Carina's father, was keeping a similar watchful eye on his daughter, not that he expected her to collapse – she was made of sterner stuff than that – but simply because his heart was breaking for her. Hester Dallimore was there too, wearing her best black coat and a tragic expression that she clearly thought befitted the occasion.

Carina had hoped her aunt would offer to look after the children so that Daisy, her mother, could come to the funeral with her – both her parents had travelled to Somerset from Pontypridd for the sad occasion. But Hester had not offered. She didn't want to pass up the chance of being one of the key figures in a drama that would give her plenty to talk about for weeks. So Daisy had remained at the farm with Meg and Mattie while Hester paraded her connection with the young widow for all to see.

Quite a few folk had come along to pay their respects, filling the pews in the tiny church, though Carina, seeing everything through a dark haze as she followed the coffin, was almost unaware of them. David Perkins was there with his parents, Dick and Ellen, along with the families from the other tenant farms and half of Dunderwick village. In a small, tightly knit community such as this, funerals were always well attended, and with Robert having been so young and dying so tragically, the turnout was even higher than usual.

Now they stood in knots around the perimeter of the church-yard, watching from a distance in near silence. As the mourners began to move away from the graveside, some of the onlookers went to offer their condolences, while others talked amongst themselves in low voices.

'What a terrible thing! And him so young.'

'However are they going to manage now?'

'They'll have to sell up.'

'That'll be the death of Luke.'

'Looks to me as if he's on his last legs now.'

A few people going about their business had stopped on the other side of the street, outside the village shop – a couple of women with shopping bags on their arms, an old man, bent as a crooked stick, another woman with a baby in a pram. And further along, on the forecourt of the Dunderwick Arms, a young man with a half-empty beer mug in his hand.

Clem Porter, the landlord, emerged from the door to the public bar.

'Sorry, mate, you'll have to drink up. It's closing time.'

'Oh, right.' The young man gestured in the direction of the churchyard. 'There's a funeral, I see.'

'Oh ah. Young Robert Talbot. Got kicked in the head by his horse. Bad business. Now . . . if you've finished . . .'

'Yeah, I've done.' The young man emptied his mug and passed it to the landlord. 'Cheers, mate.'

He wiped the foam off his mouth with the back of his hand and walked off along the street.

'Why don't you come home with us, my love?' Daisy Button suggested.

It was early evening. Much to Carina's relief, Hester, who had accompanied the family back to the farmhouse, had at last left, and the children were in bed. Daisy, who was very concerned about her daughter and wanted to talk to her alone, had made them all a cup of tea and suggested she and Carina should have theirs outside, sitting on the bench outside the kitchen door. The heat had gone out of the day now, but Carina's cheeks were still flushed in her otherwise ashen face, and she seemed to be lost in a world of her own. Daisy hoped she wasn't sickening for something; shock, she knew, could lower a person's resistance and bring on all kinds of ailments.

'Carina?' she prompted her. 'I don't like to go home tomorrow and leave you like this.'

Carina seemed to come back from a long way off.

'Sorry – what?'

'I said, why don't you come home with us? For a few days at least. Just until you're feeling a bit better.'

'Oh Mam, I can't do that. What about Sally and Grandpa Luke? I couldn't leave them on their own. And there's so much to do here.'

'That's what's worrying me. You're not up to dealing with it.'

'Someone has to,' Carina said. 'And anyway, I'm trying to keep things as normal as I can for the children. This is their home. They've got their daily routine. I don't want to upset that any more than can be helped.'

Daisy sighed, finishing her tea and putting the mug down on the ground beside her.

She should have known Carina wouldn't agree to her suggestion. She was stubborn, always had been, and she'd feel she was letting Robert down if she walked away from her responsibilities, even if it was for only a few days. But the thought of her beloved daughter having to cope with everything alone when she was devastated by grief and shock was worrying her to death.

'What if I stayed on for a bit?' she suggested, but again Carina shook her head.

'I've got to get used to it, Mam, and the sooner I start the better. Besides, how would Dad manage? He can't so much as boil an egg. No, I'll be all right. You mustn't worry about me.'

'But I do,' Daisy said emphatically. 'You're my daughter. You might be grown up, with children of your own, but that doesn't mean I feel any different now than I did when you were little.'

Carina smiled faintly. 'I know. They go from being a weight in your arms to a weight round your heart. I've heard you say that plenty of times, when Harry was getting into scrapes.'

Harry, her younger brother, had gone through a bit of a wild stage before he'd finally settled down with Dilys, the pretty Welsh girl he'd got in the family way, much to his mother's dismay and his father's disgust.

'I expect I said it when you wanted to marry Robert and

81

move back here, miles away from us,' Daisy said. 'Doesn't make it any less true, though. I just wish you were nearer, so I could help out, with the children if nothing else. As it is . . .'

'We'll be all right,' Carina reiterated.

'But what are you going to do? How are you going to manage?'

'I don't know, Mam. I haven't had a chance to think yet.'

'Well you can't keep the farm on, can you? Not without Robert.'

Carina's head jerked up; her eyes were feverishly bright.

'Why not?'

'Oh Carina, talk sense! Stands to reason – two girls and an old man who can hardly get out of his chair without help?'

'Sally can turn her hand to anything. She's brilliant. She's worked on the land all her life. And you'd be surprised what I've learned, too.'

'But she's not a man, and neither are you,' Daisy argued. 'Two girls running a farm? I can't see it. It was hard enough when Robert was alive, I seem to recall. You'll have to sell up, my love. There's no other way around it.'

'The farm's not mine to sell,' Carina said. 'It belongs to Luke, and as long as he's alive, it's up to him. Besides, what would we do?'

'You could always go back to your trade. You were a lovely seamstress and dressmaker, and there'll always be people who want sewing done.'

'And where would we live? Meadow Farm is Luke's home, and Sally's, and mine and the children's too.'

Daisy shook her head helplessly.

'I still say you're going to have to think again. But it's early days, I suppose. Given time, I dare say you'll come to realise you don't have any option.'

'We'll see.' Carina's tone was mulish, her mouth a hard line.

Although she wished she'd been able to persuade her differently, at least that was more like the old Carina, Daisy thought. Headstrong and stubborn. And eventually she'd come to her senses – she'd have to. For the moment, if it helped her to cope with her grief, perhaps it wasn't such a bad thing.

As she turned into the last stretch of road before reaching the track that led down to Fairley Terrace, Hester Dallimore was surprised to see her husband Sid waiting for her. After he came home from work, Sid didn't usually go out again. He wasn't one for a drink, apart from the occasional drop of whisky, and neither was he the sociable sort: as a deputy at New Grove Colliery, he hadn't made himself popular, and had few mates. His usual routine was to sit down after he'd had his bath and his tea and read the paper or snooze until bedtime, although at this time of year he did sometimes do a bit in the garden, pulling a weed, or putting Derris Dust on the broad beans, which were always later than anyone else's because he'd had to be nagged into remembering to put them in.

Today, knowing she'd be out at the funeral when he got home, Hester had left him a plate of cold meat and cheese, and some bubble and squeak left over from yesterday that he only needed to put in the pan to warm through, though whether he'd be able to be bothered, she wasn't sure. After he'd eaten, he'd leave the dirty dishes on the table, more likely than not, and sit himself down for what he considered a well-earned rest.

What in the world had got into him to make him come and meet her?

'This is a surprise!' she said when she reached him.

'Well, I were a bit concerned about you.'

Sid was a slightly built man, thin, and several inches shorter than Hester, with a weaselly face and thinning hair that straggled over a peeling pink scalp. The previous Sunday he had fallen asleep in a deckchair on their patch of scrubby lawn, not realising that the knotted handkerchief he'd covered his head with had blown off in a sudden breeze. As for what was left of his hair, Hester always cut it herself these days. 'No sense wasting good money on a barber when you haven't got enough to cover a hard-boiled egg,' was her acid assessment.

She took his arm now.

'Concerned? Why? You knew I'd gone to the funeral.'

'Oh ah, I knew that. But I thought you'd be home before now, and with this varmint on the loose, I were starting to get worried.'

'Varmint?' Hester repeated. 'What varmint?'

'I don't s'pose you'll have heard. But it was all the talk when we came out of work. Some thug walked into Ticker Bendle's this afternoon, threatened Ticker with a knife and made off with all his takings.'

Ticker Bendle was the local bookmaker, with an office in a gaggle of buildings that were mostly used as storerooms by a builder's merchant.

'Good Lord!' Hester was shocked. 'In broad daylight?'

'Well, seeing as 'twere about four o'clock in the afternoon, couldn't have been anything else! I s'pose 'twere quiet enough then, though. Not like on a Saturday.'

'All the same . . . anybody could have walked in!'

'Could have, I s'pose, but they didn't.'

'Is Ticker all right?'

'Far as I know. He's shook up pretty bad, though.'

'And in a way about losing his takings, I expect. A good job it wasn't a couple of weeks ago, on Derby day!'

'Right enough. Well, you never know what's going to happen,

do you? And I thought, with a man like that on the loose, and you out on your own, walking round all them lanes . . .'

'Hah! I'd like to see the man who tried to steal my bag!' Hester snorted. 'Not that he'd get much if he did.' But she was gratified all the same that Sid had been concerned for her safety. It was a long time since anyone had shown a desire to protect her.

They reached the track leading down to Fairley Terrace, and as they turned the corner came upon Dolly Oglethorpe and May Cooper, who were outside their houses deep in conversation. It didn't take much to work out what they were talking about; in fact, the robbery was probably being discussed all over town, and Hester felt put out. She'd thought she'd be able to hold court with all the details of the funeral, which was, after all, a terrible tragedy given Robert's young age. But Ticker Bendle being robbed at knifepoint trumped that all right, and she hadn't even known about it until Sid had told her!

'Have you heard if they've caught him yet?' Dolly asked Sid as they drew level with the two neighbours. Sid, not her. Hester fumed inwardly.

'Haven't heard, Mrs Oglethorpe. Weren't a local, I shouldn't think.'

'I should hope not!' Dolly said, and May added:

'What a thing! And Ticker couldn't even give the police a description, from what I heard. The rascal had a handkerchief over his face, just like the bandits in the Wild West, and a cap pulled well down.'

'Still, just as long as Ticker's all right,' Dolly said. 'That's the main thing. Money can always be replaced.'

''Specially if you're in Ticker's line of business,' Sid said wryly. 'There's always going to be some fool ready to throw it away.'

'How was the funeral, Hester?' May asked belatedly.

'A sad do,' Hester said. 'I don't know how our Carina's going to manage, and that's a fact.'

'Well, give her our best when you see her.'

And that was it. Her moment of glory ruined by some thug who'd shown the law a clean pair of heels and was probably well away by now, looking for the next likely target.

'Did you hot up that bubble and squeak I left you?' Hester asked Sid as they walked on along the rank to number 9.

'I thought I'd leave it till you got home,' Sid said. 'You'll make a better job of it than me.'

And that's why you were worried about me, Hester thought bitterly. You didn't fancy having to get your own meal.

She let go of Sid's arm and stalked, annoyed, into the house.

No matter that it was the day of Robert's funeral, life on the farm had to go on, and Sally was not altogether sorry. It was a relief to escape from the claustrophobic atmosphere in the farmhouse. Luke was exhausted, sitting silently in his chair, though not asleep for once but awake and brooding. Carina's Aunt Hester had been nothing but a trial until she eventually left, and although her parents were nice people, Sally didn't know them well enough to be altogether comfortable in their presence.

At least in the milking shed with only the cows for company she could be alone with her thoughts, and the solid, steaming bodies were familiar and comforting.

Once she'd finished the milking, she turned the cows out but lingered in the cooling early evening air, reluctant to go back and join the others. After a few minutes sitting on an upturned pail, she made her way to Captain's stable.

The big old shire lumbered towards her as she went inside,

nudging her gently with his nose. He knew from experience that she usually had a carrot or some other treat for him in her pocket.

'Sorry, Captain, I haven't got anything for you tonight.'

As if he understood her, he turned away, peacefully cropping the hay she'd replenished before going to the funeral, and she leaned against his solid shoulder, gaining comfort from the scratch of his coarse hair on her cheek and the familiar smell in her nostrils.

'Oh Captain, I can't believe you killed Robert,' she said aloud, voicing the doubts that still assailed her. 'You wouldn't harm a fly.'

It was dim in the stable, but a ray of late sun slanted in through the small window high up in the wall, and motes of dust and particles of hay danced in it like minute bits of confetti tossed at a wedding. It glanced off the bridles and harnesses on their hooks, making the brass gleam dully, and lit a long section of the side wall. Sally winced as she noticed a dark stain, half covered by straw, on the floor beneath.

In a stable, of course, it could be any manner of things, but she couldn't escape her conviction that it was blood. Robert's blood. She couldn't think why she hadn't noticed it before, when she'd been mucking out, but that was normally one of her morning jobs, when the sun was quite the other way. And in any case, she had been too preoccupied to take much notice. Now, however, she was unable to tear her eyes away from it.

Gruesome though it was, much as it made her stomach turn, she was somehow drawn to it as if by a powerful magnet. It was something of Robert that was here with her still. His body was buried now beneath six feet of earth, but his blood was here – or at least she thought that was what it was.

She slid down on to her haunches, staring at the stain

mesmerised, then leaned over, brushing the straw aside so as to touch it. As she did so, she saw something winking up at her from beneath the dry, light covering. Puzzled, she picked it up.

A button. Just a button, brown and shiny, with a few threads of cotton clinging between the four central eye holes. But a cold shiver was prickling up her spine, and she realised she was scarcely breathing.

There were plenty of ways to explain what it was doing here, of course. The casual labourers had been in and out of the stable during the harvest – it could have been dropped by one of them, though she didn't recall any of them wearing coats or jackets. They'd been either shirtsleeved or, in the heat of the day, bare-chested. But that didn't mean they hadn't brought a coat to put on if it turned cool late in the evening. Or perhaps the button had lain here for years, somehow missed each time the stable was cleaned out, pushed from here to there by the rake and the broom, falling from a shovelful of straw and mulch to hide away again.

But Sally wasn't buying any of that. She was now more convinced than ever that it was not Captain who was to blame for Robert's injury, or at least, not without provocation.

It was her firm belief that they had not been mistaken when they'd thought an intruder was on the premises the night before Robert died. And whoever he was, he had still been on the premises the following morning. Perhaps he had bedded down in the stable and Robert had discovered him there. There could have been a scuffle, Robert had fallen, and inadvertently Captain had kicked out.

Or maybe it hadn't been the horse that had caused the injury at all. She hadn't noticed any blood on his hoof, though of course he might have trampled it into the straw. Was it possible that the intruder had lashed out with a heavy instrument of some kind and it had been assumed Captain was responsible for the fatal injury simply because Robert had been found here in the stable?

Carried away now by her reasoning, Sally began hunting for a likely weapon. Goodness knows, there were plenty to choose from – shovels, a pickaxe, even a length of metal piping discarded in a corner. But she could see no evidence on any of them that they had been used in an assault.

As she realised the futility of it, she bent her head, covering her face with her hands and feeling the grief and loss overwhelm her once more. No tears came – she thought she had cried herself dry – but never before in the whole of her life had she felt as lonely and bereft as she did now.

At last she straightened and patted the horse once more.

'It wasn't your fault, boy, I'm sure of it. But whether I can ever prove it . . . well, that's another matter.'

She spat into her handkerchief and wiped her face, which she felt sure must be filthy. Then she went back to join the others in the farmhouse.

By evening, the news of the robbery at the bookmaker's office had spread all over the district. It was dramatic enough to dominate most conversations, and the talk in the bar of the Dunderwick Arms was no exception.

'Have 'ee 'eard if they've got anybody for it yet?'

'Shouldn't think so. Whoever it were would've bin long gone afore Sergeant Love came on the scene.'

'He'd have bin called quick though, wouldn't 'er? Ticker's got one of them thar telephone gadgets. Has to, I s'pose, in his line of business.'

'Couldn't have called the coppers till the thief had legged it, though, could he?'

'True enough. An' Sergeant Love don't get about as quick on that bike of 'is as 'er used to.'

The public bar of the Dunderwick Arms was small enough for the conversation to be a general one. Those seated round the tables or on the padded window seats were able to join in with the men who leaned on the bar or perched on the high stools dotted along its length.

''Tweren't anybody local, I don't s'pose. Would've bin some varmint out o' Bath or Bristol.'

'How come they knew about Ticker, then?'

'Ev'rybody d'know Ticker. An' they know he don't go to bank with his takings as often as he ought to neither.'

'Wouldn't 'ave bin anybody local. They'd know Ticker 'ould recognise 'em and they'd be done for.'

'How come he weren't spotted anyway? A stranger in High Compton 'ould stand out like a sore thumb.'

'There were a stranger in here at dinner time.' Nobby Clark, a wizened little man sitting in his usual seat in the inglenook with his pint, spoke for the first time.

'In here?'

'A stranger?'

'Did you see 'im then, Nobby?'

'Oh ah.'

Nobby was a regular whenever the pub was open. Common conjecture was that he came to escape the nagging wife who had made his life a misery since he'd retired.

'You seen 'un, didn't 'ee, Clem?' he called to the landlord for confirmation. 'Well, you must'a done seeing as you served 'un.'

''Course I seen 'un. An' he weren't in no hurry to leave neither. But he were a respectable enough young chap. I wouldn't have served 'un otherwise.'

'What were he like, then?'

'Like I say, respectable.' Clem Porter was bristling at the suggestion that he might have offered hospitality to a common criminal.

'Where'd he go?'

'How the dickens am I supposed to know that? I don't ask you lot where you're going when you leave here. Which is just as well, if you ask me.'

He cast a dark, meaningful look at a couple of his regulars who, he suspected, didn't always go straight home to their missuses.

'Let's just hope that whoever did Ticker over has hightailed it back wherever he came from,' ventured Petey Perkins, known for a peacemaker.

'Let's hope so, ah.'

The topic having been exhausted, the pub's customers turned their attention to other things, namely the forthcoming village flower show and the annual cricket match between Dunderwick and Hillsbridge, and for the time being the hold-up at Ticker's office, as it was being described, was forgotten.

Chapter Eight

Carina sat at the kitchen table, the leather-covered farm accounts book open in front of her, a heap of bills that needed to be paid to her left, a cup of tea gone cold to her right, desperately trying to make sense of it all.

This was a side to the running of the farm she'd never been initiated into. She'd learned to milk a cow, churn butter, sort eggs, and a hundred and one other everyday tasks. But Robert had always dealt with the financial aspect of things.

Carina had once offered to take on the chore that often kept him up late when he should have been in bed after a long day out on the land and was faced with an early start again the following morning, but he had refused point blank to even discuss it. Now she wondered if his reluctance had been because he hadn't wanted her to see just how tight things had become since Grandpa Luke had been unable to work and they'd had to bring in hired help. And of course there was the added expense that came with two children to feed and clothe, not to mention herself. From what she could make out by looking back to earlier times, the farm had been profitable once. The accounts recorded in the early pages, the figures entered in what she imagined was Grandpa Luke's firm sloping hand, looked to be quite healthy. Now every penny, it seemed, was spoken for.

No wonder Robert had been so angry with her for damaging his precious Rover, and, worse, Lord Melbrook's motor. He must have been wondering how on earth he was going to cover the extra expense.

Tears sprang to Carina's eyes as she remembered the terrible row the night before he had died, and wondered, as she had wondered so often in the days that followed, if it had been to blame for the accident. Had Robert been careless around Captain because his mind was elsewhere?

Even if it hadn't had anything to do with what had happened, she still felt a huge weight of guilt that she had ruined what had turned out to be the last day they would ever spend together through her unforgivable recklessness. Robert had been so angry with her – and understandably so. And, she thought, he had still been angry with her when they'd gone to bed. He'd denied it was the reason he'd rebuffed her overtures to lovemaking, saying he was just dog tired. But Carina couldn't get it out of her head that his fury at her stupidity had had something to do with it too. Oh, if only they'd been able to share one last night of tenderness! But they hadn't, and she had only herself to blame.

Grief and guilt and an overwhelming sense of despair knotted together in her stomach, but somehow she dragged her attention back to the task in hand.

How on earth she was going to keep things going where even Robert had struggled, she didn't know. But somehow she had to. She owed it to him, and to Sally and Grandpa Luke and the children.

Suddenly she was remembering the promise she had made to Meg, that had also felt like a solemn vow to Robert.

Somehow she would find a way to keep Meadowbrook, which he had loved so much, and ensure a safe and happy future for what was left of their precious family.

* * *

It wasn't just the finances causing problems, of course, but also the day-to-day running of the farm.

At least the harvest was in now, though given the weather, there might be a second one, but there was still so much to do, and Sally was struggling to keep on top of things. Only this morning the man collecting the milk churns had come down to the house to warn them that some of the cows had broken through the fence and were wandering in the road. Carina had had to leave Grandpa Luke in charge of Meg and Mattie while she helped Sally to round them up. Then Sally had had to spend half the morning repairing the fence, something Robert would have done in half the time.

'We're going to have to get some help,' she'd said when she came in for her dinner, her hands covered in blisters.

'I don't know if we can afford it,' Carina admitted. 'And who could we ask? Wally and the others are all committed at this time of year with their regulars. I don't suppose they could fit in extra hours for us even if we could afford to pay them.'

'Are things that bad?' Sally asked, keeping her voice low as Carina had done so that Grandpa Luke wouldn't hear what they were saying. Neither of the girls wanted to worry him.

Carina nodded grimly.

'They're not good, that's for sure. But I suppose we're going to have to find the money somehow. We can't go on like this.' She paused, thinking. 'I wonder if Mr Perkins or Mr Harvey would be prepared to loan us one of their hands until we can find someone permanent?'

'Not Mr Perkins,' Sally said firmly.

Carina cast her a questioning look. 'But you and David . . .'

'Exactly. David might come over himself, and the last thing I want is to be beholden to him. He's a nice chap, I know, and

I am fond of him, but I don't want to give him more ideas than he already has.'

Carina sighed, biting her lip. 'Mr Harvey, then? He was good enough to drive Grandpa to the funeral, after all.'

'I suppose it's worth asking. Just a few hours every now and then would make all the difference.' Sally took a long pull of the cider that she'd taken to drinking as the men did, and refilled her mug from the earthenware jug.

'You'll be falling asleep on the job if you drink any more of that,' Carina cautioned.

'Chance would be a fine thing!' Sally retorted.

'Well, it's your funeral.'

The moment the words were out, she regretted them. How could she have been so crass? But Sally didn't seem to have noticed. She was too lost in wondering, like Carina, how they were going to manage. Goodness only knew, she was not afraid of hard work, but there was only so much she could do on her own.

'So will you have a word with Martin Harvey, or shall I?' she asked.

'I think it might come better from you.' Carina brushed a strand of hair from her face, and began mashing up potato and carrots with a drop of gravy in Mattie's bowl. 'You've known him ever since you were a little girl.'

'Without a care in the world.' Sally laughed bitterly. 'All right, leave Martin Harvey to me. But we really have to get something sorted out.'

'I know.'

The weight of responsibility was pressing heavily on her shoulders once more.

Oh Robert, Robert, why did you have to die? I miss you so much . . .

But wishing he were still here, coming in ravenous for his

dinner, dropping a kiss on her hair, swinging Meg into the air, chucking Mattie under the chin, would do no good at all.

The kitchen door slammed suddenly and Carina whirled round, half expecting to see him there. But of course it was no one, just a sudden gust of wind.

'D'you think the weather is on the change?' Sally asked, and Carina simply shrugged helplessly.

She had no idea, and in the great scheme of things, it hardly mattered.

Mid-afternoon. Carina was preparing vegetables for a stew, not the most suitable meal when the weather remained so hot, but it was cheap, and she still had onions and turnips stored from last year that needed to be used up. Grandpa Luke would peel the potatoes for her later – it was one of the jobs he could still do, sitting with a bowl between his knees and paring off the skins into long curling strips with his old wooden-handled knife that had been sharpened so often the blade was no more than a short tapering strip. At the moment, however, he was fast asleep in his chair – his afternoon naps seemed to get longer and longer each day – and for once the children were playing together quite nicely, building a structure of some kind with Mattie's wooden blocks. Sally, of course, was back out on the farm, trying to finish a few more jobs before it was milking time again.

The peace was shattered suddenly by the sound of a motor engine. Startled, Carina looked up and saw, through the kitchen window, a car she instantly recognised as the one she had collided with, turning into the farmyard. Her heart came into her mouth with a sickening thud.

Lord Melbrook. Oh no!

She dropped a half-peeled turnip into the sink and hurried to the door, her hands flying over her hair to tidy it, and horribly conscious of the fact that she was wearing one of her oldest working dresses and that her apron was stained with the mashed carrots Mattie had been throwing everywhere at dinner time. She went out into the yard, half closing the door behind her so that the children wouldn't follow her out.

Lord Melbrook climbed out of the Benz, slammed the door behind him and strode purposefully towards her, making light of his obvious limp. In an open-necked white shirt and narrow grey trousers, there was a casual elegance about him, but there was nothing casual in the way he was approaching her, and his expression was stern. This was no social call.

Feeling every bit as embarrassed as she had been when she had crashed into his motor, Carina wished with all her heart that she could run away and hide. But of course she couldn't. She had to stand her ground, not behave like some naughty child.

And in any case . . . how dare he come here, pestering her, when Robert was scarcely cold in his grave! A sudden flash of anger gave Carina courage. She folded her arms, lifted her chin and met his gaze defiantly.

'Lord Melbrook. This is a surprise.'

'Really? I would have thought you would be expecting me. As I have been expecting to hear from you. You'll notice my motor has been repaired now, so I have an exact figure for what it cost.'

Staggered by the sheer insensitivity of the man, Carina was rendered speechless for a moment. Then the anger and disgust she was feeling ratcheted up another notch and she found her voice.

'How dare you!'

Lord Melbrook looked surprised and a little affronted.

'Mrs Talbot, you agreed to make good the damage, as I recall. Damage for which you were undoubtedly responsible. Is

97

your husband at home? If so, perhaps we can settle the matter here and now and be done with it. If not, then here is the garage bill – perhaps you would be so good as to give it to him.'

'I don't believe this!' Carina was shaking now, but still defiant. 'Of course my husband isn't here, as I think you very well know. But don't worry, you'll get your money. I pay my debts, just as he did.'

'I beg your pardon?'

Carina was too upset and angry to notice the look of bewilderment on the scarred but still good-looking face.

'I suppose you think you can come here and bully me now I'm alone, just because you are who you are. Well let me tell you, there's not a single one of your tenants who'd stoop to such . . . such . . .' For a moment she was unable to think of an appropriate word to describe his despicable behaviour. 'Callousness!'

'Mrs Talbot—'

'Oh, I know I damaged your precious motor,' Carina rushed on. 'I was in the wrong, I admit it. But to come here, hounding me for money, when I've only just buried my husband . . .'

'What are you saying?'

'Don't pretend you don't know! It's been the talk of Dunderwick, I should think.'

'I've been out of the country for the past week, Mrs Talbot. I only got home last evening. I'm afraid I don't—'

'Robert is dead.' Carina's chin quivered, but her voice was as strong and full of fury as before. 'He was kicked in the head by our carthorse and killed. So now you know, if you didn't before. But don't worry, you'll get your money. I'll make sure of that.'

She reached out and snatched the sheet of paper from his hand, then turned and went into the house, slamming the door behind her.

* * *

Cal Melbrook stood for a moment staring at the solid oak of the kitchen door, completely shocked by Carina's outburst and the dreadful news that Robert Talbot was dead, and appalled that he had unwittingly trampled all over his widow's grief.

But how was he to know what had happened? As he'd said, he had been out of the country for the past week, but even if he had been at home, it could have passed him by. Busy as he was trying to sort out the mess his brother had left the estate in, he had no time for idle gossip, and it wasn't as if the Talbots were his tenants.

But all the same . . .

Cal hesitated, wondering if he should knock on the door again and apologise. She'd given him no chance to do that, and it would go some way to easing his conscience. But beyond that, what good would it do? He could tell her that under the circumstances he'd forget about pressing for payment for repairs to the Benz, but it could be that that would only make matters worse. He *wouldn't* press her, of course. He wasn't that heartless, or that desperate for a few pounds. But he rather thought that telling her so in her present mood might very well offend her. She'd assume that he thought she couldn't afford to pay, and perhaps with her husband dead, she couldn't, but her fierce pride would never allow her to admit it.

She wasn't likely to accept his apology either. Perhaps it would be better to write to her. At least she would have cooled down by the time a letter arrived. Though if she knew it was from him, she might assume it was a further request for money and throw it away unopened . . .

Cal swore to himself, annoyed by the indecisiveness that was not normally a part of his nature. Then, making up his mind, he rapped on the door and stood back, not wanting to appear threatening in any way when she opened it.

For long moments nothing happened, though he could hear voices within the house. Then he heard the click of the lock, the creak of a hinge, and the door opened. To his surprise, however, it was not the young widow who stood there, but an old man, leaning heavily on a stick and holding on to the door jamb for extra support.

'I'm sorry, Lord Melbrook, but she don't want to see you. She's said all she's got to say, and that's an end of it.'

This must be Luke Green, Cal realised. He had vague memories of a strong, well-built figure, glimpsed occasionally working in the fields or driving a horse and cart, but it was years now since he'd seen him, and the change in him was shocking. This man was frail and wasted, his eyes clouded above sunken cheeks and a neck that might have belonged to a Christmas turkey after it had been plucked. But there was nothing feeble about his voice. Despite the slight tremor in it, it was firm and decisive.

'Mr Green, I can only apologise if I've upset Mrs Talbot,' Cal said. 'I really had no idea that she had lost her husband – and you your grandson. It's unforgivable that I should have come here at such a time.'

'Ah, you'm right there, my son,' the old man said, with none of the deference usually shown to the gentry. 'She's got enough on her plate without you adding to it.'

'I'm sure. Will you please tell her I was totally unaware of what had happened, and of course I shall not be pressing her for payment of the debt.'

'I'll tell her.' Luke nodded shortly. 'Now if there's nothing else, perhaps you'll leave us alone to grieve in peace.'

'There's nothing. But I am truly sorry.'

Cal turned and crossed to the Benz without so much as a backward glance, unaware that behind him Luke was cursing him for an arrogant swine without realising it was Cal's natural dignity that made him appear cold and unfeeling. And certainly, as he started the car and turned it around, Cal was also cursing himself.

How could he have put his foot in it so badly?

But then again, how was he to have known the circumstances?

Guilt made him irritable, but at the same time he couldn't help but admire Mrs Talbot. She was a firecracker, and no mistake. Though clearly devastated by grief, she had stood her ground with courage and spirit. She was pretty, too, or would have been if it hadn't been for the dark circles under her eyes. Robert Talbot had been a lucky man.

As he drove back along the rutted track to the main road, the prime location of Meadow Farm struck him, not for the first time. No doubt about it, it had far more potential than any of the tenant farms. Cal felt sure it had once been a profitable holding, and, with the right stewardship, could be again. Claud Robbins – before Cal had given him his marching orders – had said as much. He had intimated that in his opinion the place had been allowed to go downhill in recent years, and now that Cal had seen for himself the state of Luke Green's health, he could understand the reason for that. It had been left to the grandson to run the property, presumably, and he had been too young and inexperienced to make a go of it.

So what hope was there for it now?

Cal's eyes narrowed as the likely opportunity presented itself to him. There was nothing he'd like more than to have Meadow Farm back in the fold of the Dunderwick estate where it belonged. If he put in a good, experienced tenant farmer at a rent that reflected the possibilities the place offered, it would provide a much-needed boost to the estate finances.

And thanks to the collector, who had paid a good price for the antique china he'd taken to France last week, he had some ready cash. More than enough to make an offer for Meadow Farm, which was almost certain to be put on the market at a knockdown price when old Luke Green and Carina Talbot realised they could no longer keep the place going.

Cal's spirits rose.

He was sorry, of course, that young Talbot was dead, but these things happened. He'd seen too many men and boys of Robert's age meet their maker in South Africa to feel overly sentimental about it. He was sorry, too, for his young and spirited widow, left alone with two children and an elderly man to care for, but they weren't his problem.

It was an ill wind that blew nobody any good, as the old saying went. He thought it was about time some luck was blown in his direction.

'Well, that's seen him off with a flea in his ear,' Grandpa Luke said as the Benz drove out of the farmyard. 'Now, d'you want me to peel the spuds for you, m'dear?'

'If you like.'

Carina didn't want to talk about the unpleasant encounter, and Grandpa Luke seemed to have dismissed it in the matter-of-fact way that was so typical of him. He didn't believe in wasting time and energy on going over and over things, agonising about what couldn't be changed, or harbouring grudges. It was an attitude Carina had grown used to, and it had made his outburst when Robert had lost his temper over her accident all the more surprising. Now, it seemed, he had reverted to his usual acceptance; basically he was a quiet man who liked a quiet life, though as he had just demonstrated, he could stand his ground when it was called for.

She waited until he was settled in his chair, then took him the potatoes, a bowl and his knife. At once Meg and Mattie abandoned the wooden blocks they'd been playing with and scooted over to sit at his feet. They were endlessly fascinated by those long curling ribbons of peel, picking them out of the bowl as they fell to see who could get the longest, though Mattie inevitably managed to break his, so Meg was always the winner.

With any luck the competition would keep them occupied for a bit, and Carina was glad of it. The contretemps with Lord Melbrook had upset her far more than she cared to admit. Her hands were shaking now as she finished the turnips and started on the onions, which would certainly make her cry, but which would provide a good excuse if she was unable to hold back the tears of reaction to the horrible encounter as well as a fresh wave of grief that was welling up in her.

Oh, how she despised that man! she thought, cutting savagely into the skin of an onion. He had been horrible to her when she'd had the accident, and even more horrible today. Even if it were true that he hadn't known about Robert dying, he'd been all too ready to come here and demand his pound of flesh, no matter that he could buy and sell their farm a dozen times over. He must have realised that paying for the damage would be hard for them, yet he hadn't been prepared to let it go, and although Carina knew that he was well within his rights, and the accident had been entirely her fault, it didn't excuse the arrogant way he'd treated her.

Well, she'd find the money and pay him somehow. She wouldn't be beholden to the likes of him.

But how would she do it? Paying the casual labourers for their time bringing in the harvest had eaten into her reserves, and most of the rest would have to go to the undertaker. She still had to buy food for the family, and there would be no more money coming in until market day, when hopefully Sally would come home with decent takings from the sale of their butter, bacon and cheese. There would be money at the end of the month from the dairy for the milk they'd supplied, but how far would that go? Meg had complained that her boots were pinching, and Mattie couldn't wear Meg's old dresses for ever. Carina had wanted to put him into rompers soon, but what hope was there of that now? The meagre income would be eaten up by necessities. And on top of all this, as Sally had said, they really needed to take on a hand to help out if they were to keep the farm running. How in the world could she afford to pay Lord Melbrook for the repairs to his motor?

The juice from the onions was really beginning to sting her eyes now, so that they were squeezing tight involuntarily and the tears were running down her cheeks. She brushed them away with the back of her hand and stuck the peeled onion into a saucepan of water.

Damn Lord Melbrook! Damn him! Somehow, of all her problems, it was being in debt to him that irked her the most. She had to find a way to get him off her back.

The solution came to her in a flash, though in that first instant she recoiled from it. Her engagement ring. It was the most precious thing she owned, really the only thing of any value. How much it had cost Robert she didn't know, only that he had told her, as he slipped it on her finger, to be sure not to lose it.

'As if I would!' She had gazed down in wonder at the five little diamonds, arranged in a row with the largest in the centre, that winked up at her. 'Don't worry, I'll keep it safe for ever.'

He'd kissed her then, and she had swelled with so much love and happiness she had thought she would burst.

Oh, how she had treasured that ring, a symbol of their love and a constant reminder of that happy day when he had put it on her finger. She'd worn it with such pride, finding ways to show it off to the world without appearing to be doing it deliberately, using her left hand rather than her right whenever she could, and refusing to wear gloves though the cold of winter had frozen her fingers.

After they were married, she'd worn it less often; the chores meant that her hands were often in water, washing dishes, washing clothes, washing eggs. The ring had remained safe in its leather box on her dressing table, and she took it out now only for special occasions and to look at it sometimes, just for the sheer pleasure of gazing at those tiny sparkling stones and remembering how much joy they had brought her.

The thought of selling it now was a dreadful one, but it seemed to Carina it was the only solution. Tomorrow she would find an excuse to go into town and pay a visit to the jeweller; she didn't want Sally or Grandpa Luke to know what she was planning to do. That they had come to such dire straits would cause Sally distress, and goodness only knew, she was suffering enough. Carina had never seen the usually carefree girl so low. And it was possible that Grandpa Luke might have some items of value that he would feel obliged to offer to sell to prevent her from making the sacrifice: the pocket watch whose face he was no longer able to read but which had belonged to his father, or perhaps some items of Margaret's jewellery that he treasured. They would be of just as much sentimental value to him as the ring was to her, and this was her problem. She'd been the one who had caused them to end up in debt to Lord Melbrook; why should Grandpa Luke have to suffer for it?

Her mind made up, Carina picked out another onion from the basket and, resigning herself to yet more tears, began to peel it.

Chapter Nine

Sitting at her dressing table, Carina slid open the smallest drawer and took out the leather box. Her hand was shaking and there was a lump in her throat. It was one thing to come to the decision that she would have to sell the ring in order to pay Lord Melbrook what she owed him; quite another to actually part with it. But what choice did she have?

She opened the box, took out the ring and slipped it on her finger. As she spread her hand, the light from the window caught the tiny diamonds, making them wink, and tears stung her eyes as she remembered the happiness it had brought her.

She was so lucky, she thought. Lucky to have met Robert, lucky to have had such a happy marriage, and two lovely children. Some people lived their whole lives without ever knowing half the joy and satisfaction that she had been blessed with. That was what she had to hang on to. The ring . . . it was just a bit of jewellery. She might have to part with it, but she still had her memories, and no one could take those away.

Filled with new resolve, she replaced the ring on its velvet cushion, closed the box and slipped it into her bag. Then she went downstairs.

Sally had come in for a little break from her chores; she was sitting at the kitchen table with a mug of tea and a hunk of bread and butter, and the children were happily occupied playing some game that involved a lot of crawling about under the table, which had, it seemed, become a make-believe house where Meg was the mother and Mattie her child.

'Could you keep an eye on them for an hour or so?' Carina asked Sally. 'I have to pop into Hillsbridge.'

'I've got an awful lot to do,' Sally objected.

'I know, but I promise I'll be as quick as I can, and I can always give you a hand when I get back.'

Sally eyed her suspiciously.

'How are you getting there?'

'I'm taking the Rover, of course. I'd never get there and back in an hour on foot.'

'Are you sure that's wise after what happened last time?' Sally asked.

'I'll make sure it doesn't happen again. It wouldn't have happened at all if it hadn't been for that darned wasp. The motor's there; we might as well make use of it.' And she headed for the door before Sally could raise any further objection.

Some of her confidence ebbed away, however, as she approached the Rover. All very well to pretend bravado, but inwardly she quaked at the thought of getting back into the driver's seat.

Come on, you can do it! she urged herself. You'll be fine. Lightning never strikes in the same place twice.

Sure enough, when she had got the motor going and man-oeuvred out of the farmyard and on to the track, her confidence began to return.

This time the drive was uneventful, though she was relieved to reach Hillsbridge without mishap. As she pulled up outside the jeweller's, a small boy running ahead of his mother was so astonished by the sight of the motor that he forgot all about the hoop he had been bowling and it ran into the road, whirling in a crazy circle before crashing into the pavement on the opposite side, causing his mother to shout at him.

'Look what you're doing, our Winston! Go and fetch it, quick, before another motor comes along and runs over it.'

Carina smiled to herself. There was not another motor in sight, and if she was lucky, there wouldn't be.

She climbed out of the car and went into the jeweller's shop. It was empty, no customers, and no one behind the counter, but when he heard the jangle of the bell, Mr Johnson, the jeweller, came hurrying out from the back room.

'Good morning, good morning! And how can I be of assistance this lovely morning?'

Mr Johnson was of Jewish descent, a small, wiry man with round-rimmed spectacles pushed up onto a high forehead. Besides the jewellery business, he also repaired clocks and watches in the little workroom behind the shop.

Carina decided this was no time to beat about the bush.

'I have a ring to sell.' She delved into her bag, retrieving the box, opening it and placing it on the glass counter, beneath which various items were set out on display shelves. 'As you can see, it's diamonds and gold, and I'm hoping you can offer me a good price.'

'Hmm.' Mr Johnson opened a drawer, extracted a small magnifying glass and, lowering his spectacles, fitted it in one eye to examine Carina's precious ring.

'Diamonds, yes, but very small.'

'And set in gold.'

Mr Johnson examined the ring again, then replaced it in its box, popped out the magnifying glass and shook his head.

'I'm sorry, but I don't think I am able to make you an offer on this occasion.'

Carina's heart sank.

'But why not? What's wrong with it?'

'This is an engagement ring, if I'm not mistaken.'

'Yes, but . . .'

'I don't have much call for second-hand engagement rings, I'm afraid. Young couples, on the whole, tend to be superstitious. They like to buy new. If the stones were of high quality I might be tempted to make an exception, but unfortunately they don't fall into that category.'

'Oh.' Carina really didn't know what to say, not only disappointed at his refusal to buy her ring but also hurt by the way he was dismissing it as if it were just some cheap trinket.

'I'm sorry.' Mr Johnson looked at her shrewdly. He didn't know who she was, but he could sense her desperation, and he had spotted the wedding band on her ring finger. It wasn't just a case of some snap decision made after a lovers' tiff. This was a woman so much in need of money that she was prepared to part with a ring that clearly meant a great deal to her.

'I think your best option would be a pawnbroker,' he suggested.

'A pawnbroker?'

He nodded. 'He would make you a cash advance, and when your circumstances improve, you would be able to buy back your ring. Though of course he would also have the right to sell it should that take too long.'

Carina's heart leapt with sudden hope. A chance to buy her ring back! When she'd be able to afford to do that was another matter entirely, of course. But the possibility was there, remote as it might be.

'Where would I find a pawnbroker?' she asked. Such a place was completely outside her experience.

Mr Johnson smiled faintly.

'Not in Hillsbridge or High Compton, I'm afraid. You'd need to go to Bath. There are several there. I could give you an address.'

He tore a sheet of paper from a notepad that lay on the counter and wrote on it.

'Take the street opposite the station and head into town. You'll pass a public house on an island where two or three roads join. Take the left fork rather than the right, and you should come upon it.'

'Thank you.' Carina folded the piece of paper and tucked it into her bag along with the box containing her ring.

'I wish you luck, my dear.'

Carina nodded and smiled wanly. She felt flat and emotional both at the same time. All the determination she'd summoned to drive into town and offer her ring for sale had been for nothing.

As for the jeweller's suggestion, the prospect of going all the way to Bath was a daunting one. She had only ever been there once or twice in the whole of her life, and she knew that taking the Rover was out of the question. Quite apart from the fact that it was a good nine or ten miles, there would almost certainly be far more traffic there than in sleepy Hillsbridge. She imagined busy streets teeming with horse-drawn delivery vehicles and other motors and knew it was a challenge far beyond her capabilities. She'd have to go by train, and the trip would take her half a day, or maybe more. How could she manage that?

And even leaving aside the practicalities, could she go through the whole upsetting business of offering her precious ring to a stranger again? Much as she wanted the money she had hoped it would bring, it was immensely comforting to still have it in her possession rather than having to walk out of the shop leaving it behind and knowing she would never see it again.

With an effort, she pushed the dilemma to the back of her mind. The most important thing was concentrating on getting the Rover back to Meadow Farm without a repeat of the disaster that had marred her first attempt at driving alone, and which was still casting its long shadow over her efforts to restore some stability to her precious family.

Soon after Carina had driven out of the farmyard, the children became restless.

'Where's Mammy?' Meg demanded.

'She's gone out for a little while,' Sally said. 'I'm afraid you're going to have to put up with me.'

'Ma-ma!' Mattie emerged from beneath the table and pulled himself up by the seat of Sally's chair, tottering uncertainly on his plump legs.

'Mattie! You naughty boy! What are you doing out of the house?' Meg scolded in perfect imitation of Carina.

Mattie ignored her.

'Ma-ma!' His eyes were tragic, his lower lip thrust out.

'Mattie, I won't tell you again!' Meg gave him a push. He lost his balance and fell, banging his head against the table leg, and began to scream.

'What's going on?' Luke, who had been snoozing, came to with a jolt.

'Oh, nothing, Grandpa.' Sally scooped Mattie up on to her lap, but he continued to scream, tears rolling down his cheeks, which had turned scarlet.

'Ma-ma! Ma-ma!'

Sally examined his forehead, where a swelling had begun.

'We'd better put some butter on this. We don't want your mam coming home and finding you with a lump the size of an egg on your head.' She poked her finger into the butter, still on the table from breakfast, and smoothed some on to the swelling. 'What did you do that for, Meg?'

'He was being naughty,' Meg retorted mulishly. 'I told him he had to stay in our house.'

'You're the naughty one, pushing your little brother over. When your mam gets home I shall tell her so, and she'll say you're not to have any sweets today.'

'Not fair!' Meg's small face contorted and she began to cry too.

'Oh, will you stop this, the pair of you!' Sally snapped, losing patience. 'I can't stand it!'

'Best take them out for a bit,' Grandpa Luke said. 'Where's their mother, anyway?'

'Gone into Hillsbridge.'

'What for?'

'I don't know. She didn't say. She's taken the motor.'

'Well, well.' Luke considered this. 'Let's hope she don't have another accident.'

'We all hope that.' Sally got up. 'Come on, you two. We'll go for a walk over to Mr Harvey's farm. I promised Carina I'd go and see him and ask if he could spare one of his lads to help out until we can find a man of our own,' she said to Luke. 'It might as well be now, seeing as I can't do anything else until she gets back.'

'Ah, he's a good chap, Martin Harvey.'

Sally fetched Mattie's pushchair and plonked him in it. He was still crying, and he kicked against the footrest in a paddy and wriggled so hard that Sally had some difficulty fastening the restraining strap around him.

'Come on, Meg.' She headed for the door. 'A walk will do you good.'

Meg's tears had vanished with the distraction. She ran ahead of Sally. Cymru, who had been lying in the sun outside the back door, got up and began to follow them.

'No, Cymru, you stay here,' Sally told him. He looked up at her pleadingly, but Sally remained firm. She didn't want him to follow them on to another farmer's land. It wouldn't help her cause if he started chasing the chickens who wandered free in Martin Harvey's farmyard, or, worse, decided to round up the sheep. 'Stay!' she repeated, holding up a commanding finger, and the dog did as he was told, though his tail had lowered to half-mast and his reproachful eyes followed them until they were out of sight.

It was a fair walk to Martin Harvey's farm, and Sally set a fast pace so that Meg had some difficulty in keeping up. At last she gave in and allowed Meg to ride on the pushchair, standing on the strut between the back wheels and holding on to the handle. It made the load heavy and awkward, but Sally didn't have the patience to take it more slowly.

As luck would have it, though, she didn't have to go all the way down to the farm. Martin Harvey was out checking fences. A tall, rangy man with baggy trousers tied at the knee with baling twine and a battered hat, he could, at a distance, have been mistaken for a scarecrow.

He straightened when he saw them approaching and walked towards them with a rolling gait.

'Sally? Is everything all right?' He sounded anxious.

'Yes. Well, as right as it can be these days.'

'You're missing your brother, I expect.'

'In every way, Mr Harvey. That's why I'm here, to tell you the truth. We're really struggling, and we were wondering if you could lend us one of your lads for a few hours every so often until we can find someone suitable for ourselves. We'd pay him, of course,' she added.

'Oh, m'dear, now you'm asking. I'm short-handed myself, what with it being that time of year.'

Sally's heart sank, though if she was honest, it was no more than she had expected.

'I understand.'

'I'd help if I could – you know that.'

Now that the comforting motion of the pushchair had stopped and there was no longer anything to distract him, Mattie had started grizzling again.

Meg jumped down from her perch, ran around and gave him a sharp slap on the leg.

'Shut up, Mattie!'

The little boy wailed more loudly, rubbing his hands over his face so that dirt mixed with tears in grimy streaks.

'What is the matter with you, Meg!' Sally exploded. 'How dare you hit your little brother!'

'He's bad,' Meg retorted mutinously.

'He's just a baby, and you're big enough to know better.' Sally tucked a loose strand of hair behind her ear, shaking her head helplessly. 'I'm sorry, Mr Harvey. I don't know what's got into them today.'

'You've got your hands full, Sally, I can see that.' He thought for a moment. 'Look, no promises, but I'll see what I can do. I might be able to spare our Corky for a bit, if it's all right with him. Let me have a think.'

'Oh, Mr Harvey, we'd be so grateful!'

'Like I said, no promises.'

'I know. Look, I won't hold you up any longer . . .'

'That's all right, m'dear. And you know where we are, don't you?'

'Thanks. That's kind. I'd better get these two home.'

Meg climbed back on to the rear of the pushchair, and as

soon as they moved off, Mattie's anguished cries lessened once more.

Perhaps it had been no bad thing that they'd both kicked off, Sally thought. She rather thought it was that which had persuaded Martin Harvey to have second thoughts about sparing one of his sons occasionally. He'd felt sorry for her. But grateful though she was for the offer of even a few hours' help, she felt guilty. Martin Harvey was probably struggling himself, and she'd really put him on the spot.

Sighing deeply, Sally set out for home.

She had covered about half the distance along the road when a cyclist came into view, riding in her direction. David Perkins, it had to be. He was the only person she knew who owned a bicycle and who was likely to be on this road. Sally's heart sank. She hadn't seen him since the funeral, and she really didn't think she could cope with talking to him today. He'd ask questions she didn't want to answer, and be sympathetic, and she couldn't bear that. At this moment she just wanted to be left alone with her grief.

There was no avoiding David, though. As he reached her, he slowed and stopped, a slimly built yet well-muscled young man with a shock of reddish hair. His shirt was open at the neck and the sleeves were rolled up to reveal freckled arms that had turned pale gold working out in the sunshine, while his trousers were caught at the ankle by cycle clips.

'Sal . . .' He was still in the saddle, the bicycle leaning at an angle as he balanced on one long leg.

'David.'

'Sal – I'm so sorry . . . I don't know what to say . . .'

'That's all right. There's nothing to say, really.'

'It's just terrible. I couldn't believe it when I heard.'

115

'No.'

'I wanted to come over, but Mam said best not.'

'Yes.'

An awkward silence. Meg was fidgeting, making the pushchair rock.

'I've got to get these two home . . .' Sally made to move away, but David was right in her path.

'How are you managing?'

'It's not easy, but . . .'

'If there's anything I can do . . . I could come over and give you a hand . . .'

'It's all right. I've just been to see Mr Harvey. He's going to let Corky help us out if we need him,' Sally said, glad that she had met David after she had been to see Martin Harvey and not before. Much as they needed assistance, kind as it was of David to offer, she really didn't want to be beholden to him. If he helped out on the farm she would feel obliged to be a little nicer to him. She really didn't know why she was treating him so badly; she'd just come to feel there was more to life than sticking with the same boy who'd been her companion through her growing-up years, and losing Robert had done nothing to change that.

'Oh, right . . .'

A flush was creeping up his neck, and from his tone, deliberately offhand, Sally could tell she had hurt his feelings. She was sorry for that. It wasn't his fault that she didn't feel the same way about him as he did about her, even if she'd once thought she might.

Meg was leaning into the pushchair, tugging at the curls that were growing down over Mattie's collar, and Mattie was squirming and grizzling again.

'I'm sorry, David, I really have to go,' Sally said.

'Yeah. But don't forget . . . if you need anything . . .'

Reluctantly he moved the bicycle out of Sally's path and she manoeuvred her way past him. But she knew he was still watching her over his shoulder as she headed back along the road to the track leading to Meadow Farm.

Carina had decided she had no option but to explain to Sally why she had been to Hillsbridge today and needed to go to Bath tomorrow. She could hardly concoct an excuse for that.

By the time Sally arrived back with the two children, she had been home for almost an hour and was wading through the chores that had been left undone this morning. She was at the big stone sink, elbow deep in suds as she washed nappies, when she saw them come into the farmyard, Meg trudging mutinously behind Sally – who had eventually tired of struggling to balance the pushchair with her riding on it – and Mattie crying.

Carina grabbed the kitchen towel and hurried out to meet them, drying her hands roughly as she went.

'Oh thank goodness you're back!' Sally greeted her. 'These two have been driving me crazy.'

Carina draped the towel over her shoulder and crouched down beside the pushchair. Luke had told her that Sally had gone to see Martin Harvey, and also that there had been a bit of a spat between Meg and Mattie that had ended up with him bumping his head.

'Oh Mattie, what have you done? Let Mammy have a look . . .' She ran her fingers gently over the swelling, big as a small bird's egg.

'It's just a bump.' Sally had reached the end of her tether. 'I put butter on it. It'll be better by bedtime.'

Mattie was holding his arms out to Carina.

'Ma-ma!' he managed between sobs.

Carina lifted him out of the pushchair, cradling him against her shoulder.

'It's all right, my baby. Mammy's here now.'

She carried him into the kitchen, Sally and Meg following.

'You'm back, then,' Grandpa Luke said to Sally. 'How d'you get on?'

'Give me a chance to get my breath and I'll tell you.'

'Me thirsty!' Meg pouted.

Sally cast a glance at Carina, but she was still preoccupied with Mattie.

'All right, I'll get you a drink, and then for goodness' sake find something to occupy yourself with.' She poured milk into a cup and gave it to the little girl. 'Try not to spill it.'

She watched anxiously as Meg settled herself on her three-legged stool, then sat down herself.

'Mr Harvey is up to his neck in work at the moment, but I think he took pity on me in the end. He said he'd do his best to send one of the lads over for a few hours to help out now and then.'

'That's something, I suppose,' Grandpa Luke said. 'I just wish I could do what I used to.'

'But you can't, so there's no point wasting time and breath talking about it,' Sally said shortly. Then: 'I'm sorry, Grandpa. I didn't mean to snap. I've just had enough for one morning, that's all.'

'Think nothing of it, m'dear.'

Carina seemed almost oblivious to the conversation.

'I think Mattie's tooth is bothering him too,' she said. 'He didn't hit his cheek, did he, when he fell? It's really flushed. And he keeps putting his hands in his mouth.'

She slid her own finger inside his mouth, and sure enough there was another hard mound on the other side to the tooth that had broken through. She got up with Mattie still tucked against her shoulder and went to the sideboard. She'd replaced the quarter-bottle of brandy as she liked to keep some in the house for medicinal purposes, and she thought it would help Mattie. Robert might have objected, but he wasn't here now. The decision was hers, and she couldn't see the harm. Her own mother advocated the remedy, and nothing dire had happened to her or her brother.

She unstoppered the brandy, dipped her finger into the bottle and rubbed it on Mattie's sore gums. Then she fetched the bottle of gripe water. He was a little old for it now, but a dose still worked wonders, and usually settled him. If she could get him to go down for a nap, he'd feel better when he woke.

By the time she eventually managed to get him to sleep, Sally had gone out again to resume whatever she had been doing when Carina had left the children in her care. Explaining that she needed to go to Bath tomorrow would have to wait.

Chapter Ten

In the event, when she set out for Bath next morning, Carina took Mattie with her. He was still restless, and after yesterday's debacle she was reluctant to leave him with Sally even if she had been willing.

'I've got too much to do to spend so much time looking after him,' Sally had said bluntly. 'I can take Meg with me and hopefully get things done, as long as she behaves herself, but Mattie needs too much attention.'

Once the children were in bed, Carina had taken her aside and confessed what she intended to do, and to her surprise, Sally had agreed with her decision.

'Needs must when the devil drives,' she said. 'And it would be good to know Lord Melbrook was off our backs.'

Really, Carina thought, she should have known that Sally's practical side would come to the fore. Her sister-in-law had little time for sentimentality. But she was a bit hurt that Sally seemed to have no real comprehension of the sacrifice she was making.

She wasn't going to dwell on that, though. She should thank her lucky stars that Sally was as single-minded as any man, and as competent when it came to dealing with the day-to-day running of the farm, even if she was struggling under the load.

With a little more confidence than she had felt the day before, Carina drove the Rover into Hillsbridge with Mattie sitting on her lap. It was far from an ideal arrangement, but the novel experience held Mattie's attention for long enough to keep him still and quiet, and she reached the town without incident and parked outside the railway station. Then she unloaded the pushchair, dumped Mattie in it and went on to the platform to buy a ticket.

'That pushchair will have to go in the guard's van.' The porter, whose job also entailed manning the ticket office when no train was actually in the station, never failed to enjoy the prestige of serving passengers instead of carrying cases and wheeling trolleys, and made the most of his increased authority.

'That's all right,' Carina said. 'My son can sit on my lap.'

'Just as long as you know.'

'I expect you'll help me with it anyway,' Carina said sweetly, leaving him in no doubt that she was well aware of his less prestigious alter ego.

Sure enough, when the train came puffing into the station and clanked to a halt, the porter emerged from his office donning a navy blue cap and manhandled the pushchair into the guard's van. Carina found a seat in one of the carriages and sat Mattie on her knee. There was a short delay while the driver took on more water from one of the big tanks, then the guard blew his whistle and they were off, chugging along slowly at first, then building up speed as they left the town behind and headed towards Single Hill halt.

All in all the journey took about half an hour, passing through green countryside, dusty black embankments and several stations before coming to a halt at Bath Green Park. To Carina's relief, Mattie had been so entranced by this novel experience he had behaved perfectly, and a woman in the same carriage had

121

remarked on what a beautiful child he was, making Carina flush with pride.

She was feeling extremely nervous, though, as the guard lifted down the pushchair and she settled him into it. She only hoped she could find the pawnshop from the directions Mr Johnson had given her, and that the outcome would be successful.

The town was busy. Carina had to manoeuvre her way past shoppers and round the feet of a blind beggar, whilst carts and a few motor vehicles passed by on the road. But she found the street Mr Johnson had mentioned without too much trouble, and spotted the three golden balls suspended on a bracket over the door which advertised that the shop beneath was a pawnbroker's.

She stood for a moment looking in the window, which was depressingly grimy. Watches and various items of jewellery were laid out on a red cloth that was speckled with dust and faded by sunlight. Most of the items had small white price tags attached to them by cotton threads, and Carina was interested to know what they were selling for but was unable to decipher the figures.

Taking a deep steadying breath, she opened the door, and an overhead bell jangled.

As far as she could see, the shop was crammed with valuables that customers had presumably left in exchange for money. A number of clocks, ornaments of all kinds, even a stuffed owl in a display case, which seemed to stare at her with disconcertingly beady eyes. She didn't care for the look of the man behind the counter either. His forehead was low and jutting, his eyes set too close together, and much of the rest of his face was hidden by hair, long sideburns that reached almost to a straggly beard and mutton-chop whiskers. He was also sweating profusely.

'Good day to you, my dear. And what may I help a pretty

young lady with this fine day?' His tone was oily and over-familiar.

Carina took the ring box out of her bag and placed it on the counter.

'I'm told you may be able to make me an advance on my ring.'

'That's what I'm here for.'

He examined the ring as Mr Johnson had done, but Carina was repulsed at seeing it held between those thick, none-too-clean fingers capped with horny nails that didn't look as if they'd been cut in a long time. Bad enough having it pored over by nice, pleasant Mr Johnson, but this man . . . She could hardly bear it and had to look away.

'Very well, my dear, I'll make you an offer.' He named a sum far less than Carina had hoped for. It would cover Lord Melbrook's bill, yes, but there would not be a lot left over to help with the other expenses that were piling up.

'Couldn't you give me a little more?' she asked, without much hope.

The man scratched his fleshy nose.

'An extra two pounds, perhaps, and I'm being generous here, since you are such a pretty young lady. But that's my final offer, I'm afraid. Unless you have anything else to sell . . . ?'

It took Carina a moment to realise what he was implying, and she shivered in disgust.

'No, there's nothing else,' she said coldly.

'Pity.' He leered at her. 'In that case, we'll call it a deal. And you know you have one month to retrieve your ring.'

'For the same amount?' Carina asked, though she couldn't see how she would be able to afford to buy it back, much as she would like to.

'Now surely you know better than that, my dear. It will cost you more, of course. How else would I make a living?'

By selling at a profit all the things people like me can't afford to buy back, Carina thought.

'So you'd like me to take it?' the man pressed her.

Carina nodded wordlessly. She could no longer look at her precious ring, but as the horrible man's hand closed over it, her jaw trembled and it was all she could do not to cry.

The ring safely back in its box, the man counted out the agreed sum and pushed it across the counter towards her.

'Nice doing business with you, my dear. And if you should change your mind and decide you have something else to sell after all . . . you know where I am.'

Carina thrust the money into her bag, grabbed the handles of Mattie's pushchair and hurried out of the shop as fast as her legs would carry her.

The sun had disappeared behind gathering storm clouds. It seemed a perfect metaphor for the turn her life had taken, though of course Carina did not think of it in those terms. She just knew that her world was darker even than it had been before.

She started back along the street the way she had come. Unshed tears were blinding her, and she didn't even see the two people walking along the pavement towards her until she practically collided with them.

'Mrs Talbot, isn't it?'

She looked up into a face she knew. A face she hated. A man she hated.

Lord Melbrook. Of all the people in the world.

There was a lady with him, as finely dressed as one might expect, and wearing a large hat at a jaunty angle. But Carina scarcely noticed her. All she could see was the man who had just cost her her precious ring.

'How very surprising that our paths should cross again,' he said. 'And in the city, too! You haven't motored here, I hope?'

The sarcasm in his tone stung her.

'And if I have, what business is it of yours?'

'None at all, of course.' He smiled faintly. 'I just hope you are not going to cause more havoc and run up bills you are unable to pay. But as you so rightly point out, that is not my problem.'

In that moment Carina saw red, and shelved her fierce pride.

'I expect you're wondering what I'm doing here in Bath. Well, I'll tell you. I've just pawned my engagement ring so as to pay you for the damage I did to your motor. I have the money here. You might as well have it now and be done with it.'

Her hand shaking, she opened her bag, removed the notes the pawnbroker had just given her, counted out enough to cover her debt and held them out, glaring at him defiantly.

Lord Melbrook made no move to take them.

'Really, I don't think—'

'It's beneath you, I suppose, taking my money in the street?'

A man unloading crates of vegetables at the kerb for a nearby greengrocer's shop turned to look at them curiously, and a woman pushing a perambulator had come to a stop behind Carina, waiting for the trio to move out of her way.

'We're causing an obstruction, Cal.' The fine lady's voice was clear and cultured, with the ring of a spoon rapped against a crystal glass, and for the first time Carina turned to look at her.

She was perhaps in her mid thirties, tall, slender and elegant in a dress of royal-blue silk. Upswept copper-coloured hair was just visible beneath a wide-brimmed straw hat decorated with ostrich plumes, and her eyes were as green as emeralds.

Lord Melbrook stepped aside into the gutter, raising his hat slightly to the woman with the pram by way of apology as she passed. But still he made no effort to take the notes Carina was holding out to him.

'You've pawned a ring in order to get this money?' He was frowning.

'Yes, I have. It's what we're reduced to, I'm afraid. But I pay my debts. At least I still have my pride.'

'Really, Mrs Talbot—'

'Oh, for heaven's sake just take it, Cal! She's making an exhibition of us. If you won't take it, I will.' The fine lady reached out a gloved hand and took the notes. 'Now, have we quite done here? Or do you have anything else to say, Mrs . . .' She left the name hanging in the air, perhaps because she didn't remember, perhaps because she was making a point. That Carina was an anonymous nobody. Certainly the scorn in her voice and her haughty demeanour suggested it might be just that.

'Quite done.' Carina returned the icy green stare with all the dignity and defiance she could muster. 'If you'll excuse me . . .'

Lord Melbrook stepped into the road again, and without another word or a backward glance Carina set off along the pavement.

'What a bitch!' she said aloud, glad that Mattie was too young to understand and she was able to give vent to her feelings without restraint; if Meg had been there, she would have made sure to moderate her language or risk her daughter copying it. 'They're well suited, I must say. Horrible jumped-up . . .' Words failed her. 'Let's just get you home, Mattie.'

Her hands, gripping the pushchair fiercely, were trembling, she realised, and her knees felt weak. A result of the unpleasantness of the encounter? But she couldn't help feeling it was more than that. There was something about Lord Melbrook that unsettled her. Hardly surprising given the embarrassing circumstances under which she had met him, she supposed, and of course he was landed gentry while she was just a poor farmer's widow. But that did not explain her shaking limbs or the way her pulse was racing and her stomach tying itself in knots. It was an unfamiliar feeling to her and she didn't like it any more than she liked him . . .

Oh, forget him! Carina told herself sternly. It's done and dusted now, and you'll never have to see him again.

Setting her jaw determinedly, she set off in the direction of the station.

'I'm home!'

The door was ajar, Carina pushed it fully open and man-oeuvred the pushchair inside. Then she stopped short, her eyes widening in surprise. A young man she had never seen before was seated at the kitchen table, a plate of bread and cheese in front of him. Sally was sitting opposite him, Meg beside her.

'Oh Carina, I'm glad you're back!' But Sally didn't sound anxious, rather eager and excited. 'This is Frank Bailey. We knew him when we lived in Bristol.'

'Goodness me . . .' Carina was at something of a loss.

'He was over this way and called by to catch up with Robert. But of course he didn't know . . .' Her voice tailed away and she bit her lip, holding back the tears that threatened.

'Gave me quite a shock to find out he's no longer with us.' The young man stood up, and Carina saw that though not tall, he was strongly built, with a face that stopped just short of handsome and a head of thick brown hair. 'I was really sorry to hear such awful news, Mrs Talbot.'

'Carina,' she said mechanically.

'Carina.' He nodded. 'But I'm pleased to meet you, anyway. Robert and me were good mates when we were boys. We had a lot of fun together, though mostly it was getting into scrapes, I'm ashamed to say.'

'I can imagine.' Carina lifted Mattie out of his pushchair, but he clung to her legs, gazing at the stranger, his eyes huge in his rosy face.

'Well, he's a chip off the old block and no mistake.' The young man bent to ruffle Mattie's hair and Mattie flinched away, but Frank seemed unfazed. 'And that's a very pretty young lady you've got over there.' He winked at Meg. 'You must be proud of them. And I bet Robert was too.'

'He was.' Carina managed to keep her voice steady. 'I'm really sorry you've had a wasted journey.'

'It might not have been, though!' Sally's face was animated in a way Carina had not seen it since Robert's death.

'What do you mean?'

'Sit down and we'll tell you.'

Puzzled, Carina put away the pushchair and Sally poured her a cup of tea from the pot that was keeping warm on the hob.

Carina sipped it gratefully. 'Go on then.'

'Well, as Frank's already said, he and Robert were friends in Bristol, and when he found himself over this way he decided to look Robert up. What he hasn't told you is that he was looking for work. He'd had enough of labouring in the docks, and fancied getting out of Bristol into the fresh country air. He thought Robert might know of a job that was going.'

Carina began to see where this was leading.

'What sort of job?' she asked, looking at Frank, but he seemed content to allow Sally to do the explaining.

'Any sort really,' she said. 'But especially . . .' She could contain herself no longer. 'Oh don't you see, Carina? Frank could be the answer to our prayers! I've explained our position to him, and—'

'Whoa! Slow down!' Carina said. 'Aren't you putting the cart before the horse?'

'Oh, I said I'd have to talk it over with you and Grandpa, of course . . .'

'Do you have any experience of farming?' Carina asked the young man, but again Sally answered for him.

'Of course not, if he's been working in the docks. But he'd soon learn – I can teach him. And he's young and strong and . . .'

Exhausted as she was by having to do all Robert's work as well as her own, Sally, it seemed, had already made up her mind. This young man turning up on the doorstep looking for employment must have seemed like manna from heaven. But surely she must know it wasn't that simple.

'We can't afford full-time help, Sally. You know that,' Carina said. 'I hope you haven't given Robert's friend the impression that we can.'

'She hasn't.' Frank glanced at Sally and smiled. 'She's made me well aware of your situation. I've got savings – I wouldn't have given up my job and taken my chances elsewhere if I hadn't. I've got enough to live on, whatever you can afford to pay me for the time being. When the money runs out, of course, well . . .' he shrugged, 'I'll have to think again. But it should last me quite some time if you've somewhere I could stay so I don't have board and lodging to pay for.'

'I've told him there's accommodation over the barn,' Sally put in eagerly.

'But it hasn't been lived in for years,' Carina pointed out. 'Goodness, Grandpa Luke hasn't had hired help for I don't know how long! It must be in a terrible state.'

'Nothing that can't be fixed,' Frank said.

Carina looked at him in surprise.

'You've already seen it?'

'I showed him.' There was a slight defensive edge to Sally's tone now.

'I could sort it out, no trouble,' Frank said breezily. 'I'm not looking for luxury – not yet, anyway. Get it cleaned up, make a few repairs to the stairs and the floor, put in a palliasse and maybe a new chair, and Bob's your uncle.'

Carina was silent, trying to get her head round all this. She couldn't imagine anyone willingly living in that musty little room and working full time, and all for a pittance.

'Why?' she asked Frank. 'Why would you want to do that?'

'I'd do it for Robert,' Frank said. 'We were good mates, me and him. I don't like to see his wife and sister struggling so, and if I can help out for a bit, well, I reckon I should. He'd have done the same for me.'

'That is so kind of you!' Sally gave him a beaming smile. 'And we are really grateful, aren't we, Carina?'

Carina still had some misgivings, though she couldn't put her finger on exactly what they were. On the face of it, this was the answer to all their problems – for the time being, at least. It was as if fate had decided to be kind to them after dealing them such a bad hand; almost as if Robert had sent his old friend to help them out in their hour of need. Frank seemed personable enough, and Sally had clearly taken a shine to him. She should grasp this opportunity with both hands and be grateful for it.

And yet . . . and yet . . .

'We'll need to talk it over with Grandpa Luke,' she said, playing for time. 'He still owns Meadow Farm, remember.'

'Talk what over?' Luke was in the doorway. How on earth had he managed to miss out on all that had been going on? Carina wondered. Fast asleep again, presumably.

'Taking on someone who's going to make life a whole lot easier for us.' Sally went to help Luke to his chair, then squatted down beside him, explaining the situation. 'So what do you say, Grandpa?' she asked when she'd finished. 'Should we take Frank up on his offer?'

For a long moment Luke was silent. Then he nodded.

'Seems like the best thing, m'dear.'

'There you are – it's settled!' Sally got up, smiling at Frank. 'What do you say we make a start cleaning up your room until dinner's ready?'

'Are you sure we're doing the right thing, Grandpa?' Carina asked when Sally and Frank had left, Meg going with them.

'Don't think we've got much option, m'dear.'

'But . . .' Carina glanced at the carpet bag Frank had dumped beside the kitchen dresser. 'It doesn't look as if he's got much to his name. We don't know him from Adam, and we're having him more or less live with us.'

'If he were a friend of Robert's, that's good enough for me,' Luke said. 'And you and Sally can't manage on your own, can you?'

Carina shook her head.

'Well then, there's your answer. If he turns out to be a useless git, just out for a bed and a free meal, we can always give him his marching orders.'

'Yes, I suppose.'

'What did you go to Bath for, anyway?' Luke asked, changing the subject so abruptly it took her unawares.

'Oh . . . just trying to sort out Robert's affairs,' she answered vaguely.

'Ah well, I s'pose there's that.' To her relief, the old man seemed satisfied.

But his question had reminded her of the money she'd had over after paying Lord Melbrook what she owed him. Sometimes the children took it into their heads to turn out her bag; she needed to put the money away safely.

Though she doubted Grandpa Luke's sight was good enough to be able to see what she was doing, she turned her back towards him anyway while she extracted the notes. Then, with them folded tightly into her fist, she crossed to the dresser and slipped them into the biscuit barrel that served as a makeshift bank, before making a show of getting a biscuit out of its twin and offering it to Mattie. The little boy took it and stuffed it into his mouth, sucking on it so that dribbles ran down his chin. Though there was still a high spot of colour in his cheek, it seemed the emerging tooth was no longer hurting him so much.

'I'll just go and get changed, then I'll make a start on the dinner,' Carina said, heading upstairs.

The dressing-table drawer was partly open; in her haste this morning she must have failed to close it properly. Now it only served to remind her that her precious ring was not there, and never would be again.

Oh Robert . . .

Grief washed over her, catching her off guard, and suddenly she was sobbing, deep, rending sobs that seemed to tear her body apart. She sank down on to the edge of the bed that she and Robert had shared, bent double, and gave way to the tidal wave of emotion that was consuming her.

As Carina had said, no one had been in the room over the barn for years. Cobwebs festooned every corner and the remains of a dead bird – now nothing more than a heap of dusty feathers – lay beneath the window. There was a wooden bunk, a small table and an old easy chair, but there was no mattress on the bed, the table was rickety and in spite of the recent hot weather the upholstery of the chair felt damp to the touch.

'It really is in an awful state,' Sally said.

But Frank only grinned at her.

'I've slept in worse.'

'You can't. At least not until we've given it a thorough spring clean, and we're not going to have time to do that today. We'll have to make you up a bed in the kitchen for tonight.'

'I'll be fine. You worry too much. I'll get this chair out in the sunshine. That'll dry it out in no time.' He hoisted the chair on to his shoulders as easily as though it were a feather pillow. 'Watch out, Meggie. I'm coming through.'

Meg, who had been hanging back, scuttled down the rickety stairs, then began to giggle and point.

'He's a monster, Auntie Sally! Look, he's got great big shoulders and no head! Doesn't he look like a monster?'

Sally laughed. 'You're right. He does.'

But she was thinking that far from a monster, Frank Bailey was the most attractive man she had ever laid eyes on, and she couldn't believe her luck that she was going to be working alongside him, teaching him the ropes. As he unloaded the chair into a patch of sunshine and straightened, his muscles rippled, and Sally felt an unfamiliar but very pleasant sensation prickle deep inside.

She was very glad indeed that he had turned up on the doorstep this morning.

Chapter Eleven

'What on earth was that all about?' Isobel Luckington slipped the notes she had taken from Carina into Cal's top pocket, tucked a gloved hand into his arm and glanced enquiringly at him from beneath finely arched brows. 'And who was that perfectly dreadful woman?'

'She's the granddaughter-in-law of a farmer whose land adjoins mine, and recently widowed. Hardly dreadful, Isobel.'

'Any woman who makes such a scene in the street is dreadful as far as I'm concerned. As for giving you *money* . . . how very common.'

Cal ignored the remark. Usually he was amused by Isobel's snobbishness, but today it irritated him, perhaps because he was feeling guilty for harassing Carina to the point where she had felt it necessary to pawn her engagement ring to pay for the damage she'd caused to his motor. The ring must have meant a great deal to her, especially in view of her recent loss. Cal wasn't especially proud of the high-handed attitude he'd taken towards her in any case; given that she was recently bereaved, it was unforgivable. And 'common' was the last word he would use to describe her. Dignified and brave would have been more apt.

'So – shall we think about luncheon?' he asked in an effort to change the subject.

'You mean you've tired already of looking at fabric for drapes for your drawing room? Really, Cal, sometimes I despair of you!' Isobel chided.

'I never wanted to do it in the first place. The whole damned thing was your idea. There's nothing wrong with the ones I have already,' Cal retorted.

Isobel shook her head despairingly.

'Only you could fail to notice the dreadful state they're in. They are quite disgusting, as I told you when I last came to see you and your dear mother. How you can live with them, I really don't know – they'll be in tatters soon. What sort of impression must that give to visitors?'

'I don't have many visitors, and those I do have can think as they like,' Cal said drily. 'Besides, I'm not sure I can waste money on something so trivial when there is so much else that needs doing on the estate.'

'Oh pooh! Anyone would think you were down to your last farthing.'

'If Stafford had lived and continued to indulge himself, we probably would be,' Cal said grimly. 'I'm having to sell off the family silver to bail us out.'

'Poor dear Stafford . . .'

'Poor dear Stafford indeed. He'd have bankrupted the estate if his wild life hadn't caught up with him. Look, I'm hungry if you're not. Let's call it a day and head for the Francis Hotel.'

'It's barely noon,' Isobel objected. 'I think we should make one more stop first. Jolly's is just around the corner from the Francis, and perhaps you'll find something there to take your fancy. Then our day won't have been entirely wasted.'

Cal chuckled. 'You're a hard woman, Isobel. If I didn't know you so well, I'd despair of you.'

'But you do, don't you, Cal? That's the thing about us.

There's very little we don't know about each other. And I think that gives me the right to try to take you in hand when I think it necessary.'

It was probably no more than the truth, Cal thought, as he followed Isobel along the racks of fabrics lining the walls of the home-furnishings floor of the renowned department store. No other living person knew him better than Isobel did. They'd played together as children, running wild in the fields that surrounded the Dunderwick estate and the woods on the hillside above the house, or in the grounds of Isobel's home, Parkleigh, three miles down the road. It had been Isobel – three years older than him – who had initiated him into the art of kissing, and later more; Isobel who had shared his darkest moments after the death of Alice, the love of his life. It had been Isobel who had encouraged him to leave the past behind and follow his ambition to become a soldier. Their lifelong friendship had brought them closer than many brothers and sisters; each knew the other's faults and failings and loved one another as much because of them as in spite of them. And they had remained close though their lives had followed very different paths, always able to take up where they had left off even if they had not seen one another for months or even years.

Isobel lived in Bath now, and had done since she had married fifteen years earlier. Her husband, a wealthy banker, had been thirty years older than her, the last choice anyone who knew the headstrong girl with a zest for life would have expected her to make. It was his money and the grand house in the Royal Crescent that had attracted her, the gossips said, and they might well have been right. Percy Luckington had died of a massive heart attack when barely into his fifties, and after a brief period of mourning – all show, according to the gossips – Isobel had made the most of her situation. She still lived in the grand house, dressed in the latest fashions and took long holidays in France, Italy and Switzerland. Between these she occupied herself with what she self-deprecatingly called 'good works': prison visiting, fund-raising, and sitting on various charitable committees.

And there were, of course, her gentlemen friends. Isobel had a fancy for much younger men, and they in turn were all too happy to squire a rich older woman who had kept her good looks and had few inhibitions. Cal teased her about them sometimes. 'My dear, they are what keeps me young!' she would say, and the gleam in her emerald eyes left him in no doubt of her meaning.

Cal knew that his mother still entertained hopes that perhaps one day he and Isobel would finally take their friendship a stage further and marry. She was blissfully unaware of Isobel's flighty ways, seeing only an attractive woman with the right breeding to make a future Lady Melbrook, something she frequently pointed out to Cal. He, however, had no intention of doing any such thing. If he and Isobel lived under the same roof, there would soon be ructions, he knew, and a lifelong friendship would be destroyed. Besides which, he had had no desire to marry anyone since he had lost his beloved Alice.

He had been just nineteen when he had met her. Her father, until recently an admiral of the fleet, had retired to a country home on the outskirts of Hillsbridge, and his own father had invited the family to share their Christmas celebrations. It had been love at first sight – forever afterwards the season would be for Cal a time of bittersweet memories.

He still visited her grave in Hillsbridge churchyard, taking fresh flowers in season – and always pink roses, which she had loved, for her birthday – and arranging them clumsily in the stone pot that sat beneath the headstone. At Christmas he made sure to lay a wreath of holly, ivy and Christmas roses. He chided himself for the sentimentality – she wasn't there, and Cal had serious doubts about the panaceas offered by the clergy and other religious folk that she was in 'a better place'. She was gone, and that was the end of it. Yet sometimes, even now, so many years later, he would catch sight of someone walking towards him on a crowded pavement, and for a heart-stopping moment he would believe it was her, only to realise that of course it was not. Sometimes he would dream of her, the curve of her lips, the scent of her hair, the feel of her in his arms, and when he woke to reality would feel as bereft as he had done when he had first lost her, the pain in his heart as sharp as it had ever been. Perhaps, he thought, he might have come to terms with her death more easily if it hadn't been so sudden. The last time he had seen her she'd not been well, it was true, but he'd thought it was no more than a common cold or influenza. Pneumonia had set in, though, and within just a few short days she was dead.

He was thinking of her now as he followed Isobel around the department store and wondering what she would say if she knew how badly he had behaved towards the farmer's widow, who must be going through much of what he had gone through then. She'd be horrified, he was sure. He could almost hear her voice: 'Cal! How could you?'

'Now, this would be perfect!' Isobel, who had stopped in front of a bolt of deep red plush velvet, touched his arm, interrupting his reverie. 'See how the light catches it? I can just see it at the windows of your drawing room. What do you say?'

'Oh, very well, Isobel, you win,' Cal said resignedly. 'Order the wretched stuff and have done with it.'

'Only if you're sure . . .'

'Yes, yes, I'm sure. And then perhaps we can go and get something to eat.'

* * *

'Now we've got Frank to help us, perhaps you could go back to what you were trained to do and take in sewing,' Sally suggested. 'You know you've always wanted to, and we could certainly do with the extra money.'

It was supper time, and they were all seated around the kitchen table eating bread, cheese, and tomatoes fresh from the greenhouse that were ripening as fast as Carina could pick them.

'You can sew?' Frank asked, turning an admiring glance on Carina. 'That's handy! My work trousers could do with taking in a bit around the waist.'

'I don't think that's quite what Sally had in mind,' Carina said, bridling at what she couldn't help seeing as his over-familiarity. He seemed to have wasted no time in getting his feet under the table, and Sally was clearly taken with him, but for some reason that she couldn't quite put her finger on, Carina didn't like him, and she was surprised that he and Robert had been friends. Really, they were chalk and cheese. Robert had been quiet and reserved; Frank . . . well, the best word she could think of to describe him was 'cocky'. It had been a long time ago, when they had been just boys, of course, but did people change that much? She just couldn't see Robert palling up with someone like Frank.

'No, she's far too good to be wasted in taking in your dirty old trousers,' Sally said, but there was a hint of flirtatiousness in her tone, and she was dimpling as she said it, making Carina feel even more uncomfortable.

'Do you know, I think I might just do that,' she said, trying to ignore her misgivings about taking this stranger into their house. 'I could put a card in the post office window, and if I get a job or two, word would soon get around. It's not the best-paid trade in the world, but every little would help.'

'Robert would be proud of you, my dear,' Grandpa Luke said gruffly, and glancing at him Carina could see there were tears in his rheumy eyes.

'And he'd be really pleased to know that you were helping us out, Frank,' Sally said, treating him to one of her warmest smiles. 'Do you really think you'll be all right in the room over the barn tonight, or would you rather sleep on the sofa in here until we can make it a bit nicer?'

'I'm sure he will be fine in the barn,' Carina said quickly. 'After all the work you've put in, it must be fit for a king. And I'm sure Frank would prefer his privacy,' she added slyly, echoing her own feelings on the subject. Though he was probably harmless, she really didn't care for the idea of having him here, just downstairs.

'It's certainly looking a lot better than it did,' Sally agreed, though Carina thought she sounded disappointed. 'The chair dried out nicely in the sun, and I always knew that old palliasse would come in useful one day. Goodness, I quite fancy it myself!'

'You'd probably wake up with a rash,' Carina said. 'Girls' skin and straw don't go together very well.'

'You're the one who gets rashes,' Sally retorted. 'And wasp stings . . .' she added wickedly.

'Don't remind me.'

'What's all this?' Frank asked without missing a beat.

Carina ignored the question.

'I think I'll write out a postcard offering my services when we've finished tea and walk over to Dunderwick in the morning,' she said instead.

'You mean you're not going to take the motor?' Sally asked in mock surprise.

For the first time in a long while Carina felt a wave of exasperation with her sister-in-law. Was this how it was going to be from now on? Sally trying to look clever in front of this stranger who had walked so unexpectedly into their lives? But little as she liked him, they needed Frank Bailey. And if this was the price they had pay for the help they so badly needed, then she would just have to swallow her irritation and get on with it.

Cal was sitting, as he so often did, in the wicker chair in the orangery. Another sleepless night, another bottle of whisky. It had almost become a habit with him, and he was lucky, he supposed, that he could survive on just a few hours' sleep a night. He'd wake early next morning with a clear head, ready to face another day. Which was just as well, given all that he had to contend with.

Tonight, however, it was not the problem of the estate that was playing on his mind. Try as he might, he could not get Carina Talbot, and the way he had treated her, out of his head. Bad enough that he had called on her as he had, trampling all over her grief with his high-handed demands for compensation for the damage to his motor, but that she had actually pawned her engagement ring in order to pay him was something that made him cringe. Once he was aware of the circumstances, he would certainly not have pressed her, and he would have refused to take the money from her this morning if Isobel hadn't done it for him. The trouble was that the harm had already been done. Mrs Talbot was a proud woman who would be sure to pay her debts no matter what it might cost her. And pawning her precious engagement ring had, he felt sure, cost her a great deal. The family must be really struggling for her to take such a drastic step.

The realisation stirred yet more feelings of guilt. Wasn't that exactly what he had wanted – that they would be unable to keep the farm going and he would be able to buy it back cheaply for the estate? And yes, it *was* what he wanted. But if he got his wish, it would mean that brave young woman and her children would be homeless, perhaps destitute. And the one in the pushchair this morning had been barely more than a baby.

Cal tossed back a good slug of whisky, then rolled the glass between his hands before refilling it. For all that he wanted to make the estate profitable and prosperous, he couldn't do it on the back of a grieving widow like Carina Talbot. Quite the opposite, in fact. Just at this moment, he was wishing there was something he could do to help her, or at least make up for his outrageous behaviour in some way. Should he offer practical assistance? But he didn't have any farmhands working directly for him; his employees were foresters and gamekeepers who would be of little use to a farmer, and in any case he could imagine she would be too proud to accept help from him, given the background to their relationship.

Certainly she would be too proud to allow him to return the money she had forced on him this morning.

But there was one thing he *could* do next time he was in Bath.

Feeling more at ease with himself, Cal finished the whisky and decided he would call it a night.

Carina, too, was having a sleepless night. She had fallen into bed exhausted, both mentally and physically, but the events of the day kept buzzing around in her head and it was a long time before she fell asleep. Then, soon after she did, she was woken by the sound of Mattie crying. She got up and went upstairs to his room under the eaves without bothering to put on a dressing gown, intent on reaching him before he disturbed Meg too.

It was hot in the attic room, and Mattie's firm little body felt like a furnace when she lifted him out of his cot, though he had kicked off his covers and was wearing only his nightgown and nappy. He was teething again, she guessed – by the light of the moon streaming in through the window she could see that one of his cheeks was flushed scarlet. She took him downstairs, rubbed some brandy on his gums and sat rocking him in Grandpa Luke's chair until his screams quietened to sobs and then to a muted intermittent grizzle and his head fell heavy against her shoulder.

Then and only then did she take him back upstairs, kissing his damp forehead and laying him gently in his cot. She stood on a stool, opened the window a little wider to let in some cooler air, and tiptoed away.

It was as she reached the landing that she heard the sound of muffled weeping coming from Sally's room, and then, loud in the silence, an anguished wail. 'Robert! Oh Robert, why did you have to die?'

Carina paused, her first instinct to go to her sister-in-law, put her arms around her and cry with her. But Sally was quite a private person – probably it would be best to leave her. Biting her lip, Carina crept across the landing to her own room.

It wasn't the first time she had heard Sally crying in the night, and in spite of her own overwhelming grief, Carina worried about her. Beneath the seemingly tough exterior she presented to the world, she was quite vulnerable, and she and Robert had been so close, especially as they had had only each other since Sally was quite young.

She had seemed so much better today, brighter and full of life, even flirting with Frank Bailey. Perhaps he would be good for her. Little as she liked him, Carina thought that having a good-looking young man on the premises might give Sally something else to think about besides her terrible loss. If so, then whatever she herself thought of him, she would just have to bite her tongue.

And besides – if she had any hope of fulfilling her promise to keep the farm going as Robert would have wished, and ensuring the family's future, she needed help with the day-to-day running.

But as she glanced out of her bedroom window towards the barn where Frank Bailey would now be fast asleep, the sense of unease was still nagging at her, and she thought it would be a long time before she was comfortable with him living and working at Meadow Farm.

Chapter Twelve

'What I want to know, sir, is what you mean to do with all those rolls of material that are cluttering up my linen room.'

Biddy Thomas, Cal's housekeeper, had come into the study where he was working on the accounts, and now stood, hands on hips, mouth set in a determined line, triple chins wobbling indignantly above the collar of her pristine white blouse.

Cal glanced up, impatient at being interrupted.

'Oh I don't know, Biddy. I haven't had time to think about it.'

'Well I suggest you do find time, and soon, unless you want me to up and leave you high and dry.'

It was an idle threat, Cal knew. If he had a guinea for every time he'd heard that, he wouldn't have any money worries, he thought wryly. Biddy trotted it out every time something upset her.

But perhaps she had a point. The fabric for the new drapes had been delivered from Jolly's almost a week ago, and it couldn't stay in its wraps for ever.

'There's nothing I can do until I find someone to make it up for me,' he said. 'Do you know of anyone who would be able to do that?'

Mrs Thomas removed her hands from her hips, clasping them in front of her, and a self-satisfied smile twitched at her lips.

'As a matter of fact, I do,' she said. 'This morning, when I was in the village, I saw a card in the post office window – someone advertising to take in sewing.'

Cal suppressed a smile. So that was what had prompted Biddy to make an issue of the bolts of fabric.

'Well in that case, I suggest you make the necessary arrangements.'

Mrs Thomas bridled. 'You can't expect me to do that, sir. I'm not walking all the way over to Meadow Farm.'

Cal put down his pen, where it made a dark splodge on the pink blotter.

'Meadow Farm?'

'That's right. Mrs Talbot, it said. So I take it that's Luke Green's grandson's wife.'

'Widow,' Cal said automatically.

'Whatever. Anyway, I reckon it would be a lot easier to use someone local than go further afield, somebody Miss Isobel might recommend.' Her lips pursed as she mentioned Isobel's name – she didn't have a lot of time for that one, and had never approved of her friendship with the master. 'That's what I think, anyway,' she went on. 'You could send for her, get her down here to measure up, no trouble at all.'

'Yes, thank you, Biddy.' Cal picked up his pen again, hoping that the housekeeper would take the hint and go about her business.

'You will do it, won't you? Otherwise . . .'

'Yes, Biddy, I understand. You can safely leave the arrangements to me.'

* * *

Life had returned to some semblance of normality at Meadow Farm. With the harvest now in and Frank doing much of the heavy work that Robert had once done, there was much less pressure on Sally, and, as a result, on Carina too. If she needed to go into town, she could ask Sally to mind the children without feeling guilty at eating into her day, and Sally could help out with some of the heavier household tasks – turning mattresses, folding wet sheets to put through the mangle, chopping logs for the fire.

Carina still didn't care for Frank, or his overfamiliarity, didn't like him being there across the table at mealtimes, intruding into what had always been family time. But she had to admit he was a hard worker, and Sally was certainly much brighter when he was around. Carina hadn't heard her crying in the privacy of her room since the night she had been up with Mattie, and that could only be a good thing. She only hoped that Sally wasn't expecting too much out of a relationship with him – she rather thought Frank was a drifter who would soon tire of both country life and Sally, and she didn't think Sally was emotionally strong enough at the moment to have her heart broken.

This morning, something had happened that had brought this particular concern to the forefront of her mind.

Captain had lost a shoe and they'd had to send for Dick Brimble, the farrier from Hillsbridge. He'd arrived just as they were finishing breakfast, and Sally had gone with him to the stable. While she was washing nappies at the sink beneath the kitchen window, Carina had seen him leave, seen Sally walking the horse round the yard, checking his gait, then taking him back into his stable. But by the time she'd hung the nappies out to dry and was ready to go into town for a few odds and ends, Sally still hadn't come back, though she had promised to look after the children while Carina was gone.

'Have you seen Sally?' she asked Grandpa Luke, who was sitting outside the back door puffing on his pipe.

'She's in the barn, I think.'

'What on earth can she be doing? I need to get going.'

She headed for the barn. The door was ajar. She pushed it open and went inside, a shaft of sunshine following her but making only a triangle of brightness in the gloom.

'Sally?' she called.

A rustle in the silence.

'Sally?' she called again. 'Are you there?'

A dark shape moved from the corner of the stacked bales of hay and into the triangle of light.

'What's the matter?' Sally sounded flustered.

'What are you doing?' Carina asked.

Another dark shape materialised, and she knew. Sally and Frank had been canoodling in the hay. She felt her cheeks flush hot, with both annoyance and embarrassment.

'I thought you were going to keep an eye on the children for me,' she said.

'I am. I'm just coming . . .'

As Sally passed her, going out into the sunlight, Carina saw that she too was flushed. Bits of hay had stuck in her hair and one button too many was undone at the neck of her shirt. Carina averted her eyes. She didn't want to see the evidence of what Sally had been up to with Frank; it was all too obvious. As for Frank, he sauntered out totally unabashed, looking a sight too pleased with himself.

'It's gonna be another hot one,' he said carelessly, cocking a glance at the cloudless sky, but Carina suspected his words had a double meaning.

'Can I go into town now?' she asked Sally, ignoring him.

Sally shrugged. 'Yes, if you want.' She turned to Frank.

'Do you fancy a cup of tea before you get back to work?'

'Wouldn't say no.'

Carina wasn't at all happy about that. How could she be sure Sally would look after the children properly if that man was there, distracting her? But she couldn't see that she could object, and it didn't seem likely that Sally and Frank would carry on where they had left off with the children playing around them and Grandpa Luke just outside the back door. The best thing was to just go to town and get back again as quickly as possible.

She'd finished her shopping and was making her way back to the motor when David Perkins emerged from the doorway of the hardware store, carrying an oil can and manoeuvring his way around a display of gardening equipment and brooms, baskets of cheap bulbs and seeds.

'David!' she greeted him.

He nodded, a little awkwardly. 'How are things going? No, that's a stupid question. What I meant was—'

'We're managing,' Carina said.

'I did say to Sally when I saw her the other day, if there's anything I can do . . . She said that Martin Harvey's Corky was going to help you out, but if he's too busy, you know where I am . . .'

'That's very kind of you, David, but actually we haven't had to call on Corky. An old friend of Robert's turned up out of the blue and he's staying with us and doing a lot of the donkey work.'

'Oh, that's all right then . . .' But David looked crestfallen, and Carina, who knew he was sweet on Sally, guessed that he wasn't very enamoured of the idea of another young man on the scene. He was right to be worried, she thought, given Sally's

149

behaviour and the scene she had stumbled across this morning.

If only Sally was as interested in David as he was in her! He was a really nice boy; she liked him a lot and felt sorry for him. Besides which, he wouldn't toy with Sally's affections as she feared Frank might.

'Did you walk into town?' she asked. 'If you did, I could give you a lift back in the Rover.'

Momentary surprise flickered across David's face, then he shook his head.

'You're all right. I came in on my bike.'

'Oh yes.' Sure enough, there was his bicycle propped up against the wall beyond the stack of garden implements. 'Can you manage to ride carrying that, though?' She nodded in the direction of the can of oil.

'No problem.' David grinned. 'Don't you know I was the champion when we used to muck about on the batch?'

'You were one of those daredevils, were you?' Carina was glad to be back on safer ground. 'Robert's told me about those races between the local lads when everybody went home covered in coal dust. Not something I'd fancy, I must say.'

'Nor me nowadays. But it certainly taught me how to ride a bike.'

'I must be going,' Carina said. 'I have to get home and relieve Sally of looking after the children.'

'How is she?' David asked.

'Oh . . .' Carina hesitated, not knowing quite how to answer. 'Up and down, you know.'

As she said it, it struck her that the vague generalisation described Sally's moods perfectly. She was on a see-saw – no, more than that: a swing boat, perhaps, or a scenic railway, veering between almost manic extremes, desperately unhappy in her grief, but also, at times – the times when she was with Frank

– elated to the point of silliness. Her sister-in-law was on a knife edge, she thought.

'I really must go,' she said abruptly.

'Course you must.' David retrieved his bicycle. 'Give her my love, won't you?'

'I will.'

Carina made her way back to where she had left the Rover, still thinking anxiously about the effect Robert's death had had on Sally.

Suddenly she couldn't wait to get home and make sure everything was all right there.

As she pulled into the farmyard, Carina's heart gave a jolt of shock and surprise. There was no mistaking the motor standing outside the door. Lord Melbrook! But what in the world was he doing here?

Slowing to a snail's pace, she manoeuvred her way past the gleaming cream contraption; the last thing she wanted was to clip the recently repaired rear fender – repairs she had paid dearly for, she reminded herself bitterly. Surely Lord Melbrook couldn't be here with yet another bill for some damage that had been missed? But she wouldn't put it past him.

She pulled the Rover up under the wall, reached into the rear footwell for her bag of shopping and walked apprehensively back to the kitchen door.

There was quite a gathering inside the house, Grandpa Luke sitting in his favourite chair, wide awake, it seemed; Sally at the range, where the kettle was coming to the boil; the children round-eyed and silent for once, Meg clutching her doll; Mattie hanging on to Sally's trousered legs. Even Cymru was sitting to attention near the door, eyes trained watchfully on the visitor. And Lord Melbrook himself at the head of the kitchen table, for all the world as if he owned the place.

'Well!' she said, a little sharply. 'To what do we owe this honour?'

'Mrs Talbot.' He got to his feet, ever the perfect gentleman. 'I hope I haven't called at an inconvenient time.'

'No.' No time is convenient for you to come here unannounced, she was thinking, but of course she didn't say it. She dumped her shopping bag on the floor, leaning it against the table leg, then added coldly: 'I'm just surprised to find you here, that's all.'

He smiled, the movement of his facial muscles accentuating the white scar that ran from the corner of his eye to his mouth.

'I must say I'm quite surprised myself.'

'So?' Carina challenged him.

'Lord Melbrook is after your services, Carina,' Sally said, pouring boiling water into the teapot.

'I'm sorry?'

'As a seamstress.' There was a wicked twinkle in his eye, as if he thought she had hold of the wrong end of the stick and wanted to waste no time in putting her right. 'I have need of one, and my housekeeper tells me you are advertising for work along those lines.'

'Oh!' Carina was totally taken by surprise; she had more or less forgotten about the card she had placed in the post office window, as she had heard nothing since and no potential clients had been forthcoming. And Lord Melbrook coming here in person to ask her to do some work for him was quite unbelievable.

'I have purchased fabric for new drapes for my drawing room,' he went on easily. 'I was wondering if you would be prepared to make them up for me. Although of course I realise furnishings may not be the sort of work you undertake.'

Carina wished she could tell him in no uncertain terms to find someone else to do the work, but pride wasn't a luxury she could afford.

'I'm trained in all aspects of my trade,' she said stiffly.

'Well, that is good news. My housekeeper is plaguing me about the bolts of fabric she claims are in her way. In fact she's threatening to resign, and the household would fall apart without her. So . . .'

'Your tea, Lord Melbrook.' Sally had used one of the best cups and saucers, Carina noticed – in fact, perhaps the only matching cup and saucer they possessed. She set it down on the table.

'Do please sit down,' Carina said because she thought she should – and because it made her feel uncomfortable with him towering over her. 'So what is it you want me to do?'

'The drapes are for three large windows, and if there is any fabric over, it could be used for cushions. If you are agreeable, perhaps I could drive you over to the house, and you can take measurements and collect the rolls of fabric at the same time,' he suggested.

'Very well.' She was doing her best to remain civil and businesslike, though inwardly she was still burning with resentment at being placed in this position by the man who had humiliated her. 'When . . . ?'

'Since I'm here, I suppose there's no time like the present.'

'I'm not sure that . . . Sally?' Carina glanced helplessly at her sister-in-law, but the support she had hoped for was not forthcoming.

'It's all right. I'll look after things while you're gone.'

Her heart sank, but she tried to muster a professionalism she was far from feeling.

'I'll need to collect my tape measure and things.'

'No rush. I'm perfectly happy with the cup of tea your sister-in-law has made me.'

And so he was! she thought, furiously. They weren't tenant farmers who had to kowtow to the lord of the manor, but that was exactly the way it seemed, with everyone gathered in awe while he sat in state as if he was the King of England, perfectly at ease.

She fetched her sewing basket, trying to think what she would need. The tape measure, certainly . . . but where was it? It should be here, along with her needles and pins, thimbles and reels of thread. But it wasn't. She tried to remember the last time she had used it. Last week she'd taken in another old shirt of Robert's for Sally when she'd caught the one she'd been wearing on barbed wire while repairing the fences and torn it too badly for repair. That was probably it. She ran upstairs, and sure enough the tape measure was in Sally's room, sitting on top of the chest of drawers where she'd left it.

She'd also need a notebook or paper to write down measurements or any special instructions. But her writing pad wasn't where it should be in the bureau drawer either, and when she eventually found it, after rifling through a pile of old papers heaped on a chair, she realised it was useless. Meg had obviously been using it to draw on; almost every sheet was covered with bright childish scrawls.

'Oh no! I'm sorry, it looks as if the children . . .'

'Don't worry, I have plenty of paper at home,' Cal said easily, but Carina thought he sounded amused and she felt more cross, foolish and flustered than ever.

Why hadn't she made sure all the tools of her trade were up together before placing the postcard in the post office window? Failing to do so made her look unprofessional. The trouble was, she simply hadn't had the time to think about it.

Well, too late now.

'Shall we go, then?' Cal asked when he'd finished his tea.

Carina followed him outside, and he opened the passenger door of the Benz and helped her up.

'You're still driving, I see,' he said with a nod in the direction of the Rover.

The comment, delivered with a half-smile, needled her beyond the bounds of caution.

'I'm getting quite good at it,' she returned tartly. 'And don't worry, I steered well clear of your car when I saw it here.'

The half-smile disappeared.

'Look, Mrs Talbot, I know we got off to a very bad start. I saw red when you ran into my motor and probably said things I shouldn't have. But when I came to see you about paying for the damage, I honestly didn't know about your tragic loss. If I had, I'd never have pursued it. I wanted to apologise there and then, but understandably you were too upset to speak to me again, though I did ask your grandfather to tell you how sorry I was. I hope he passed the message on, but I expect the damage was done by then. As for the day I met you in Bath . . .'

Carina huffed slightly and turned away. The pain of having to part with her precious engagement ring and the humiliation of her encounter with him and that horrible lady was still too raw.

'I am really sorry that you had to go to such lengths to repay me,' he went on. 'I had no intention of taking your money, and wouldn't have done if it hadn't been for Isobel.'

'I'd have insisted.' Carina turned back to him. 'As I think I said at the time, I pay my debts, Lord Melbrook.'

'I know. You're a proud woman, Mrs Talbot, and I won't insult you by trying to return the money to you now. But please, can we put all this behind us and begin again?'

155

It occurred to Carina then that this work he was offering her was his way of making amends.

'Are you sure you really need my services as a seamstress?' she asked. 'Because if it's charity . . .'

'I really need your services.' He smiled again. 'You wouldn't have me lose my housekeeper because of our differences, would you?'

And I really need the work, Carina thought, but she didn't say so.

'Well, if you're sure.'

'Absolutely. And I hope my apology for my previous behaviour is accepted.'

'Yes.' What else could she say?

'Good. Then let's get going, shall we?'

As they turned out of the farm track and on to the road, a figure on a bicycle came into view ahead of them – David Perkins, riding one-handed, with his can of oil dangling beside his knee. As they passed him, he glanced in their direction, wobbling slightly, and Carina saw the look of surprise on his flushed face when he realised who was in the passenger seat.

'That was young Perkins, wasn't it?' Cal said. 'Didn't I hear that he was courting your sister-in-law?'

Carina was surprised that his lordship should have heard anything of the sort, but she realised he was trying to ease the somewhat strained atmosphere between them and did her best to reciprocate.

'He'd like to be,' she said. 'Sally's not really interested, though, more's the pity.'

'Yes, the Perkins family are doing a very good job with High Combe Farm,' Cal said, and again Carina was surprised, though she supposed she shouldn't be. As their landlord of course he would know all about the success or otherwise of his tenants' farms.

As they drove, she felt herself relax. Really, holding on to her resentment would do no good, and perhaps Lord Melbrook wasn't as bad as she had thought. If he was making an effort to put the past behind them, perhaps she should do the same.

They descended the long hill into the village of Dunderwick, which was more or less deserted – most folk would be getting their dinner ready, Carina supposed, and hoped Sally would think to make a start at getting theirs. The children were used to regular mealtimes and she had no idea how long she would be gone. One old man sitting outside the Dunderwick Arms raised his cap as the Benz passed, and Cal acknowledged him by raising his left hand briefly. Then they were climbing up the other side of the valley and turning into the drive that led through the woods to the house.

Though she had often walked around the walls that bordered the estate, Carina had never set foot inside. It was dim on the roughly laid drive, with the trees forming a canopy overhead, so that when they reached the bottom of the gentle slope and Cal swung sharply to the right, it was like coming out of a tunnel. There in front of them was the house, set behind a swathe of lawn and gardens, and bathed in sunlight as it was, everything was so bright that it almost hurt her eyes: tumbling rose bushes, yellow, red and salmon pink; the house itself built of local white lias stone, its many windows reflecting the rays of the sun; a fountain drooping a sparkling spray of crystal droplets, a peacock strutting across the smooth emerald expanse of lawn. Carina almost gasped; she had never seen anything so beautiful, so unexpected.

Cal swung the Benz again in an arc, pulling up between the house and a row of outbuildings, stopped the engine and went round to hand Carina down.

'We'll go in this way.'

He indicated what Carina took to be a large conservatory, but which was in fact his favourite night-time haunt, the orangery. The door stood ajar; as he pushed it fully open, indicating that she should go first, a black Labrador emerged, pushing a wet nose into Cal's hand before turning its attention to sniffing Carina's skirts.

'Away, Cleo!' Cal snapped.

The dog looked up at him, hurt.

'It's all right, I'm quite used to dogs,' Carina said.

'But not all visitors are, and she should know better. Away, Cleo!' he repeated, and still looking soulful, the dog slunk off back into the house.

Cal indicated the doorway again. 'Do please go in.'

As she stepped inside, the sharp scent of citrus struck her instantly.

'It smells like Christmas!' she said before she could stop herself.

'Except that at Christmas it doesn't smell like this,' he said with a smile.

She gazed at the trees, shaking her head, all resentment and awkwardness forgotten in the wonder of them.

'The only oranges I've ever seen are the ones in the fruit bowl, or in the stocking I used to hang up for Father Christmas.'

Cal picked one of the ripe fruits and handed it to her.

'Try it. I think you'll find it tastes even sweeter.'

About to tear off the peel, Carina hesitated.

'Better not. I shall get all sticky.'

'Take it home with you, then. And have some for the children, too.'

He picked another three or four of the little oranges.

Carina put them in her bag. 'Thank you. They'll be thrilled.

They don't get many treats . . .' She broke off, wishing she hadn't said that. 'They're happy, though,' she added defensively.

'I'm sure they are.' There was a small silence. Then he said abruptly: 'To business, then. I'll show you the fabric and the windows it's meant for so that you can measure up.'

He led the way and she followed, manoeuvring her way round a low table and cane chair, through a room that judging by the bookshelves lining the walls was a library and into a broad passageway hung with portraits.

'Don't be put off by my ancestors,' Cal said with an apologetic grin. 'I think they must have been a pretty grim lot.'

Carina looked up, taking in the stern faces above the stiff collars of the men and the tightly corseted waists of the women.

'They were rather uncomfortable in those clothes, I imagine. I don't think I'd feel like smiling if I could hardly breathe,' she said, and couldn't believe she had dared to say such a thing.

A voice called from a doorway on the left of the passage. It was low-pitched and imperious, with just a hint of a quaver, and Carina wasn't sure if it belonged to a man or a woman.

'My mother.' Cal set her straight.

'Yes, Mama,' he called back. 'I've brought the seamstress to measure up for the drawing room drapes.'

'Don't creep about, then. Bring her here.'

Cal threw Carina an apologetic glance. Clearly Lady Melbrook was a woman to be obeyed. Feeling uncomfortable again, Carina approached the door that he was indicating.

The room she stepped into was small but elegantly furnished in shades of pink, cerise and gold. In a brocaded chair beside the window sat a woman who might have stepped straight out of the Victorian era. Upswept snow-white hair was topped with a black lace cap, and her high-necked black gown fell all the way down to the pink and cerise rug that covered most of the varnished wooden floor. Her face was smooth and almost unlined, but the thin lips and pale mottled hands, one of which clutched an ivory-topped cane, were those of a woman who had probably reached her allotted three score years and ten. Beady eyes regarded Carina appraisingly from beneath hooded lids.

'So.' Her voice seemed to come from deep in her throat. 'You are the seamstress. Are you a local girl?'

'Yes, ma'am . . .' Carina was uncertain whether this was the correct form of address, or even if she was expected to curtsey, so regal was this old lady.

'This is Mrs Talbot, Mama.' Cal stepped into the breach. 'Her late husband was the grandson of Luke Green at Meadow Farm.'

A tiny frown puckered the smooth skin of the woman's forehead.

'*Late?*'

'Unfortunately he died a few weeks ago after being kicked in the head by his horse,' Cal explained.

Her ladyship snorted slightly.

'Hmm! Dratted horses! One was the death of my dear husband too.'

'Yes, Mama, but the circumstances were rather different.' He turned to Carina. 'This is my mother, Lady Melbrook. As you can see, she's not one to mince her words.'

'Life is too short for that, Calvert.' Those dark beady eyes were on Carina again. 'So you are here to make new drapes for the drawing room, I understand? Well, I hope you'll make a good job of it. Though why it is necessary at all, I fail to comprehend.'

'You and me both, Mama,' Cal said drily. 'You have Isobel to blame for that. "Disgusting" was the word I think she used for the old ones.'

A slight shake of that snow-white head, but a softening of the hard lines of her mouth.

'That's Isobel for you. I dread to think what changes she would demand if you and she should ever . . . She would take you in hand, certainly, which could be nothing but a good thing.'

'If you say so, Mama.' Cal was clearly less comfortable having this conversation in Carina's presence than his mother, who was used to open discussion in front of the servants; like so many of her class, she treated them as if they were as deaf and lacking in understanding as the alabaster busts on their plinths. 'If you'll excuse us, I think Mrs Talbot is anxious to measure up and get back to her family.'

'Very well.' Another imperious nod, this time one of dismissal.

Relieved to have escaped, Carina followed Cal to the drawing room. In contrast to her ladyship's sitting room, it was spacious and very light, with the large windows taking up most of the front wall, but it was no less elegantly furnished, with spindle-leg chairs, heavily brocaded sofas, a velvet-covered chaise and small ornate side tables. A grand piano occupied one corner, and Carina noticed several glass-fronted display cabinets, which, surprisingly, appeared to be empty.

She crossed to the windows and saw at once that the drapes, which reached from ceiling to floor, were indeed old and in need of replacing. Around the edges and in the folds they were badly faded, and the hems looked ragged and worn, even rotten in places, as if damp had seeped in beneath the windows and saturated the thick fabric, which had then failed to dry out properly. Little as she had liked the woman who had been so rude to her that day in Bath, and whom she assumed to be Isobel, she couldn't help agreeing with her in her opinion of the drapes, even if Lord Melbrook and his mother did not.

'We'll need a stepladder to take the measurements,' Cal said.

'And I doubt my tape is long enough,' Carina added, feeling inadequate again.

'I'll see what I can find.'

He left the room and Carina took the opportunity to look around. There were fewer ornaments than she would have expected, and a large patch of wall in one of the alcoves beside the chimney breast was a slightly different shade to its surroundings. It looked as if a picture that had once hung there had been removed, and recently, she thought. In fact, for all that the first impression was one of timeless elegance, she couldn't help feeling that the whole room, and not just the drapes, would benefit from freshening up.

Cal was back with a stepladder, a retractable metal tape measure and a pad and pencil.

'Don't worry, I'm not expecting you to climb up,' he said. 'I'll do that.'

'Are you sure?' She was thinking of his limp, the result of being wounded in the Boer War, Sally had said. 'If it's difficult for you, I don't mind.'

That she had touched a raw nerve was immediately obvious.

'Quite sure. Just write down the measurements.' Cal's tone was clipped, almost aggressive.

He climbed the stepladder decisively if a little awkwardly, hooked the end of the tape over the curtain rail and let it drop. But when Carina had noted the depth to which it had fallen and he climbed down again, he was grimacing slightly, and she guessed that for all his protestations he was in pain.

'We can do the width from down here,' she said. 'It's going to be the same at the bottom as at the top.'

The measurements completed, Cal went off to fetch the rolls

of fabric and spread one out along one of the sofas. It fell smooth and glowing to the floor.

'It's beautiful.' Carina ran her fingers over the soft ruby-red velvet.

'There's no doubt about it, Isobel has an eye for these things, even if her tastes do veer alarmingly to the extravagant.'

Carina experienced a stab of panic as it struck her just how expensive this fabric must be. The very thought of cutting into it was scary; supposing she got it wrong? It was a long time, after all, since she had undertaken anything more demanding than making up clothes for the children or a cheap cotton frock for herself. As for having to do it on the kitchen table with Meg and Mattie playing close by, Cymru shedding hairs on everything he brushed against . . . and oh, horror of horrors, the children perhaps touching the lush velvet with sticky fingers before she could stop them, or Grandpa Luke slopping tea from his cup as he carried it across the room, not to mention the smells of fried bacon and boiled cabbage that hung about in the kitchen and might well permeate the rich fabric . . .

'I don't suppose I could make the drapes here?' she suggested tentatively.

'Well, I don't see why not.' But he looked surprised and Carina rushed on:

'I think it would be safer. At home I'd have to do it on the kitchen table, and that's far from ideal when it's such a big job.'

'You'd bring your sewing machine?'

'Yes. I could drive over in the Rover . . .'

'Or I could collect you and take you home.' The corners of Cal's mouth lifted slightly and the eyes that met hers held a mischievous twinkle. 'I don't disbelieve you when you say your driving skills have improved, but I wouldn't want to be responsible for you having another mishap.'

Something about the way he was looking at her was oddly unsettling. It felt as if a dozen butterflies were fluttering in her stomach. But at the same time Carina was infuriated by the fact that he was still making fun of her and something that had had very serious consequences for her.

'If I'm going to be working here, I'd appreciate it if you'd stop bringing that up,' she said sharply.

'I'm sorry.' He raised his hands in submission. 'I put my offer very badly. What I should have said is that collecting you and taking you home on your first day is the very least I can do. What time shall we say? Would about nine suit you?'

'Well . . . yes, I suppose so.' Backed into a corner, Carina had little choice but to agree.

'Good.' He was still looking at her in that way she found so strangely disturbing. 'That's arranged then. And now I expect you are anxious to get home to your family.'

It was well past one by the time Carina was back at Meadow Farm.

'Mattie's gone down for his nap,' Sally informed her. 'And Meg and Grandpa have eaten too, but I waited until you got back.'

'What about Frank?' Carina asked.

'He ate with Grandpa.'

'Right.'

It was a conciliatory gesture on Sally's part, Carina thought. She would probably much rather have eaten with him.

'How did you get on?' Sally asked, taking the remaining baked potatoes out of the oven.

Carina told her.

'It's going to mean that I'll have to ask you to look after the children while I'm working, though,' she added.

'That's all right,' Sally said. 'With Frank here, I'm relieved of a lot of the heavy work.' She went a little pink as she spoke his name, but her acquiescence was another sign that she was doing her best to make amends for this morning's behaviour.

'I can't risk them touching that beautiful velvet with their sticky fingers,' Carina said. 'And speaking of sticky fingers, I have a treat for all of us. These are from Lord Melbrook's orangery.'

She produced the oranges from her bag.

'Good Lord!' Sally was flabbergasted. 'He grows *oranges*?'

'It's another world up there,' Carina said, and felt a glow of pride that for a few days at least she was going to be experiencing it.

Chapter Thirteen

The weeks that followed were unlike any that had gone before, and Carina found that although she was busier than ever, she also had a renewed energy that came from a sense of purpose. Bedtime might be later than it had ever been by the time she had finished her chores, but she was still awake early next morning, fresh and invigorated, and with none of the lethargy that had dragged her down in the early days following Robert's death. Now she buzzed with enthusiasm, and though of course she was still grieving, there was less time for indulging it.

Her new lease of life had begun with the days spent at Dunderwick House. Although at first she felt guilty and anxious about leaving the children in Sally's care, those feelings were quickly negated by relief that she was able to work without worrying about either them or Cymru spoiling the expensive curtain fabric. Besides this, she couldn't help but enjoy her new surroundings. Lord Melbrook had set up a work table for her in the library, and here, with the citrus scent that wafted in from the orangery and only the whirr of the sewing machine and the buzzing of bees in the honeysuckle outside the open window to break the restful silence, Carina was able to recapture the almost forgotten satisfaction and pleasure that came from doing what she had been trained for, and was good at. She even found herself humming softly as she turned the handle of her sewing machine and guided the lengths of material beneath the foot with an expertise that had come back to her quickly and easily despite her lack of practice. For those few hours each day she might almost have been the carefree girl who had met and fallen in love with Robert in what had seemed, until now, to be another lifetime.

Lord Melbrook had collected her as arranged on the first day, and driven her into Hillsbridge so that she could buy cotton that exactly matched the ruby velvet. He had waited in the Benz while she went into the shop, but when she emerged, he had got out and come round to help her up into her seat, and for some reason that had made her feel unsettled again – because he was upper crust when she was just a seamstress, she supposed. But that didn't quite explain the strange flutters in her stomach, and she wished he wouldn't look at her in that teasing way when she was trying to be serious. But at least he wasn't turning out to be quite the ogre she had thought him, and for that she should be grateful, she told herself.

When he drove her home, she suggested that the following day she should drive herself. She was half expecting him to make some sarcastic comment again, but to her surprise he did not. He had to go to London for a day or two, he told her, so if she was happy to do that, it would save him having to get one of his staff to collect her.

Until recently, Carina would have been mightily relieved that she would not have to face him on a daily basis; now she was surprised to find herself feeling almost disappointed.

'Don't let Cleo bother you while I'm away – she will if she gets half a chance,' he warned her. 'And don't let my mother bully you. Just remember that unlike Cleo, her bark is worse than her bite.'

And goodness knows, that's pretty fearsome, Carina thought. But aloud she said: 'Don't worry, I won't.'

'No, I think she might have met her match in you,' he said with a smile.

In the event, Lady Melbrook kept her distance and the only reminder that she was in the house at all was that distinctive voice calling instructions to some hapless servant from time to time.

Cal was back by the time the drapes were finally finished. He, Carina and a satisfied Biddy Thomas watched as two of the servants hung them.

'You've done a splendid job, Mrs Talbot,' he said when they were in place.

Carina had made up her mind not to allow herself to be overawed.

'They do look good, even if I do say so myself,' she said.

'You've every right to be proud,' Cal told her, and she felt a flush of pride. 'I'll get Mama to take a look. She can be very critical, but I don't think even she will be able to find fault this time.'

He went to fetch Lady Melbrook, and she came into the drawing room leaning heavily on her stick. She twitched the edges of the curtains before standing back to regard them critically.

'Perhaps Isobel was right, Calvert,' she admitted eventually. 'Even I can see these are something of an improvement. And –' with a glance in Carina's direction – 'very well made. Perhaps we should think about refurbishing some of the other rooms. My sitting room, for instance.'

Carina's heart gave a little leap of anticipation. She couldn't think of anything she would like better than to spend some more time working in this pleasant environment, and the money would certainly come in useful too. But her hopes were quickly dashed.

'Perhaps, Mama, but there are other things that need attending to first. The barn roof at Rookery Farm, to name but one,' Cal said.

He turned to Carina.

'Don't worry, the moment we decide to replace some of the other drapes, it will be you I shall call on. And I shall be recommending you to anyone else I hear of who is in need of a seamstress.'

'Thank you.' The praise almost made up for her disappointment. And she had just earned enough money to not only pay the week's bills but also put some aside in the biscuit barrel, she reminded herself.

Perhaps Cal had been as good as his word, or perhaps the card in the post office window was finally yielding results, but in the days that followed, Carina had suddenly found herself inundated with requests for her services. They were minor jobs only compared with the huge task of making the drapes for Dunderwick House, but she attacked them with the same meticulous care and diligence. Since she now had to make do with the kitchen table at Meadow Farm, she took to working in the early morning before the children were up, and the late evening when they were in bed and Cymru had been banished to his kennel.

She took no less care with a tea dress for the vicar's wife or pinafores for the Dunderwick schoolmaster's brood of daughters than she had with the drapes, and soon her growing reputation meant she could barely keep up with the work that was coming her way. But she felt it would be folly to turn down any potential clients until her business was firmly established, and besides, it was gratifying to see the pot of money growing steadily even after she had paid the bills and bought a few small treats for the family. 'I never expected to eat a biscuit that wasn't broken ever again!' Sally had said, digging into the bag of custard creams that Carina had added to the weekly shop.

Sally seemed to be much more her old self, with far fewer of the violent mood swings that had been so worrying Carina. Now that Carina was at home during the day once more, her sister-in-law had resumed her old routine, spending her time out on the farm. She was still just as besotted with Frank, and Carina couldn't help but wonder anxiously just what they got up to when they were out of her sight.

Once, when she was working especially late to finish a confirmation dress for a little girl from the village, she had heard the stair boards creak as if someone was creeping down; then, after a pause, a reversal, as if they were going back up again. It had occurred to her to wonder if it was Sally, intending to steal across to Frank's quarters over the barn, then having to abandon her plan and beat a hasty retreat when she had seen the light from the kitchen and realised Carina was still there, and the possibility had worried her.

Supposing Sally should be foolish enough to overstep the mark and do something silly? The very thought made her go cold. Sally in trouble would be the last straw, and somehow Carina couldn't imagine Frank would be the sort to hang around if he thought he was likely to be caught in a domestic trap. But she couldn't be watching her sister-in-law twenty-four hours a day; she just had to trust her. And though she didn't like Frank any more than she had ever done, she had to admit that he seemed to be good for Sally.

He was a hard worker, too. She didn't know how they could have managed without him, and soon they were going to be even more in need of all the help they could get. A spell of rainy weather followed by yet more hot sunshine meant the grass was growing again apace; there would be a second harvest this year, good for supplies of winter fodder, but tiring and time-consuming. No, really they would never be able to manage without Frank, and Carina knew she had no choice but to bite her tongue where he was concerned.

By the end of those weeks of summer, Mattie had cut a second tooth and Meg had grown another full inch, so that Carina thought she was going to have to somehow find time in her busy schedule to make her a new dress. Well, at least now she wouldn't have to worry about how she would find the money for it, though she would use a thicker fabric, she decided, so it would see Meg through the winter. She didn't want to dip too deeply into her stash – she was hoping that one day she might have enough to spare to go to Bath and buy back her precious engagement ring. The month the pawnbroker had stipulated had passed now, but remembering what Mr Johnson, the Hillsbridge jeweller, had said about young couples thinking it unlucky to plight their troth with a second-hand ring, she was clinging to the hope that the pawnbroker might not have been able to find a buyer for it.

For the moment, however, the most important thing was to build up her business and still manage to look after the children and keep the house running smoothly. The ring would just have to wait.

Cal and Isobel were having lunch again at the Francis Hotel, the first time they had met up since the day she had railroaded him into buying the fabric for the drapes, as Isobel had only just returned from a month's holiday in Italy.

Ever since he had returned to Dunderwick following the death of his brother, the two of them had tried to meet at least once a month. Their easy friendship was important to both of them – much as she enjoyed the company of her young gentlemen admirers, Isobel had to admit it was good to spend time with someone closer to her own age, and Cal liked to be able to put his responsibilities to the back of his mind for a while, even let off some of the head of steam that built up as he tried to sort out the mess Stafford had left behind.

Invariably they chose the Francis, five tall town houses with Georgian facades on the south side of Queen Square that had been opened up to make one imposing hotel. The food, they agreed, was the best in Bath, and the Regency elegance of the place appealed to Isobel.

'So – your mother approved of my choice of fabric?' she asked once they had perused the menu and the waiter had taken their order.

'My mother approves of just about everything where you are concerned,' Cal said drily. 'Though I doubt she would if she knew you as well as I do.'

'Oh Cal! What a dreadful thing to say!' she objected, but there was a wicked gleam in her emerald-green eyes.

'True, though.' He returned her twinkle. 'But yes, Mama is very impressed with the new drapes. In fact she's pestering me now to do up the dining room and her sitting room too. You'll bankrupt me between the two of you.'

'Fiddlesticks! You can afford it.'

'That's just the trouble – I'm not sure that I can.'

'Well, at least I hope you took my advice about the seamstress and employed mine. When we spoke on the telephone before I went to Italy, you were threatening to use that ignorant woman who created such a scene in the street.'

'I did indeed use her – though I wish you didn't have such a low opinion of her, Isobel. She is far from ignorant. And a very good job she made of the drapes too.'

'Well, I dare say you might think so. What do you know

about these things? As for your mother, her eyesight is failing, I imagine.'

'There's nothing wrong with my mother's eyesight. And you're a fine one to talk.'

'That's a very low blow, Calvert.' Isobel had put on a pair of wire-rimmed spectacles to study the menu, and quickly slipped them back into her bag again as soon as she had made her choice. 'You know I only need them for reading.'

'Nevertheless . . . Mama seems to manage perfectly well without. Though I have to admit, her hearing isn't what it used to be.'

'Whilst mine is perfect. If you mutter something unpleasant about me under your breath, I assure you I shall hear every word. But to get back to the drapes. Why on earth would you trust a country bumpkin with that beautiful velvet when you could have used my seamstress, who is the best in Bath, if not the whole of Somerset?'

'She's not a bumpkin,' Cal said, 'and she needed the work. She lost her husband recently, as I think I told you, and the family are really struggling. In fact the whole family seems to attract bad luck. Robert Talbot's parents both died young – there's some sort of mystery surrounding the circumstances, according to local gossip, but maybe that's all it is, gossip. You know what country folk are like when it comes to embellishing a story. Anyway, Talbot Senior was a dock worker in Bristol, and the Greens' daughter had moved there when she married him. They had two children, Robert and Sally, and after the parents died, their grandparents took them in. Then the grandmother passed away, and Luke – the grandfather – had an accident that left him crippled. And as if all that isn't bad enough, now Robert Talbot is gone too. Kicked in the head by his horse, as I understand it.'

'Dear, dear, a very sad tale,' Isobel murmured, but her eyes had narrowed thoughtfully.

'It is actually, yes.'

'Don't look so disapproving, Cal. Flippancy is my middle name. But actually . . .' She paused for a moment, then asked: 'Did you say the father's name was Talbot?'

'Yes.'

'And the children were quite young when they were orphaned, presumably.'

'From what I can make out, Robert was in his early teens and his sister some years younger when they came to Dunderwick. But why all the interest, Isobel? It isn't like you to want to know the ins and outs of the family lives of my tenants and neighbours.'

Isobel's eyes met his teasingly.

'A couple of reasons really. For a start, I'm interested because I think you have a soft spot for your Mrs Talbot.'

'She's not *my* Mrs Talbot.'

'Maybe not . . . but I think you'd like her to be.'

'For goodness' sake, Isobel! Just because I employed her to make the drapes . . .'

'You fly to her defence at every opportunity, Calvert. But actually that's not the main reason for my interest. There's something—'

The waiter was at her shoulder, ready to serve their first course – potted salmon for her, mulligatawny for Cal. When he had finished and glided away, Cal gave her a questioning look.

'You were going to tell me why you are so interested in the Talbot family.'

Isobel shrugged, picking up her fork.

'Oh . . . it's nothing. I'm probably mistaken. Let's forget about your little seamstress and enjoy our lunch.'

Curious though he was, Cal let the subject drop. Whatever it was, Isobel would tell him when she was good and ready. If indeed there was anything to tell. He knew only too well that there were times when nothing pleased her more than being frustratingly mysterious. This, clearly, was one of them.

'When is my daddy coming home?'

Meg had tugged at Carina's skirt to attract her attention. Now she gazed up at her mother, her eyes puzzled and pleading.

A lump rose in Carina's throat.

'Oh my darling, I thought I'd explained. Daddy won't be coming home any more. He's in heaven with the angels.'

'But I miss him so!'

'I know.' Carina swallowed hard. 'We all do. But—'

'If I got the stepladder, couldn't I go up and see him?'

Tears welled in Carina's eyes.

'If I promised to be ever so good,' Meg added.

'I'm afraid it doesn't work like that, sweetheart.'

But how could she expect Meg to understand what she herself barely could? Even now she didn't feel she had accepted the cruel reality that Robert had gone for ever. *I've done my best and carried on without him – now please can I have him back?* The words were sometimes there in her head, unspoken but heartfelt. She knew it was impossible, yet somehow a tiny part of her clung to the desperate hope that it had all been a horrible dream.

'But why did he go?' Meg persisted. 'Was it because we were bad, me and Mattie? Doesn't he love us any more?'

'Oh Meg . . .' Carina dropped to her knees, wrapping her arms round her daughter. 'Of course it wasn't because of anything you or Mattie did. And of course he loved you, very much, and still does. But sometimes . . .' Words failed her. 'Sometimes these things just happen,' she went on after a moment. 'None of us can understand why.'

'But I want him!'

'I know, Meg. So do I, very much.'

'You won't go away too, will you, Mummy?'

'No, Meg, I'm not going anywhere, I promise.'

God willing, she added silently. Who knew what the future held for any of them? But the thought of Meg and Mattie orphaned as Robert and Sally had been was so horrendous she couldn't allow herself to dwell on it for even a moment. She had to be here for them. She would be.

She cradled Meg in her arms, her face buried in the little girl's silky-soft hair, and soon it was damp with her tears.

'Hey, beautiful!'

Sally was crossing the yard on her way back from afternoon milking. Her heart gave a flip and she turned to see Frank lounging against the barn door, sun-bronzed arms folded casually, chewing on a length of straw.

'Ignoring me, are you?' he taunted. 'We'll have to do something about that.'

Quick colour had risen in Sally's cheeks. She'd never known anyone quite like Frank, never known anyone who could make her feel this way, excited, eager, happy – yes, happy, even though she was still mourning Robert. And in some strange way, he reminded her of her father. Not to look at; rather it was something in his manner.

'I just didn't see you there,' she said, pretending nonchalance.

'Well now you have seen me, aren't you coming over to say hello?'

She knew very well what saying hello meant. He'd pull her inside the dark barn and kiss her until she was dizzy, and then . . . he'd try to go further. He always did. So far Sally had resisted, but she wasn't sure how much longer she could hold out. It wasn't that she didn't want him – she did. Wanted him so badly that it hurt, deep in the pit of her stomach. But she was a little bit afraid too, and so far that fear had held her back so that she would push away his hands however good they felt on her body and tell him no. To begin with he'd only laughed, and told her she was a rotten tease who would one day get what was coming to her, but more recently he'd seemed genuinely put out, pushing her away and then ignoring her for the rest of the day. On the last occasion he'd turned his attention to Carina all through supper and even flirted with her. Sally had been very hurt, and she was dreadfully afraid that if she continued to stop Frank in his tracks she might lose him altogether. So she had been doing her best to avoid being alone with him, much as she longed to be.

'It's nearly teatime,' she hedged now.

'Well, if that matters to you more than me . . . I had something for you, but if you don't want it . . .'

I'll find somebody else who does . . .

The unspoken threat alarmed her. If Frank took up with another girl, she just couldn't bear it. And he'd only have to walk down into the village to find plenty who would be eager for his attentions. Young men as attractive as he was didn't grow on trees, and she should know. Until he'd arrived on the doorstep, she'd never really fancied anyone.

Trying to appear insouciant, she sauntered towards him.

'Okay – what is it?'

'Come inside and I'll show you.'

He led the way up to his room. Though still far from luxurious, it had been much improved since the day he moved in, with a blanket of squares that Grandma Margaret had knitted and crocheted together years ago covering the palliasse, cushions in the old armchair and a rag rug that had once lain in front of the kitchen hearth covering part of the bare board floor.

Sally stopped in the doorway, thrusting her hands into the pockets of her trousers. 'I don't believe you've got anything to show me at all.'

'Well that's where you're wrong.'

The rucksack he'd arrived with lay in a corner; he crossed to it now and extracted something from one of the pockets, concealing it in the palm of his hand.

'How about a kiss first?'

'No. Not until I see what it is.'

'You're a hard woman, Sally. All right. You win.'

He uncurled his fingers, and a shaft of sunlight slanting in through the small high-up window glinted on something silver and blue.

A pendant; a tiny stone that might have been a sapphire or just a piece of pretty blue glass on a fine chain.

'Oh!' Sally was so surprised, she didn't know what else to say.

'Well – do you like it?'

'It's lovely! But . . .'

'A lovely necklace for a lovely girl.'

'It's for me?'

'I'd look a bit silly wearing it, wouldn't I?'

'Oh Frank . . .'

'Shall I put it on for you then?'

Sally didn't usually care much for jewellery. But this was different.

'Well . . . yes . . .'

He fastened the chain around her neck, then slid his hands down to her waist, holding her fast.

'Very nice, if I do say so myself.'

'But Frank, it must have cost you . . .' She broke off, embarrassed. That wasn't the right thing to say, even if it was what she was thinking. 'You shouldn't have,' she finished lamely.

'You're worth it, Sally.' His breath was hot on her face; he nibbled her earlobe. 'So – are you going to thank me properly?'

'Oh Frank . . .'

'You know you want to.'

She did. Of course she did. Especially now that he had proved how much she meant to him by spending his hard-earned money on something so lovely.

'Oh Frank . . .'

It was the last thing either of them said for some time.

On the opposite side of the yard, Luke Green was sitting in his favourite chair and enjoying his pipe and the afternoon sun when Sally appeared on her way back from turning the cows out into the field after milking. Though his sight was not good, he knew it was her. Who else could it be? Besides, there was no mistaking the slender boyish figure in trousers. He heard Frank call to her – his eyes might be bad, but there wasn't much wrong with his hearing – and he saw the pair of them disappear into the barn.

Luke frowned and pulled a little harder on his pipe. Generally he was the most pragmatic of men, but now his usual calm acceptance was tinged with a feeling of unease.

Sally was getting a deal too involved with that one, and he didn't think it boded well. In fact, he was beginning to wonder if it had been a mistake to take Frank Bailey on. They hadn't had much choice, of course, and certainly his being here had lightened the load on Sally and Carina, but he didn't like the man. He was too much like Joel Talbot, a sight too full of himself and all easy charm. He'd never liked Joel either, but when Essie had fallen head over heels for him, Luke had kept his reservations to himself.

And look how that had turned out. Luke still blamed himself for not speaking out. He should never have agreed to let her marry the man. If he'd made her wait until she was twenty-one, maybe she'd have been old enough to see sense. But she'd begged and pleaded and he'd gone along with it because he didn't have any concrete reason to refuse his permission and he couldn't bear to see her upset. In the end, his instincts had proved correct and Joel Talbot had shown his true colours. But by then it was too late.

Well, it was no use harking back to that now. What was done was done and there could be no changing it. But Essie was still a bleeding scar on Luke's heart and he couldn't stand to think the same fate might befall her little girl. If Frank reminded him of Joel, Sally was certainly her mother's daughter, every bit as wilful and headstrong, yet soft as butter underneath and just as able to twist those who loved her round her little finger.

This time, though, it wouldn't work. Sally didn't think her grandfather noticed things. She thought, like all of them, that because he was old and crippled and half blind, he'd also lost some of his marbles, and that because he so seldom spoke out or allowed anything to ruffle him, he wasn't capable of strong emotion. But they were wrong. He felt grief deeply, and beneath his usually calm exterior lay a burning rage.

He'd failed Essie, and he'd never forgive himself for that. But he wouldn't stand by and see the same thing happen to Sally.

Luke puffed on his pipe, his rheumy old eyes narrowed against the smoke, and wondered what would be the best way to set about it.

Chapter Fourteen

It was eight o'clock in the evening, and the regulars at the Dunderwick Arms were chewing the fat over a pint and a pickled egg as they did almost every night.

Most of the talk was of the upcoming flower shows and fetes. There was fierce competition among the men for the longest runner bean, the biggest marrow and the straightest carrot – not the easiest class, since many of the gardens in the Dunderwick valley were riddled with stones. There were prize dahlias blooming in several of the men's gardens, and almost everyone's wife competed in the baking, needlework and flower-arranging classes.

The serious conversations and the good-natured joshing was interrupted, though, when the door opened and Sergeant Love from Hillsbridge police station lumbered in, sweating from his cycle ride up the long hill and down again.

'Evening, Sergeant.'

The unexpected visit made Clem Porter, the landlord, straighten from his usual position, resting on his elbows on the bar. He was always wary of the law, and his first thought was to wonder anxiously if someone had reported a lock-in after hours that he'd allowed last weekend when one of the regulars had been celebrating the birth of a new addition to his family.

'What can I get you?' he asked now, anxious to mollify the policeman.

'Nothing, thank you, Clem. Can't you see I'm on duty?'

'Well . . . ah . . . I s'pose you be. Look, if it's about Saturday night, I can explain . . .'

'A glass of lemonade wouldn't go amiss, though,' the sergeant conceded.

'Course. Anything you like.' Clem hastily filled a pint glass and set it down on the counter. 'That's on the house.'

Sergeant Love drank thirstily and mopped his perspiring face and the nape of his neck with a handkerchief. Then he turned and addressed the gathering in the bar.

'There's been another robbery. I'm here to make inquiries.'

'Oh – a robbery!' Clem relaxed visibly, realising he was off the hook. 'Where were that, then?'

'Out at Ivy Cottages.' Ivy Cottages comprised three terraced houses on a quiet lane on the outskirts of Dunderwick. 'Mrs Deacon from number two came into Dunderwick to do a bit of shopping, and when she got back, somebody had broken in and ransacked the place. Well, I say broken in, but she'd left her door unlocked, so they just walked in and made off with quite a few bits and pieces, including her late husband's war medals.'

'Walked in in broad daylight? Whatever is the world coming to when you can't go out and leave your door unlocked?'

'You may well ask,' the sergeant said heavily. 'Old Mr Peck next door was having his afternoon nap and Mrs Blanning the other side was in her back garden pruning her roses. So I'm here to ask if anybody saw anything suspicious . . .'

'Well, I seed Artie Small hanging his wife's bloomers on the line to dry,' one wag offered to ribald laughter. 'That were mighty suspicious if you do ask I.'

'You reckon he's done away with her at last, then?' another put in.

'An' who could blame 'un?'

'It's no laughing matter,' the sergeant said testily. 'This is the third robbery we've had on my patch in as many weeks.'

'Not in broad daylight before, though,' Clem pointed out.

'No, it's true the others were at night, where access was gained through windows left open to combat the heat.' Sergeant Love spoke in the sort of official language he might have used to record the incidents in his pocketbook. 'But the robbery at Mr Bendle's bookmaker's shop was in the middle of the day, if you recall, and that was aggravated. The offender confronted Mr Bendle and threatened him with a knife.'

'And you never got anybody for it neither, did you?' Clem remarked.

'Unfortunately no, not yet. But it seems to me we've got new criminals out here, from Bath, perhaps. I've never known any of our local rascals do anything like it.'

'And they wouldn't shit on their own doorstep.'

Sergeant Love gave him a stern reproving glance.

'What I meant was, Sergeant, all the local varmints know you'd be on to 'em in a flash and give 'em what for,' the landlord amended hastily.

'I certainly would. No, I don't think whoever is responsible for this crime wave is local. Which is why I'm asking you all to keep a sharp eye out for anything suspicious.'

'I told 'ee about that fellow who was in here the same day Ticker Bendle got done over,' called Nobby Clark from his usual seat in the inglenook. 'And what did you do about that? Nothing, I suppose. I might as well 'ave saved me breath.'

The policeman patted his breast pocket and extracted his notebook.

'Perhaps you can give me a description of him, then.'

''Ow am I s'posed to remember after all this time? That were weeks ago.'

'How about you, Mr Porter?'

'He was respectable enough,' Clem said defensively. 'I told you that at the time. I'd never have served him otherwise.'

'And he hasn't been in since?'

'Not to my knowledge when I've been on duty, no.'

It seemed there was little else the policeman could do.

'Well, I'll just ask you all to keep your eyes skinned,' he said, replacing his notebook in his pocket. 'Let me know straight away if you see anything of interest. I don't like this sort of thing happening on my patch.'

With that, he drained his glass and left the pub, not relishing the thought of the long climb back up the hill. Even now, in what should be the cool of the evening, it was still too hot to ride a bicycle in comfort.

For a while the men in the bar chewed over what they'd just learned – that it seemed it wasn't safe to go out leaving your door unlocked any more. For them, that was the most disturbing part of the whole thing. Then, the topic exhausted, they went back to discussing their runner beans, marrows and carrots.

It was when she went into Dunderwick to pay for her card to remain in the post office window that Carina heard about the burglaries. She'd almost decided against renewing the advertising since so much work had come her way, but another month would cost only a few pence and she didn't want her business to dry up, as it might if her current clients ran out of jobs they wanted doing.

'Terrible what's going on, isn't it?' said Madge Charlton, the postmistress, as she gave Carina her change. 'It's come to

something when you can't leave your door unlocked in broad
daylight without somebody coming in and helping themselves
to whatever they can lay their hands on.'

'What do you mean?' Carina asked, puzzled.

Madge told her.

'And nobody's ever been caught for the armed robbery at
Ticker Bendle's, have they?' she finished.

'Armed robbery?' Carina didn't know anything about that
either.

'Oh, some time ago now, that were. Must have been . . . Yes,
it were. The day of your husband's funeral. Some varmint
walked into Ticker's, threatened him with a knife and made off
with his takings.' Madge liked nothing better than to be able to
share all the talk she was party to, and from her position behind
the post office counter she was party to plenty.

It was no wonder she hadn't heard of the robbery if it had
been on the day of Robert's funeral, Carina thought.

'That's awful,' she said, slipping her purse into her bag.

'Well, you just go careful,' Madge advised. 'Out in the wilds
where you are, and with your poor husband gone . . . There's
some bad lots about all right, and Sergeant Love don't seem to
know what to do about it.'

'I wouldn't think a criminal would come as far out as us,'
Carina said, as much to convince herself as Madge.

'You never know. Ivy Cottages are pretty well out of the
way, and whoever it was found them all right.'

As she walked home, an uncomfortable thought occurred to
Carina.

Last time she'd checked her savings in the biscuit barrel,
there had been less than she'd been expecting. She'd reasoned
she must have dipped into it for something she'd forgotten
about, but for the life of her she couldn't think what. The weekly

bills . . . she always kept a careful check when she paid them. The material for Meg's dress . . . she had been sure she had counted what was left before she had bought that. But there must be something. Either that or she'd been so tired she'd made a mistake.

Now, however, she wondered: had someone crept in when she and Sally were out and Grandpa Luke was snoozing? But that was just silly. If that were the case, surely they would have taken all the money, not just some of it. And she hadn't noticed anything else missing – not that there was a great deal in the house worth stealing.

But she felt uneasy just the same. It would be wise to take more care than they were used to doing, and she must warn the others to watch out for anything suspicious.

She broached the subject over lunch, waiting until the children had finished their meal and been allowed to get down from the table to play. Mattie was much too young to understand, of course, but she didn't want to alarm Meg.

'I heard some disturbing news in Dunderwick,' she said. 'It seems there has been a lot of crime round here lately and folk are worried that some of the Bath villains are moving out this way.'

She went on to repeat what Madge Charlton had told her.

'I think we should all be a bit more careful,' she finished. 'When you have a nap, Grandpa, perhaps it would be wise to lock the door if Sally and me are both out. And we should all keep an eye open for any suspicious characters. I don't suppose they'll be likely to come this far out, but you never know. And if whoever it was threatened Ticker Bendle with a knife and made off with his takings is still in the area . . . well, he sounds dangerous to me. Someone who could do a thing like that would be up for anything.'

'Oh my God!' Sally said. Though her tone was low, they all turned to look at her.

'The intruder the night before Robert was killed,' she said. 'Could that have been the same man?'

'What's this?' Frank asked.

Sally turned to him.

'Robert thought there was someone creeping about in the yard. We hunted around and couldn't find anything, but he was so sure . . . and I thought I'd seen something too. What if we were right all the time and there was someone there? It could well have been the same man who robbed Ticker Bendle. The same man who's carrying out all these break-ins.'

'Oh surely not.'

'But it fits! And what if he was still here the next morning and Robert surprised him? And the man lashed out and killed him!'

'I thought it was Captain kicked Robert to death,' Frank said.

'But supposing it wasn't. I've never believed Captain was responsible. He's so placid and gentle. And a man who can carry out an armed robbery in the middle of town in broad daylight . . . well, who knows what he'd be capable of?'

Warm though it was in the kitchen, a shiver ran down Carina's spine. Was it really possible? Though Sally had suggested much the same in the aftermath of Robert's death, she had been too grief-stricken to give it any thought. It had seemed simply too far-fetched.

'Oh Sally, I don't think—' she began. But Sally rushed on.

'I'll tell you something else. I found a button in the stable the day of Robert's funeral. It was just there, in the straw. I'll show you.'

She jumped up from the table and darted up the stairs to her room. A few moments later she was back.

'See?' She uncurled her fingers, revealing the shiny brown button that lay in the palm of her hand. 'Robert didn't have a coat with brown buttons, did he? Nor have you, Grandpa.'

'It could belong to anyone,' Carina said. Somehow the thought of someone attacking Robert was too horrible to even contemplate. 'One of the labourers, perhaps? There were three or four of them here for the harvest.'

'But they weren't wearing coats. It was so warm, they were even taking off their shirts and tying them round their waists,' Sally argued hotly. 'Besides, this button didn't just come loose and fall off. Look at the bits of cotton still in it. It looks to me as if it was yanked off. As if Robert managed to get hold of his attacker's coat before . . .' She broke off, tears welling in her eyes.

Carina had begun to tremble. 'Surely you can't really think that . . . ?'

'You're letting your imagination run away with you, Sal. You're just upsetting everybody,' Frank said with a surreptitious nod in Carina's direction.

'Maybe I am, but it's my brother's death we're talking about here,' she flared. 'If that robber killed him, he's a murderer, and he's out there walking about, free to do it all again. I'm going to take this button to the police station. If Sergeant Love ever manages to get anybody for the burglaries, this might tie them to Robert's death too.'

'No use going over it, Sally.' Grandpa Luke spoke for the first time. 'You'll only upset yourself, and none of it will bring Robert back.'

'Grandpa's right,' Carina said, desperate to bring this to an end. 'And so is Frank. It's easy to think all sorts when you're in a stew. Goodness, this morning when Madge was talking about an intruder walking into houses and helping themselves, I even thought he might have been in here, taking some of the money I've been saving from my sewing. As if he'd just take some and leave the rest! How ridiculous is that? But I think I shall put it somewhere safer all the same,' she added. 'That money means a lot to me. I'm trying to save up enough to buy back my engagement ring.'

Sally ignored her. She scraped back her chair and got up, still visibly upset. 'Well, I'm going to Hillsbridge in the morning, and don't any of you try to stop me!' she declared.

'Sal . . .' Frank tried to mollify her, but ignoring him too, she headed for the back door and went out, slamming it shut behind her.

'Best leave her be,' Grandpa Luke said, then turned to Carina.

'What's this about your engagement ring, my girl?'

Reluctantly Carina explained. She hadn't wanted Grandpa Luke to know what she had done.

'Dear, dear. And yet you've been buying all sorts of luxuries for us since you've been earning. You mustn't even think of doing that until you've saved enough to get your ring back.'

'How close are you?' Frank asked.

'Well, I thought I was nearly there.' Carina got up, fetched the biscuit barrel and emptied the money out on to the table, hoping in vain that she'd made a mistake the last time she had counted it. 'If I could buy the ring back for what the pawnbroker gave me, I might just about manage it,' she said wretchedly. 'But the trouble is, he made it clear he'd want extra.'

'Rogues, that's what they are, the lot of 'em,' Grandpa said, shaking his head.

'I suppose he has to make a living the same as the rest of us. But I was so sure I had enough after I got paid for my last job . . .' The tears that had been so close when Sally had been talking about Robert's death threatened again. 'I just don't know how I could have made a mistake like that.'

'It would be easy enough,' Frank said. 'How much are you short?'

'I don't really know,' Carina snapped, irritated that this man who was still virtually a stranger was party to, and even interfering in, their private affairs. 'I don't know how much extra the pawnbroker will want, do I?'

'Would this cover it?' He pulled out his wallet and put some notes down on the table.

Carina stared at the money stupidly and he pushed it towards her.

'Go on, take it.'

She shook her head. 'I couldn't do that.'

'Why not? You've been good to me, and I told you when I first arrived, I've got a few pounds put aside.'

'But . . .'

'If I can help, I'd like to. I reckon it's what Robert would want.'

Carina hesitated. Tempting as the offer was, she really didn't see how she could accept it.

'I should take it while the going's good,' Grandpa Luke said. His tone was unusually harsh – perhaps he was touched by Frank's generous gesture, Carina thought. She certainly was. She was feeling ashamed, too, of the way she'd snapped at him a moment ago, and of all the negative thoughts she'd had about him since he had arrived.

'All right. But on the understanding that it's a loan. I'll pay you back as soon as I'm able.' She reached across and picked up the notes, adding them to the money she had tipped out of the jar. 'And thank you. You're very kind.'

'You're welcome. I reckon it's the least I can do.' Frank

pushed back his chair and got up. 'I'll go and see if I can find Sally, calm her down a bit.'

Grandpa Luke watched him go, his face set, eyes narrowed and watchful. But Carina didn't notice. She was too busy counting the money once again, hoping against hope that it would be enough, and that she wouldn't be too late to retrieve her precious ring.

Now that she had accepted Frank's money, Carina was buzzing with a sense of urgency; she couldn't wait to have her ring back where it belonged. Next morning, she asked Sally if she could take care of Meg for a couple of hours while she went to Bath.

'And what if I want to go over to the police station?' Sally asked.

Carina's heart sank. She'd been hoping Sally had forgotten about that. She'd be driving into Hillsbridge to catch the train and could give her a lift, but Sally would have to walk back. That was much too far for Meg's little legs, and she couldn't expect Sally to carry her.

'Couldn't it wait?' she asked.

'You mean you getting your ring is more important than catching Robert's killer?' Sally clearly still had the bit between her teeth.

'One more day wouldn't make any difference, would it?' Carina reasoned. 'But the longer I delay, the more likely it is that the pawnbroker will find a buyer. Please, Sally . . .'

'Oh, all right,' Sally agreed, but with bad grace.

Carina wanted to try to dissuade her from going to the police at all; it was only opening up old wounds, and she really didn't think the button had anything to do with Robert's death. But she didn't want to get into an argument now. Better to let it go for the moment, before Sally changed her mind.

She was concerned about Grandpa Luke, though. Always a man of few words, he seemed quieter than ever this morning.

'Are you feeling all right, Grandpa?' she asked him when she was almost ready to leave.

'Yes, don't you worry about me.'

'Your leg's not troubling you, is it?' She hadn't liked the look of his ulcer when she had dressed it yesterday afternoon, and she wondered now if it was paining him. If it was, it would be just like him to keep it to himself.

'No, it's much the same as usual.'

'I'll have a look at it before I go, if you like.'

'You'll do no such thing. You get off to Bath and see if you can get your ring back. Me and my leg will still be here when you get back.'

'Well, if you're sure . . .'

'I'm sure. You get off or you'll miss your train.'

What a trouper he was, Carina thought as she got Mattie and his pushchair into the Rover. With all his afflictions, not to mention the many tragedies that had blighted his life, Grandpa never complained, and always put others first. It was his way, even down to the small, unimportant things. If there was one piece of cake left, or one pikelet, he'd always say, 'Go on, you have it,' so that the others round the table felt quite guilty as they did so, because Grandpa would never have taken it even if he *had* wanted it. Sometimes it exasperated Carina that he was so selfless, but at the same time she loved him dearly for it.

The train to Bath was more crowded than it had been the last time she had made the journey, and she had to sit with Mattie on her lap for most of the way. But she didn't mind that. She loved the feel of his small firm body nestling into her, and the clean, soapy smell of his freshly washed hair that filled her nostrils when he fell asleep with his head tucked underneath her chin.

At last they were climbing down on to the platform, and Carina hoped she would remember the way to the pawnbroker's shop. She did make one mistake, heading into the wrong street, but she retraced her steps and found it at the next attempt, spotting the three golden balls over the door as soon as she turned the corner. A cart was unloading greengroceries outside the shop next door, just as on the morning of her previous visit when she had practically bumped into Lord Melbrook and his awful hoity-toity lady friend. Carina cringed inwardly as she remembered the altercation. But it was strange to think how much she had despised him then and how differently she thought of him now.

Perhaps it was mostly that she was in awe of him, she thought. After all, she'd never met any of the gentry before. And although he was horrible and arrogant when she had run into his motor and when he'd called to ask for his compensation, she supposed he'd really had every right to be.

All very well to make excuses for Lord Melbrook, but the woman was a different kettle of fish entirely. Who in the world did she think she was, putting in her five penn'orth as she had? Carina still steamed with anger when she remembered how cutting and dismissive she had been. Lady Melbrook seemed to approve of her – in fact, if she had not been mistaken, there was some suggestion that she and Cal might be more than friends. The very idea made Carina bristle all the more. Not that it was any of her business, of course, but goodness, he could do far better than that horrible bitch!

She couldn't resist looking in the pawnbroker's window to see if her engagement ring was displayed there. It wasn't, or at least it wasn't immediately visible, but she felt dreadfully sad at the collection of items that were. Many of them, she supposed, were treasured trinkets and keepsakes that had meant a great deal to someone, and to see them lying there on the dusty velvet to be picked over by greedy hands was heartbreaking.

The bell over the door tinkled as she pushed it open and manoeuvred Mattie's pushchair inside. Much to her relief, there was no sign of the obnoxious man who had made such disgustingly suggestive remarks. Instead a woman stood behind the counter, half-heartedly rubbing silver polish on to a tarnished trophy. She was grossly overweight, with small, mean features that might have been dotted on to her pasty face by a child with a colouring stick and lank, greasy hair that drooped over her low forehead.

'Yes?' Her greeting was as abrupt as the man's had been effusive.

Carina got out her purse and laid the receipt for her ring on the grimy counter.

'I left a ring with you some weeks ago,' she said. 'I was hoping to buy it back.'

The woman looked at the date on the receipt, her mean little eyes narrowing as she struggled to read it so that they almost disappeared into the folds of her cheeks. Then she grunted dismissively.

'You'll be lucky. We don't keep stuff that long.'

'But if it hasn't been sold . . . ?'

The woman grunted again and waddled to a doorway that presumably led into the rear of the shop.

'Jacob!'

A few moments later, the man appeared. A baggy cardigan over a flannel shirt looked to be the same ones he had been wearing the last time Carina was here, and had probably not been washed in the meantime judging by the state of them.

'What's up?'

'This woman is looking to redeem a ring she left with us. Have we still got it?'

Carina held her breath as the man looked from her to the receipt and back again.

'You're too late.'

Her heart sank. 'Are you sure?' She gestured towards a tray of rings. 'Couldn't you please look?'

'I don't need to,' the man said shortly. 'I remember you, and I remember the ring. I sold it, soon as your month was up. And a good price I got for it too.'

'Oh.' Carina felt ready to burst into tears.

'Anything else I can do for you? Another ring take your fancy, perhaps? There's a nice ruby over here might suit you.'

As if anything could ever take the place of her precious ring!

'No thank you.'

'Sure there's nothing I can show you? You'd get a real bargain . . .'

At least today he wasn't making those horrible suggestive remarks that had made her skin crawl. Probably he wouldn't dare in front of the woman, who must be his wife, or maybe his sister. But he was repellent, none the less – they both were – and Carina couldn't wait to get out of the shop with its claustrophobic atmosphere and musty smell that was making her feel sick.

She turned the pushchair and manoeuvred it out of the door, then started back along the street in the direction of the station. Unshed tears were almost blinding her, and there was an ache in the back of her throat. Too late. Her ring was gone for ever. She'd never see it again, never be able to slip it on her finger and remember the happy times she and Robert had shared.

At least I'll be able to give Frank his money back, she thought. That she would no longer be in his debt should be some consolation. But it wasn't. She couldn't imagine anything that would be.

A brief moment of anger flared. If it hadn't been for Lord Melbrook, she would never have had to pawn the ring in the first place. How could he have done that to her when he had so much and she had so little? But it wasn't his fault really. She had no one to blame but herself.

She glanced down at the dark head lolling in the pushchair – Mattie was fast asleep.

'Oh my darling, at least I've got you,' she murmured.

But at that moment, not even her beloved son could lighten the heavy load that lay on her heart.

Chapter Fifteen

For a day that had started out so full of promise, this one was going from bad to worse, Carina thought. Well, perhaps not *worse* – what could be worse than discovering she was too late to buy back her precious ring? But certainly it seemed that there was more than a grain of truth in one of her mam's sayings: 'It never rains but it pours.'

When she reached the station, she discovered she had more than an hour to wait for the next train, and Mattie, refreshed from his earlier sleep, was now wide awake and grizzling. Perhaps he was just tired of being in his pushchair for so long, or perhaps he was cutting another tooth. That was most likely it, she thought. His cheek was glowing again and he kept stuffing his fingers into his mouth.

She bought herself a cup of tea from the station tea stall and tried to keep him entertained while she drank it, but there was no pacifying him, and by the time the train pulled in to the platform and she had managed to find a seat, he was crying hard. The other passengers gave her dirty looks, and one woman tutted loudly, muttering something about bad mothers. But there was nothing Carina could do about it apart from giving him her finger to suck on. She didn't have his teething rings with her, or any brandy to rub on his gums. It wasn't the sort of thing she carried in her bag!

Thinking of the brandy reminded her of how angry Robert had been with her for doing just that, and it made her feel worse than ever. That last night they had spent together had been spoiled by rows and recriminations. If only they could have put it all behind them by making love, but instead she had fallen asleep feeling miserable and rejected. Had Robert really been too tired for lovemaking, or had he still been angry with her?

Overwhelmed by desolation, she hugged Mattie tightly and fought back the threatening tears. She couldn't cry here in the crowded railway carriage; her pride simply would not let her. But the tears were gathering inside her until she felt she would burst with them, and the weight on her heart was unbearable.

When had she last been able to cry – really cry? She couldn't let go in front of the children; she didn't want to frighten and upset them. Even in her own bedroom she felt constrained by the fact that Sally was just the other side of the dividing wall. In the early days, when they had all been consumed by grief, it had been acceptable, but now she felt almost guilty if she gave way to the despair that sometimes dragged her down into the depths.

Oh Robert, I need you so much! I want you so much! Where are you?

The thought occurred to her out of nowhere. It was weeks now since she had visited his grave, taking flowers on what would have been his birthday. There simply weren't enough hours in the day, and in any case, what was the point? He wasn't there, or so it had seemed to her. Now it occurred to her that although maybe he wasn't there, it was the closest she could ever be to him now, and she burned with a sudden urgent need.

She'd go this evening, when the children were in bed. She'd talk to him there in the peaceful churchyard, with the late-evening sun filtering through the trees and the swifts circling overhead, snatching at insects, and perhaps he'd answer her. It was a vain, desperate hope, but it was all she had to cling to.

By the time the train arrived at Hillsbridge, Carina had regained control of herself. Thankful to be able to escape the disapproving stares of the other passengers, she carried a still-grizzling Mattie to the guard's van, retrieved his pushchair and headed out of the station.

Now all she had to do was get home and admit to the others that her mission had been unsuccessful, and her precious ring was lost to her for ever.

She had left the Rover in the road outside the station, on the side of the track that took trains headed for Bath. Her train had come in on the opposite platform, of course, and now she had to cross the line to get to it. The level-crossing gates were closed and would be until the train had departed, but Carina decided she would wait rather than take one of the other options: the subway, an extension of the road that ran under the railway line; or the footbridge that crossed it further down. She didn't want to have to manhandle the pushchair up all those steps and down the other side, and for some inexplicable reason she hated going through the subway. In very wet weather it flooded, and although there was no danger of that today, it would be dusty and dirty – the wind invariably blew any rubbish down the steep slope, where it gathered in heaps until Teddy Vranch, the road sweeper, could be bothered to go down and clear it up. Added to which, though it was both high and wide, she found it claustrophobic.

She made for the picket gate beside the main crossing gates. The train had stopped well clear of them to take on water from the big tanks at the end of the platform, so there was a clear view across to the other side of the track, and she saw at once that there had been an accident of some kind.

A horse and cart had stopped a little way back from the gates, and in front of it a knot of people were clustered around something – or someone – in the road.

Carina's heart gave an uncomfortable lurch. Witnessing an accident was upsetting at any time; today, in her fragile state of mind, it was the last thing she needed. Instantly her imagination began painting lurid pictures. Had someone been run over? Gone beneath the horse's hooves or under the wheels of the cart? Were they badly hurt? Dead, even? She gripped the handles of Mattie's pushchair with hands that had begun to tremble violently and she felt sick with dread. She didn't want to know, didn't want to go anywhere near the accident, but if she was to get to the Rover, there was no alternative.

At last the engine had finished taking on water, the guard blew his whistle, and the train moved away, temporarily blocking her view. But as it cleared the crossing and the gates were opened, the knot of men were still there on the opposite side.

Well, nothing for it, she'd have to cross the line and pass them. But she wouldn't look. At least, that was what she told herself. But somehow she couldn't help it, and when she saw a bicycle lying on the ground, she couldn't tear her eyes away no matter how she tried. She couldn't see a body, thank goodness, but that didn't mean there wasn't one, perhaps underneath the cart . . .

But somebody was picking up the bicycle now, moving it out of the way, and as the cluster dispersed, Carina recognised a figure being helped towards the side of the road.

David Perkins! Her heart gave another jolt of shock. But at least it looked as if he was relatively unhurt. At least he was on his feet and walking, even if he was being supported.

There was no way she could give the accident a wide berth now. She couldn't turn her back on a friend and neighbour.

'David!' she said anxiously as she reached him. 'Whatever's happened? Are you all right?'

'That horse and cart went right into him.' One of the men who had gone to his aid spoke for David. 'You're lucky to be alive, mate.'

And: 'Know him, do you, missus?' the other said.

'Yes, of course I do! David . . .'

'Carina.' David looked very shaken. A gash on the side of his head was streaming blood, and angry grazes ran the length of one bare arm.

'Knocked him out cold, it did,' the first man said. 'I thought 'e was a goner.'

A lad of twelve or thirteen came panting up the slope from the subway.

'He's not there. He's out on his rounds.'

Clearly the boy had been sent in vain to fetch a doctor.

'Well, that's sod's law, ain't it? Reckon we'd better try to get you over to the hospital, chum. Don't know how, though.' The first man had pushed back his cap and was scratching his head. The cottage hospital was three or four miles away, the other side of High Compton.

'I could take him,' Carina offered. 'I've got a motor.' She gestured in the direction of the Rover, barely registering the amazed expressions of the men. It was something she'd grown used to.

'There's no need for that.' David's voice was shaky but firm. 'I'm all right.'

'So you say. I reckon somebody ought to have a look at 'im, missus. Banged his head, he did, and you never know with something like that.'

Carina swallowed hard. A head injury was far too close to home for comfort.

'I'm not going to hospital,' David insisted. 'I've got to get home. Our mam's going to be worried to death.'

'She'll be worried all right if she do see you in that state,' said the man who was doing most of the talking.

Carina was thinking quickly. The trip to the hospital and back would take an hour at least by the time David had been seen, and it would be well past Mattie's dinner time. At least with all the excitement he'd stopped crying for the moment, but he'd be bound to start up again if they had a long wait at the hospital. Besides, chances were there wouldn't be a doctor in attendance; it was a cottage hospital only. What could the nurses do that she couldn't?

'Look, David, I'll tell you what we'll do,' she said. 'I'll drive you home, but we'll call in at Meadow Farm on the way and I can clean you up a bit.'

She delved into the pocket of the pushchair and pulled out a clean nappy that she'd brought with her in case Mattie needed changing.

'Hold this to your head and see if that will stop the bleeding. Then when we get home I'll have a good look at it. If it needs stitches we'll have to think again, but at least Mattie can have his dinner and you can pop in and let your mam know you're all right before I take you to the hospital.'

David nodded, clamping the nappy to the wound with a trembling hand.

Carina fetched the Rover and the men helped David into the front seat, then loaded his bicycle into the rear on top of the pushchair. Carina thought it was probably damaged beyond repair, but they couldn't just leave it lying in the road.

'Thanks, Carina,' he said groggily.

'What are neighbours for?' she returned. But she was thinking this was just something else she could have done without.

As she pulled into the farmyard, it occurred to Carina that this could be awkward. At this time of day it was quite likely that Frank would be in for his dinner, and knowing how David felt about Sally, he was bound to be upset if he realised he had a very real rival right here under the same roof as her. But to her relief, when she took Mattie into the kitchen, there was no sign of Frank; just Grandpa snoozing in his chair, Meg playing with her doll and Sally washing dishes at the sink.

'I've got a wounded soldier in the car,' she said. 'David Perkins got knocked off his bike by a horse and cart and I've brought him here to clean him up a bit before I take him home.'

'David's been knocked off his bike?' Sally repeated, shocked. 'Oh my goodness, is he all right?'

'More or less. He was lucky, I think. But he was knocked out for a bit, I'm told, and he's bleeding all over the place.'

'We'd better get him in, then.' Sally was already wiping her wet hands on the seat of her trousers.

'Where's Frank?' Carina asked, following her.

'He'll be late in for his dinner. The cows got out again and he's gone off to check the fences and get them mended.'

'Good. Because I wouldn't want—'

'Oh for heaven's sake!' Sally retorted. 'David knows the score. I've made it plain to him enough times.'

But there was no doubt she was visibly shocked when she saw the state David was in.

'Honestly, David, what have you been up to?'

'It wasn't my fault, Sal. They closed the crossing gates and I went to go under the subway and then . . . I don't know what happened.'

'Never mind that now,' Carina said. 'Let's get you inside and see what the damage is.'

Between them she and Sally helped David out of the car and into the kitchen. They settled him on one of the dining chairs.

'Do you think you could get Mattie something to eat while I see to David?' Carina asked Sally. 'He's bound to be really hungry.'

'It's all right – you see to him. I'll look after David.'

Sally was already at the range, setting the kettle to heat up for water to bathe his wounds and finding an enamel bowl in the cupboard beside the sink. Carina got the bottle of brandy from the dresser and put it on the table ready for her to use as a disinfectant, then picked up Mattie, who had begun to grizzle again, and gave him a rusk to chew on while she mashed him some vegetables that were keeping warm in a pan.

Sally, meanwhile, was attending to David, much more concerned about his injuries than Carina would have imagined she would be. She'd thought her sister-in-law would be irritated at having her would-be beau here, but she was fussing over him like a mother hen. Perhaps she was fonder of him than she let on, or even realised herself, Carina thought, and hoped with all her heart that was the case. When it came down to choosing between Frank and David, it was no contest in her opinion.

With Mattie settled in his high chair, the dish of vegetables in front of him, she went over to see how Sally was getting on in her unaccustomed role as nurse.

'It's a nasty cut,' she said. 'I've done my best with it, but it's still bleeding. If you ask me, it needs stitches.'

'It'll be all right,' David insisted. 'I'm not going to any hospital.'

'Well at least if it leaves a scar your hair will cover it,' Sally said. 'Anyway, scars can be very attractive – isn't that right, Carina?' She shot her sister-in-law a wicked look that left her in no doubt who she was alluding to.

Carina ignored the pointed remark.

'Can I help? I'll cut a piece of lint for you if you like.'

Together they managed to patch David up, securing the dressing with a bandage.

Sally laughed. 'You really do look like a wounded soldier now. Right, let's have a look at your arm.'

Carina emptied the bowl of bloody water down the sink and refilled it with fresh. Sally began washing the grit and gravel out of the grazes on David's arm with surprising gentleness. As she worked, she glanced at Carina.

'How did you get on with . . .' She broke off suddenly, realising Carina might not want to discuss her errand in front of David.

'No good, I'm afraid,' Carina said shortly.

'Oh dear. You mean . . . ?'

'Too late.'

At that moment the back door opened and Frank strode in, then stopped short, taking in the scene.

'What the hell's going on?'

David had stiffened too.

'Keep still!' Sally warned him.

'What's going on, I said!' Frank snarled.

Carina's hackles rose. Maybe Frank's nose was put out of joint finding Sally ministering to some other man. But he had no right to talk as if this were his house, his kitchen.

'We're looking after a neighbour who's had an accident,' she said stiffly. 'Do you have a problem with that?'

Frank's scowl said that he clearly did. But he simply shrugged and walked over to the range, lifting the lids on the saucepans.

'I'll have my dinner if that's all right with you. I've got work to get back to.'

'Please go ahead, Frank.'

But her blood was boiling, and she had to remind herself of his kindness in lending her the money to try and buy back her ring in order to control her fury.

Sally too was clearly uncomfortable; worried that she might have upset Frank, Carina supposed.

And neither of them had noticed that Grandpa's eyes were no longer closed, but half open and narrowed watchfully. He was listening and missing nothing.

That evening, when the children were in bed, Carina went to the churchyard as she had promised herself she would. She was no longer sunk in the deep depression of this morning – taking care of David had shaken her out of that – but the desire to be as close to Robert as she could was as sharp as ever. Though she hadn't given it much thought as she drove David and his damaged bicycle back to his own farm, or even as she went about her neglected duties, it was still there, just lying dormant.

Late in the afternoon, she had taken the children for a walk to pick wild flowers. Now she took them from the jam jar she'd put them in to keep fresh, wrapped the dripping stems in a brown paper bag that had contained sultanas and set out to walk to Dunderwick.

During the day, it had begun to cloud over, fluffy white puffs thickening and turning to grey. Now they obscured the sun, and Carina thought they were probably in for rain. Goodness knows, they could do with it, but she hoped it would hold off until she got home. She didn't want to be caught in what might very well be a downpour or even a thunderstorm.

She walked briskly along the road and down the long winding

hill. A few men, most of them quite old, were sitting on benches outside the Dunderwick Arms, mugs of beer on the rustic table in front of them. Their eyes followed her as she skirted the pub forecourt and crossed the road to the lychgate leading into the churchyard.

She followed the path past ancient gravestones and tombs, some crumbling with age, some green with lichen, the inscriptions so weatherworn as to be almost illegible. Only the massive stone tomb surrounded by looped cast-iron chains and closest to the church door looked cared for. The grass around it was neatly clipped, the pale grey stone clean and the names around the sides and on the top as clear to read as when the stonemason had chiselled them. Carina didn't need to read the inscriptions to know who was buried here, though. No one local needed to. That it was the Melbrook family tomb was common knowledge, and that it was still cared for while others on the same patch of grass crumbled was testament to the continuing existence and importance of that family in Dunderwick.

Who had those other graves belonged to? Carina wondered briefly as she passed them. In their way they were almost as grand as the Melbrooks' and quite unlike the plain gravestones that marked the plots in the main churchyard on the other side of the path and further from the church porch. Presumably their occupants had once been wealthy and well respected; now they were forgotten and unloved. Family lines that had died out. Descendants who had moved away. The poignancy of it touched a raw nerve and she resolved that Robert's grave would not suffer the same fate, at least as long as she lived, and when they were old enough, she'd tell the children to be sure that it was kept cared for after she was gone.

Not that there was much to care for as yet. It was too early to erect a proper headstone, even if she could have afforded it.

'You have to wait for the ground to settle,' the sexton had told her, so for the present Robert's resting place was marked only by a simple stone kerb. But my goodness, the weeds had already taken hold amidst the gravel that covered the rectangle of bare earth: dry grass and a few clumps of dandelions, even a shoot of bramble.

Carina got down on her knees and pulled them out as best she could with her bare hands, though the bramble defeated her – she'd have to come back with a fork and trowel to deal with that. Then she scooped them up and took them to the compost heap in a corner of the churchyard, along with the flowers she'd brought for Robert's birthday, bare heads and shrivelled leaves now. She refilled the jar from the standpipe tap that jutted from the wall nearby, and arranged the fresh flowers in it, wishing she'd been able to find something nicer, then sat back on her heels, staring at them and the rectangle of dry earth and allowing herself at last to think about what had brought her here today.

After all the activity, it was a moment or two before the tears came again, just an ache in her throat at first and a prickle behind her eyes. Then the terrible pain of loss was spreading through her veins and the tears began to flow freely, running down her cheeks and dripping on to her high-necked blouse. She bent double, sobs and gasps racking her body.

At least it was a blessed relief to be able to let the tears flow with only the rooks in the churchyard trees as witness, but the weight on her heart was as heavy as ever, choking her.

'Oh Robert, how can I go on without you?' she whispered. 'Help me! Please help me!'

She had scarcely spoken the words when a shaft of sunlight fell on the cold, dark earth. She raised her head, looking up. Miraculously, the dark clouds had parted and in a sliver of blue sky the sun was shining through.

And then, making her jump because she was simply not expecting it, the bells in the church tower rang out, a slow round as they were lowered, then following each other in a perfect rhythm. It must be practice night for the ringers.

Carina sat listening, and looking up at that patch of blue sky as it grew larger by the minute, and realised that the weight had lifted from her heart. The sadness hadn't gone completely – perhaps it never would – but she felt lighter somehow, at peace, and with new hope that brightened her spirit just as the sunlight was brightening everything it fell on.

Had Robert heard her? Had he answered? In that moment it seemed to Carina that he had.

'Oh thank you – thank you!' she whispered.

She remained there a few more minutes, savouring the wonder of it. Then she got to her feet. 'Goodnight, my love. Sleep tight. And I will look after the children and Grandpa and Sally too, I promise.'

As she murmured the words her throat tightened and tears pricked her eyes again, but she now felt imbued with new strength. She could go on. She could. And Robert would be beside her. Watching over her. Helping her.

At the lychgate, she paused and looked back. The shaft of sunlight was still there. And in it the wild flowers she and the children had picked no longer looked pathetic but perfectly fitting.

Chapter Sixteen

The rain started as Carina neared the top of the hill, a few heavy drops at first that quickly became a downpour. The patch of blue sky had disappeared completely now behind a blanket of heavy cloud, and she couldn't see the weather changing any time soon. Why, oh why, hadn't she thought to bring a coat or umbrella?

Hurrying along, her head bent against the rain that was already dripping down her forehead and into her eyes, she didn't hear the motor car approaching or see it round the bend in the road ahead. In fact she wasn't aware of it at all until it had almost reached her and she recognised Lord Melbrook's Benz. It slowed and pulled up on the opposite side of the road.

'Mrs Talbot? Carina?' It was the first time he had ever called her by her given name, but for the moment she didn't register that.

'Lord Melbrook . . .'

'For goodness' sake, come and get in the motor!'

She stared stupidly.

'Come on! You're getting drenched.'

She hesitated for another long moment, then dived across the road.

He leaned across and opened the door for her. The engine was still running. She climbed up into the passenger seat.

'What on earth are you doing walking in this rain?'

'I've been to the churchyard . . . I was on my way home when I got caught.'

'You certainly did.' He pulled away.

'Where are we going?' she asked stupidly.

'Well, the plan is I'll turn round when I can and take you home.'

He was going to go out of his way for her. Suddenly she was remembering another time, a lifetime ago, it seemed. Hillsbridge market in the pouring rain. Robert in the pony and trap, splattering her with water as he drove past her. Stopping. Offering her a lift. Driving her back to Fairley Terrace, though it was in quite the wrong direction for him. Lending her a waterproof sheet to keep off the worst of the rain. Asking to see her again. The start of everything. Tears pricked her eyes again.

Cal was driving back down the long hill into Dunderwick. Until they reached the village, there would be nowhere he could safely turn around.

'So how are things with you?' he asked conversationally.

Carina swallowed hard at the knot of tears that had gathered in her throat, but there was no way she could answer.

He glanced in her direction.

'Are you all right?'

With an effort, she found her voice.

'It's been a bad day, that's all.'

'How so?'

She swallowed again. There was no way she was going to tell him about her failed attempt to buy back her ring, and how much it had upset her to know she would never see it again.

'Oh . . . nothing. I don't want to talk about it.'

He was silent for a moment. Then he said: 'I hear young David Perkins was involved in an accident today.'

This was safer ground.

'Yes, he was knocked off his bike by a horse and cart. I was there, actually . . . well, just after it happened. He was lucky not to be killed.'

'And you brought him home.'

'How do you know that?' she asked, taken aback.

'You'd be surprised what I hear when I'm out and about on the estate.'

'Yes, of course . . .' She smiled wryly. 'I suppose David was happy to tell anyone who'd listen that Sally was the one who patched him up.'

Cal was swinging the car into the road between the church and the Dunderwick Arms. The benches outside the pub were empty now, the men drinking there having beaten a hasty retreat inside. Though Cal had the hood up, some flurries of rain were still able to blow in through the open side of the motor as the Benz changed direction.

'Sorry about that,' he said as he saw Carina wipe her face and push back her wet hair.

'It doesn't matter. It's a lot better than walking in it. It's very kind of you, Lord Melbrook.'

'My pleasure. And isn't it time you stopped calling me that? My friends call me Cal. That will do very nicely.'

For some reason Carina felt her cheeks grow hot.

'Oh, I don't know that I could do that!'

'Well I hope you'll at least try. "Lord Melbrook" is not a title I'm particularly comfortable with. It's not something I ever wanted or aspired to. To be quite honest, I was much happier with the way things were before my brother died.'

'That was very sad,' Carina said, uncertain as to quite how she should reply.

'He brought it upon himself, I fear.'

'Why? What happened to him?' she asked, curious. She had known, of course, of the death of the previous Lord Melbrook, but had not been party to the gossip surrounding it.

'The sort of life my brother led was not the most beneficial for his health and well-being.'

'Oh.' She wished she hadn't asked.

'The really ironic thing is that I should have been the one to meet an early death, not Stafford,' Cal went on, deftly steering the conversation away from his brother's indiscretions and excesses. 'I was in the army. Fought in the Boer War. Life was pretty cheap out there. But I escaped unscathed.'

'You were wounded, though.'

'It could have been worse. It didn't do my leg much good, it's true, and it put paid to my boyish good looks, as I expect you've noticed, but I lived to tell the tale,' he said lightly.

Involuntarily Carina glanced at him. In the dim light the scar stood out white and ridged, but she didn't think it spoiled his looks at all. There was something romantic about it, just as there was about his manly profile. But she could hardly say so!

'You miss the army, then?' she said instead.

'I enjoyed the life, certainly. And I miss living on the edge, though I suppose at my age I should know better.'

The rain was beginning to ease now.

'If you can find somewhere to turn around, I could walk from here,' Carina suggested.

'And have you caught in another storm? I don't think so.'

They had reached the top of the hill; the road stretched before them, long and more or less straight, with only gentle bends. Cal opened up the engine and the car shot forward so suddenly that Carina gasped. The surge of power was exhilarating; she hadn't realised a motor could do that. Certainly the Rover didn't. At least, not when she was driving it.

Cal cast her a sideways glance.

'All right?'

'Yes! I'm fine.'

He kept his foot on the accelerator. Hedges, gateways, trees rushed past, and the throb of the engine reverberated through her whole body, a sensation she had never experienced before. She caught her lip between her teeth, thrilled but just a tiny bit afraid, and the fear only heightened the thrill.

All too soon they were approaching the track that led to Meadow Farm and Cal eased off, then braked to a more sedate pace to turn in to it.

'I think you enjoyed that, Mrs Talbot,' he said, grinning.

'I didn't know a motor could go that fast!'

'Oh, the Benz is quite a car. They race, you know. On a track. And they are very successful.'

'But we weren't on a track.'

'No, but it was fun, wasn't it?'

'You didn't go fast like that before, when you took me to your house to make your curtains.'

'That was in the middle of the day. There would have been other people using the road. Besides, I wouldn't have wanted to frighten you.'

'But you don't mind frightening me now?'

'Carina,' he said, 'don't try to tell me you were frightened. You were enjoying every minute of it.'

'You're right, I was,' she admitted.

'I'll take you for another ride some time. Show you what she can really do. If you'd like to.'

Carina was dumbstruck. But before she could think of a suitable reply, he was going on: 'I have some more work I'd like you to do for me, too. Drapes for my mother's sitting room. She's given me no peace since she saw the new ones in the drawing room. Would you be able to manage that?'

'Well, yes . . . though I do have one or two other jobs I've committed to.'

'But you think you could fit me in?'

Carina thought she would be stupid to turn down Lord Melbrook, however busy she was. There were so many windows at Dunderwick House, she wouldn't have to worry about her work drying up.

'I'm sure I could,' she said.

They had reached the end of the track and were pulling into the farmyard. As they did so, Cymru emerged from his kennel, barking madly and straining on the end of his chain. Sally must have already put him out for the night. Carina was surprised. Usually they allowed him to stay in the kitchen or roam free until bedtime.

'Here we are then.' Cal drew the Benz to a halt, jumped out and came round to open the door and help Carina down.

There was nothing remotely intimate in the way he took her hand, but quite suddenly Carina was sharply aware of him. As her foot touched the ground, she stumbled slightly. For a moment, before he steadied her, she was thrown against him, and the awareness intensified, prickling over her skin and also somewhere deep inside where her every nerve throbbed faintly still from the vibration of the powerful engine of the Benz.

'Hey – careful!'

She straightened abruptly.

'Sorry!'

'My fault. All that speeding has made you dizzy. I hope it won't put you off riding with me again.'

'Of course not. I just turned my ankle, that's all,' she said, confusion making the words come tumbling out.

'That's good. So you'd be happy for me to pick you up in the morning?'

'What?'

'To go to Bath and choose some fabric for the new drapes. Isobel came with me when I bought the first lot. But she's away on one of her Continental jaunts and I wouldn't have the first idea what to choose. I'm sure you have just as good an eye for these things as she does.'

The thought of having to decide on suitable fabric to please the redoubtable Lady Melbrook was a daunting one.

'I don't know about that,' she protested.

'Don't underestimate yourself, Carina. Shall we say about ten?' He was behaving as if it were a fait accompli, leaving her no room to argue.

'Well . . . yes . . . I suppose so.'

'Good. I'll see you then.'

In something of a daze, Carina walked towards the farm-house. Behind her she heard the motor pulling away; as she reached the door, she turned and saw it disappearing out of the yard.

She stood for a moment trying to gather herself. Her skirts were clinging wetly to her legs, and loose strands of her hair lay damp across her forehead, but she was almost unaware of it. She needed to still the confusion raging inside her before she faced the others.

What in the world had happened? The events of the last half-hour seemed unreal, as if she'd fallen asleep in the churchyard and dreamed the whole thing. The sense of peace that had come over her when she'd begged Robert for help. The sudden downpour. Lord Melbrook stopping, picking her up, talking to her as if she were his equal, urging her to call him Cal. The exhilarating burst of speed. The way he'd made her feel, like nothing she'd ever experienced before. And then to top it all, more or less ordering her to go to Bath with him tomorrow to choose fabrics for drapes . . . Unbelievable.

It wouldn't happen, of course. She couldn't understand what had possessed him to suggest such a thing. He'd have thought better of it by the morning. Realised she had no qualifications whatever for deciding what would be suitable in his home.

At the thought, Carina experienced a tiny shard of something that might almost have been disappointment, and quickly pushed it away. She didn't know what had got into her, but whatever it was, she'd better come to her senses, and quickly.

Her breathing had steadied now, her pulse no longer raced, and the thrumming deep inside from the vibration of the engine was lessening. She brushed the damp hair off her face and went into the house.

Only Grandpa Luke was in the kitchen, sitting in his chair, his pipe, unlit, clenched between his teeth.

'You got caught, didn't you?' he said. 'That were a hard storm. Fair rattled against the windows and down the chimney.'

'I did, but luckily Lord Melbrook happened to be passing. He gave me a lift.'

'Did he indeed!'

'It was really kind of him. He must have been on his way home, but he turned round and brought me all the way back.' She looked down at her skirt. 'I'm still pretty wet, though. I must go up and change. Where's Sally?'

'Hmm. Her and Frank have gone off somewhere. Don't ask me where.' Grandpa Luke sounded uncharacteristically disapproving. 'All I can say is they'll be like drowned rats if they were out in that storm. But I don't reckon they were. They're up in that room over the barn, if I'm not much mistaken.'

Carina's heart sank. Well, that would explain why Cymru had been turned out to his kennel so early – they wouldn't have wanted the dog following them. But . . .

'Oh dear. I don't like it, Grandpa. I just hope . . .' She broke off. All very well to be worried that Sally might allow Frank liberties that could have disastrous consequences; quite another thing to actually say it out loud.

But Grandpa was clearly thinking along the same lines.

'Trouble is, she's young and silly. And I wouldn't trust that one any further than I could throw him. I wish to God he'd never come here. He's a bad lot, Carina.'

'Oh, I don't know, Grandpa. It was very good of him to lend me that money, even if it was too late.'

'He were quick enough to take it back again, though, weren't he, when you came back from Bath empty handed?'

'Well, it was his money.'

'You reckon?' His voice was deep with suspicion, but before she could ask him what he meant, he went on: 'And you want to go careful too, my girl. There's something a bit fishy going on with Melbrook, if you ask me.'

'Cal?' Considering he had only just asked her to call him by his given name and she had never yet done so to his face it slipped out with surprising ease, and she immediately felt herself flushing scarlet

'Oh, *Cal*, is it? Well, whatever you like to call him, he's been a bit too friendly since our Robert died. That's all I'm saying.'

'He's just been kind, that's all. There's nothing . . .' But again she was becoming flustered.

'Look, Carina, I might be doing him wrong. But the Melbrooks have never liked it that we got given the freehold of this place back in my father's day. Good land, better than most, and slap bang in the middle of the estate. I know for a fact they'd have it back if they could. The old Lord Melbrook, your one's father, came to see me once. Made me an offer. I sent him off with a flea in his ear. Told him Meadow Farm weren't for sale, and never would be. But that didn't stop him trying again, more than once, right up till he fell off his horse and broke his neck. I never heard a word from that Stafford when he were lord of the manor, though from what I can hear the estate never interested him much. But now there's a new one in, and all of a sudden he's in the picture, giving you work to do, picking you up in his fancy motor . . . Our Robert dies, and the next thing we know, Melbrook's worming his way in . . . Just you be careful, my girl. That's all I'm saying.'

It was just about the longest speech Carina had ever heard Grandpa make, and though she felt sure he must be mistaken, it disturbed her all the same.

'Oh Grandpa, I really don't think—'

'You might not be as young and silly as Sally, but there's a lot you don't know about the ways of the world, m'dear,' he said sadly. 'Not everybody is as straight and honest as you.'

'All right, Grandpa, I'll remember what you've said,' she tried to pacify him. 'But he's coming to pick me up in the morning – he wants me to do some more work for him, and he's taking me to Bath to buy the fabric – so please don't say anything to upset the applecart. And now I really must go and get out of these wet clothes before I catch pneumonia.'

'Ah. You don't want that.' His eyes had gone far away, and Carina could have kicked herself for her careless choice of expression. Wasn't it pneumonia that had taken Grandma Margaret?

'Are you going to bed soon?' she asked. It was well past his usual bedtime.

'No, I'm all right here for a bit.'

Carina took a long time over changing into a dry skirt and blouse. Her head was spinning. What a day! She seemed to have ridden a roller coaster of emotion from hope, grief and despair to giddy elation and back again. Worry about Sally and Frank was nagging at her too. Supposing they were up to something in the room above the barn? Supposing Sally was to fall pregnant? What a disaster that would be!

But most of all she was thinking about Lord Melbrook. Grandpa was wrong about his motives, surely. Or was it just that she didn't want to believe something like that about him? As she remembered the sharp awareness of him that she had experienced as he had handed her out of the car, she felt a flush creep up her cheeks.

How shameful was that? How could she have felt that way for even a moment, and when she had just come from Robert's grave, too? And how was she going to face him tomorrow if he did indeed turn up to take her to Bath?

Suddenly everything was too much for her and she felt heavy with exhaustion. Hardly surprising – she'd been up since the crack of dawn, and she might yet be up again in the night if Mattie was teething. She undressed again and put on her nightgown. Then she padded barefoot down the stairs.

Grandpa was still in his chair, sucking on his unlit pipe, but there was no sign of Sally. Well, she couldn't worry any more about that tonight. Short of going over to the barn, there was nothing she could do, and that was a step too far. She would have a word with her sister-in-law tomorrow, but for now she could only hope for the best.

'Do you mind if I go to bed, Grandpa?' she asked. 'I'm really tired and I wouldn't be surprised if Mattie didn't wake me up later.'

'No, you go on, m'dear.'

Carina went upstairs again, turned back the covers and climbed into bed. But with all the turbulent thoughts chasing one another round inside her head, it was a long time before she fell asleep.

'Carina! Wake up! Carina!'

Someone was shaking her. Shouting her name. She didn't know what was happening, or even, for a moment, where she was. She'd been dreaming. She was back home in Pontypridd. In her old room. Now . . .

'Carina!'

She came to with a start, trembling all over from the shock of it.

Sally. It was Sally.

'For God's sake, Carina, wake up! The barn's on fire!'

Chapter Seventeen

Still thick with sleep, Carina stumbled down the stairs and outside to a scene that might have been part of a continuing nightmare.

The door of the barn was wide open, and clouds of black smoke were billowing out, shot through with bolts of scarlet and orange. Beyond it was the flickering glow of the stacks of burning hay.

Panic gripped her, thoughts tumbling wildly. How had this happened? She simply couldn't imagine. What was to be done? The awful realisation – nothing! Nothing! Buckets of water from the pump would be worse than useless against the inferno that had taken hold. And what about Frank? Was he trapped in the room upstairs? But no, that was him running towards her across the yard, silhouetted briefly against the glow of the fire as the smoke subsided, then billowed again.

'Frank!' she gasped. 'What happened?'

'Christ knows! I woke up and my room was full of smoke. The whole bloody stack's gone up.' His voice was hoarse and the effort of talking set him coughing.

'Oh my God!' Carina clapped a hand to her mouth, fighting waves of paralysing horror. Never in all her life had she seen anything quite like this; never had she felt so terrified and

222

helpless. 'All that hay! All that work! Our winter feed for the animals! What will we do?'

'At least it's contained . . .'

'But what if it's not?' She had a sudden terrifying vision of the fire raging through the room above the barn, bursting through the timbered roof. There would be sparks, hot flying ash . . . already there were burning bits of hay blowing about the farmyard. Supposing the surrounding buildings were set alight? The stable, even the farmhouse itself . . .

Dread somehow clarified her chaotic thoughts. 'We need the fire brigade.'

'It'll be too late by the time they get here.' Frank, controlling that rasping cough.

'They can stop it from spreading. I'll go for them.' She turned to her sister-in-law, who stood hugging herself in petrified silence. 'Sally – get the car started for me.'

She ran back into the house, grabbed a coat from a hook on the back of the door and pulled it on over her nightdress. For a moment she hesitated: should she wake the children? Take them with her? But no, best leave them where they were, just as long as they were in no danger. She didn't want them witnessing the terrifying scene outside unless there was no alternative.

As she emerged again, she heard the cough and rattle of the motor engine as Sally cranked it to life, and another sound, more ominous even than the low roar of the flames – the crack of timbers burning and falling. The floorboards of the room above the barn must have caught alight.

'Sal – get Captain out if there's any chance of the stable going up. And keep an eye on the house, too. Grandpa and the children . . .' She was climbing up into the driving seat as she spoke.

'Course I will. Just go!'

Her hands shaking, she shoved the gearstick into position and let off the handbrake. The Rover shot forward: thank God it was already facing towards the track. She put her foot down hard on the accelerator and realised she was only wearing her carpet slippers. Well, too late now.

As she bumped along the uneven track, the Rover finding every pothole and ridge, or so it seemed, Carina was again thinking furiously. The fire brigade in Hillsbridge was a volunteer service, manned by local men from all walks of life who were summoned to duty by a hooter, set off on the instruction of a policeman. Should she go to the police station, or was there anyone closer to home who would have a telephone she could use to raise the alarm? None of the farms had one, she was fairly sure. Only people with money had telephones. People like the Melbrooks . . .

At the end of the track she hesitated momentarily, trying to come to a decision. Dunderwick House was nearer than Hillsbridge, but would she be able to make anyone there hear, no matter how hard she knocked? It was the middle of the night, after all. But then, Sergeant Love might well be in bed and fast asleep too, and there wasn't always a constable on night duty.

For a split second longer she deliberated, then made up her mind. She swung the Rover to the right, in the direction of Dunderwick.

It wasn't just her hands that were shaking now; her whole body was trembling as if a colony of ants were feeding on every nerve ending, and the sense of urgency was making her breath come short and uneven, so that she was almost gasping. Her mouth was dry, too, as if she hadn't had a drink for days, and her lips felt thick and swollen. Desperately she tried to gain control of herself as she negotiated the long hill down into the village and up the other side, driving as fast as she dared. She almost missed the entrance to the drive to Dunderwick House, saw it at the last minute and swung across the road, the Rover lurching perilously.

Oh, let me be able to make someone hear! Please let me be able to make someone hear . . .

She emerged from the tunnel of trees, and as the house materialised before her, she saw them. Lights! There were lights in the orangery! Had a lamp been left burning? Or did it mean that someone was up?

She brought the motor to an abrupt halt in the courtyard, jumped down and flew towards the orangery, banging on the glass door so hard that her knuckles felt as if they had been skinned. Somewhere within the house a dog began barking furiously – she'd disturbed Cleo, at least, and hopefully she would wake the rest of the household. Beyond caring about the proprieties of such things, she peered in through a window. And saw a figure seated in the wicker chair stir.

Cal had come downstairs as he so often did and taken the whisky decanter into the orangery. As he sipped the drink, his aching leg propped up on a footstool, he thought about his earlier encounter with Carina. What in the world had got into him to make the sudden decision to ask her to go with him to buy fabric for drapes he didn't much want and couldn't really afford? He felt sorry for her, of course, tonight more so than ever. She'd just paid a visit to her husband's grave, and he knew as well as anyone how upsetting that could be. And to make matters worse, she'd been getting soaked to the skin. He'd have had to be utterly heartless not to have picked her up and driven her home. But that didn't explain why he'd not only offered her more work, but actually said he'd collect her in the morning to take her to Bath to choose the fabric!

As for talking to her about his brother's shortcomings and his own army experience, he could scarcely believe he'd done that either. Both were subjects he took pains to avoid. Stafford's carryings-on were not something he was proud of and were a matter to be kept within the family as far as possible, though he did sometimes discuss his brother with Isobel. His own feelings, though, he did not. He preferred that they remain private.

But there was something about Carina that had made him open up, and it puzzled and disturbed him. She'd got under his skin in a way no woman ever had since he'd lost his beloved Alice, and he didn't like it. Even now, after all these years, it felt like a betrayal. He poured himself another drink and drank it in one gulp.

It wasn't like him to fall asleep in the orangery. Generally when the whisky took effect he went back to bed. Tonight, however, his leg had been paining him badly, and when it finally eased he hadn't felt like climbing the stairs and perhaps setting it off again. So instead he had propped a cushion behind his head and stayed where he was. He wasn't aware of falling asleep, but he must have done because suddenly his dreams were invaded by a loud knocking and Cleo's barks.

Cal came to with a start and was instantly wide awake – one of the legacies of active service in the Boer War. With the darkness outside and the oil lamp still burning in the orangery, he couldn't see who was on the other side of the glass, and he rescued the stick that he sometimes reverted to using when his leg was especially bad. If the late-night caller was a tramp or a ne'er-do-well, it might prove useful.

He raised it in readiness as he opened the door.

'Oh Lord Melbrook! Oh thank goodness!'

Cal lowered his stick. Carina! What in heaven's name was she doing here in the middle of the night? But clearly something was terribly wrong – she wouldn't be here otherwise – and he could see at a glance that she was in a dreadful state, shaking and almost sobbing.

'What is it?' he asked sharply.

'Our barn's on fire! Oh please, can you ring for the fire brigade?'

'Come in.' He opened the door. 'Wait here.'

For the moment he didn't waste time with any more questions, but hurried through to where the telephone sat on an occasional table in the hall. Only when he had made the call did he go back to the orangery and Carina.

'Right. Hopefully they'll be on their way soon.' He tried to sound reassuring, but he knew that in reality it would take some time to rouse all the members of the fire crew from their beds, as it was unlikely any of them would hear the hooter at this time of night, with the possible exception of Bert Rawlings, who lived in a row of cottages opposite the wagon works where it was situated. Then they all had to make their way to the fire station and get the engine going. They did their best, but all too often it wasn't good enough.

'It's the house I'm worried about, and the stable. If they catch too . . .' The words were tumbling out, followed by a sob of panic.

'Take a deep breath and calm down, Carina.' Cal laid a steadying hand on her arm.

'I've got to get back . . .'

'You're in no fit state to drive. Just let me put some clothes on and I'll take you.'

'But I've got to . . .'

'Stop it!' he instructed. He fetched the whisky decanter and his glass – the only one to hand – poured a glug and handed it to her. 'Drink this. It will steady your nerves.'

Jennie Felton

'Oh, I couldn't . . .'

'Drink it!'

Obediently Carina put the glass to her lips and sipped. The amber liquid ran a scalding river down her throat, making her cough. But there was something comforting all the same about the instant rush of warmth through her veins, and she sipped again, and again.

'Good girl. I won't be a minute.'

As he opened the door to the library, Cleo came trotting out and went straight to Carina. Automatically Carina fondled the dog's silky ears and rubbed her chest, finding momentary comfort in that too. She seemed fatter than Carina remembered her, but the observation was only a fleeting one. All she could think of was the burning barn.

Upstairs, Cal slipped off the silk dressing gown that had once belonged to his brother and dressed hastily. Then he hurried back to the orangery, where Carina was pacing, one hand pressed to her mouth, the other, still clutching the empty whisky tumbler, wrapped around her waist.

Ordering Cleo to stay, he ushered Carina out and helped her up into the Benz. This time there was no frisson of awareness, nor any thrill in the drive as he raced the engine and hurtled along the drive and down the hill into Dunderwick. She hunched in her seat, willing him to go even faster.

'How did it start? I just don't understand how the fire came to start!' She was babbling, the only release from the panic that was choking her.

'Spontaneous combustion? It happens.'

'Don't you think we know that? We're always really careful to make sure the hay is properly dry . . .'

As they climbed the hill on the other side of the village, Carina fancied she could smell smoke in the still night air, and

228

by the time they turned in to the track to Meadow Farm, there was no mistaking it. A pall of black smoke, darker than the night sky, hung over the farm, lit occasionally by shooting flames and spiralling sparks.

'Looks bad,' Cal commented.

'It is! We'll never save the barn. But I'm so scared it's going to spread.'

'It shouldn't. There's no wind to speak of,' Cal tried to reassure her.

'But if it does . . .'

'We'll make sure it doesn't. We'll fill every bucket and bath you can find with water and have it ready. And the fire brigade will be here soon.'

But rather than take the Benz too close to the blazing barn and risk that too being set alight, he stopped on the track, well out of danger.

Carina was opening the door and preparing to jump out even before he had the handbrake on.

'Careful!' he warned her, but she took no notice, levering herself out and down and running towards the farmyard without waiting for him.

As Cal followed, the scene that met his eyes reminded him of paintings he had seen of the fires of hell, a nightmare in orange, vermillion and scarlet. The acrid smell of burning was sharp in his nostrils, the roar of the flames and the crack of falling timbers loud in the still of the night. From the stable came the sound of a frightened Captain whinnying and kicking at the confines of his stall. Carina had run to a couple of figures who stood helpless, watching the barn burn. As he approached them, he recognised Sally Talbot; the young man he had never seen before. His arm was around Sally, who looked to be in much the same state of distress as Carina.

'Lord Melbrook!' Sally gasped as he reached them.

He didn't waste time in returning a greeting.

'Come on,' he said abruptly. 'We need to collect as much water as we can in case the fire should spread. Where's your pump? And bring all the buckets you can find.'

'There are some in the stable. But watch out for Captain. He sounds terrified. I'll get the tin bath from the kitchen.'

Carina set off at a run towards the house; Sally headed for the stable. The young man made no move.

'Are you going to let her do it?' Cal asked sharply.

'I'm not used to horses. She's better with them.'

'Oh for God's sake!'

Cal followed Sally, catching up with her as she drew back the bolts of the stable door.

'Leave this to me. Just open the top half first.'

Sally slid the bolt of the bottom half back into place and opened the upper section. Captain's large head appeared; his eyes were wild and he was foaming at the mouth.

'Steady, boy.' Cal laid one hand on the rough muzzle and with the other patted and stroked Captain's neck, whispering softly into the horse's ear. 'It's all right. You're all right. You're fine. Nothing to be afraid of.'

After a few minutes he felt the animal began to relax, and he could almost believe he was back on the veldt, calming horses in the heat of battle. It was something he'd always been able to do; some of his men had said he had the magic touch.

When he deemed it safe, he motioned to Sally to unbolt the lower section of the door. He went in and stood beside the horse, restraining him and still whispering soothingly in his ear, as Sally fetched three large buckets.

'Stay with him,' he instructed her when they were outside again. 'Keep him calm. We don't want him kicking down the door.'

Sally nodded wordlessly, but it was almost as if Cal's soothing whispers had calmed her too.

He picked up two of the buckets and headed across the yard to where Carina and the young man were filling a tin bath at the pump.

'Do you have a ladder?' he asked. 'It might be a good idea to damp down the stable roof.'

'There was one in the barn, but that's no good.' The young man straightened from working the pump handle, and brushed his hair back from a forehead that was shiny with perspiration. His grimy hands made black smears across his face.

'There might be one by the hayricks,' Carina said.

'Where are they?'

'I'll show you.'

Together they half ran across the field. Carina had been right: there was a ladder resting against one side of the haystack. It should have been put away when the stack was finished, but thank goodness it hadn't been or it too would have been destroyed.

Cal took one end, Carina the other, and together they carried it back to the yard, where Cal leaned it up against the stable wall.

The young man had finished filling the bath and started on a bucket by the time they were back at the pump.

'What's your name?' Cal asked him.

'Frank.' He sounded resentful at being asked.

'Well, Frank, if Carina takes over the pump, can you help me get this to the stable?'

He took one handle of the bath, the young man – Frank – the other; he also picked up one of the empty buckets. There was no way they'd be able to get the bath up the ladder, and in any case, the water could be spread more easily with a smaller container.

For perhaps a quarter of an hour they worked ceaselessly, filling buckets and climbing the ladder to pour water on to the roof of the stable. At last the jangle of a bell carried across the fields from the track. The fire brigade had arrived.

Cal descended the ladder as the fire engine, pulling a water tank on wheels behind it, chuntered into the farmyard. He wiped his wet hands on the seat of his trousers. His leg had begun to throb unbearably; strangely, concentrating on nothing but the task in hand, he'd scarcely noticed it. Now that the cavalry had arrived, the pain had become excruciating.

The firemen were clambering down from their perches along the sides of the fire engine; their helmets and the brass buttons on their tunics gleamed as they reflected the flames.

Reg Box, the chief fireman, was also the proprietor of the hardware shop in Hillsbridge. He strutted over to Cal, scratching his neck above the stiff collar of his uniform jacket and full of his own importance.

'Phwr! Looks like we'm a bit on the late side.'

'But not too late to damp everything down,' Cal said. 'We've been concentrating on the stable, but it was only a bucketful at a time.'

'Lord Melbrook, isn't it?' Reg sounded taken aback. 'What be you doing here?'

'It was I who telephoned the police station to raise the alarm.'

'One of your farms, in't it?'

Cal didn't bother to correct him.

'I suggest you get on with putting out this fire,' he said shortly.

'Will do, milord.' Respectful now. And officious. 'Get to it, men!'

They did, unwinding the hose and playing it first on the stable and surrounding sheds, then on the seat of the fire. The barn roof had completely collapsed now. Pockets of flame shot up within the confines of the blackened stone walls, died down under the weight of the water, then shot up again. Steam hissed, the farmyard was turning to mud, but by the time the water truck was empty, it seemed the fire was under control.

Reg Box approached Cal. 'Reckon that's about all we can do.'

'You can stay until we're sure it's not going to flare up again. Collect water from the pump as we did, if necessary.'

'If you say so, squire.' Like most of his men, Reg was anxious to get back to his bed. Night-time call-out pay was always welcome, but each and every one of them had a day job to go to tomorrow.

'Thank you so much.' Carina had joined them.

'Pity you didn't call us sooner. We had no chance of saving the barn or your hay.'

'We called you as soon as we could,' Carina said. 'We were all in bed when it started. It's just lucky Frank woke up when he did – he lives in the room over the barn.' She shuddered. 'He could have been burned to death in his bed.'

'Frank? Who's Frank?'

'Our hired hand. That's him . . .' Carina pointed in the direction of the young man, who was now sitting on an upturned bucket.

'Hmm. Can't say I know him.' Reg was eyeing Frank curiously.

'You wouldn't. He's only been here a matter of weeks. He comes from Bristol.'

'Bristol? A Bristol bloke working on a farm?' The chief sounded scathing and incredulous.

'This is no time for idle gossip,' Cal interrupted. 'But perhaps you could make the men a cup of tea, Carina?'

'Oh yes . . . of course . . .' She broke off as a sudden thought struck her. 'Where's Grandpa?'

She said it quietly at first, almost wonderingly. Then, as her concern mounted, she yelled across the yard to Sally, her voice rising in panic.

'Sal – where's Grandpa?'

Sally came over to her.

'In bed and asleep, I suppose.'

'With all this going on? Surely it must have woken him up?'

Without another word she turned and ran towards the house, emerging a few moments later in a state of near hysteria.

'He's not there! He's not in his room! Oh dear God, you don't suppose . . .'

She was running now towards the burning barn.

'Carina!' Cal chased after her, caught her arm. 'What do you think you're doing?'

She tried to shake herself free. 'Grandpa . . .'

'You can't go in there! Don't be foolish.'

'But Grandpa . . .'

'If he is in there, he's beyond help. But he isn't. Why would he be?'

'I don't know . . . I don't know!'

'Come on now.'

The heat from the smouldering ruin was scorching his face. Gently he began to ease her away, but quite suddenly she jerked to a halt, her eyes fixed on the ground beneath her feet, her whole body tensed and trembling.

'Carina?'

She wriggled free of his restraining grasp and dropped to her haunches, picking something up, staring at it as if mesmerised.

'Oh my God.'

'What is it?

She straightened.

'His pipe. Grandpa's pipe.' She uncurled her fingers and he saw it there in the palm of her hand: an old briar with a chewed stem.

'Oh my God,' she whispered again. 'He was smoking it when I went to bed. Sitting in his chair. What's it doing out here? How did it get out here? Unless . . .'

'Carina, don't jump to conclusions. There could be any number of reasons . . .'

'No, there couldn't. His pipe is always with him. He's in there, Cal! I know he is! Grandpa was in the barn and now . . . Oh no! No – no – please no . . .'

Without thinking, Cal took her in his arms and held her as she sobbed hysterically against his chest.

Chapter Eighteen

Once again Meadow Farm was in mourning. Just as Carina had feared, Grandpa Luke's remains had been found in the burned-out barn.

Dawn had broken before the fire brigade eventually left, the soft pearly grey light and the pink-streaked sky signalling another fine day. Numb with shock, Carina had made yet more tea, and she, Sally, Cal and Frank sat around the table drinking it.

'I don't understand! I just don't understand any of it!' Tears were running unchecked down Sally's face. 'How did it happen?'

'As I said to Carina, it was probably spontaneous combustion.' Cal rubbed his leg, which was aching badly.

'And as I said, we're always so careful to make sure the hay is properly dry,' Carina said.

'But perhaps this time it wasn't.'

'And what was Grandpa doing in the barn anyway?' Sally went on as if neither of them had spoken.

'Maybe he woke up, discovered the fire, and was trying to put it out,' Cal suggested.

'It doesn't make sense that he'd be the first to realise what was happening. He sleeps like a log. And if he did happen to wake up and saw the barn was on fire, he'd have woken us . . . or Frank at least. He knew Frank was asleep upstairs. He didn't wake you, did he, Frank? It wasn't him calling to you that disturbed you, was it?'

'It was the smoke that woke me. I told you. I didn't hear a sound till then. I was out like a light.'

'A light! His pipe! You found his pipe, Carina. Perhaps he was trying to light it . . .'

'His pipe was *outside* the barn, Sally.'

'But he might have thrown away the match and it went into the barn and set the hay alight. Then when he saw what he'd done, he tried to put the fire out and . . . oh, I don't know . . . fainted? Had a stroke? Fell over and couldn't get up? Do you think that might have been it, Carina?'

Carina didn't reply. She was staring down at the mug of tea held between her trembling hands. The most terrible thought had occurred to her.

Grandpa had taken against Frank in a big way. It wasn't like him to harbour such strong feelings towards anyone, but like most quiet folk, when he did, those feelings ran deep and were perhaps even more extreme than in people who gave free rein to their emotions. And he had been greatly concerned about what was happening between Frank and Sally. What was it he had said to her, only last night? 'I wouldn't trust that one any further than I could throw him', and 'I wish to God he'd never come here. He's a bad lot.'

Suppose, just suppose, Grandpa had started the fire deliberately, to get rid of Frank? He'd still been up when she had gone to bed, which was very unlike him; he usually liked to retire early. She couldn't bring herself to believe that Grandpa had meant to burn the hired hand in his bed; more likely that he thought with the accommodation and all his belongings gone, Frank would have to move on. He'd meant to call to Frank, warn him, but then things had happened as Sally had suggested, and his pent-up anger had brought on a stroke or something of the kind. At least, she hoped that was how it had been . . .

'There's no point speculating,' Cal said, almost as if he had read her mind. 'What's happened has happened and nothing can alter that.' He drank the last of his tea and stood up. 'You'll be needing your motor, Carina. I'll get it back to you as soon as I can.'

'Oh . . . I suppose I will.' She stood up too. 'If I can come with you now, I'll drive it back.'

'I don't think you're in any fit state at the moment,' he said firmly. 'Leave it to me.'

'I can't put you to that trouble,' Carina protested. 'You've been so kind. I can never thank you enough.'

'I'm only glad I was able to help. Though heaven knows, it was little enough. I'll see you later.'

'You're not thinking . . . ?'

'Of our visit to Bath? Hardly. That will have to wait for another day.'

He'd left then, and another nightmarish day had begun. The doctor had come to certify death – certify death, when there was nothing left of Grandpa Luke but charred remains! Sergeant Love. The undertaker. David Perkins, sent by his parents to find out what had happened. Other neighbours, offering their condolences. And all the normal everyday things. The cows to be milked. The hens to be fed. The children to be cared for.

Meg, to Carina's disbelief, seemed more excited than anything else by what had happened. She ran outside, stared round-eyed at the ruins of the barn. 'Oh, we missed it, Mattie! The fire brigade and all! Fancy we missed seeing the fire brigade!' She scarcely seemed to take in that Grandpa Luke had died in the fire, and when Carina tried once more to explain, she simply said: 'He's with Daddy, then? I'm glad. Daddy won't have to be lonely any more.'

And then: 'Who's going to peel the potatoes now?'

Carina, her nerves in tatters, wanted to slap her.

'Is that all you can think of, Meg?'

Meg's lip quivered, and Carina regretted having spoken so sharply. The child was only three years old, and Grandpa Luke, snoozing much of the time and saying very little when he was awake, must have been a shadowy figure to her, just an old man who was part of the backdrop to her young life. Peeling potatoes in those long continuous strips was one of the few things he did that she and Mattie had taken an interest in. It was what she would remember him for.

Cal returned with the Rover, which he'd driven himself. He would walk home, he said. The exercise would do him good. And although Carina tried to persuade him to let her drive him, he remained insistent. When he had left, striding out along the track, his limp noticeable but determinedly ignored, she had felt bereft, abandoned. Cal couldn't change anything that had happened, he couldn't bring Grandpa Luke back, but his simply being there was a comfort.

With him gone, the weight of responsibility had fallen squarely back on her shoulders, and she didn't know how she was going to cope.

The fire, of course, was the talk of Dunderwick and Hillsbridge, more gossip-worthy even than the fact that there had been another burglary overnight, at the home of the well-to-do owner of a timber yard who lived in a big house on the outskirts of the town. This time, it seemed, the burglar had been even bolder than before – a window had been forced and cash and valuables stolen with the family upstairs in their beds. Rumour had it that jewellery had gone missing from the bedroom in which the man and his wife were sleeping, and though no one knew for sure whether that was true, it didn't stop them from passing on the story.

As for the fire at Meadow Farm and the demise of Luke Green, there were those who relished the gory details, and the hardware shop in Hillsbridge was doing a roaring trade as, eager to hear all about it from the horse's mouth, people found the sudden need to buy all manner of small items. Reg Box was only too happy to oblige, all the while stressing that the fire had been well out of control by the time he and his men arrived, and boasting about the fact that Lord Melbrook had been there. 'Talked to him just like I'm talking to you!' he said, his ego swelling as his customers' faces reflected their awe at such a thing.

He also took a delight in hinting that he had his suspicions about the strange young man Luke Green had had working for him and wondered if he might have had something to do with the fire starting. 'A bloke from Bristol working on a farm? What's he after, I'd like to know. Seems fishy to me.'

It didn't take long for folk to begin to link the two stories. The spate of burglaries, even the robbery at Ticker Bendle's bookmaker's, and a stranger from Bristol in the district. The general consensus of opinion was that people from the city, and Bristol in particular, were not to be trusted. The fact that the young man had been asleep in the room over the barn when the fire started and so was unlikely to have been the burglar who stole into the timber yard owner's house didn't put a stop to the talk. People shook their heads and tapped their noses knowingly as they passed on the titbits of gossip. They didn't like to think that one of their own was responsible; far better to have an outsider to blame.

But whoever he was daft enough to have there working for him, Luke Green hadn't deserved an awful death like that. And whatever would Sally and Robert's young widow do now?

Oh, there was plenty to talk about that day, and the people of Hillsbridge and Dunderwick made the most of it.

On that first night after the fire, Frank slept on the kitchen sofa, but it was clearly no long-term solution. Apart from anything else, it was much too small to accommodate him – he'd had to dangle his legs over the arm, and next morning he complained bitterly that every muscle in his body was aching and he thought he'd cricked his back.

'There's a perfectly good bed in there,' he'd said, nodding in the direction of Grandpa Luke's room. 'Why can't I sleep in that?'

The very idea was abhorrent to Carina, and she wanted to hit him for daring to suggest such a thing with Grandpa Luke not even yet laid to rest. She wished with all her heart that she could give him his marching orders, but she couldn't see that they could manage without him. Apart from anything else, the second harvest was almost ready, and they now needed the hay it would yield more than ever. Perhaps when that was finished she could find a way to get rid of him, but for the moment she couldn't even begin to contemplate it.

In any case, she had Sally to contend with. And Sally, unsurprisingly, was all for the idea.

'It makes sense, Carina,' she said. 'We need Frank fit and healthy, not tired out and half crippled by trying to get a night's sleep on that old sofa.'

'Well in that case we'd better turn Grandpa's room out,' Carina said. She couldn't bear the thought of Frank poking about in the old man's things. 'You can help me.'

'Oh Carina, I've got so much to do. And I was going to go into Hillsbridge with Frank to help him buy replacements for all the things he lost in the fire . . .'

'He'll just have to manage without you,' Carina said crossly. 'Luke was your grandfather, after all, and it's only right you're there to make the decisions about what to do with his things.'

It crossed her mind to wonder how Frank was going to manage for money to shop for replacements, since everything but the clothes he stood up in had been lost in the fire. But she decided she didn't want to know. She had too many other things to worry about.

When Frank had left for Hillsbridge – he'd even had the cheek to ask if he could drive the Rover, a suggestion she'd quickly stamped on – she shut Cymru out of the house, put Mattie down for a nap and settled Meg with a box of coloured pencils and some paper. Meg liked to draw; hopefully it would keep her quiet long enough for Carina and Sally to do what they had to do.

The task that faced them was a horrible one, the very thought of going through Grandpa Luke's things and disposing of them dreadfully upsetting. Just seeing his dressing gown hanging on a hook on the door and his nightshirt folded on the pillow was enough to make Sally break down, and Carina's heart went out to her. Grandpa Luke had been like a father to her ever since she was a little girl; to lose both him and the brother she adored in such a short space of time must be unbearable for her.

But even as she comforted Sally, Carina was wondering. It didn't look as if Grandpa had undressed ready for bed. Could it be that the awful thought that had occurred to her – that he had been the one to deliberately start the fire – was correct? She hoped it wasn't so, but certainly everything seemed to be pointing in that direction. With an effort she pushed the thought to the back of her mind.

'Come on, Sally. The sooner we start, the sooner we'll be finished.'

Sally wiped her wet cheeks and blew her nose.

'I'm sorry, Carina, but it's just so awful. I can't believe it . . .'

'I know, love. You've got to be brave. And you can be. I know you.'

'I don't feel very brave. I feel . . .' She broke off, blew her nose again. 'Okay, where do we start?'

'Let's strip the bed.'

Together they removed the sheets, pillowcases and coverlet and piled them on the floor ready for washing. Carina fetched clean ones, patched and worn but smelling of soap and fresh air, and they made up the bed. They turned then to Grandpa's clothes, emptying the wardrobe and the drawers of the tallboy, folding and stacking neatly, though as yet they had no idea what they would do with them. Probably even a tramp would turn up his nose at the shirts with frayed cuffs, the vests and long johns that were a little stained for all Carina's efforts with the washboard, the old baggy trousers, the cardigans felted and stretched out of shape. The best solution would probably be a bonfire, but Carina shrank from the thought. It was, as yet, too soon for that.

She struggled with the sudden threat of tears as she remembered Robert's clothes still hanging in the wardrobe as if he might still need them. She hadn't been able to bring herself to turn them out yet, and he had been dead for almost three months. Yet here they were doing just that with Grandpa's, only a day after his death.

'I'll just check on Meg.' She popped her head round the door. Meg had abandoned her colouring, but she was busily setting out the cups, saucers and plates of her toy tea set, chattering to herself as she did so, and Carina went back into Grandpa's room without disturbing her.

The last job that needed to be done was turning out the cupboard beside the bed. This would be the hardest of all, Carina thought, because it was where Grandpa had kept his most personal possessions. But if Frank was going to move into the room, it was also the most important.

'Can you do it, Carina, please?' Sally was obviously thinking the same thing.

'If you like, but it's up to you what we do with it all.'

Carina opened the top drawer while Sally sat on the newly made-up bed.

The first thing she found was a bible with a book plate stuck inside the flyleaf, recording that it had been presented to Luke Green for regular attendance at Sunday school. It looked in remarkably pristine condition considering it must be at least sixty years old and probably more. Grandpa Luke's devotions had stopped at the church door, she guessed, and the regular attendance had most likely been down to pressure from his mother. There was also a well-used pouch of tobacco, a box of matches and a little wooden-handled knife, not dissimilar to the one he used for peeling the potatoes, as well as a pile of handkerchiefs, some old and frayed, some much newer – the ones she herself had laundered.

In the second drawer was a bag containing humbugs that had gone sticky and were dripping syrup through the paper, a box of dominoes, a pack of cards, and a bundle of letters tied together with a length of string. Luckily they were far enough away from the sweets not to have been damaged by the melting sugar.

'What about these, Sally?' Carina passed them to her, unwilling to pry herself into something so personal. She watched, though, as her sister-in-law untied the string and spread the first letter out on her knee.

'They're from Grandma!' Sally said, surprised. 'It looks as if she wrote them before they were married. She came from Dorset, of course. I'm not sure how they met, but they must have had quite long separations in the beginning.'

Unlike the bible, the letters looked to have been read and pored over many times, judging by the slightly grimy marks along the fold lines and the crumpled edges.

Sally was crying again. 'Fancy keeping them all these years! He must have loved her very much.'

'I'm sure he did. But it wouldn't be right to read them.'

'Oh, I wouldn't dream of it!'

'I suppose we should burn them. Or perhaps we could ask the undertaker to put them in his coffin . . .'

'That would be a good idea,' Sally said through her tears.

Carina opened the third and last drawer, which seemed to contain nothing but a stack of papers.

'What on earth . . .' She broke off suddenly, listening, as a door slammed somewhere in the house. Meg had been very quiet for a long time – had she finally become bored, climbed on a chair, managed to open the door and gone out? 'I must check on Meg,' she said, getting up.

Even before she reached the door, though, it opened and Frank came in, Meg and Cymru following him.

'What's to do?' he asked.

'We're turning out so that you can use this room,' Carina said brusquely.

'Oh? And what have you found? Anything of interest?'

'These things are private,' Carina snapped as anger flared – how dare he? 'Perhaps you wouldn't mind keeping an eye on Meg while we finish.'

Frank shrugged. 'Suit yourself. Come on, Meg. We're banished.'

He went out, taking the child and the dog with him and leaving the door open behind him.

'What is it?' Sally asked, putting down the letters and leaning forward.

'I don't know . . .' The papers were not so much paper as thick vellum, covered with copperplate writing and tied with pink ribbon. The vellum had yellowed with age and the ink had faded, but when Carina held the pages up to the light, the writing was still legible. 'It looks like the deeds to the farm,' she said. 'Grandpa must have kept them himself rather than leaving them with the solicitor.

'Good Lord! Can I see?'

Carina passed them to her. There was something else in the drawer, also vellum but not nearly so yellowed, and much thinner – a double sheet at most. Carina lifted it out, looking at it.

'This is a will, Sally! Grandpa made a will!'

'Really? He never mentioned it.'

'It's dated 1899. That must have been . . .'

'The year we lost our parents and came to live with him and Grandma Margaret. What does it say?'

Carina was trying to make sense of the legal jargon.

'It leaves everything to Robert, I think.'

'I suppose it would.'

'But that's not all . . . there's more . . .' She paused, then read slowly: '"Should my said grandson Robert predecease me leaving issue, then I give and bequeath my entire estate to any son of his to be held in trust for him until he shall become of age."' She looked up wide-eyed at Sally. 'Does that mean what I think it means? Grandpa has left everything to Mattie?'

'It certainly looks like it,' Sally said bleakly. 'Don't I get a mention?'

Flustered, Carina read on.

'I think what it says is that everything would come to you if Robert had no son. There's no mention of Robert's daughters.'

'Left out, like me.' Sally laughed humourlessly. 'And you, for that matter. No wonder the suffragettes are fighting for a better deal for women.'

'It makes sense, though.' Carina felt the need to defend Grandpa Luke. 'A farm is a man's work.'

'I'm as fit as any man!'

'I know you are, but . . .' Carina floundered. She had the awful feeling she was just making this worse. 'I'm sorry, Sally . . . I wouldn't want Mattie to deprive you of your inheritance. This is your home, and when he's old enough to understand, I'll make very sure he knows that.'

'It's not that simple, though, Carina. Held in trust until he becomes of age. What does that mean?'

'I'm not sure. I think it means someone has to look after it for him. We'll have to go and see the solicitor. He'll explain it all to us.' She got up abruptly. 'I'll put this somewhere safe.'

'Don't worry, I'm not going to destroy it,' Sally said. She sounded hurt and bitter.

'Oh Sal, I wouldn't for one moment think . . . Please don't let's fall out over this.' She cocked her head, thinking she had heard Mattie crying, and crossed to the door, opening it fully.

Outside, certainly near enough to have been able to hear what was being said, was Frank.

'I thought I told you that what we were doing was private!' she snapped.

'Keep your hair on! I'm not eavesdropping, if that's what you think. I was just coming to tell you that Mattie's awake and crying, that's all.'

Carina pushed past him. She didn't believe a word of it. Mattie was grizzling, it was true. But Frank had been listening, she was sure of it.

She ran up the stairs to her son's room, still clutching the will and the deeds of the farm to her chest. Mattie's tears turned to chuckles when he saw her, and he held out his arms to be picked up.

Her heart contracted with love. For want of a better hiding place, she tucked the will and the deeds under the cot mattress and lifted the child into her arms.

'Oh Mattie! You'll never guess what's happened . . .'

As the enormity of it struck her, she wasn't sure whether to be glad or sorry. Grandpa might not have been a rich man, but everything he possessed now belonged to this little boy, her pride and joy. Would it be a blessing or a burden? She didn't know, but to some extent at least his future was secured.

At Sally's expense. Carina wished fervently that it were not so; as she had said, the last thing she wanted to do was to fall out with her sister-in-law. But Grandpa Luke had intended the farm and everything else to go to Mattie. He might have made the will long before his grandson was born, but he'd done nothing to change it since. When he came of age, Mattie would inherit Meadow Farm. And Carina would fight with her last breath to ensure that he did.

'I think I'm going to turn in since I've got a decent bed tonight.' Frank got up from the supper table, stretched and yawned. 'What with that bloody sofa last night, and no sleep to speak of the night before, I'm ready for a good long kip.'

'I think we all are, Frank,' Carina said. She'd hardly slept herself the previous night, and she guessed neither had Sally. But she couldn't imagine tonight would be any better.

'Night, then.' Frank winked at Sally and headed for the door.

Carina piled the plates together and carried them over to the sink. She couldn't bear to watch him go into Grandpa's room, and she hadn't liked that wink either. Surely, surely he wasn't expecting Sally to creep downstairs and join him in Grandpa's bed? And even if he was, surely Sally would never dream of doing such a thing? But she wasn't going to say anything about it. She'd upset Sally enough for one day, and the last thing she wanted was to fall out with her sister-in-law. With emotions running so high, it would be all too easy. And goodness knows, they needed one another now more than ever.

'We've got to decide the details of Grandpa's funeral,' she said as she poured hot water from the kettle into the sink and dunked the used crockery. 'Seward Moody is coming to see us tomorrow to make the final arrangements, and the rector is very likely to call too.'

'Oh, you can talk to them, can't you?' Sally was as tight as a drawn bowstring. 'Do whatever you think best.'

'But Sally, he was your grandpa,' Carina protested. 'You really should be the one . . . What hymns did he like, for instance?'

'I don't know . . . Moody and Sankey, I think.'

'But which ones?'

'How would I know? It wasn't the sort of thing we talked about.'

'Well, the rector will want to do a eulogy. You're the one who has memories of Grandpa.'

Sally attacked the glass she was drying so violently it shattered, and broken bits showered the floor.

'Yes, I have memories all right. But what do they mean? He didn't really care about me.'

'Oh Sally! That's not true and you know it!' Carina gently took the remains of the broken glass from Sally's hands, putting them on the cupboard top out of harm's way, and steered her sister-in-law away from the shards at her feet. 'He thought the world of you.'

'Well he had a funny way of showing it.' Sally was crying again.

'He just wanted the farm to pass down through the male line,' Carina said gently. 'It didn't mean he thought any the less of you.'

'It still hurts.'

'Oh, come here.' Carina put her arms round Sally's shaking shoulders and let her cry for a while. She could feel the tears pricking her own eyes but she blinked them back. Sally was at breaking point – small wonder – and although she was devastated herself, one of them had to remain strong.

'I think we ought to go and see the solicitor tomorrow,' she said when Sally's sobs had subsided. 'We need to get this sorted out.'

'What's the point? A will's a will, Carina.'

'We don't know that he didn't make another one,' Carina said. 'This one is very old.'

'Then where is it?'

'The solicitor could be holding it.'

'I don't think so. The one we found is the one he kept. The deeds were with it too, remember. If he had made another will and left it with the solicitor, then surely he'd have left the deeds with him too?'

'Well we still have to find out what we need to do. I don't understand anything about this sort of thing, and neither do you.'

'You can go and see the solicitor, Carina. I really don't want to. I'll look after the children.'

'We'll talk about it again in the morning. Right now, we're both too tired to think, let alone make decisions. Come on, let's clear up and go to bed.'

She fetched a dustpan and brush and swept up the bits of glass. By the time she'd done that, Sally had taken on the washing-up, so she dried instead.

'That's it, then,' she said as she put the last of the crockery away. 'And now we both need a good night's sleep.'

She went round putting out the oil lamps but didn't bother to light a candle. The moon streaming in at the windows made it light enough for them to see without the need of one. Then, putting her arm round Sally's waist, she guided her to the door and followed her up the stairs.

But she couldn't sleep. For more than an hour she lay tossing and turning, one worry after another chasing around in her head. Try as she might to still them, the moment she began to feel she might be about to doze off, one or the other was there again, nagging her back to full wakefulness.

She almost jumped when she heard a sound from downstairs. For a moment she lay alert and listening, wondering if she had imagined it, but she was sure she had not, and another soft thud confirmed it. Her first thought was that it was Sally, creeping down to visit Frank. But then she remembered the burglaries. Perhaps it was an intruder. Tired and distracted as she had been when she had come to bed, had she left the door unlocked? Or a window?

Scared though she was, Carina knew she had to investigate. Everything was quiet now, but she had heard something, and if sleep had been reluctant to come before, now it would be impossible. She slipped out of bed, looking round for something she could take with her for protection, and settled on one of the heavy brass candlesticks that stood on the mantelpiece. Gripping it tightly in a hand that was trembling, she crept down the stairs.

As soon as she was level with the doorway to the kitchen, she saw the faint glow lighting the room beyond and recognised it. Someone had lit an oil lamp. Then it wasn't a burglar, surely? More likely Sally, come downstairs because she was also unable to sleep. If she was with Frank, Carina would creep away again; whatever they were up to, she didn't feel like confronting them tonight. But if she was just sitting here alone, then perhaps they could have a warm milky drink together before going back to bed.

Her bare feet making no sound, Carina crept down the last few stairs. Then she stopped short, her eyes widening in disbelief.

Frank was at the dresser, one of the drawers pulled out and half its contents on the floor. As she watched from the doorway, he bent down, picked it all up and put it back in before opening the next. Incensed, Carina flew into the room.

'What do you think you're doing?'

Frank looked round, startled. Guilt was written all over him.

'I was just—'

'I can see what you're doing. Poking around in our things. How dare you?'

'Don't be like that, Carina. I was looking for something to use for a handkerchief. I lost all mine along with everything else in the fire. You keep your drying-up cloths and stuff in here, don't you?'

That much was true. For some reason Carina felt wrong-footed.

'If you want a handkerchief, I'll get you one. But I'd really rather you didn't go rooting around in our drawers.'

She went upstairs and reluctantly fetched a couple of Grandpa's handkerchiefs from the pile of his things they had put ready for disposal. As she gave them to Frank, her heart twisted, but she told herself Grandpa had no more use for them.

She waited until Frank had returned to his room and closed the door before she went back to bed herself. She wasn't convinced he had been telling the truth. But if not, why had he been rifling through the drawers? Was it just nosiness, or had he been looking for something? And if so, what? An image popped into her mind – Frank right outside the door when she and Sally had discovered the deeds to the farm and Grandpa's will. Was that what he had been looking for? The will? But why would he do that?

Oh, it made no sense at all, and she was too tired to think. Carina plumped up her pillow, climbed into bed, and once again tried to get to sleep.

Chapter Nineteen

Next morning, after Meg and Mattie had been washed, dressed and fed, Carina set off for Hillsbridge to see the solicitor. She'd asked Sally again if she would come with her, but Sally was adamant she didn't want to. Besides, as she pointed out, they could hardly take the children with them, and Carina was bound to agree. It would be difficult enough to sort things out without having to keep them out of mischief as well.

Her stomach knotted with nerves, she drove into Hillsbridge and parked at the kerb on the main street. The offices of Willoughby and Clarence were situated above a row of shops, marked by an impressive brass plaque on the wall beside a firmly closed door. Taking her courage in both hands, she pushed open the door and started up a steep flight of stairs.

As she neared the top, she was intercepted by a wiry little man, stooped and balding, who introduced himself as Josia Horler, the solicitor's clerk.

'May I help you?' His voice was dry and dusty, as cracked as the vellum on which the will and deeds were written.

'I've come to see Mr Willoughby,' Carina said.

Josia uttered a small crackling sound midway between a cough and a laugh.

'I'm afraid Mr Willoughby retired some years ago.'

'Oh.' Carina pulled the documents out of her bag. 'He's the solicitor named on these . . .'

'It will be Mr Clarence now. Do you wish to see him?'

'Yes please.'

'Very well. I'll see when he will be free.'

'Oh, but . . . I was hoping to see him now,' Carina said.

'You should really have made an appointment. Mr Clarence is a very busy man.' Josia gave a small, impatient shake of his head. 'Wait here, and I'll see if it will be possible.'

He showed Carina into a tiny room, hardly larger than a glorified cupboard. Three chairs were lined up against the wall, but Carina didn't sit down. She was feeling far too tense and anxious.

A few moments later, he was back.

'Mr Clarence is able to spare you a few minutes. If you would care to follow me.'

Arthur Clarence's office was scarcely bigger than the waiting room, small and frowsty, with bookshelves lined with legal tomes and stacks of documents tied with pink ribbon stacked against the walls. Behind a large leather-topped desk the man himself sat in a swivel captain's chair. He rose to greet her, then sat down once more, indicating that she should take the chair opposite him.

'I understand you are here to discuss a will made by my partner,' he said, steepling his fingers and regarding her solemnly from behind owlish spectacles.

'Yes, sir.' Carina laid the documents on the desk and explained.

'May I . . . ?'

Carina pushed the pages across the desk and he took his time examining them.

'Hmm.' He removed the spectacles and fixed her with a beady stare. 'You are the mother of the beneficiary?'

'Mattie. Luke's grandson. Yes.'

'And he is still a minor?'

'He's only just over a year old.'

'I see.' He pressed a finger to his lips. 'In that case—'

'Is the will legal?' Carina interrupted.

'Perfectly legal. Provided this is Mr Green's last will and testament. Are you quite sure there is none other?'

'This is the only one we found.'

'Things would have been a good deal simpler if the will had been lodged with us. There would then be no room for doubt. However, unfortunately Mr Green did not see fit to take that route, and we must work with what we have.' He studied the document again. 'It would appear that Mr Willoughby is both executor and trustee.'

'That's what I said in the first place.' Carina felt flustered and inadequate, but she was determined not to let the solicitor see it.

'And by extension, this firm. Do you want me to obtain a grant of probate, Mrs . . . ?'

'Talbot. That's what's needed, is it?'

The solicitor smiled slightly.

'Probate, certainly. And then an arrangement regarding the trustees until your son comes of age. There is no stipulation as to a minimum age, so it would be assumed to be when he reaches legal majority, at twenty-one years. In the meantime, the trustees will be responsible for looking after his interests.'

'Mr Willoughby?'

'Myself as representative of the firm of Willoughby and Clarence. But as a safeguard I would recommend an additional trustee be appointed. You yourself could be that person, although,' he smiled slightly, 'I think it might be advisable to choose someone with some knowledge of commerce and the law. Is there anyone you think might be suitable to hold that position?' He waited a moment, then: 'No? Then might I suggest—'

'Lord Melbrook,' Carina interrupted him. She said it almost without thinking. His name was just there, on the tip of her tongue.

'Lord Melbrook?' Arthur Clarence looked taken aback. 'I think it highly unlikely his lordship would have the time or the inclination.'

'Well, I'd like you to ask him.'

'I really don't see . . .' The solicitor seemed lost for words. 'What is your connection with Lord Melbrook?'

Carina bristled. She had no intention of going into details, and she wished she dared tell this stuffed shirt to mind his own business. But she simply said: 'He's been very kind to me.'

'Very well. If that's what you want, I'll write to him.' He paused. 'You do realise all this is going to cost money, don't you?'

Carina's heart sank. She'd known, of course, that there would be a fee – if solicitors worked for nothing, they wouldn't be living in far nicer houses than ordinary folk and keeping offices in the centre of town. But she'd been hoping it wouldn't be too much. Now she wondered if it would be more than she could afford, and where the money would come from. But what choice did she have?

She lifted her chin.

'I pay my bills, Mr Clarence, don't worry,' she said.

'I'm sure you do, Mrs Talbot. So you'd like me to set things in motion?'

'Yes please.'

He nodded, made some notes, asked some more questions and then stood up, indicating that the interview was at an end.

'Good day to you then, Mrs Talbot.'

'Good day.'

Leaving the deeds to the farm and Grandpa Luke's will on the solicitor's desk, she went back through the tiny waiting room and down the steep flight of stairs, and headed for home.

Cal couldn't decide whether he should attend Luke's funeral. He'd been at the farm on the night of the fire and when the old man's remains had been found, so he felt an involvement, and besides, he would like to pay his respects. But his presence in the church would be sure to cause a stir – landed gentry didn't attend the funerals of farmers unless they happened to be tenants – and he didn't want to detract from an occasion that should be all about the deceased. The funeral should be dignified, not some sort of spectacle with villagers whispering among themselves and speculating about why he was there.

When the day dawned, drizzly and overcast as few days had been that summer, he still hadn't made up his mind. The church was sure to be full; if the weather had been fine and sunny, the menfolk would most likely have been out in the fields, getting in the second harvest, but as it was, a lot of them would no doubt accompany their wives. No one would expect him to be there, no one would miss him. But still the urge to attend nagged at him.

'What am I going to do, Cleo?' he asked the dog stretched out at his feet.

Cleo didn't move. She was carrying a litter of pups and growing heavier every day, and from the look of her swollen nipples it wouldn't be long before they arrived. She did cock an ear, though, as the grandfather clock in the hall outside the study door whirred and began to chime out the hour. Twelve o'clock. The funeral, he knew, was at one. If he was going to attend, it was time he told Biddy Thomas that he wouldn't be in for luncheon and ask her to cut him a piece of cold pie that he could eat quickly while getting ready.

At last he made up his mind. He'd walk into the village – he didn't want his Benz attracting attention – and slip into the back of the church. With any luck, it would be dim enough for him to keep a low profile. Then, when the funeral was over, he'd slip out again, hopefully unnoticed.

The rain had stopped by the time he was ready to leave, but he put on a light overcoat anyway in case it started again. As he walked down the long hill into the village, his thoughts turned to Carina. Why was it that some people seemed to get more than their fair share of misfortune? But then, he supposed, that was life. In the end, no one escaped unscathed.

He thought of Alice, but for once he found it difficult to conjure up her face. Instead he could see only Carina's. Understandable, he supposed, since it was her husband's grandfather's funeral he was on his way to. But strangely, the image in his mind's eye wasn't that of the terrified girl who had come banging at the door of the orangery on the night of the fire, nor the grief-stricken one when Luke's remains had been discovered. Instead, he was seeing her as she had looked the night he had given her a ride home in the Benz, laughing, exhilarated, joyful. And then the proud set of her jaw, the anger sparking in her eyes the day he had called at the farm to demand compensation for the damage to his motor, and again when he and Isobel had met her in the street in Bath after she had pawned her engagement ring. That was the real Carina. Brave, spirited, determined. How many women would do such a thing? He still felt ashamed that he'd driven her to it, but at least he'd gone some way to putting that right, though she didn't yet know it. Now he pictured her face when he told her what he'd done – not dissimilar to the way she'd looked when she'd been enjoying the car ride, he imagined – and a faint smile lifted the corners of his mouth.

That woman is turning you soft, he told himself.

And realised that one of the reasons he had wanted to attend the funeral today – perhaps the chief one – was that he wanted to be there for her, even if the only support he could offer would be silent and, most likely, unnoticed.

Carina didn't see Cal in the church. Her eyes blurred with tears as she and Sally followed Luke's simple coffin, and she saw no one. The service seemed interminable, the words she had heard so recently at Robert's funeral washing over her in waves. The one thing that stood out clearly was the Sankey hymn they had settled on. The congregation sang lustily – with Moody and Sankey it was almost impossible not to. But it was the words of the fourth verse that really hit home.

> *Thro' the water and the fire*
> *This, O Lord, my one desire;*
> *With thy love my heart inspire,*
> *And lead me on.*

Through the water and the fire . . . She hadn't realised how apt the words were. Had Sally? Carina held tight to herself. She had got through the ordeal of Robert's funeral, and she would get through this.

It was when the interment was over and they turned away from the graveside that she saw him, standing at a distance under the trees at the edge of the churchyard, and her heart missed a beat.

The rector was murmuring some words of consolation; she hardly heard them. Villagers and farming folk were waiting in awkward knots to offer their condolences; David Perkins was making his way over to Sally. Carina pushed past all of them, anxious only to get to Cal to thank him for coming.

But by the time she had escaped, she could no longer see him, and the jolt of despair that ran through her brought it home to her that her eagerness to reach him had not just been to thank him. It was the same feeling of abandonment she had experienced when he had left on the morning Grandpa Luke had died. When Cal was there, nothing seemed quite so bad. But now he'd gone, without waiting to speak to her.

Had he received the letter from Arthur Clarence asking if he would become a trustee under Grandpa's will? Was the reason he hadn't wanted to face her because he was going to refuse? Carina felt sick suddenly. She shouldn't have asked it. It was an imposition, a liberty.

But he'd come to the funeral, even if he hadn't wanted to see her. That, at least, was some small comfort. And it was, she told herself, a great deal more than she had any right to expect.

Two days after the funeral, Tommy Dix, a miner who lived in Dunderwick, came knocking at the farmhouse door. A week or so before the fire, his wife, Gwen, had asked Carina if she would make a skirt for their oldest girl, who was going to start working at one of the grocer's in Hillsbridge. Carina had promised to fit it in as soon as she could, but with all that had been going on, she'd had no time to even think about her dressmaking. Now, when she saw Tommy standing on the doorstep, perspiring from the cycle ride up from the village and twisting his cap awkwardly between his hands, her first thought was that Gwen and the girl were getting impatient, and Tommy had been sent to ask if she could see her way to making a start.

'I'm really sorry, Mr Dix,' she said, wiping her hands on her apron. 'With everything that's been going on, I just haven't had time to—'

'No, missus, I'm the one that should be sorry, bothering you at a time like this. But Gwen asked me to come and let you know that she's changed her mind. She's going to make Dolly's skirt herself.'

'Oh, I will get round to it, really . . .'

'No, don't you worry about it, missus. Gwen's made up her mind. She made a start on it last night.'

'I'm so sorry to let her down, Mr Dix.'

'That's all right. No trouble.'

He retrieved his bicycle, which he had leaned against the wall, and rode away.

Carina sighed heavily as she watched him pedalling off down the track. A skirt wasn't a big job, it wouldn't have paid very much, but every little helped, especially now that she had the solicitor's expenses to think of. She was puzzled, too. When Gwen had asked her to do the work, she'd confessed that she herself was ham-fisted with a sewing machine, but perhaps she had thought Carina wouldn't get it done in time, given all that had happened these last few days.

'What did Mr Dix want?' Sally asked her when she went back in.

Carina told her.

'I can't understand it really,' she finished. 'And we could have done with the money, too. Never mind, I've still got the kitchen curtains to make for the schoolmaster's house. Perhaps I ought to go down and measure up, or they might think I'm not going to do it now.'

'Perhaps you should. You get off, I'll mind the children.'

Carina tidied herself up, collected her tape measure, notebook and pencil and walked down the hill into Dunderwick.

The school house was at the end of a narrow lane, just across from the school itself. Carina knocked on the door and waited. A lace curtain moved at the window of the front room, but it was a few minutes before she heard footsteps in the hall and the door was opened.

'Ah, Mrs Talbot.' The schoolmaster's wife was a thin woman whose shoulders sloped as if she too spent her days poring over books, and who looked permanently harassed. 'I'm glad you're here. I've been meaning to get in touch to let you know – I've changed my mind about the curtains.'

'Oh!' This time Carina was really shocked at the loss of an order. 'But I thought—'

'Really, it won't be long now before it's time to put the winter ones up, so I don't think there's much point having new summer ones just at the moment. Perhaps in the spring . . .'

She looked on the point of closing the door, anxious to bring the conversation to an end.

'Well, you know where I am when you're ready,' Carina said.

'I do. Yes.'

This time she did close the door, leaving Carina staring bemusedly at the shiny brass knocker.

She simply couldn't understand it. To lose one order in a morning was bad enough, but two . . . Well, there was nothing for it, she'd have to put a new postcard up in the post office window. After the first time she'd let it lapse as the work seemed to be pouring in. Now, it seemed, she'd have to begin advertising again.

She retraced her steps to the main street, wrote out a card at the post office counter and paid for it to go in the window for a month. Mrs Bray, the postmistress, was far from her usual chatty self; people felt awkward after the string of tragedies and troubles at Meadow Farm, Carina assumed. She stopped to pick up a few bits and pieces of shopping and a packet of Woodbines for Frank – he'd taken to smoking and asked her to buy them for him – and was just hesitating over whether she could afford some sweets for the children when the bell above the door rang and Ellen Perkins, David's mother, came in. She, at least, was not unwilling to talk to Carina.

'Oh my dear, what can I say? You must be in such a state up there. Look – I've only got to get a pound of currants and a couple of other things and I'll be on my way home. We can walk back together.'

'I'll wait outside.' The uncomfortable atmosphere in the post office was making Carina feel quite claustrophobic. She decided against the sweets – really, she couldn't afford luxuries just now – paid for her shopping and left. A few minutes later, Ellen Perkins joined her, shopping basket, now full, over her arm.

'How are you getting on?' she asked kindly as they started out along the road home.

'Coping – just.'

'Well, the family's got to be fed, that's for sure. But look, I could always do a bit of shopping for you, save you having to come into Dunderwick. Our David could bring it along to you on his bike.'

'That's very kind,' Carina said. 'The real reason I came in today, though, was to see about a sewing job I was going to do for the schoolmaster's wife. But she's changed her mind – the second one today – and I was just putting a card in the post office window to try and drum up some more business. I just can't understand it. No one's ever cancelled a job before, and I really do need the work.'

'Oh dear.' To Carina's surprise, Ellen sounded flustered. 'You've had two cancellations today, you say?'

'Yes, the schoolmaster's wife and Mrs Dix, too. Tommy came to the door with a message, on his way to work, I suppose. All I hope is that Mrs Bray puts the card where people can see it.'

'Oh dear,' Ellen said again.

Carina looked at her. 'What?'

'I'm not sure a card's going to do any good. And I can make a fair guess why folk have been cancelling their orders.'

'What d'you mean?'

'Look, Carina, don't take this the wrong way, but there's been a lot of talk in the village. You've got a young chap from Bristol working for you, haven't you?'

'Well, yes, but—'

'And you know there's been a lot of burglaries lately. And Ticker Bendle, of course, that awful do when he got threatened with a knife.'

'What's that got to do with Frank . . . ?' Carina's voice tailed away as light dawned. 'You mean people think that Frank is responsible?'

'That's the talk. You know what folk round here are like. They don't trust strangers, especially one from Bristol.'

'But that's ridiculous!' Carina exploded.

'Ridiculous or not, I wouldn't mind betting that's the reason your clients have been cancelling. They don't want you going in their houses.'

'You mean they think I might be working with Frank to rob them? I can't believe this!'

'Now don't get upset, Carina,' Ellen soothed. '*I* don't think anything of the sort, of course I don't. But everybody knows you must be struggling to make ends meet, and most of them know girls and women who have done all sorts when they're in dire straits.'

'Like going on the streets, you mean? Are they saying that about me too?'

'Course they're not. They know you better than that.'

'But not well enough not to think I'm in cahoots with a burglar. Giving him a so-called job so he can go round robbing houses and threatening folk and bring home the proceeds.'

'Carina, love, please . . . I wish I hadn't said anything now, but I thought you ought to know what's being said, and why your work is drying up.'

Carina took a moment to answer. What Ellen had said had upset her dreadfully, but deep down she knew that she had spoken as a friend.

'I'm sorry to bite your head off, Ellen, and I'm glad you've told me,' she said at last. 'I'm just really shocked that anyone could think such a thing.'

'Well, like I say, folk round here are wary when it comes to strangers.' Ellen hesitated. 'I must say, I was a bit concerned myself when I heard you'd got a chap you don't know from Adam living there. I mean, there's all sorts of rogues in the world, and when it's just you and Sally . . . He's all right, is he?'

'I might as well tell you straight, I don't like him, Ellen. But what choice do we have? And he's a good worker. It's surprised me how quickly he's learned about farming. Anybody would think he'd been born to it.'

'There you are, see. You never can tell.'

They had reached the track leading to High Combe.

'Well, just you take care, love.' Ellen gave Carina's arm a quick squeeze. 'And don't forget where we are if you need anything.'

Carina walked on along the road leading home feeling suffocated by anxiety. Wherever she turned, whatever she did, it seemed the fates were conspiring against her. What was she going to do now, if the villagers were going to stop giving her work? The bills were piling up, the second harvest was due to begin tomorrow and the extra hands would have to be paid. Really, there was only one chink of hope. Before the fire, Cal had said he wanted more drapes made for Dunderwick House. She'd heard nothing from him since, but perhaps he was giving her a breathing space. She didn't like the thought of going to him and begging for work, but she didn't see that she had any option.

She'd take the car and drive over just as soon as she could find the time. She only hoped that he too hadn't changed his mind.

But her hopes were to be dashed.

When she called at Dunderwick House a few days later, Biddy Thomas answered the door and told her that Lord Melbrook was away.

'He's gone to France for a bit of a holiday,' she said. 'Meeting up with Miss Isobel. They'll be having a high old time of it, I shouldn't wonder.'

Carina's heart sank.

'When will he be back?' she asked.

'Not for a couple of weeks at least. What did you want to see him about?'

Carina told her.

'Oh, not more bolts of cloth cluttering up my linen room!'

'Don't worry, it hasn't been ordered yet,' Carina assured her.

'Oh well, that's all right then. If his lordship should ring, I'll let him know you've been here asking about it, and if he doesn't, I'll tell him when he gets back.'

It was the best Carina could hope for, but her spirits had sunk even lower, and as she drove home, she felt as if she was motoring through a dense black fog. A couple of weeks at least before she could even begin to earn some much-needed money. And there was something else . . . something she couldn't at first identify. A nagging misery in the pit of her stomach . . .

She had almost reached Meadow Farm before she realised what it was. Cal was in France with the hateful Isobel. Having a high old time of it, as the housekeeper had said. She shouldn't mind, of course. They were old friends – very likely more. And it was absolutely none of her business. But the very thought of it hurt.

What in the world is the matter with me? Carina asked herself. And really did not like the answer her heart gave her at all.

Chapter Twenty

By September, the second harvest was under way and Carina was almost too busy to think. Besides all her usual chores, there was a ploughman's lunch to prepare for the casual workers as well as the family, and cups of tea to make or mugs of ale to pour when they took their hard-earned breaks. The plums had ripened too on the trees in the patch of orchard beyond the barns, and she wanted to get them picked before they rotted so that she could make jam and bottle some to help feed them through the winter.

That afternoon, she was alone in the kitchen making rissoles for the evening meal. Sally was out with the men in the fields and Meg and Mattie were both fast asleep, curled up together on Meg's bed. It was unusual for Meg to nap in the day now, but she'd been running around all morning chasing after the threshing machine and tired herself out. It was only when Carina had gone to look for them because they were so quiet that she had found them there, dead to the world, and her heart had warmed, seeing the two heads close together on the pillow. She only hoped the snooze wouldn't mean Meg wouldn't be able to get to sleep tonight.

She had put the leftover meat through the mincer with an onion, a slice of bread and a handful of parsley, mixed the whole lot together with a beaten egg and formed it into patties. Then she heated some dripping in a pan on the stove and began to fry the rissoles. If she didn't overcook them, they could be heated up later.

She was turning one carefully with a knife and fork when a sound behind her made her jump, and she whirled round to see Frank standing there. The rissole plumped back into the pan and hot fat splashed up on to her wrist. She squealed, dropping the fork and grabbing her burned hand.

'Oh! Look what you've made me do!'

Frank was across the room in a couple of quick strides.

'You'd better wash that off.'

He grabbed her by the arm, pulling her over to the sink, where a bowl of cold water was waiting for the potatoes to be washed, and dunking her hand into it.

'I should leave it there a minute,' he advised.

Carina yanked it out again.

'I've got to see to the rissoles.'

She hurried back to the pan; already she'd left them too long, and bits of onion on the edges were burning.

'Oh, now they're done too much. And look at those fat splashes on my skirt! I'll never get them out.'

'You worry too much,' Frank said lazily.

'Perhaps I've got things to worry about,' Carina snapped. 'And what are you doing in here anyway? I thought you were supposed to be helping with the harvest.'

'Mm. Thought I'd take a break and come and see you.'

'What for?'

'Ah, that's for me to know and you to find out.'

Carina frowned. She didn't at all care for the way he was looking at her: quizzical, teasing. Much the way he looked at Sally. The way he'd looked at her a few times lately, now that she came to think of it.

'I hope you don't mean what I think you mean. Because if you do, you'd better leave right now.'

'Oh, Carina, don't be like that . . .'

'Go on. Get out.' She turned back to her rissoles, pulling the pan off the heat, hoping he'd realise this was out of order and do as she said. Instead, she felt his hands on her waist.

'You know you don't mean that.'

'I most certainly do!'

But he was close behind her, his chin stubbly and rough against her ear, his hands still holding her and pulling her against him. His breath was hot on her skin, and then she felt the pressure of his mouth against the nape of her neck.

'Stop it!' She tried to turn and push him away, but somehow succeeded only in facing him whilst being held as firmly as ever.

'Let me go! This instant—' Her words were cut off as his mouth covered hers.

'Oh!' She twisted her head to one side, managed to free one hand and hit out at his face. It wasn't a hard slap, but it was enough to make him release her.

'What d'you do that for?' He looked shocked, but also angry, and for a moment the snarl on his lips and the cold fury in his eyes sent a wave of fear through her. Then his expression changed and he grinned at her. 'Dear, oh dear, you've got a temper and no mistake, Carina.'

'Is it any wonder? What were you thinking of?'

'Well – you, obviously. I've wanted to do that ever since the first time I saw you. And I'm a man that takes my chances.'

'Well please don't try to take them with me. You might have charmed Sally, though I wish to goodness you hadn't, but I'm not so easily won over. And I'm not so sure she's going to want anything more to do with you when I tell her . . .'

'But you won't, Carina, will you?'

'I most certainly will!'

'And I shall tell her you've been leading me on, making eyes at me when her back's turned. Which of us do you think she'll believe?'

Suddenly Carina wanted nothing more than for this obnoxious man to be out of her kitchen. Out of her house.

'I think it would be best if you were to pack your bags and leave, Frank,' she said.

He cocked his head to one side, still looking at her with that assured smirk.

'Are you sure about that, Mrs Talbot? I think you ought to have a word with your sister-in-law before you do anything too hasty.'

A frisson of alarm ran through Carina.

'What are you talking about?'

'You'd better ask her that. Perhaps it's just as well you did knock me back. Under the circumstances.'

With that, he strolled confidently to the door.

'What are you talking about?' Carina repeated.

He ignored her but for one last self-satisfied glance over his shoulder.

Carina stared after him, her heart in her mouth. *Oh please don't let him mean what I think he might mean . . .*

The nightmare scenario of a pregnant Sally flashed before her eyes, as it had done more than once since she had begun to suspect she was allowing Frank more liberties than she should. It would be a total disaster. At least, from what he had said, it didn't sound as if he was going to take off and leave her in the lurch, but Carina felt sure that would be only a matter of time. He was a chancer, a womaniser; in the long run he'd never make Sally happy, never settle down to family life, never be the stable influence a father should be on a child.

She only hoped she was wrong and that it was not too late to make Sally see sense. Warning her about Frank was sure to cause more friction between them, but Carina knew she had to try.

Her chance came that evening as she and Sally washed the dishes.

Supper had been an awkward meal, Carina horribly conscious of Frank, sitting opposite her at the kitchen table, and Sally quieter than usual to her now suspicious mind. But then she had been quiet ever since she'd found out that Grandpa Luke had left everything to Mattie and nothing whatever to her, and she had eaten every scrap of her rissole, even though it was a little charred around the edges.

Perhaps, please God, she'd misinterpreted what Frank had said. But she had to be sure, all the same, and she had to warn Sally what Frank was really like.

When the meal was over, Frank had gone outside to smoke one of the Woodbines she'd bought for him and the two girls were left alone.

Carina dunked dirty plates into a bowl of hot water and soap flakes, wondering how best to broach the subject. Really there was no ideal opening, so she decided that the only way was to take the bull by the horns.

'Are you all right, Sally?' she asked bluntly, turning to face her sister-in-law.

Sally frowned. 'What do you mean?'

'There's nothing you want to share with me?'

'What are you talking about?' Sally looked genuinely puzzled, and Carina's resolve faltered. Suddenly it seemed quite inappropriate to ask the question that had been tormenting her ever since her altercation this afternoon with Frank. But she'd gone this far; she could hardly stop now.

'I'm worried about you and Frank,' she said.

Sally scowled. 'Why?'

'Because the two of you seem to be getting very close. And I think you're going to end up getting hurt. He's a philanderer, Sally. He's taking advantage of you.'

'What makes you think that?' Sally's dark eyes were sparking, her tone sharp and aggressive.

'All sorts of things. He's not to be trusted. Look, it gives me no pleasure to say this, but you're not the only one he turns on the charm for. He's tried it with me, too. And this afternoon he came in here when I was on my own and tried to kiss me.'

For a moment Sally's face registered shock, then disbelief, then anger.

'You don't expect me to believe that? You're just jealous, Carina. You don't like seeing me happy with someone when you are on your own.'

'That's not true, and you know it. There's nothing I'd like better than for you to find someone to love you the way Robert loved me.'

'Frank does love me!' Sally countered. 'He's told me so.'

Carina shook her head sadly.

'Words are cheap, Sally, and I rather think Frank is a born liar.'

'And you think Robert wasn't?' Sally flared.

'Of course he wasn't. Robert couldn't tell a lie to save his life.'

'Well you're wrong there.' Sally had the bit between her teeth now in defence of Frank. 'I'm pretty sure he lied to me about what happened to our parents. And I expect he lied to you too.'

Carina started, all her unasked questions about Robert's family history rushing to the forefront of her mind.

'He would never talk to me about that,' she said.

'No? Well that's not surprising really. Either he wanted to forget, or he was ashamed. Both probably. He always maintained they died in an accident. But there was more to it than that, I'm sure of it.'

For a long moment, Sally was silent, and Carina waited, tingling now with apprehension.

When she spoke again, Sally's anger seemed to have burned itself out in a quick burst of flame like a Roman candle on Guy Fawkes night. Tears sparkled in her eyes, and she was wringing the tea cloth between her hands.

'I think something terrible happened. Mammy and Daddy used to have the most dreadful rows. I was only a little girl at the time, and it happened so often – Mammy screaming, things being broken – I thought it was just a part of normal life. But now I know that sort of thing isn't normal. I think Daddy would get drunk, lose his temper and take it out on Mammy. And one day things went too far. He wouldn't have meant to hurt her, of course. Not the Daddy I knew. But he was a big man, a docker, and he probably didn't know his own strength. I think he killed her. And then when he realised what he had done, perhaps he killed himself.'

'Oh Sally, that's terrible!'

Carina scarcely knew what to say. But little as she wanted to believe it, there was no denying it made sense. It would explain Robert's refusal to talk about his parents' deaths, and why he hated alcohol so. She could even believe that Joel might have killed himself in a fit of remorse.

'Did you never ask him outright what happened?'

Sally shook her head. 'No, more's the pity. I think there was a part of me that didn't really want to know.' She hesitated, then rushed on. 'You see, there was something else . . . Sometimes I wondered if there was another reason why Robert would never talk about what happened. I wasn't there that night – I was here, staying with Grandma and Grandpa. But Robert was. He'd have heard everything. And . . . Oh, I know it sounds crazy, but suppose he intervened? Walked in and found Mammy badly beaten, bleeding, unconscious . . . already dead . . . with Daddy standing over her? Suppose he went for Daddy with whatever was to hand? I think that was what I was most afraid of finding out if I asked too many questions . . . that Daddy didn't kill himself at all; Robert did.'

'Oh Sally, I'm sure that's not the case,' Carina said, shocked. 'He was only a boy. Thirteen, fourteen . . .'

'Strong, though. He'd been going to the gym to build himself up and to learn to box. I think now that the reason he did that was so that he could take on Daddy. Oh, I don't suppose he meant to kill him. Just get him off Mammy. But he hit him harder than he intended. Or perhaps Daddy fell and hit his head – that could have been it, or what he told the police anyway, and it's why he was never charged with anything. I think that's the real reason I never pressed him for the truth. I was too afraid. If that's what happened, I didn't want to know.'

'I'm sure you're wrong, Sally,' Carina said. 'Robert would never . . .'

'He had an awful temper when he was roused,' Sally went on. 'He got that from Daddy, I suppose.'

A shiver ran through Carina. She was remembering that last night, the way Sally had lied that she was the one who had been driving the Rover when it had damaged Cal's Benz, remembering how Robert had almost struck her, and remembering too the things Grandpa Luke had said. She could see him now, standing there in the kitchen doorway in his flannelette nightshirt, waving his stick at Robert: 'You'd better calm down, my lad, before someone gets hurt.' And then, to her: 'His father all over again. And see where that led.'

Oh, Sally was wrong. She must be.

'I can't believe that's the way it was, Sally,' she said. 'You've got to put such ideas right out of your head.'

'I only wish I could.' Sally's eyes were full of tears again. 'He was my brother, and I couldn't have wished for a better one. He always took good care of me. Always! I loved him so . . . and now he's gone . . .'

The tears spilled over and ran down her cheeks, and Carina's heart bled for her. No wonder she could be moody, no wonder she looked for love in all the wrong places. To have lost both her parents when she was so young and not to know what had really happened to them was bad enough, but to secretly harbour such terrible suspicions about her beloved brother, and then to lose him so tragically, was terrible. And now Grandpa, her last living blood relative, was gone too, the one person left who might have known the truth and could set her mind at rest . . .

'So please don't get on to me about Frank,' Sally said, wiping the tears away with her fingers. 'I know you don't like him, but . . .' She forced a small, wan smile. 'At least he didn't kill anyone.'

'No, I don't suppose he did,' Carina conceded.

There was no way now she could tell Sally just how aggressive Frank had been with her this afternoon, or that she dreaded to think what might have happened if she had not slapped him and brought him to his senses. And she certainly couldn't ask her if she was pregnant.

'Just be careful, Sally,' she said gently. 'The last thing you need is to get your heart broken. Or get yourself into trouble.'

'Frank *is* careful.'

Those three words confirmed all Carina's suspicions, but

again, she didn't think this was the time to lecture Sally about the possible consequences. And what notice would she take anyway?

A shadow fell across the window. Frank was coming back indoors.

'You'd better go and wash your face if you don't want him to see you've been crying,' she said.

Sally departed hastily and Carina returned to the washing-up. The water had gone stone cold now, but it would have to do. She couldn't be bothered to fill another kettle and wait for it to come to the boil. She felt too laden down, both by the things Sally had told her about Robert, and by her fears for her relationship with Frank.

But somehow life had to go on. And it was up to her to see that it did.

The letter was delivered next morning.

Carina, glancing out of the kitchen window, saw the postman cycling across the farmyard and went out to meet him. Getting mail was a rare occurrence; apart from letters from her parents, and the occasional bill, no one had occasion to write to them. Much to the relief of the poor postman, she imagined. Having to deliver to outlying farms couldn't be much fun, especially when the weather was bad – or hot, as it had been this summer.

'Do you want a cup of tea, Bias?' she asked.

The postman mopped his sweating brow.

'Better not, missus. Got to get on, but thanks all the same.'

He fished in his bag, which he wore slung around his neck, and pulled out an envelope. 'Here you are. Just the one.'

The envelope was foolscap, manilla. Not from her mother, then. Mam used blue writing paper and envelopes. And when she took it, Carina noticed that it was postmarked Hillsbridge.

Her heart gave a thud. The solicitor. It must be! She was glad now that Bias had declined her offer of tea – she couldn't wait to open it. Though of course it might very well be the bill, which she had no idea how she was going to pay . . .

She took the letter into the kitchen, sat down at the table and slit the envelope open with the bread knife. Mattie was clawing at her legs, reaching up for the knife.

'No, Mattie, you can't have that. It's sharp and you'd cut yourself.' She pushed it well back on the table, out of his reach.

'What's that?' Meg had abandoned her dolls and joined Mattie.

'It's a letter. For me. Nothing exciting. Just go back to your dolls' tea party, Meg.' But she hoisted Mattie up on to her knee before extracting the single sheet of paper.

As she had thought, the legend printed at the top of the page was 'Willoughby and Clarence', and the writing beneath, in jet-black ink, was sloping copperplate.

Dear Madam,

Further to your recent visit, I am pleased to inform you that Lord Melbrook has agreed to be named as a trustee of the estate of Luke Jeremiah Green deceased, and to assist in the management of the aforementioned Luke Jeremiah Green deceased's assets until such time as the beneficiary, Matthew James Talbot, shall become of age. I am presently preparing the necessary documentation, which will be signed and sealed on Lord Melbrook's return from the Continent.

'Oh!' Carina breathed. 'Oh Mattie, he hasn't refused!'
But there was more.

I further beg to inform you that Lord Melbrook has asserted his willingness to remunerate this firm with regard to any legal expenses incurred in the said trust, and there will therefore be no invoice forthcoming in this matter.

I remain,

Yours faithfully,

The letter was signed with a flourish 'Arthur Clarence', though as the writing differed slightly from the text, it was clear that the long-suffering clerk had been the one to pen the bulk of the missive.

'Oh!' Carina said again. She could scarcely believe it. Not only had Cal agreed to become a trustee, he was also offering to foot the bill! Why on earth would he do such a thing? Out of pity for her? Well, she certainly couldn't let him do it. Little as she could afford to pay the solicitor, her pride simply would not allow it. She'd write back to Mr Clarence and tell him so.

But for all that, the kindness of the gesture warmed her heart.

She decided she wouldn't mention the letter to Sally. It would only be rubbing salt in the wound, and Sally had been in one of her dark moods ever since their conversation yesterday. Mentioning Mattie's inheritance would only make things worse.

Carina was not the only one to notice that Sally seemed to have gone into herself.

'What's up with you?' Frank asked.

They were putting the finishing touches to the last hayrick – the casual labourers had all gone home, and they were alone.

'There's nothing wrong with me,' Sally snapped.

'Come off it. You've been like a bear with a sore head all day.' He tossed his pitchfork aside and reached for her.

'Get off!'

'Don't you fancy me any more?'

He made another grab for her, sweeping her off her feet and dumping her on top of a waist-high bale of hay. 'Come on, Sally, I reckon I've worked hard enough today to earn a kiss.'

She turned her face away.

'Is that what you said to Carina?'

'What?' He raised himself on his elbows, looking down at her, the picture of innocence.

'You tried to kiss her, didn't you?'

'Kiss Carina? Why would I want to do that when I've got you?'

'Well, she says you did.'

'Then she's telling porkies.'

'Are you sure?'

'Course I am! Kiss Carina?' He chortled scornfully. 'She's trying to turn you against me. She doesn't like me. Never has. You're not going to let her come between us, are you? She's jealous and bitter and spiteful, that's all.'

Ignoring Sally's doubtful expression, he bent over again, kissing her firmly on the mouth, and this time she didn't resist.

'See? We're good together, Sally. I'll show you how good.'

His hands were on the buttons of her blouse, undoing them one by one. She raised one of her own hands to stop him.

'You do love me, don't you, Frank?'

'Course I do.'

'And if something . . . happened, you wouldn't go off and leave me?'

'No chance. But nothing is going to happen. Trust me.'

She was weakening, he could tell.

'You're my girl, Sal.'

He kissed her again, harder and deeper, and now, when he

loosened the belt of her trousers, she didn't try to stop him.

But as he whispered sweet nothings in her ear, his mind was elsewhere. Things weren't really working out as he'd planned. He'd had to have a rethink, not once but twice. But he'd be damned if he'd give up now. He'd risked too much to let it all slip through his fingers.

Melting, Sally let him have his way. And when it was over, she was far too lost in a rosy glow to notice the triumphant gleam in his eyes.

Chapter Twenty-One

The very last place that Carina would have expected to encounter Cal Melbrook was Hillsbridge market.

Whereas in the old days Robert had taken Sally into town with the butter, cheese, eggs and bacon and collected her again later in the day, now mostly it was Carina who ran the stall. It seemed silly to make two journeys to Hillsbridge when one would do, and for some unfathomable reason, Sally seemed happy enough to be left at home minding the children while Carina went to the market. Perhaps because the elderly man who ran the toy stall just across the way had been paying her more attention than she was comfortable with, Carina thought. He did seem to be a bit of an old lecher.

That Saturday morning Carina had driven in as usual, parked the Rover as close as she could to the side entrance of the market hall – their stall was situated just inside – and set out her wares. As usual, business was brisk – Meadow Farm had a good reputation amongst the locals – and Carina had to work fast to keep up with the stream of customers.

She was just cutting a slab of cheese when she saw him sauntering down the aisle between the greengrocery stall and the one that sold all manner of novelties and knick-knacks, the shoppers moving respectfully aside for him so that his progress resembled that of an ocean liner carving its way through a channel of water. Carina was so startled, the cheese wire slipped and she almost cut her finger.

The queuing customers looked almost as startled as she was; there was a great deal of tugging of forelocks and some of the women bobbed a curtsey.

Lord Melbrook in the market, like any Tom, Dick or Harry! Unheard of!

Cal, however, seemed completely oblivious to the stir he was causing. When he reached Carina's stall, he stood to one side while she finished serving the customer and motioned to the next one, who was all prepared to let him jump the queue, to carry on. Flustered, Carina wrapped cheese and a pat of golden yellow butter, totalling up the cost with a blunt stub of pencil on the corner of the greaseproof paper because she didn't trust herself to do it in her head with him watching.

At last the queue diminished and no new customers joined it. They were hanging back, unwilling to approach with Lord Melbrook there, Carina guessed.

'You're not doing my business any good,' she greeted him, her heart hammering and the heat creeping up her neck beneath the high collar of her blouse.

Cal was smiling. 'Don't worry, I won't stay long. I just wanted a word, and I thought I might find you here.'

'I'm usually here on a Saturday.' She glanced around and lowered her voice. 'I heard from the solicitor. Thank you so much for agreeing to be a trustee of Grandpa's will . . .'

'My pleasure.'

'. . . but I can't possibly let you foot the bill. It's very kind of you, but—'

'Let's not argue about it here. The reason I wanted to see you

284

was to enquire if you are still able to make the drapes for my mother's sitting room.'

'Oh! Oh yes . . . of course.'

'Then perhaps we could go to Bath to choose the fabric one day next week?'

'Oh, yes . . . if that's what you want . . .'

'Good. We can talk about all the other matters then. Which day would suit you?'

'Any, really.'

'Then shall we say Tuesday? I'll come and collect you at about ten.'

'All right.' She felt heady, breathless; she must sound like the village idiot. What on earth was wrong with her?

He smiled at her. 'Till Tuesday, then.' And with that he was gone, taking the short exit route this time through the side door.

Desperate to collect herself, Carina wiped her hands, greasy from the cheese and also, she rather thought, from perspiration, on the big white apron tied around her middle, and busied herself wiping down the slab.

'Well, Carina Talbot, I never did!'

She spun round at the sound of the familiar voice.

'Aunt Hester.'

Hester Dallimore didn't often come all the way to Hillsbridge to shop, but it seemed she'd chosen today of all days to visit her niece's stall – and managed to arrive just as Lord Melbrook was there talking to her too.

'Hobnobbing with the gentry! Whatever next!'

Hester was wearing the satisfied expression she couldn't help when she happened upon a juicy piece of gossip. And this, to her mind, was gold dust, Carina guessed. She'd be boasting to all the neighbours for days that her niece had been engaged in a private conversation with his lordship.

'I wasn't hobnobbing,' Carina said.

'Well, I didn't see him buying anything.'

'I do sewing for him,' Carina said defensively. She could feel the flush in her neck beginning again. 'What can I get you, Aunt Hester?'

'Oh, I'll have a bit of cheese. Not too much – I've got to carry it all the way back home.' But she hadn't finished yet with the subject of Lord Melbrook. 'Sewing, is it? What sort of sewing? You don't make his trousers, I hope.'

She looked ready to be scandalised by the prospect of Carina taking intimate measurements.

'Of course I don't,' Carina said shortly. 'I'm a seamstress, not a tailor.'

A queue had begun to form again.

'Look, I'm sorry, Aunt Hester, but I need to get on.'

'Huh! Well, of course *I'm* not gentry,' Hester huffed.

Carina ignored the jibe. Aunt Hester was Aunt Hester and always would be. She'd never change. How did she and Mam come to be sisters? Carina had often wondered. But just now she had other things on her mind. As well as a queue of customers to serve.

The Benz pulled into the farmyard at one minute to ten precisely. Carina was ready and waiting; she'd guessed that Cal would be a stickler for punctuality, and in any case she was spurred on by a restless eagerness that seemed to prickle in her veins and tremble in her stomach.

'He's here!' she called to Sally as she opened the door.

Meg, who had been changing her doll's dress, jumped up and ran outside, and Mattie began to scuttle after her on all fours. Carina scooped him up before he could get over the doorstep and skin his knees, but she wasn't quick enough to stop Meg running right up to the motor, where she came to an abrupt halt, gazing up at Cal in open curiosity.

'Hello. You must be Meg,' he said, taking off the dark goggles he was wearing.

Overcome by sudden shyness, Meg dipped her head.

'I'm sorry,' Carina said. 'Say good morning to Lord Melbrook, Meg.'

Meg glanced up at him from beneath her lashes, but remained silent.

'I'm sorry,' Carina said again. Why did she keep apologising? 'Come on, Meg, don't be so rude.'

'It's all right, Meg,' Cal told the little girl. 'That's a very pretty doll you have there. What's her name?'

'Elsie,' Meg muttered, picking at the doll's skirt.

'Well, make sure you look after Elsie while your mother is out. I'm taking her to Bath, but she'll be back by lunchtime.'

A puzzled frown puckered Meg's face.

'She thinks you mean by the time she has a biscuit and a glass of milk, which will be pretty soon. What you call lunch, we call dinner,' Carina said, embarrassed by the differences in terminology that highlighted the social chasm between them.

Cal, however, seemed unfazed.

'Ah. By dinner time then, Meg. And this,' he said, turning to the chubby little boy in Carina's arms, 'must be Mattie.'

Carina smoothed a curl off his forehead.

'Yes, this is Mattie. Really, I can't thank you enough for agreeing to act as a trustee until he's old enough to take responsibility for his own affairs.'

Cal smiled slightly.

'I'm flattered you should think of me. And, as I said before, it's my pleasure.'

'But as for paying the solicitor's fees – I couldn't possibly let you do that. It's very kind of you, but—'

'Can you afford them?'

'That's not the point.'

'Just swallow your pride for a moment, Carina, and admit you're struggling.'

'Well . . . yes, we are. But . . .'

'Look on it as a loan. When you're back on your feet, you can pay me back. How does that sound to you?'

She still didn't like it. 'Neither a borrower nor a lender be' had been one of Mam's endless supply of maxims, and Carina thought it was a good one to live by. But she had worried about how she was going to pay the solicitor, and how big the bill would be. Fairly large, she imagined. And almost every penny piece of their income was spoken for.

'Well . . . if you're sure, but I shall pay you back just as soon as I can. I don't like being in debt to anybody.'

Mattie was wriggling in her arms, and Meg, growing impatient, was tugging at her skirts.

'Perhaps we ought to be on our way,' Cal said. 'The children aren't coming with us, I take it?'

'Oh no, my sister-in-law is going to look after the two of them while I'm gone.'

She glanced back at the house. Sally was standing in the doorway but making no move to come over and collect the children, unwilling, Carina guessed, to have to engage in an exchange with the gentry.

'I'll just hand Mattie over to her,' she said. 'Come on, Meg. Say goodbye to Lord Melbrook.'

Still Meg remained mute, but she did glance back over her shoulder as her mother led her by the hand to where Sally was waiting.

'Be good for your Auntie Sally,' Carina told the two children, before hurrying back to the Benz.

Cal had got out and opened the door on the passenger side for her. As he handed her up, a thrill tingled in her veins. Why was it he had this effect on her?

'They're beautiful children,' he said easily as he climbed back up into the driver's seat. 'You must be very proud of them.'

'I am.' She felt on safer ground now. 'Meg can be a bit of a handful, but she's a good girl really. And Mattie . . . well, he's the image of his father,' she said, somehow spurred to mention Robert, as if the frisson of attraction she felt towards Cal was a betrayal of her late husband.

'That must be hard for you,' Cal said.

'Yes, but I'm glad of it all the same. It means . . .' She broke off, unable to say what she felt – that Mattie's likeness to Robert meant that it was as if she still had something of him.

'He lives on,' Cal finished quietly for her.

'Yes.'

They drove on in silence for a while, the breeze cooling Carina's hot cheeks and neck.

At the bottom of the long descent into Hillsbridge, a hearse drawn by four black horses was pulling up at the steps to the high pavement that led to the church. Carina's heart came into her mouth; she'd seen more than enough funerals in recent months to last her a lifetime. Cal slowed to a crawl to pass it so as not to frighten the horses, and though she didn't want to look, her eyes were drawn towards the ornate vehicle, designed like a stagecoach, with turrets at each corner and velvet-curtained windows through which she could glimpse a black coffin. She couldn't help contrasting it with the simple wooden boxes that had taken both Robert and Grandpa to their last resting places, on a farm cart pulled by one plodding horse.

'Ridley Reeves,' Cal said, naming the well-to-do owner of one of the local wagon works. 'A stroke, I believe.'

Carina was silent, and he added: 'Death is no respecter of wealth and position, Carina. But now, let's turn to more cheerful things. Are you ready for me to open up the Benz and show you what she can do?'

'Not here in Hillsbridge!' Carina gasped, horrified.

'Hardly. Once we get through the town.'

With an effort, Carina pushed her sad thoughts to the back of her mind. It wasn't often she was relieved of responsibility and had the freedom to enjoy herself. She mustn't let the opportunity slip through her fingers.

'I'm ready,' she said recklessly.

The streets of Bath were busy. Cal found a place to park in leafy Queen Square, where the trees were beginning to turn red, gold and ochre for autumn, and glanced at Carina sitting beside him. Her cheeks were flushed, her eyes sparkling, and some locks of hair had come loose, curling about her face. It was good to see her looking happy for a change.

'Did you enjoy that?' he asked unnecessarily.

'I did,' she admitted. 'It's not at all like our poor Rover.'

'Well I'm sorry, but I'm not going to offer to let you drive her,' he said, smiling. 'I'm afraid you'll have to put up with riding with me.'

'I wouldn't dream of it!'

'Riding with me?'

'No, of course not. Me trying to drive the Benz. I know my limitations!'

'I'm glad to hear it. Now, shall we go and look for some suitable fabric for my mother's drapes?'

He climbed out and went around to help her down. Her hand

felt slightly rough and dry in his. Not at all the way Alice's had once felt – hard work had taken its toll. But for all that . . .

He glanced down at the wedding ring on her finger. The same finger where her precious engagement ring had once sat. He'd very much like to be able to give it back to her. Even more . . .

He cut off the thought that had popped unbidden into his head.

It wasn't ever a good idea to mix business with pleasure. He'd heard that somewhere, and it had the ring of truth. Cal thought that whatever his inclinations might be, it should be a maxim he took heed of.

Although she was a seamstress, Carina had never seen so many fabrics together at any one time. The basement room was stacked full of them, piled high and end to end. She felt a moment's panic. How on earth was she going to select one of them? Where to start? And why on earth had Cal thought for one moment that she was capable of such a thing? Last time it had been his friend Isobel who had made the selection – and chosen perfectly. Surely if Cal was back from France, she must be too? And if so, why hadn't he enlisted her help again?

'I'm not sure I'm the right person . . .' she began.

'Is madam in need of some assistance?'

A woman had approached them; in her pristine white blouse and black skirt, her hair piled elegantly on top of her head, she was every bit as daunting as the stacks of fabric. Carina wasn't sure how to reply, but luckily Cal stepped into the breach.

'We're looking for fabric for drapes for a small sitting room.'

'As you can see, we have a splendid selection.' The shop assistant spoke with pride, for all the world as if she were the owner of the shop and the impressive display. 'What colour did madam have in mind?'

'Carina?'

'What's your mother's favourite colour?' she asked him desperately.

'I'm not sure she has one. But I think she favours florals.'

'Then allow me to show you some. If you would care to follow me . . .'

The assistant glided off along the aisle, stopping now and then to pull out a bolt of fabric and let a length fall from shelf to floor. Some were flamboyant, with overblown roses, some covered with small delicate designs with no more than an inch between the repeat patterns. Carina tried to picture Lady Melbrook's sitting room. She'd been in there only once or twice, but she rather fancied the drapes had been heavy and dark. Though winter was coming, it would be nice to choose something that would make the room lighter and more airy, perhaps bring something of the garden indoors. But which one?

'If madam likes green . . .' The assistant loosened a length of printed cotton with a design of formally sculpted bay trees on a mottled ground.

'That's very nice,' Carina said.

'The Liberty Anton,' the saleswoman informed her. 'And this is the Liberty Fawley. Also one of the very newest additions to our range.'

The moment she draped the fabric, Carina was in no doubt whatsoever. Clusters of daisies and poppies, single tulips and snowdrops, all in delicate shades of pink, green and a soft red, were set against a white background, the softly curving leafy stems between them palest blue. She loved it on sight, and knew it would be perfect for the little sitting room.

'That one,' she said without hesitation.

'And how much does madam require?'

Cal extracted a notebook from the pocket of his jacket.

'I have the measurements of the window here.'

They followed the superior saleswoman to a counter, where she deposited the roll of fabric and summoned a much younger and rather harassed-looking assistant.

'Miss Jones will look after you now.' She turned a stern gaze on the junior. 'Be sure to get the measurements correct, Miss Jones.' With that she stalked away.

Carina immediately warmed to the girl, who appeared very nervous.

'I'm sure you'll get it right,' she said by way of encouragement.

As the girl measured and blocked the fabric, Carina was suddenly aware of someone close behind her.

'An excellent choice! Your little seamstress has taste, Cal.'

She looked round. Isobel Luckington was standing there, even more supercilious and intimidating than the senior saleswoman.

'Isobel!'

But Cal didn't actually appear that surprised to see her, and Carina suspected he had told her what he had arranged and what time they were likely to be in the store. That suggested that not only had he been in contact with Isobel since Saturday – a thought that made Carina prickle with unreasonable jealousy – but also that despite what he had said, he didn't entirely trust Carina to make the right choice. Nervous as she had been about her own ability to do just that, the confirmation of it still stung.

Yet here was the sophisticated woman of the world actually approving her decision! She didn't much care for being referred to as Cal's 'little seamstress', though.

She lifted her chin, determined not to let Isobel think she was intimidated by her.

'I'm glad you like it,' she said as coolly as she could manage, 'and I hope Lady Melbrook likes it too.'

Isobel merely smiled by way of reply, though her slightly arched brows suggested amusement.

'So – are you taking Mrs Talbot for lunch at the Francis?' she asked Cal. 'If so, perhaps I might join you.'

'No, we're going straight home,' Cal said. 'Mrs Talbot is anxious to get back to her children.'

'Ah yes, of course.' The same patronising smile. But Carina breathed a silent sigh of relief. The very idea of eating with the gentry in a grand hotel was a terrifying one. There would be a mystifying array of cutlery and glassware, she felt sure, and she wouldn't have the first idea as to which she was supposed to use. At least she knew how to hold a knife and fork properly – Mam had been very particular about that, along with other basic table manners – but as to the niceties of fine dining . . . she wouldn't know what to order, and supposing the menu was in French?

'Your children must be very important to you since you lost your husband,' Isobel went on.

'They always have been,' Carina replied defensively.

'I'm sure. But in the light of all the tragedies . . . Your husband's grandfather has died in dreadful circumstances too, I understand.'

'Yes.' Carina didn't want to go into details. She felt sure Cal must have already told Isobel all about what had happened.

'And your husband's parents . . . are they not able to assist?'

'They are both dead,' Carina said. 'They died when Robert and his sister Sally were children. That's the reason they came to live at the farm.'

'Dear me! It does seem your family is cursed.'

Carina said nothing, but the words struck home. It was much what she had thought recently, and told herself not to be silly. She was surprised, too, at Isobel's interest in her family's affairs.

She would have thought the lives of humble farm folk would have been far beneath her.

'Well, you must come to Bath again soon,' Isobel was saying to Cal. 'I've missed you, Calvert, since we returned from the Continent.'

'Flattering, Isobel, but patently untrue. You're hardly short of male company.'

'But there are no friends like old friends, are there?' She laid a gloved hand on his arm in a manner that looked to Carina to be much more than merely friendly, and the imp of jealousy taunted her again before she firmly drove it away.

'I'll see you soon, Isobel.'

'Make sure you do.'

With that she glided away.

The purchase was ready, packed neatly in brown paper. The amount of fabric was much less than what had been required for the drawing room drapes; no need to have it delivered this time.

Cal tucked it under his arm and they made their way back to Queen Square, passing the vast and impressive frontage of the Francis Hotel. Through the windows that looked out on to the street Carina glimpsed formally set dining tables – white napery, silver and crystal, just as she had imagined – and thanked her lucky stars Cal had not suggested they dine there.

But why would he? She was, after all, just his little seamstress, as Isobel had so disparagingly referred to her. Such a thing would never have entered his head, and Isobel had just been being unpleasantly mischievous when she'd asked if he was taking her there.

Back in the Benz, however, driving through the city streets, she couldn't help but feel a moment's pride.

Maybe she wasn't of a class to dine at a grand hotel, but here she was riding in state like a lady. And being treated almost as an equal by a man who not only owned half of Dunderwick, but was also handsome and charming. Mam and Dad would scarcely believe it if they could see her now. And Robert . . . what would Robert think?

A shard of guilt punctured the balloon of satisfaction and pleasure. Oh, he'd be proud of her for soldiering on, keeping things going in the only way she could. But as for the thoughts she sometimes had about Cal, as for being happy in his company and accepting his favours, that was a different matter entirely.

Much as she loved to think that Robert was still with her, watching over her, she hoped that at this moment he was not able to read her thoughts or see inside her heart.

'So will you come over to Dunderwick House to sew the drapes as you did before?' Cal asked as they turned into the farmyard.

'Well . . . yes, provided Sally is able to mind the children. But I know there's a batch of cheese that needs pressing, so she'll be busy with that, and I don't like them in the cheese loft. And a couple of our cows are due to calve soon.'

'In that case, why don't you bring them with you?' he suggested. 'I'm sure one of the maids could be spared to keep an eye on them. Besides, Cleo has just had a litter of puppies. I expect they'd like to see them.'

'Oh my goodness, I'm sure they would!' Carina remembered thinking Cleo had put on weight the last time she had seen her. 'How old are they?'

'They were born while I was in France, so it will be a few weeks yet before I find homes for them.'

'They must be adorable.'

'They are. And luckily Cleo is a very good mother. So,' he gave her a questioning look, 'that's settled, then? When you come, you'll bring Meg and Mattie with you?'

'If you're sure . . .'

'Yes. But perhaps it would be best to leave it until next week. I'm going to be out and about a lot in the next few days, and I would like the opportunity to get to know the little boy I'm going to be acting for as trustee.'

The kitchen door was open; Meg came rushing out.

'Mammy! Mammy! Did you buy anything for me?'

Inevitably, Mattie was not far behind, but as his knees encountered the rough ground, he stopped and to Carina's surprise pulled himself up by the doorpost to a standing position. He took a couple of staggering steps before tumbling over.

'He walked!' she gasped. 'At last! He actually walked!'

She ran towards her son, who had begun to cry, whether from frustration or pain she didn't know, and scooped him up in her arms.

When she had finished comforting him and congratulating him and turned around again, the Benz and Cal had gone.

Cal had not long reached home when the telephone rang. It was Isobel.

'Is your little seamstress there with you?' she enquired.

'No, of course not. I've taken her back to Meadow Farm. Why do you ask?'

'I just wanted to be sure. Cal, I was being perfectly serious when I said I hoped to see you soon. There's something I have to tell you. Something I think you should know.'

'About Carina?' Cal was mystified.

'About her husband's family. When could you come to Bath again?'

'I'm very busy this week.' As he had mentioned to Carina, he had a lot of estate business to attend to; things had been allowed to slide while he was away. 'Can't you tell me whatever it is over the telephone?'

'I'd really prefer not. It's rather a delicate subject.'

Her insistence annoyed Cal. Isobel expected everyone to be at her beck and call, doing her bidding, with no consideration for their commitments. But he knew her well enough to know that trying to change her mind would be a waste of breath, and she had aroused his curiosity.

'Very well. I'll see what I can do. It won't be tomorrow – I've already made arrangements to visit some of the tenant farmers. But perhaps towards the end of the week.'

'Not until then?'

'If this was really urgent, you would tell me over the telephone,' he said, determined not to be bulldozed into changing his plans, curious as he might be about what she wanted to tell him. 'I'm sure it will keep for a few days.'

Isobel huffed. 'I would have thought you'd be anxious to hear what I have to say, given the interest you seem to have taken in your Mrs Talbot.'

He ignored the jibe. 'I'll give you a call when I've broken the back of what I have to do here.'

But as he replaced the telephone receiver in its ornate stand, he had to admit he *was* eager to know what on earth Isobel could be talking about. And wondering whether whatever it was might have implications for his plans.

Chapter Twenty-Two

Carina was in the kitchen, elbow deep in preparing bottled fruit and making jam and chutney. There had been a bumper harvest this year, and she was surrounded by baskets and bins of plums, pears and apples, which would turn rotten if she didn't get them dealt with soon. Just as well Cal had told her to delay starting work on the new drapes until next week – Sally was too busy with the cheese and butter to help, and in any case Carina thought she'd soon tire of peeling apples and pears, chopping onions and stoning plums.

With a pan of chutney simmering on the stove and the fire stoked up beneath the oven to sterilise the Kilner jars for the bottled plums, the heat in the kitchen was almost unbearable and making the children fractious. Carina had closed the door and windows to try and keep out the wasps, which were attracted to the smell of fermenting fruit, yet still they somehow managed to get in, and she was growing worried that either Meg or Mattie was going to get stung. Meg had the sense to be afraid of them, but her wildly flapping arms when one came near her were bound to make it angry, while Mattie was more than likely to put one in his mouth if he saw it crawling on an overripe plum.

She picked up Mattie's wooden horse on wheels, which he

had been tottering round the kitchen with, and took it to the door.

'Go and play outside for a bit, children,' she said. 'I don't want you getting stung.'

Mattie toddled after her, but as usual Meg proved obstinate.

'Elsie wants to stay in here and help you make jam.'

'Well she can't. You can give her a ride on Mattie's horse instead.'

As she emerged from the kitchen with Meg still whining and complaining, she was annoyed to see Frank sitting on the bench she still thought of as Grandpa's, smoking a cigarette. Was it her imagination, or was he not working as hard as he had in the beginning.

'Having trouble?' he asked insolently.

Carina ignored him, but Meg ran to him, her face brightening.

'Will you play with us, Frank?'

'Oh, I don't know what your mam would say about that, Miss Meg . . .' He gave Carina a sly look.

'Please!' Meg had spied Mattie's pushchair, which had been left outside the kitchen door, and dumped her doll into it, bustling with importance. 'We can take Elsie for a walk. She'd like that.'

'Okey-dokey. If that's all right with you, Carina.' He flicked away the butt of his cigarette and looked at her challengingly.

Carina hesitated. She didn't like the idea, but he'd made it very awkward for her to refuse, and he had always been good with the children, especially Meg. She'd most likely kick off again if Carina said no, and Carina really didn't want to have to cope with that.

'All right,' she said grudgingly. 'But don't go too far. Meg – pick up Elsie so I can put Mattie in his pushchair.'

Meg scowled. 'Elsie wants to ride!'

'She can ride on Mattie's lap.' Carina moved the doll herself, passing her to Meg, and lifted a protesting Mattie into the seat. In the last few days his walking skills had improved immeasurably, as if he'd known all the time how to do it and just chosen not to, and now he was eager to practise at every opportunity.

'No! No!' he yelled, squirming and going red in the face.

His flailing arms knocked Meg's precious Elsie out of her arms. Luckily Frank managed to catch her before she fell to the ground, but Meg, beside herself with rage, gave Mattie's leg a sharp slap, making him scream all the louder.

'Meg, you naughty girl!' At the end of her tether, Carina's fingers itched to give Meg a taste of her own medicine, but she restrained herself. 'I've told you before, you do not hit your little brother!'

'He's annoying.'

'That's as maybe, but you still don't hit him.'

'Come on, princess. No harm done.' Frank passed the doll back to Meg and took the handles of the pushchair.

'Don't worry, they'll be fine, both of them,' he said over his shoulder to Carina.

Carina watched them out of the yard, still feeling anxious in spite of the evidence of her own eyes, and went back into the kitchen.

In her absence, a whole swarm of wasps had got in through the open door. She managed to shoo some out and squash a few others against the window pane with a matchbox, but there was no way she could deal with all of them. Resigned, she put a spoonful of jam into an empty jar, filled it with water and put on the windowsill, hoping – rather vainly – that they might be attracted to that and drown. Then she covered the pan of chutney with a lid to make sure none came to a sticky end – boiled wasp was not an ingredient anyone would favour – and went back to stoning the plums and covering them with syrup.

It wasn't long, however, before the inevitable happened. As she unloaded the sterilised jars from the oven, one of the dozy creatures, drunk perhaps on plum juice, got caught in the folds of her tea cloth and stung her on the wrist. She yelped, and dropped a jar, which smashed on the flagged floor. By the time she'd found the blue bag to put on her wrist and swept up the broken glass, the chutney was beginning to catch and burn on the sides of the pan.

Quite suddenly, it was all too much for her, and hot, helpless tears stung her eyes. Why couldn't anything go right? She was tired, so tired, of struggling to keep everything going, tired of feeling exhausted, tired of worrying, tired of being alone. Oh don't be so pathetic! she scolded herself, but it did no good. The tears still came, blinding her so that she was seeing everything through a haze.

And then she heard a car turning in to the farmyard. She looked out of the window and her heart sank. Cal. What was he doing here? Oh, she couldn't let him see her like this!

Hastily she blew her nose and dashed some cold water on her face. By now he was out of the car and at the back door; there was nothing for it but to go and open it.

'I wasn't expecting you!' Her voice was croaky from crying.

Cal could see at a glance that she was not herself.

'What's wrong?' he asked, concerned.

'Oh – nothing. I just got stung by a wasp, that's all.'

'Not again! You must be a magnet for them.'

'And I've burned the chutney, and broken a Kilner jar, and the children have been playing up and I've let Frank take them for a walk against my better judgement and . . . well, I'm just feeling a bit sorry for myself.'

'Oh, Carina! Do you want me to go?'

'No. Come in. I'm all right really, and I'm sure the children will be fine. Would you like a cup of tea or something?'

'Only if you're making one.'

'What about a glass of lemonade? I made some fresh this morning.'

'That sounds nice.'

She fetched the jug, covered with a square of muslin to keep out the flies, and poured two glasses.

'Delicious,' he said. 'I should let you have some of my lemons. They're ripening nicely.'

'That would be lovely.' She sipped the lemonade, cool from being kept on the marble slab in the larder, tart and sweet at the same time. 'So why are you here? If you want me to start on the drapes tomorrow, I don't think I can. I'm snowed under here at the moment.'

Cal hesitated. Curious to know what it was Isobel had been so anxious to share with him but been unwilling to over the telephone, he'd been to see her this morning, and what she had told him had shocked him. It was something he should talk to Carina about without delay, he'd thought, but under the circumstances now really didn't seem like the right moment. She might already be aware of the situation, of course, but if she wasn't . . . The last thing he wanted to do was cause her more distress when she was clearly at the end of her tether.

'I was passing and I thought I'd drop in,' he said.

To his ears it sounded unconvincing, but Carina seemed to accept it, reaching for the blue bag and dabbing it absently on her wrist between sips of lemonade.

'After all, I do feel a certain responsibility, since I'm now a trustee for the future owner of the farm,' he added.

To his surprise, tears welled in her eyes.

303

'What is it?' he asked. 'What have I said?'

She gulped, shaking her head slightly. Then:

'It's just all wrong. Oh, I'm glad Mattie's going to inherit, of course. And I'm really grateful to you for agreeing to be a trustee. But it should have been Robert. He worked so hard on this place, and now he'll never see it come to fruition. He's gone, and I can't bear it.'

'Oh Carina, it's hard, I know.'

'How could you?' She looked up at him, eyes blazing through the tears. 'How could you possibly know how hard it is?'

'Believe me, I do. I lost someone very dear to me. A young lady.' He saw her eyes widen slightly and he smiled ruefully.

'I suppose, like everyone else, you think I am a confirmed bachelor, but it wasn't always so. If Alice had lived, she'd be my wife now and my life would be very different. Oh, I might still have ended up inheriting the estate – as I believe I told you once before, my brother was always hell-bent on self-destruction. But I don't suppose I'd have joined the army. I wouldn't have wanted to leave her alone while I was fighting overseas, or risk leaving her a widow and any children we might have had fatherless. In fact, her death was one of the reasons I took the King's shilling – or the Queen's, as it was in those days. I thought it might help me to get over her loss.'

Carina scarcely knew what to say. For the moment, all her own troubles and worries were forgotten.

'And did it help?' she asked.

Cal shrugged his shoulders.

'Who knows? I suppose to a certain extent it did. It certainly gave me something to focus on. It's hard to wallow in self-pity when your men are dying all around you and you're fighting to stay alive yourself, no matter that previously you thought you didn't care whether you lived or died. Time, I suppose, is the real healer, just as they say. The pain of loss never goes away, but it does lessen. Nobody can go on living in that first intense grief for ever. But it doesn't mean you forget. I still lay flowers on Alice's grave, at Christmas and Easter and on her birthday. That was the reason my motor was parked where it was that day you managed to collide with it. It was Alice's birthday.'

'Oh dear, I'm so sorry . . .'

She understood now why he had been so angry. If he'd been visiting the grave of his lost love on what should have been her birthday, he would have been raw, all his emotions laid bare.

It was still hard to believe that this strong, confident, undoubtedly privileged man had suffered as she was suffering. Hard to believe that all these years he had lived with an ache of loss so deep, so life-changing. And yet, looking at him now, she did believe it. It was written in every line of his face, and in his eyes, narrowed as if he was seeing something – someone – he would never in reality see again. The scar stood out, pale and ridged, between the corner of his eye and his mouth, and suddenly she wanted to reach out and touch it. Explore the lines and furrows, run her fingertips across that full, hard mouth. The tears that glistened still in her eyes were not now only for herself and for Robert, but also for Cal, who had lived all these years with that same empty place in his heart.

As if sensing her gaze on his face, he looked up from the glass he had been turning round and round in his hands, and as their eyes met, something sharp and sweet twisted inside her. Then he took a long swig of lemonade and the moment passed.

'It will get better, Carina, I promise,' he said.

The rip tides of her emotions seemed to be splitting her in two. She wanted to believe him, and she didn't. She wanted to have days, hours even, when the weight of grief dragged her down like an invisible ball and chain, and she didn't, because to be relieved of grief was to betray Robert's memory. She'd wanted to touch Cal's face, and wanted his touch too, and that was the greatest betrayal of all.

'Well, I dare say I'd better be going so that you can get on with your jam making,' Cal said.

'I suppose I should, or it'll be time to make the children's tea,' she replied, reluctant to see him go, yet at the same time wanting to be alone with her thoughts.

'I'll see you next week then, shall I?' he said as they stood in the doorway.

'Yes.'

'And you'll bring Meg and Mattie? The puppies are growing fast and I'm sure they'd like to see them while they're still small.'

'Yes, I'll bring them.'

'On second thoughts, perhaps I should collect you. Two little ones in a motor might be a distraction.'

Tempting as the offer was, Carina didn't think it was a good idea. In fact, any proximity to Cal was a very bad idea, given the way he made her feel.

'We'll be fine.'

'If you're sure?'

'Quite sure.'

And then he was gone. Carina watched him drive out of the farmyard and went back to her chutney and jam, alone at last with her turbulent emotions.

She was not the only one experiencing conflict and confusion. As he drove home, Cal found he was unable to get Carina out of his head.

What was it about her, he wondered, that made him talk to her about things he never discussed with anyone? Once upon a time he'd opened up somewhat to Isobel, but not for a long time now. He'd sensed her impatience with the subject of Alice; she firmly believed that he should put the past behind him and move on. And in any case, he wasn't one to lay his emotions bare, though they ran all the deeper for it.

Of course, in a way he and Carina were kindred spirits, both having suffered devastating losses. But all the same . . .

Back there in her kitchen, he'd wanted nothing more than to take her in his arms. He'd even found himself wanting to kiss her. In all the years since Alice's death, he'd never felt quite as he felt now.

Cal swore to himself and stamped down hard on the accelerator pedal.

Just his bloody luck that after all this time he should find himself attracted to someone clearly out of reach. Someone who was highly unlikely to reciprocate his feelings. Someone who had only recently lost the husband she had clearly adored. Forget her! he told himself. Forget her, and concentrate on sorting out the bloody estate and all the problems that came with it.

But he had the feeling it wasn't going to be that easy.

Carina popped a circle of greaseproof paper on to the last jar of chutney and glanced at the clock. Past five! Where had the afternoon gone? And why wasn't Frank back with the children? She'd thought he'd grow tired of looking after them and be back ages ago!

A shard of anxiety, a sixth sense almost, pricked her. She dumped the chutney pan in the sink to soak – how she was ever going to get all those sticky burned bits off she didn't know – and took off her apron. She'd go out and look for them.

As she crossed the farmyard, she half expected them to

appear around the corner of the outbuildings, but there was no sign of them. Cymru was sitting outside the milking shed, where Sally was working her way steadily along a row of cows patiently waiting to be made comfortable. Carina popped her head around the door.

'Did you see Frank and the children when you were getting the cows in?' The herd had recently been moved from the field adjoining the farmyard to fresh pasture beyond the hay fields.

'Yes – they were down by the river,' Sally replied without looking up from her task.

The river marked the boundary between Meadow Farm and Low Combe, just as a row of trees and hedges delineated the end of their land and the beginning of High Combe on the one side and Rookery Farm on the other. The broad meadow leading down to it had been divided into two by a barbed wire fence. It sloped gently at first and then steeply, and as a harvest there would be difficult, they used it as fresh grazing when the fields closer to home had been cropped bare. The cows must have been in the further section, Carina realised. If they had been in the part nearer to the gate, they would have clustered there waiting, and Sally wouldn't have been able to see Frank and the children, as they would have been hidden from view by the overhanging ridge.

She was surprised that he had taken them there. She would have thought he would have kept to the road or well-worn paths rather than manoeuvring the pushchair down the steep part of the field.

'By the river? Are you sure it was them?'

'Well it certainly looked like Meg running about. And how many men would be out with children in the middle of the afternoon? I was a bit surprised, though, I must say. I mean, I know he's fond of Meg, but he hasn't got much time for Mattie. How did you persuade him to take them out?'

'It was Meg's doing, not mine. And truth to tell. I'm not happy about it.' Her tone was sharp, mainly because her anxiety was growing.

She left Sally to her milking and hurried down the drive. She considered cutting across country, but the stubble left from haymaking in the fields she'd have to cross would cut her indoor shoes to ribbons, and Frank would never come back that way with the pushchair. He'd be sure to come along the road, and she didn't want to miss them.

By the time she reached the gate leading into the field, they had still not appeared. Sally had left it open to make it easier to herd the cows back in again. Carina hurried through, picking her way across the humps and ruts where dozens of hooves passing back and forth twice daily had churned up the mud before it had dried out in the sun, and stepping over the big smelly dollops of fresh manure. She still couldn't see Frank and the children, though she could make out the pushchair, abandoned in the middle of the field.

She was just negotiating the last bit of the field, tiered like an amphitheatre, when Frank's head appeared over the ridge. A moment later, Meg, too, came into view, scrambling up. But no Mattie. Where was he? He wasn't big enough to climb up that steep ridge on his own; Frank would have to carry him. But he wasn't.

Alarmed, she began to run, her ankles twisting painfully on the grassy tussocks. Meg, at the top of the steep ridge now, was heading towards her up the field as fast as her little legs would carry her.

'Mammy! Oh Mammy! We've lost Mattie!'

Panic made Carina's heart thump and her pulse race.

Jennie Felton

'What do you mean, you've lost Mattie?'

'I was making daisy chains for Elsie. I didn't know he'd gone . . .'

'Gone? Gone where?' Frank had reached them now. 'Where's Mattie? What's happened to him?'

'God knows. One minute he was there and the next he'd gone.'

'How could you lose him?' she screamed at him. 'He can't be far. He's only a little boy.'

'He can move like greased lightning when he wants to, though.'

She whirled round, close to hysteria, her eyes scanning the empty field.

'Where did you last see him?'

'Down by the river. Meg was up here in the field making daisy chains, like she said, and me and Mattie went down to the river to look for tiddlers. I got caught short and had to go in the bushes, and when I came back, he was gone.'

'You fool!' she yelled at him. But her heart was pumping harder than ever. After the long, hot summer, the river was mercifully shallow and slow-moving, but in some places there were pools, half hidden by trees, where the water collected, and even a little waterfall. The pools wouldn't be very deep, but deep enough if a toddler like Mattie stumbled into them. And he had only just started to walk properly – more likely than not he would be on his hands and knees.

She began to run again, almost falling as she skidded down the steep slope. Frank, following more slowly, called to her from the ridge above.

'He's not here. I've looked as best I could.'

'Of course he's here! You couldn't have searched properly,' she snapped. 'You weren't even looking when I first saw you.'

'I was coming to get help.'

310

She didn't stop to reply, running towards the thicket that spread out from the riverbank to her right and calling Mattie's name as she went. As she reached the first of the pools, she was shaking with dread and half expecting to see him face down in the water. But – thank God – still nothing.

'Mattie! Mattie!'

Her voice was muted by the trees, which were thicker here. Her breath coming in shallow panicked gasps, she stumbled on. Long streamers of bramble caught at her hair and clothes, and her hands and arms were soon a network of bloody scratches, but she scarcely noticed. She could think of nothing but finding her beloved son.

Frank had not followed her into the thicket. He was walking slowly along the grassy bank, eyes shaded, stopping when he came to the fence dividing the first part of the field from the next, where Bully, the unimaginatively named Jersey bull, stood forlornly under a lone tree, flicking his tail against the flies and midges. Sally would have shut the gate into that field to keep him in when she took the cows for milking so that she could leave the one to the road open. Frank clearly did not feel like braving the bull now that he was without his harem, but Carina was worried suddenly that Meg, who was trotting after him, might have no such reservations. She loved all the animals.

'Keep an eye on Meg!' she called back to Frank, then plunged on, battling her way through the thick undergrowth.

'Mattie! Where are you? Mattie!'

Ahead was a small clearing where the river broadened into another pool and where the cows, coming down to the river to paddle and drink, had trodden any seedlings into the churned-up ground.

And there – by some miracle! – was Mattie, ankle deep in thick mud and sobbing his heart out.

'Oh thank God! Thank God!'

Tears of relief streaming down her face, Carina ran towards him. As he saw her, he tried to take a step towards her, arms outstretched, but his feet were firmly anchored in the mud, and just as she had feared, he toppled over. She made a grab for him, trying to lift him clear of the water, and his sandalled feet made a sucking sound as they were wrenched out of the quagmire. She hugged him to her, her face buried in his mop of hair, not even aware of the river water soaking her blouse and the mud streaking her skirt. Nothing mattered, nothing, except that Mattie was safe.

Protecting his face from the overhanging brambles, she fought her way back through the thicket till she reached a place where the bank was shallow enough for her to climb up whilst carrying him. When she got to the edge of the field, a curious Bully had begun to amble towards Frank and Meg.

'I've found him! He's safe!' she gasped.

Frank said nothing.

Meg's small face was still a picture of anxiety.

'He's all muddy, Mammy.'

'Yes, he is, Meg.' Her lip was wobbling and she was trembling from head to foot as reaction kicked in. 'Let's get you home, both of you. Fetch the pushchair, Frank.'

But she had not the slightest intention of putting Mattie in it. She held him tight in her arms. She didn't think she would ever let go of him again.

'What were you thinking?' she demanded furiously of Frank.

Mattie had been bathed and his filthy clothes and hers too put to soak. His sandals, the worst of the mud washed off, were drying outside the back door, but Carina thought she'd have to get him some new ones. These would probably shrink, and in any case, they still smelled of manure. She'd pacified the little boy at last, and given him and Meg a scratch tea, since they were both hungry and she had nothing ready for them. Sally had come in from milking, and Frank too – no doubt looking for something to eat – and Carina could contain her fury no longer.

'What were you thinking? How could you have let him out of your sight?'

'I told you – it was only for a minute.' Frank's tone was mutinous.

'Long enough to lose him! He could have drowned!'

'Well he didn't. The water's not deep anyway.'

'If he'd toppled over . . .' Carina closed her eyes briefly as she felt an echo of the terrible fear that had racked her. 'And you weren't even looking for him!' she went on furiously.

'I told you, I was coming to get help. I couldn't do more than I did with Meg to look after as well.'

'Lord knows what would have happened if I hadn't come to see where you'd got to. He *did* topple over, but luckily I was able to grab him in time. But he was frightened to death, and did you see the state of him? I trusted you with them, and this is the consequence.'

'He's all right now, though,' Sally intervened. 'Can't we just forget it? It's not as if Frank meant to lose him. You can't blame him. It's not his fault.'

A furious Carina turned on her sister-in-law.

'Of course it's his fault! How can you defend him? But then you would, wouldn't you? You're besotted with him.'

'I'll ignore that, Carina. Or perhaps I won't. Who are you to talk? You're besotted too, if I'm not mistaken, with a certain member of the local gentry. So if you live in a glass house, don't throw stones.'

'Oh, don't be so ridiculous!' But Carina's cheeks had begun to burn.

'You are, and you know it! And your husband – my brother – scarcely cold in his grave!'

If Sally had slapped her, she could not have shocked and hurt her more. Carina took a step backwards, as if from a physical blow, trembling all over.

'I'm just trying my best to keep this family going, as Robert would have wanted. If I accept favours it's because if I didn't we'd be penniless by now. Don't you dare accuse me of betraying Robert!'

'I never said—'

'As good as!'

'All right – I'm sorry.' Perhaps Sally realised she had gone too far, but for the moment Carina was in no mood to accept her apology. The accusation had struck too close to home.

'So you should be.'

With that she headed for the back door, desperate for some fresh air, slamming it after her.

A fresh breeze had sprung up – perhaps the weather was on the turn at last – and it cooled her hot cheeks, but not the turbulent emotions that raged inside her. She leaned against the closed door, covering her face with her hands.

Oh Robert, Robert, I haven't betrayed you! How could she think for one moment that I had? Just because she's behaving like a common trollop . . .

But even now, as she wept yet again for her husband, something deep inside her was calling out to Cal, and she knew that against her will, she was indeed guilty of everything Sally had accused her of.

It was only later, lying sleepless in bed and going over and over every word that had been spoken in anger, that something Sally had said set her off on a quite different train of thought.

It's not as if Frank meant to lose him . . .

He hadn't looked for Mattie properly; he couldn't have, or he'd have found the little boy just as she had. And much sooner. Certainly he hadn't been looking for him when she'd seen him in the field. He'd made out he was coming for help in searching, but that didn't ring true somehow.

I don't want him here, she thought. I don't like him and I don't trust him.

But how could she ask him to leave? Keeping the farm going without his help would be well-nigh impossible. And it would certainly upset Sally dreadfully if she suggested it. Already they'd fallen out badly over him. Somehow Carina had to try to smooth things over, not make them worse.

Why would Frank deliberately leave Mattie down by the river? she asked herself, trying to think rationally. That he should have done such a thing on purpose made no sense. And much as she disliked the man, it was hard to believe even he could be so callous. She was upset and imagining things.

But for all her efforts, the sense of unease refused to go away, and she felt trapped by her inability to do anything about a situation that seemed to be totally beyond her control.

Chapter Twenty-Three

Carina had mixed feelings now about going to Dunderwick House to sew the drapes for Lady Melbrook's sitting room. After Sally's accusations and the guilt they had aroused in her, she was dreading coming face to face with Cal. She didn't want those turbulent emotions stirred up all over again, and she was embarrassed too in case she'd given herself away and he'd seen the attraction she felt for him. Her cheeks burned just thinking about it. But she didn't really see that she had any option. She'd promised to make the drapes, and she couldn't let him down. Besides which, she needed the money.

'I'm going to Dunderwick House tomorrow,' she said as she and Sally washed up the supper dishes on the Monday evening.

There was an uneasy truce between them now; they'd both apologised for the things that had been said in anger, but neither had quite forgotten, and both were treading on eggshells.

'Oh, right,' Sally said, but there was a slight sneer in her voice that made Carina uncomfortable all over again.

'I'm taking the children with me, so you won't have them under your feet,' she said, pretending not to notice.

'Won't they be under yours?'

'Lord Melbrook is going to get one of the servants to mind them,' Carina said, careful to refer to him formally.

316

'That's all right then.'

And the subject was shelved, just as was any mention of Mattie's inheritance. It wasn't even alluded to next morning when Carina got the children dressed and ready as soon as breakfast was over, except for her brief assurance to Sally that she would be back in time to make tea. She hoped that if she worked hard, she would be able to finish the job in just the one day.

She settled the children in the passenger seat of the Rover, telling Meg to be sure to hold on to Mattie tightly and not let him interfere with her driving or try to climb out while the motor was moving. She felt pretty confident that Meg would carry out her instructions to the letter – there was nothing she liked better than being the big sister and bossing Mattie about.

As they drove into the courtyard of Dunderwick House, Cal emerged from beneath the bonnet of his Benz and approached them, wiping his hands on a rag.

'Forgive me if I don't help you down,' he said by way of greeting. 'I've just been checking my oil and water and I don't want to risk getting oil on your clothes.'

'We're fine.' Carina was actually rather relieved. Cal helping her out of the car was disconcerting to say the least. She opened the door, swung herself out of the Rover and went around to lift Mattie down.

'I presume you do keep an eye on yours?' Cal said.

'What?' Carina was puzzled.

'Your oil and water.'

'Oh – should I?'

'You certainly should. A motor doesn't run on petrol alone. If you run out of water, the engine will overheat, and without oil to lubricate it, it will seize up altogether.'

'I didn't know,' Carina said, worried but also feeling rather foolish. 'It was making a bit of a noise just now.'

'Is that the first time you've noticed it?'

'Yes.'

'Then let's hope you haven't done any real damage. I'll have a look at it for you before you drive it again and top it all up. I always keep a can of oil.'

'Would you? Oh dear . . . if I've done something to the engine . . . I don't know how I'd manage without a motor . . .' In her anxiety, Carina had forgotten her embarrassment at meeting Cal again.

'I expect it will be all right,' he said reassuringly. 'But just be sure to remember in future. I expect the forecourt attendant would check it out for you when you buy petrol, if you ask nicely.'

Carina bit her lip. She hadn't filled up with petrol lately either, hadn't even thought to check. But she wasn't going to mention that and look an even bigger fool. She'd just have to keep her fingers crossed that there was enough in the tank to get her to the garage in Hillsbridge. Who would have thought keeping a motor on the road could be so complicated?

Meg was still in the passenger seat, looking at Cal with the same wary expression as she had the first time she'd met him. Carina set Mattie down, lifted Meg out and picked up Mattie again.

'Good morning, Mattie,' Cal said. 'Good morning, Meg.'

Meg was hiding her face in Carina's skirt.

'Meg, will you stop being so silly and so rude!' Carina chided her. And to Cal: 'I don't know what's got into her.'

'Not to worry. This is all strange to her, and so am I. I expect she'll soon forget to be shy when she sees the puppies.'

One eye and half of Meg's face appeared from the folds of Carina's skirt.

'I thought that would do the trick.' Cal smiled. 'Let's get

your mama set up, then we'll go and find them.'

He gave his hands another wipe on the rag and tucked it into the pocket of his trousers – not smart ones this morning, but old and a little baggy. Then he lifted Carina's sewing machine from the back seat of the Rover, swinging it easily by the handle though Carina had always found it quite heavy to carry.

'Unless you want to see them too?' he said to Carina.

'I really ought to be making a start on my work.'

'You're too hard on yourself, Carina. All work and no play is no good for you. I'm sure ten minutes won't make that much difference in the grand scheme of things.'

Carina sighed. The road to hell really was paved with good intentions.

'I don't suppose it will.'

'That's more like it. Now, I think Mrs Thomas has arranged for you to have the same room as before, if you're happy with that.'

'Yes, perfectly.'

He opened the door to the orangery.

'I'll just take your sewing machine through first. If you'd like to wait here . . . I expect the children would like an orange.'

'Mammy! Look, Mammy!'

Meg, her shyness completely forgotten, was staring in wonder at the orange and lemon trees, some of which were still bearing fruit.

'Let them pick some,' Cal said.

'No, I'll do it.' Carina was afraid the children might be rough and damage the trees. But she was not in time to stop Mattie jerking a lemon off its branch.

'Mattie – no!'

Neither did she move fast enough to stop him from putting it in his mouth. The little boy recoiled, his face screwed up against the bitter taste, and dropped the lemon as if it were a hot potato.

'That'll teach you,' Carina said. And to Meg: 'Now you know where oranges and lemons come from before they get to the shops.'

'A plant,' Meg said. 'Just like our tomatoes.'

'It's called a tree,' Carina corrected her, but she felt proud of Meg all the same. She really was a bright little girl – the oranges and lemons did hang down as tomatoes did.

Cal went off with the sewing machine and Carina carefully picked two oranges and gave the children one each.

'Don't try to eat them now,' she warned. 'You'll get all sticky. Save them for when we get home.'

'Right.' Cal had returned. 'Let's go and find those puppies.'

'Are you sure we're not holding you up?' Carina asked.

'I've nothing that can't wait. And I'd quite like to see them again myself.'

He led the way out into the courtyard to a series of outbuildings on the far side and opened the door of one of them.

'Inside quickly now, before they all escape.'

He stood guard at the door while Carina ushered Meg and Mattie inside, then stepped in himself, closing the door behind him.

Although one of the windows was open, it was warm in the outbuilding, and the air was full of the smell of animals – body heat, milk and excrement – though not nearly as pungent as the cowshed or even Captain's stable. In the far corner, towels and old blankets had been spread out and heaped up to make a bed, and empty food dishes and a full water bowl were lined up along the wall. In the centre of the outhouse lay a well-chewed marrow bone, a treat that the new mother was clearly enjoying. She came towards them now, wagging her tail and pushing a wet nose into Cal's hand.

But it was the puppies who engaged the children's attention, five sturdy little bodies with short legs and stumpy tails, five squashed faces, ten brown eyes, shiny as buttons. Four of them gambolled around, bumping into one another, yapping and play-fighting, while the fifth, the smallest of the litter, followed Cleo, vainly trying to reach her swollen teats.

'Oh, they're adorable!' Carina exclaimed.

'They are cute.' Cal was fondling Cleo's ear. 'You did well, didn't you, girl?'

Meg was staring, enraptured. Mattie began to chase the puppies, his legs working like pistons as they ran away from him, bounded back towards him, then ran away again before he could catch one of them.

'Mattie – no!' Carina warned.

'It's all right, they're big enough now to keep out of his way,' Cal said. 'Another couple of weeks and they'll be going to their new homes.'

'How can you bear to let them go?' Carina asked.

'Well, I certainly can't keep six Labradors,' Cal said with a laugh.

'Won't their mammy be sad?' Meg was looking worried.

'I expect she'll be glad to get a bit of peace,' Cal told her. 'Anyway, I might keep one so she doesn't get too lonely.'

'Which one? How will you choose?'

'The little one, I expect. Nobody wants the runt of the litter. But that's exactly what Cleo was. The runt of her mother's litter. And look how well she's turned out.'

'Her mother was your dog too?' Carina asked.

'She certainly was. Queenie. A beautiful dog. We've had Labradors for generations, and all descended from the same line.'

'That's amazing!'

'They suit us. They're known for their sweet temperament and they make good gun dogs too. I have three potential buyers waiting for the pups to be weaned, so that means there's just one I have to find a home for.'

'Oh Mammy!' Meg's face was bright and eager. 'Couldn't we have it?'

Carina smiled and sighed, shaking her head.

'I've got enough to do without training a puppy, Meg.'

'But they're so sweet!'

'Yes, and a nuisance too. When they're little, they chew everything in sight, make a mess everywhere . . .'

'Oh *please*, Mammy!'

'I said no, Meg,' Carina said sternly 'And if you keep on bothering me, I shall wish Lord Melbrook hadn't let you see them at all.'

'Oh Mammy . . .'

'You heard your mother, Meg.' Cal's tone was firm but kindly. 'But you can come here and see the puppy I keep as often as you like, watch her grow. Would you like that?'

'I'd rather have one of my own,' Meg pouted.

Carina raised her eyebrows at Cal. Children! that look said.

'Come on now, Meg. You've seen them now, and I have work to do.'

'Do you want to stay here and play with the puppies?' Cal asked.

'Oh yes!'

'*Please*,' Carina prompted her.

'Please!'

'Are you happy with that?' Cal asked Carina.

'As long as someone keeps an eye on them. They can get a bit rough. And I don't want them wandering off and getting lost.'

'Mary can come and do that. It won't hurt for some of the rooms to remain undusted for once. If you ask Mrs Thomas to send her across, I'll stay with them until she's here to take over.'

'Thank Lord Melbrook nicely,' Carina instructed Meg.

'Thank you, Lord Melbrook.' Meg's shyness was completely forgotten now.

'And just behave yourselves.'

With that she left them and crossed the yard to the house. Biddy Thomas seemed less than pleased that one of her maids was to be placed on child-minding duties, but even she knew better than to openly argue with her employer's instructions, and Carina went into the library, where Cal had set her sewing machine on the table.

First the fabric had to be cut to the right lengths with the pattern matching as far as possible. Carina spread it out on the carpeted floor and got down on her hands and knees with her tape measure and scissors, checking and double-checking before she cut into it to be sure she didn't make a mistake. Then she took the cover off her sewing machine and threaded both it and the shuttle with white cotton that would blend in with the background of the design.

As before, she was enjoying herself, humming softly as she turned the handle with one hand and guided the fabric under the foot with the other.

Before she knew it, it was time for what Cal called luncheon. She had intended to work through, but Biddy Thomas told her a place had been set for her, and in any case she would need to feed Mattie, she realised. Left to his own devices, he was still quite likely to throw a bowl of food over the floor, and since he wouldn't have his high chair here, she'd have to have him on her lap.

Cal did not put in an appearance; Carina ate with Biddy and

the other servants, who were tickled pink with the children. By four o'clock, though, he was back.

'I think you ought to call it a day, Carina. The children are getting restless.'

'Oh, what a nuisance. I really was hoping to get the drapes finished today.'

'There's always tomorrow.'

'I suppose.' And she really needed to get into Hillsbridge and fill up with petrol before the garage closed . . .

'Did you manage to look at my car?' she asked. 'Is it all right?'

'Caught it just in time, I think. I'll see you tomorrow, then?'

'Do you mind if I leave my work out? I'd rather not have to pack it all away and get it creased in the wrong places.'

'Feel free.'

'And I think perhaps I'll leave the children at home tomorrow if Sally is able to look after them. Then I can work through . . .' She was about to say 'dinner', but caught herself just in time. 'Luncheon,' she said, feeling proud of herself. She was learning!

'If that's what you'd prefer.'

She looked up and their eyes met. There was a faintly amused expression in his eyes . . . and something else. Something that made her tummy twist in that disconcerting way that was becoming all too familiar.

Why, why, why? She'd been so determined not to let him affect her this way. She just couldn't help herself, it seemed.

'Yes . . . yes, I think that would be best.'

The quicker she could finish the job and not have to see him again the better, she thought.

Doing her best to avoid looking at him, yet aware that his eyes were still on her, she got her things together. The children were still in the outhouse with the puppies, watched over by

Mary the housemaid. Meg was as rapt as ever, but Mattie did look tired, sitting on the dogs' bed rubbing his eyes and grizzling a bit. He'd missed his nap, of course.

'Time to go, children,' she said.

'O-oh . . .' Meg protested.

'Look – Mattie's falling asleep.' She picked him up. 'Come on now.'

'Can we come back tomorrow?'

'Not tomorrow.'

'O-oh!' Meg wailed again. 'Me want to!' She always reverted to baby language when she was upset, or trying to get her own way.

'You can come back another day,' Cal said.

'When? When?'

'Shall we say next Tuesday?'

'But that's a whole week!' Meg complained.

'I'm going to be away for a few days, visiting Aubrey O'Leary, an old army friend of mine. And it will be next Tuesday in no time. That will be all right, won't it, Mama?'

Carina hesitated. As far as she was concerned, it wasn't all right at all. She'd intended to put as much distance between herself and Lord Melbrook as she could once the drapes were finished and hung. But what could she say? And in any case, a small, treacherous part of her wanted to see him again very much.

'I expect so,' she said.

'Lord Melbrook!' The door of the outhouse had opened a crack and Biddy Thomas was calling through it. 'You're wanted on the telephone!'

'Ah. That'll be Aubrey, finalising arrangements. I must go and speak to him. I'll see you tomorrow, Carina. And you two . . .' he ruffled Mattie's hair, 'I'll see you next Tuesday. Be sure not to let the puppies escape when the door's open,' he instructed Mary. And then he was gone.

Carina, Mary and the children followed soon afterwards, ensuring the outhouse door was safely shut behind them. Carina lifted the children up into the Rover and got it started. At least she'd avoided Cal helping her up and setting her off again! she thought. But all the same, she drove out of the courtyard and up the track beneath the trees as if all the hounds of hell were after her.

Luckily she caught the garage in Hillsbridge just before it closed. 'You were darned near empty there,' the proprietor told her – he'd had to attend to her himself since his forecourt assistant had already gone home. She had to put it on the slate, too, as she didn't have enough money on her to pay for it, but she promised to come back and settle up the following day. Hopefully by then Cal would have paid her for the work she'd done. With Mattie fast asleep and leaning against Meg in the front passenger seat, she headed for home.

In the farmhouse kitchen, she was surprised to find that Sally had made a start on preparing tea – it was very unlike her to take on any household chores beyond helping with the washing-up.

'How did it go?' Sally asked.

'Quite well. But I didn't get finished. I'm going to have to go back tomorrow. In fact . . .'

Reluctant as she was to ask Sally to mind the children tomorrow, little as she wanted them anywhere near Frank, if she was to finish the drapes quickly she really could do without the distraction. In any case, the chances were that Frank would be well out of the way, working in the fields. Somehow, as she asked the favour, she managed to bite her tongue so as not to mention him and create further problems with Sally. But: 'It will be the last time, I promise. From now on I'll only work from home,' she finished.

'Good. I hope you stick to that,' Sally said.

'Don't worry, I will,' Carina rejoined. And, for more reasons than one, she absolutely meant what she said.

Next morning, Mattie still seemed tired, although he'd had a good long rest, sleeping right through the night and needing to be woken when it was time to get up, which was very unusual for him. Normally he was awake with the birds and full of beans. As for Meg, she was still hanging on to Carina's skirt, whining and begging to be allowed to go with her. And she hadn't given up hope of having the puppy that hadn't been spoken for, either.

'Me want a doggie!'

'We've got a doggie,' Carina said flatly. 'Cymru.'

The collie cocked his ears at the mention of his name, but Meg only stared at him disdainfully.

'Cymru's no fun. He won't play like the puppies do.'

'That's because he's old. And the puppies won't stay little and frisky for ever. Now will you please sit up to the table and eat your breakfast. I want to go soon.'

At last the essential chores were finished and she was able to set out for Dunderwick House.

To her relief – and also a treacherous twinge of disappointment – Cal did not appear to be at home. Biddy Thomas let her in and brought her a cup of tea, which Carina left on a side table, afraid to have it anywhere near her work in case she spilled some on the pretty fabric.

She worked steadily throughout the morning, and at one point heard Cal's voice, and his mother's, trumpeting as usual, as she replied, but he did not come into her room.

By midday, she'd finished all the seams and hems and was

stitching the hooks into place, a long and tedious job but one that was very important if the drapes were to hang properly. Biddy Thomas appeared and told her luncheon was ready, but Carina was unwilling to stop. Biddy brought her another cup of tea and a sandwich, which she nibbled carefully, making sure her fingers were clean before going on with her work.

Plates were clattering somewhere in the house, indicating that the meal was being cleared away, when the door opened and Cal came in.

'Good afternoon, Carina. How are you getting on?'

'I've almost finished.' She bit through the cotton securing the last of the hooks and spread the drape out across her knees. 'They're ready for hanging now.'

'Well done. And good timing, too. Mama is taking her afternoon nap. It will be a pleasant surprise for her when she comes down again and sees them.'

Hanging the drapes in Lady Melbrook's sitting room was easier than it had been in the drawing room, as the windows were smaller and not as high. It was also more complicated, however, as there were three of them, angled like a triptych. But at last they were up.

'An excellent job,' Cal said. 'Mama will be delighted.'

'I hope so.' But Carina was feeling well satisfied with her work. The drapes were perfect, and they made the room much lighter and brighter than before. 'I'll go and pack up my things.'

'And I'll find some money to pay you.'

She went back to the room she had come to think of as her sewing room, feeling regretful that she wouldn't be working here again. She had so enjoyed it, being able to do what she loved best, what she had been trained for, in such lovely and peaceful surroundings. But accepting more work from Cal – even if he had some he'd like her to undertake – wouldn't be a good idea.

She'd just have to hope that the talk about Frank in the village soon died down and people began bringing her commissions again. And she'd have to get used to working on the kitchen table, with all its drawbacks.

She packed her cottons, needles, tape measure, scissors and thimble back into their proper homes in her workbox, and was just slotting the cover of her sewing machine into place when Cal came in.

He counted out the money he owed her and she put it safely away in her purse.

'I shall miss you, Carina.'

There was warmth in his tone; somehow Carina knew that if she looked up, she would see that certain something in his eyes that played havoc with her emotions.

'I've only been here two days.' She tried to say it lightly, jokingly, but somehow her voice sounded a bit wobbly. *I'll miss you too*, she wanted to say, but of course she did not.

'I've a little something else for you too,' he said. 'Though I don't think it is little to you.'

She did look up then, surprised and mystified.

'You've already paid me.'

'But this, I think, belongs to you.'

He fished in his pocket, held out his hand, then slowly uncurled his fingers. In his palm lay a small box, a box she instantly recognised. Her mouth fell open. It was all she could do not to snatch the box from his hand. Yet still she couldn't believe it.

'It's . . .' Words failed her.

'Yes. Your ring. I didn't like to think of it going to someone who might not treasure it as I'm sure you do, so I bought it back for you.'

'But . . . when?'

'Oh, some time ago. I found the pawnbroker quite ready to sell. But I've been waiting for the right moment to return it to you.'

'So that's why he said it had gone when I went to try and buy it back. I thought I'd never see it again!'

'My fault, I'm afraid.' He smiled. 'Take it, then. Put it back on your finger where it belongs.'

He opened the box, and her precious ring winked up at her as she took it from its velvet cushion. But her hands were trembling so much she couldn't get it over her knuckle, swollen by years of hard work.

'Let me.'

He took her hand and gently eased the ring on to her finger. She gazed down at it wonderingly, then, before she could stop herself, threw her arms round Cal.

'Oh thank you! Thank you!'

'My pleasure.' His breath was warm on the nape of her neck, his hands on her waist.

Suddenly Carina was very aware of him, aware too of the temerity of her impulsive action. She tried to draw away, but his hands were holding her fast and she succeeded in nothing but coming face to face with him, close, so close. Those mesmerising eyes were narrowed, his lips slightly parted below the white scar. Her heart thudded in her chest, that forbidden desire twisting deep inside her. He was going to kiss her, and oh, she so wanted him to! Every nerve in her body was alive and tingling, drawn to his as if magnetised, and she could scarcely breathe . . .

The knock at the door was a loud rap, breaking the spell. His hands were no longer on her waist; she took a step backwards as the door opened.

'Lord Melbrook, sir . . .'

It was Mary, the housemaid. She stopped nervously in the doorway, looking flustered, as if she realised she was intruding. Just how much she had seen, Carina did not know, but the quick colour rushed to her cheeks and shame and confusion welled.

'Yes? What is it?' Cal's tone was clipped, impatient.

'Excuse me, sir, but Mrs Thomas asked me to tell you your mother is up from her nap and wants to thank Mrs Talbot for the drapes . . .'

'Oh, very well.' He turned to Carina, a half-smile curving those lips that had, just a moment ago, been so close to hers. 'I think your presence is requested in my mother's sitting room. And my mother doesn't like to be kept waiting.'

How Carina managed to gain control of her tumultuous emotions and face the redoubtable Lady Melbrook, she would never know. She made her way to the sitting room on legs that seemed not to belong to her, somehow made suitable replies as Lady Melbrook praised her work, and bobbed a slight curtsey as she withdrew, immediately thinking that it was the wrong thing to have done. What a complete and utter fool she had made of herself!

And yet Cal seemed exactly as usual, as comfortable within his own skin as ever. He went with her to the Rover, carrying her sewing machine for her and placing it on the rear seat, then handed her up without any hint of impropriety, and seemingly unaware of the way her hands were shaking.

'So – you'll bring the children to see the puppies on Tuesday?' he said, for all the world as if those moments in the sewing room had never been.

'Yes,' she said, because really there was nothing else she could say.

And: 'Thank you so much for buying back my ring. I thought I'd never see it again. I can never thank you enough.'

Then and only then did he say something, with just the hint of a smile, that might very well refer to their earlier encounter.

'Oh, I expect I'll think of a way.'

He got the Rover going for her, raised his hand in a mock salute.

'Till next Tuesday, then.'

As she drove away, much more slowly than yesterday, because she didn't really feel in proper control either of herself or her motor, she glanced at her hand on the steering wheel, at the tiny diamonds glittering as the light caught them, and bit her lip against the sob that rose in her throat.

She was glad, so glad, to have it back. It meant the world to her. And yet scarcely had it been back on her finger but all the feelings she'd tried so hard to suppress had come bubbling to the surface, and she had nearly kissed another man.

'Oh Robert, I'm so sorry!' she whispered, and the stiff breeze blew the words back into her throat.

Chapter Twenty-Four

Mattie was poorly. No, not just poorly, but quite ill. It had all started, Carina thought, on Tuesday, when the children had gone with her to Dunderwick House. Even though he'd missed his nap, it was unlike him to be as listless and drowsy as he had been that day and the next. At first she hadn't worried too much, even when he was violently sick during the night. It wasn't the first time it had happened, by a long chalk. But the nausea continued the next day, and the next. He wasn't eating, and it took all her powers of persuasion to get him to take some sips of water; he was crying as if he was uncomfortable, and his eyes were bloodshot.

Over the weekend, the chills started, interspersed with bouts of fever; his eyes were red and sore, made even worse because he kept rubbing them, and he developed a nasty hacking cough. He lay on the sofa in the kitchen, grizzling and tossing and turning restlessly. He should be in bed, Sally said, and perhaps she was right, but Carina wanted him here, where she could keep an eye on him.

As for Frank, he was annoyingly dismissive.

'Oh, stop fussing. He'll be right as rain in a day or two,' he said airily, and Carina could have hit him.

She knew as well as anyone how a child could be down one

day and up the next, and she'd nursed both Meg and Mattie through various childhood illnesses, but her gut feeling told her that this was more serious. She debated endlessly with herself as to whether the doctor should be called, but a doctor would mean more bills that she could ill afford, and she didn't have a great deal of faith in them anyway. Give it another day, she decided, and if he was still no better then, she would bite the bullet and get the doctor in to see him.

But by the next day Mattie wasn't better; if anything he was worse, and getting hold of a doctor posed something of a problem in itself, since they had no telephone, and ill as Mattie was, Carina was unwilling to leave him while she drove into Hillsbridge.

'Do you think David would ride over on his bike?' she asked Sally.

'I expect he would, but you're not suggesting I should be the one to go over and ask him, I hope,' was Sally's response.

'For goodness' sake, why ever not? You and he used to be such friends.' *Before Frank came on the scene*, she was tempted to add, but didn't. Frank was a subject to be avoided with Sally if the old wounds were not to be reopened.

'I really don't want to leave Mattie, and you needn't stay talking. Just ask if he'd be kind enough to do this for me,' she said instead.

'Oh, I suppose so,' Sally agreed reluctantly.

She set off for the Perkins farm, and was soon back with the news that David had agreed to help, just as Carina had been sure he would.

It was past midday before Dr Mackay arrived. He was, as his name suggested, a Scot, and when he had first arrived in Hillsbridge back in the dying years of the last century, some of the locals had had trouble understanding a word he said. They'd grown used to it, however, and in any case, over the years the Glaswegian accent had become much less pronounced, though the lilt was still evident. Nowadays he was no longer 'the young doctor' or 'the foreigner', but a well-respected and popular pillar of the community.

The first thing he did when Carina went to the door to let him in was to offer his condolences. He hadn't seen her since Robert and Luke died; he wasn't the one who had been called out to issue the certificates. Because Dr Blackmore from High Compton had once been a police surgeon, it was he that Sergeant Love called on in cases of sudden or violent death.

Dr Mackay crossed the kitchen to where Mattie lay, set down his medical bag and folded his long, lean body into a squat beside the sofa.

'So what's up with you, m' laddie?'

Mattie twisted restlessly, keening in the way he had been almost incessantly these last days, and which tore at Carina's heart, and fighting to push down the blanket she had covered him with.

Dr Mackay laid a hand on his flushed forehead.

'Hot are ye', wee man? Aye, you most certainly are. He's running a high temperature, Mrs Talbot. He needs to be uncovered if we're to get that down.'

'He was icy cold a minute ago,' Carina said defensively. Like all mothers with a sick child, she felt guilty, as if the illness was all her fault.

'And is that the pattern?' Dr Mackay looked up at her, no hint of accusation in his very blue eyes. 'A chill and then a fever?'

'I suppose it is, yes.'

'Aye.' He said it thoughtfully. 'Well, let's have a good look at y' then, m' wee man. Would you be taking his clothes off for me, Mrs Talbot?'

Carina undressed a protesting Mattie, who screamed as she eased his arms out of his gown and vest and pulled them over his head, but even his cries sounded weak to her anxious ears. Beneath the vest and above his terry napkin his whole body was scarlet, the heat radiating from it.

His screams quietened to pathetic sobs as the doctor examined him, listening to his chest, taking his pulse and prodding him with firm but gentle fingers.

'He has a nasty infection, without a doubt,' he said at last. 'But what is causing it? That's the question. Has he been in contact with illness at all?'

Carina shook her head.

'No, we're all perfectly well, and he hasn't been with anybody except us. Living on a farm, we don't get many visitors.'

'Quite. A farm. The animals, perhaps . . . ?'

'He hasn't been near them. Only Cymru, our dog, and Cleo, a friend's dog, and her puppies. He's afraid of the cows.'

'What about your water butts? Has he been playing near them?'

'No . . .' She broke off as a thought struck her. 'He was down by the river last week.'

'Paddling?'

'Not paddling, no. At least, not intentionally. Frank, our farmhand, took him for a walk, but he ran away and got lost. He was ankle deep in mud in one of the little pools when I found him.'

'Ah.' The doctor frowned. 'Then there I think we may have our answer.'

Carina thought of the way Mattie's sandals had reeked of manure, even after she had washed them.

'You mean the pancakes? The cows leave a lot of mess where they go down to the river to drink and keep cool.'

'Possibly. But more likely it's the rats and other vermin that are to blame. The weather has been very hot and dry this summer, and the water in those pools will have become stagnant. It's a breeding ground for bacteria, Mrs Talbot. Rats and suchlike can carry some very nasty diseases.'

Carina was shocked. She had no idea what kind of disease Dr Mackay was talking about, but she certainly didn't like the sound of Mattie picking up something from rats.

'Surely if it was that, it would have come out before now?'

'Not necessarily. These things take some time to develop. Has he been vomiting?'

'He was sick the other night,' she said.

'And is he still vomiting?'

'Not really, but I don't think he'd have anything to bring up. He's not eating and it's all I can do to get him to drink.'

'That's not good.' Dr Mackay's face was grave and he was clearly deep in thought.

A growing panic made Carina's stomach knot.

'It's not serious, is it, Doctor? He will be all right?'

Dr Mackay straightened, looking at her directly.

'I'm not going to lie to you, Mrs Talbot. It could well be serious. I think the best thing would be to get him into hospital, where we can get some liquids into him and keep an eye on how things develop.'

'Hospital!' The knot of panic in Carina's stomach tightened.

'I think so, yes. It would be the best place for him. You know the cottage hospital on the other side of High Compton? He'll be well looked after there, though if his condition deteriorates it may be necessary to move him to one of the Bath hospitals, where there are doctors who specialise in this kind of thing. So if you could get some of his things together—'

'Now?' Carina interrupted him. 'You want him to go *now*?'

'I think it would be best. I can take him in my motor. And you can come as well, to settle him in, though of course you won't be able to stay with him. Matron wouldn't allow that, I'm afraid.'

Carina's hand flew to her mouth. This was all happening so fast. And the thought of having to leave her precious son in the care of strangers was unbearable. But she couldn't argue. She had to do what was best for Mattie.

In a daze, she got together clean nappies and a freshly laundered vest and gown – all his others, sweat-soaked, were waiting to be washed. Then she found his favourite toy – a blue rabbit she had knitted herself and stuffed with old socks – and a bottle with a well-chewed teat. Though Mattie was mostly drinking from a cup now, he still liked a bottle for comfort. She put them all in a hessian shopping bag and went to dress Mattie again.

'Best not,' Dr Mackay said. 'We have to get that temperature down or he may begin fitting.'

He glanced at Meg, who had been standing in a corner, sucking her thumb and hugging her doll while watching the drama unfold with big serious eyes.

'Your daughter is quite well, I take it?'

'Yes. You feel all right, don't you, Meg?'

Meg nodded wordlessly.

'Will she have to come with you?' Dr Mackay asked. 'A hospital is not really the place for small children.'

'Oh no – I'll get my sister-in-law to look after her.' Carina hurried outside and found Sally in one of the sheds with a very pregnant cow that was lowing loudly.

'Sally, you're going to have to look after Meg for a bit.'

Sally looked round, pushing a strand of hair off her face.

'I can't, Carina. This cow has started calving, and she's having a hard time.'

'Damn the cow, Sally! Is she more important than your own flesh and blood?'

She went on to explain what was happening, and visibly shocked, Sally nodded.

'All right, I'll keep an eye on her. She can come in here with me. Just as long as she keeps out of the way. Or I could get Frank to watch her . . .'

'No! Not Frank!' Carina said decisively. She didn't want him anywhere near the children, and if the only way to avoid him being responsible for Meg was for her to go into the barn with Sally, then so be it. Growing up on a farm she'd have to see animals giving birth at some time. It might as well be now.

She went back into the house.

'Come on, Meg. Auntie Sally is going to look after you while I take Mattie to hospital. But you've got to be a really good girl and not bother her. Just sit quietly and play with your doll.'

'Why?' Meg demanded.

'Because she's helping one of the cows to have her baby.'

'Oh!' Meg's face lit up. 'Is there going to be a calf?'

'Yes. But you're to stay well out of the way, do you hear?'

Dr Mackay packed his instruments back into his bag and Carina picked up Mattie, wrapped only in a thin shawl. There was quite a cold breeze blowing and having him so exposed went against all Carina's instincts, but she knew she must accept that the doctor knew best.

An eager Meg ran ahead of her towards the barn, but at the door she stopped, looking up at Carina anxiously.

'You will bring Mattie back, won't you, Mammy?'

There was a lump the size of an egg in Carina's throat.

'Not today, sweetheart.'

'But he will come home again, won't he? He's not going for ever?'

'No, not for ever. Just until he's better,' Carina said.

She only hoped and prayed that would be the case.

By the time Dr Mackay had driven them to the cottage hospital, got Mattie admitted and driven Carina home again, the calf had been born, and in her excitement Meg seemed to have forgotten all about her concern for her brother.

'I seed the calf come out!' she squealed excitedly. 'And the mammy licked it all over, and it tried to stand up and it fell over again.'

'Well, well,' Carina said. Anything more was beyond her at present. 'I hope she behaved herself, Auntie Sally.'

'She was as good as gold. You enjoyed it, didn't you, Meg?'

'Yes, and when I'm growed up, I'm going to be a farm lady like Auntie Sally.'

'Is that right?'

Meg followed her into the house, still chattering animatedly, but all Carina could think of was how dreadfully empty it seemed without Mattie there. She picked up his little mug, which had rolled under the sofa, and folded the blanket that had covered him, burying her face in it and breathing in the scent of him. How she was going to get through the hours until she could go back and visit him she didn't know, but the most important thing was that the care he would receive would make him better. It was clear from Dr Mackay's reaction that Mattie was very seriously ill, and Carina found herself praying as she had not prayed for years.

Oh dear God, please let Mattie be all right! Please make him better! I'll do anything – anything – if only you'll make him better!

And: *Dear God, don't take Mattie too! I can't stand it! I just can't stand to lose him too!*

But nothing seemed to help. The world was a dark place

again, and Carina wondered if she would ever emerge into warm, unbroken sunshine.

David Perkins had made up his mind. He was going to see Sally and try to win her back. What they'd shared in the old days hadn't been perfect. He'd never been able to get as close to her as he'd wanted. But they'd had plenty of good times – really good times – and he missed them. Missed her. The sound of her laugh, the fresh smell of her hair when she'd washed it after a long day out in the fields. The feel of her in his arms. The taste of her lips.

He missed the hopes he'd had, too, that one day soon she would come to feel about him the way he felt about her. That she'd become a proper girlfriend rather than just someone he walked out with sometimes or took to a dance or social. And maybe . . . He had usually tried to stop himself there for fear of being disappointed. But sometimes he'd even dared to imagine them married. The mundane, everyday things, like Sally churning butter, making cheese, looking after the poultry; but the exciting ones too – having her in his bed, waking in the morning to see her face next to his on the pillow, making love to her . . .

But then that Frank had come on the scene and everything had changed. She'd stopped seeing David; in fact he thought she was avoiding him. She had eyes only for that big-headed sod whom his mother reckoned was a bad lot. He'd wrapped her around his little finger.

Though it made him sick at heart, David had thought he had no option but to try and forget Sally, at least until his rival got tired of country living and her and moved on. But this morning, when she'd come to the farm asking if he'd go for the doctor for Mattie, he'd been smitten all over again.

Riding his bicycle to Hillsbridge and back again, he hadn't

been able to get her out of his head. What sort of a man was he if he gave her up without a fight? he'd asked himself. Why should he keep out of the way and leave the coast clear for that arrogant blighter? Oh, he'd probably end up making a fool of himself, and getting his heart broken all over again, but at least he'd have tried. He could do no more than that.

Just how to set about it he wasn't yet sure, but there was nothing like working on the land to give you time to think.

And he would think of something.

Tuesday. The day she was supposed to be taking the children to see the puppies again. There was, of course, no way that was going to happen. Instead Mattie was in hospital and Sally was going to have to look after Meg again while Carina went to see him. Visiting wasn't until after midday, but she didn't think she could wait until then; she was much too anxious to find out how he was. She'd scarcely slept a wink last night for worrying. If she drove over to the hospital this morning, at least she could ask how he was and maybe they'd let her sit with him. If not, she'd just wait in the car, and she'd be on hand if he took a turn for the worse.

First, though, she owed it to Cal to let him know they wouldn't be coming to see the puppies as arranged. She'd go to Dunderwick House on her way to the hospital. She couldn't let him wait in all morning when perhaps he had better things to do. That just wasn't right. Carina had been brought up not to let people down, and anxious as she was to be with Mattie, reliability was so ingrained in her nature that she knew it would play on her mind all day if she didn't go and tell Cal what had happened.

Not that she wanted to see him. The very thought was making her stomach curl. She'd just say what she had to say and leave again. At least she wouldn't have to spend the best part of a morning in his disturbing presence knowing what a fool she'd made of herself.

An unwelcome, frankly awful thought occurred to her. She'd been dreading it. Wishing she could think of an excuse not to go. Suppose it was her fault that Mattie was ill? Be careful what you wish for, her mother had always said. Could it be she had somehow manifested a reason not to spend time with the man who had such a devastating effect on her? She told herself she was being stupid, but she couldn't quite get it out of her mind, any more than she could forget the fear for her son that hung over her like a dense black fog, making her feel physically sick.

Meg was subdued this morning too, clearly missing her brother and worrying about him. Carina got her washed and dressed, doing everything at a hectic pace, not because she thought it would mean she could leave sooner, but because her nerves wouldn't let her slow down. She cooked breakfast for Sally and Frank but couldn't eat a thing herself; though she tried, it simply stuck in her throat. Then she cleared away the dishes as usual. She didn't want to make extra work for Sally.

At last she decided it was a reasonable time to make her calls. Leaving Meg in Sally's care, she drove over to Dunderwick House. Her heart was pounding as she rang the bell. Since he was expecting her, would Cal himself answer it?

But it was Biddy Thomas who opened the door.

'I'm sorry, but you've had a wasted journey,' she said shortly. 'His lordship has been delayed on business. He won't be home today and maybe not tomorrow. He's asked me to pass on his apologies and hopes the children won't be too disappointed.'

Carina felt a huge surge of relief.

'I haven't got them with me anyway.' She went on to explain what had happened.

'Dear, dear, I'm sorry to hear that,' Biddy said. 'Let's hope he'll be better soon. Anyway, I'll tell his lordship when he gets back, and he'll be in touch to find out how the little lad is, I wouldn't wonder.'

'Thank you,' Carina said. But she wasn't at all sure Cal would be in touch. She couldn't help thinking that this business trip overrunning was a bit convenient. Given what had happened between them last week, she wouldn't be at all surprised if he was avoiding her on purpose.

She got the Rover going and set off again as fast as she dared. She was driving erratically, she knew, her mind far from being on what she was doing. But somehow she managed to complete the journey without incident.

The cottage hospital had once been a grand private house that had been donated to the community when its last occupant had died and his widow moved away. A square grey-stone building, it stood in an acre or more of grounds at the brow of the hill overlooking High Compton. From this vantage point it was just possible to see the chimney stacks of Fairley Terrace, where Carina had been born and lived when she was a little girl. But looking for them today was the furthest thing from her mind. She parked the Rover on the broad turnaround at the end of the drive and climbed out.

'Hoi! You can't leave that there!' A squat, red-faced man in a porter's uniform of smock and cap was approaching her, waving his arms indignantly.

Carina bristled. 'I'm not doing any harm.'

'You're in the way. There could be ambulances wanting to turn, or others needing the space.'

'There's plenty of room,' Carina protested.

'You can't stop there,' he repeated officiously. 'Either you move that thing, or I'll have the police on you.'

Carina was sorely tempted to argue. She couldn't see that she was causing an obstruction or that it would be of any interest to the police, but she didn't want to get into a spat. Her nerves were already shredded, and besides, she didn't want to fall out with the hospital staff. She was still hoping to get them on her side with regards to staying with Mattie. This obnoxious man might only be a porter, but he could well have the ear of the nurses.

Rather than risk a further altercation, she drove the Rover back to the road, parked against the kerb and walked back to the hospital. The surly porter was still watching her to make sure she wasn't breaching any more rules, but by the time she reached the door, he had disappeared.

The broad tiled lobby was empty. There was a brass bell on the counter of a small reception desk. Carina rang it, startled by its piercingly clear sound, and half expecting to be reprimanded again for making a noise when there were sick people just the other side of the big swing doors into the main hospital.

A nurse in starched cap and apron appeared.

'Yes? Can I help you?'

Carina explained why she was there. 'How is he?' she finished anxiously.

The nurse, who was very young, looked worried, and Carina's heart leapt into her throat.

'He isn't . . . ?' She couldn't bring herself to utter the awful word that was hovering on her lips. Suppose Mattie had slipped away in the night and no one had yet been able to reach her to tell her?

'I don't know anything about your little boy, I'm afraid,' the young nurse said. 'He isn't on my ward, and in any case it wouldn't be my place. If you wait here, I'll fetch the sister who's looking after him.'

She disappeared through the swing doors into the main hospital, and it was all Carina could do not to run after her and search for Mattie herself.

Somehow she controlled the urge, pacing fearfully and impatiently, jumping when the swing doors opened again. But it was only the surly porter, pushing an empty trolley. He glowered at her and disappeared through another, smaller door at the side of the lobby, which must, she supposed, lead to storerooms or perhaps even kitchens.

Just when she could bear it no longer, the swing doors opened once more and another nurse appeared. She was much older than the first one, perhaps in her thirties or forties, and though she also wore a starched cap and apron, her uniform dress was dark navy rather than the light blue of the junior's.

'Mrs Talbot? Matthew's mother?' She had a lilting Welsh accent that made Carina warm to her instantly. It was a voice from the valleys, her second home.

'Yes.'

'You're wanting to see him, I expect. But before you do, I should warn you, he is very seriously ill.'

'But he will be all right?' Carina asked anxiously.

'I'm afraid only time will tell, Mrs Talbot, and there is very little we can do but wait. Hopefully the symptoms will subside in a few days, but there is always the risk that they will worsen. If they do . . . then I'm afraid you must prepare yourself for the worst.'

Carina's hand flew to her mouth. She had begun to tremble all over.

The sister patted her arm.

'It hasn't happened yet, Mrs Talbot, and we hope and pray it won't. But it's only right I should be honest with you. Now, under the circumstances, Matron has agreed that you can spend some time out of visiting hours with your son. Shall we go and find him?'

'Oh yes please!'

Grateful as she was that she was being allowed to see Mattie, Carina was only too aware that it was an indication of just how seriously his illness was being treated.

There were just two cots in the side room that served as a children's ward, and Mattie lay in one of them. He was naked but for his nappy, so Carina realised his temperature must still be high, and he was keening softly although his eyes were closed.

'Mattie!' she whispered.

He opened his eyes, but seemed not to recognise her. She bent over the cot, smoothing some of his curls away from his face. They were damp to her touch.

'Oh Mattie, my darling . . .'

Quite suddenly his hand came up and grasped hers, his fist tightening around her fingers.

He knew she was here! He must do! Her heart in her mouth, Carina bit back a sob. Just let them try to throw her out! She'd fight tooth and nail to stay by her beloved son's side until – please God! – he was well again. Nothing else in the world was of the slightest importance.

Chapter Twenty-Five

Mattie was fighting for his life; Carina was in no doubt of it. Even if she couldn't see it for herself, the fact that she was being allowed unlimited visiting would have been all the confirmation she needed. Each day she drove to the hospital, hope that she might find him improved tempered with dread that he might be worse, and sat beside his bed praying as she had never prayed before.

Let him be all right! Just let him be all right and I'll never do anything bad ever again. Oh dear God, let him get better. Please . . . please . . .

Sometimes she addressed her prayers to Robert.

Help us, Robert, please! Do what you can to make your son better . . .

Just as she was leaving on the second evening, another child was brought in to the side ward and placed in the other cot, a baby younger even than Mattie, still and white as death, not even crying. The nurses and a doctor were fussing around him, looking worried, and next morning when she returned, the second cot was empty again. They must have lost him in the night.

Carina's heart bled for the grieving parents she had never even seen, but at the same time she could only be grateful it was not Mattie's cot that was empty.

At least he was holding his own, or so Dr Mackay told her when he looked in on that third day, but there was still a chance that his sickness could take a turn for the worse and his little body, drained of resistance through the fight he was putting up, would not be equal to the added strain. Carina listened without really understanding the talk of possible organ failure. All she knew was that they were trying to prepare her for the possibility that Mattie might yet die. She seemed to tremble incessantly and she was cold all the time, her hands and feet freezing. The ward windows were open to help keep Mattie's temperature under control, but it wasn't that that made her shiver, she knew. The chill came from deep inside.

The strain seemed to be telling on Sally, too. She'd looked decidedly peaky that morning, Carina thought, and she hoped Mattie hadn't passed on to her whatever it was he was suffering from, this unnamed but deadly illness. But she tried to put it to the back of her mind. Sally was a grown woman, fit and strong. She'd be all right. It was Mattie who was small and vulnerable; Mattie whose life was in danger, and she had no energy left to worry about anyone else.

She stayed at his bedside as long as they would let her, and drove home physically exhausted and emotionally drained, not knowing whether she'd see her son alive again.

The fear and anxiety covered her like a shroud, and she couldn't imagine that life could ever be good, or even normal, again.

Frank came up behind Sally as she peeled potatoes for the evening meal, putting his arms around her waist. Peeling potatoes was a job she hated, as she hated all domestic chores, and like everything else, it took her twice as long as it took Carina because she just wasn't adept at it. She wielded the knife clumsily, taking out chunks that she didn't mean to and leaving slivers of peel where there should be none.

Now, she dropped the knife into the bowl of water and turned to face him.

'Do you really want potatoes? I don't know that I can be bothered.'

'Course I want potatoes. What're you trying to do? Starve me?'

'Well I'm not going to bother with these tiddlers. Carina wanted to keep the big ones for baking, but these stupid little things take forever to peel.'

'Forget them, then. Put the big ones in the oven and bake 'em. Go the easy way about it.'

'But Carina said—'

'You don't have to do what she says, do you? She's not God almighty.'

'But she is in charge of the kitchen.'

Frank smirked. 'Not for much longer, I reckon.' He grabbed her bottom, pulling her towards him.

'What are you talking about? And you can stop that too,' she said, wriggling free.

To her surprise – and disappointment – he let her go.

'What am I talking about? Well, you'll be the mistress here soon, won't you? When Mattie kicks the bucket.'

'Frank!' she exclaimed, horrified. 'How can you say such a thing?'

'Easy. He's not going to make it, is he? And when he's gone, the farm will come to you. Bound to. You're next in line, not that stuck-up sister-in-law of yours. It'll be yours, mine, and . . .' He patted her stomach. 'Still think you're in the family way?'

Colour flooded to Sally's cheeks.

'I think so, yes.'

She'd told Frank as soon as she'd suspected it, half afraid in case he decided he didn't want to know and did a runner. But to her surprise, he'd actually seemed quite pleased.

'You're not going to go off and leave me in the lurch, are you?' she'd asked, apprehensive and remembering Carina's warnings that Frank was not the sort to stick around if responsibility came his way.

But: 'What? When I've got my feet nicely under the table here?' had been his reply.

It hadn't been quite the response she'd hoped for. In fact it made her uneasy. Sometimes she did wonder about Frank. She had a horrible feeling that there was a side to him she didn't know at all. But she was too besotted with him to wonder for long. In the end, she always made excuses for him, to herself as well as to Carina.

Now, however, she was quite shocked by the way he was talking so callously about Mattie. She loved her nephew dearly, and was worried to death about him.

Frank, however, seemed not to notice that she had gone very quiet.

'By rights this place should have been yours,' he was saying. 'And it would have been if that silly old beggar hadn't left it to Mattie. No wonder you were cut up about it. But you'll be all right now. We both will be.'

'Please don't talk like that, Frank,' Sally said. 'I was upset that Grandpa bypassed me, yes. But I certainly don't want to get the farm this way.'

'But you wouldn't turn it down.'

'Will you please leave it! I don't want to discuss it any more!' Sally snapped.

'All right, all right, keep your hair on!' Frank held up his hands in mock defeat. 'Joel always said you were a fiery one.'

Sally did a double-take. It was years since she'd heard her father's name mentioned.

'Daddy said that? I always thought I was such a good little girl.'

A strange expression crossed Frank's face, but Sally scarcely noticed. She was too surprised that her father should have said such a thing to him. She didn't recall Robert ever bringing friends home; he and his mates usually played out in the street – football with their jumpers for goalposts, or tormenting the neighbours by knocking on their doors and running away. And even if he had, she couldn't imagine her father talking to the boys about her. But perhaps she'd misbehaved and he'd just said it as a throwaway remark.

'You were a handful even then,' Frank said with a laugh. 'Now come here.'

He tried to pull her into his arms again, but for once, Sally twisted away. She was still too upset by his callousness towards Mattie to want to canoodle at the moment.

'Not now, Frank. I've got work to do,' she said, turning back to the bowl of potatoes.

Frank shrugged. 'Suit yourself. But if you are in the family way, just remember which side your bread's buttered.'

He went out, leaving her puzzled and disturbed.

By the time Carina got home from the hospital, Sally had some news for her.

'Lord Melbrook called to see you this afternoon.'

'Cal did?' Carina was surprised. She'd been sure that he had deliberately extended his business trip so as to avoid her. 'What did he want?'

'Well, for one thing he wanted to know how Mattie was.'

She had finished peeling the potatoes and had been in the

352

milking shed, preparing for the afternoon milking, when Lord Melbrook had driven into the yard, and she hadn't been able to help contrasting his concern for her nephew with Frank's heartlessness.

'Did you tell him how seriously ill he is?'

'Course I did.' She hesitated. 'There's no change, is there?'

Carina shook her head. 'I did think he seemed a bit better this morning, but this afternoon he was feverish again.'

'Oh dear. Are they any further on with finding out what's causing it?'

'They still think it's something he picked up down by the river. Oh . . . how I wish I'd never let Frank take them out that day! If it wasn't for this darned stuff . . .' She pushed angrily at a jar of fresh chutney that Sally had put out ready to go with their evening meal. 'I should never have let them go with him. What was I thinking of?'

Once before, when Carina had blamed Frank for losing Mattie, Sally had leapt to his defence. Not today. In fact, the subject made her distinctly uncomfortable.

'Anyway, he's going to call back this evening,' she said.

'Frank is?' With her mind elsewhere, Carina had lost the thread of the conversation.

'Lord Melbrook. I told you – he wants to talk to you.'

'Oh.' This was a complication she could have done without. 'Did he say what about?'

'No. But it's probably to do with Mattie. He seemed concerned about him, and after all, he is his trustee, isn't he? Anyway, when he comes, I'll make myself scarce. And if it's before Meg's bedtime, I'll take her out of your way too.'

'Where is Meg?' Carina asked.

'In her room, playing with her dolls. She's been up there most of the afternoon. I think she really misses Mattie.'

'Misses having him to boss about, you mean.'

Sally laughed, but it was entirely without humour.

'Probably. But she's worried about him too, Carina. She might only be a little girl, but she's lost both her father and her grandfather, remember. She's scared of losing him as well. And she can see how worried you are, and that's bound to upset her.'

'I'll go up and get her down,' Carina said, a shard of guilt pricking at her. Since Mattie had fallen ill, she'd had no time to spare for Meg. Everything, but everything, was having to take second place.

'I'm sorry to put so much on your shoulders too,' she added.

'Carina, the only thing that matters is Mattie getting well,' Sally said.

And regardless of the fact that, as Frank had pointed out, the little boy was stealing what should have been her inheritance, she truly meant it.

The evenings were beginning to draw in for autumn, and twilight was falling when Cal's car pulled into the farmyard. Meg was already in bed, and good as her word, Sally had gone up to her room as soon as she heard the soft purr of the Benz. Where Frank was, Carina neither knew nor cared.

She'd changed her blouse, which had felt sticky and soiled after a day spent sitting beside Mattie's cot, and brushed her hair; she'd run her fingers through it so often that it had come loose from its pins and was sticking out at odd angles, so that when she'd caught sight of it in the mirror, she'd thought it resembled nothing so much as the scarecrow that guarded their crops in the growing season. And she'd lit a couple of oil lamps, one on the windowsill and the other on the kitchen table.

Now, nervous and awkward at the thought of facing Cal again, she went to open the door.

As he came into the kitchen and passed the oil lamp, his tall frame cast a long shadow, and the power of his presence seemed to fill the room.

'Carina, I am so sorry Mattie is so ill. You must be out of your mind with worry.'

'I am,' she said. 'I feel so helpless.'

'If there is anything at all I can do, you will let me know, won't you?'

'That's very kind, but I don't think there's anything anyone can do, except wait.'

'I'm sure he's in good hands.'

'They did say in the beginning that he might have to be sent to Bath, where there are specialists in . . . whatever it is that's wrong with him.'

'I expect the local medics are taking advice.'

'Perhaps. I'd hate it if they had to move him. At least I'm able to get to see him where he is. And it would mean he was worse, too . . .'

Her throat constricted as a terrible thought occurred to her.

'Do you think the reason they haven't moved him is because there's nothing to be done anyway?'

'Oh Carina, I don't know. I'm not a doctor.'

Cal was behaving as if those moments when he'd almost kissed her had never happened, and talking about Mattie had gone some way to dispelling the awkwardness she had expected to feel.

'Can I get you something to drink?' she asked. 'A cup of tea? Or some cider?'

'Cider sounds good.'

She fetched it from the larder. Cal had made himself at home, taking one of the dining chairs, and she filled a mug and set it, foaming, on the table in front of him.

'Aren't you having one?' he asked.

She shook her head. 'It's too strong for me. I'm so tired, half a glass and I'd be drunk as a lord.'

He raised his glass, looking at it with an amused smile.

'I wonder where that expression comes from? Not all lords are drunken sots, you know.'

'Oh dear,' she said. 'I didn't put that very well, did I?'

'You're forgiven. In any case, my brother did his best to live up to it.'

He was looking at her in that way, his eyes teasing. *Careful*, Carina warned herself.

'What did you want to see me about?' she asked, trying to sound businesslike.

'Could it be I just wanted to see you?'

In spite of all the worries weighing her down, her heart flipped and she couldn't think of a single thing to say. He reached across the table, took her hand and turned it over.

'You're not wearing your ring.'

'No.' She withdrew her hand as if his fingers were burning hers. 'I don't wear it every day. I like to keep it safe. It's doubly precious to me now, since I thought I'd lost it for ever.'

'I'm sure it is.'

'Mammy! Mammy!'

Carina turned at the sound of the small tearful voice. Meg was standing at the top of the stairs.

'What's wrong, Meg?' She got up, going towards the stairs, and Meg ran down to meet her, throwing herself into her mother's arms.

'I can't go to sleep, Mammy. I want Mattie!'

'Oh Meg, I know. But you have to be brave. We all do.' *Mattie will be home soon*, she had been about to say, but she mustn't make promises she couldn't keep.

'Would you like a glass of warm milk, darling?' she asked. 'That should help to send you off.'

Meg nodded, her tear-wet face bobbing against Carina's shoulder.

'Stay here then and I'll get it.'

She put Meg down and went to the larder to fetch the milk. When she came back, Meg was beside Cal's chair, her hands on his knee, looking up at him dolefully with her lip caught between her teeth.

'I expect you're wondering about the puppies,' he was saying. Meg nodded. 'They are doing well. And they are looking forward to you and Mattie coming to see them again.'

'Even the little one?'

'Especially the little one. What do you think we should call her?'

Carina set the milk to warm, grateful to Cal for taking Meg's mind off her sick brother.

'What do you think is a nice name for her, Meg?' she asked over her shoulder.

Meg thought for a moment. 'Goldilocks.'

'Goldilocks,' Cal repeated. 'Mm. But she's not gold. She's black.'

Meg thought again.

'Cinderella.'

'Ah, now you have something! Cinderella. We could call her Cinders for short. That would be easier to call out when you want her to come. And cinders are black, too, aren't they?'

Meg nodded, brushing away her tears with the back of her hand and looking much more like the happy little girl she usually was.

When the milk was warm, Carina filled the child-sized mug she used and Meg drank it, looking solemnly over the rim at Cal. He was obviously her hero.

'Let's get you back to bed then, darling,' Carina said when she'd finished.

She took Meg upstairs and tucked her in.

'Straight off to sleep now. Sweet dreams.'

It was what she said to both children each night, but now the words caught in her throat as she thought of Mattie, lying not in his own cot but in the hospital ward. Tears pricked her eyes and the now-familiar dread enveloped her in a rush.

'Is she more settled now?' Cal asked as Carina returned to the kitchen.

'I think so.' She glanced at the cider jug, standing on the table. 'D'you know, I think I will have some of that after all. I feel like getting drunk as a lord.'

She tried to say it lightly, jokingly, but somehow her voice cracked on the words and suddenly the tears were in her eyes again, and streaming down her cheeks. She sank on to a dining chair, covering her face with her hands.

'I'm sorry . . .' she muttered.

'Don't be silly.' He reached across the table, covering one of her hands with his. 'You've had a lot to contend with. Still have. Not many women would cope as you have.'

'I'm just so worried . . .'

'I know you are. But Mattie's a fighter – like you. He's proved that.'

'But what if he can't fight any longer? I'm so frightened, Cal. And so tired.'

'Of course you are. Running this place alone would be enough to wear you out, without everything else. Come on now. Are you going to have that cider?'

She raised her head, wiping her face with her free hand.

'Better not.'

'Actually, I think you need something stronger than cider. Do you have any spirits in the house?'

'There's some brandy. But—'

'Where is it?'

'In the chiffonier. But I mustn't . . .'

'Nonsense. It'll do you good.' He got up, crossed to the chiffonier and found the bottle and a glass. 'Here you are. Drink this.'

She took a sip, made a face. Could this really be the stuff Robert had been worried about her rubbing on Mattie's gums in case he became addicted to it? It was worse than medicine!

But the brandy, trickling down her throat and into her veins, was warming her, warming all the places that had been icy cold these last days.

'Mm!' she murmured, swallowing some more and wiping her wet cheeks again with the back of her hand.

Cal produced a handkerchief from his pocket and passed it to her.

'Use this.'

She dried her eyes, blew her nose. The handkerchief was finest linen, monogrammed in one corner with his initials, she noticed.

'Better?' She nodded. 'What are we going to do with you, Carina?'

'I don't know. I'm a bit of a lost cause, aren't I?'

But it felt good, so good, to have someone caring about her. Supporting her. It seemed a lifetime she had been struggling on alone, making decisions, fighting to keep the family afloat, worrying about everything from Sally's involvement with Frank to where the next penny was coming from. Alone, always alone. And on top of everything else, eclipsing it, her beloved Mattie hovering between life and death.

'You're certainly not a lost cause,' Cal said. 'You're a remarkable woman, Carina. You've been through a terrible time, and all in the short space of a few months. But things will get better. There will be light at the end of the tunnel.'

'I wish I could believe that.' She wiped the last of the tears from her cheeks, went to hand him back his handkerchief.

'Keep it.' But his hand closed over hers anyway.

She stared down at it, that big hand covering hers, and wished he'd leave it there for ever. Wished she could burrow into him, safe and warm and protected. Curl up and forget all the anxieties and problems, or at least have someone to share them with to lighten the load.

'It's too much for you alone, Carina,' he said as if he'd read her thoughts. 'And I think I may be able to help. I can't do anything about Mattie's illness, of course – that's up to the doctors, and Mattie himself. But I could take some of your other worries off your shoulders. The farm, for instance.'

She raised her eyes to his, puzzled.

'The farm?'

'It's not paying for itself, is it? But it should. What it needs is some investment, and someone who knows what they're doing to run it.'

She smiled wanly. 'Tell me something I don't know.'

'I think I may have the answer. If I were to buy it from you – or from Mattie, to be precise – you'd have some capital to live on.'

Carina had stiffened. 'Buy the farm?'

'I think it's the answer. It will be – what? – another twenty years before Mattie is ready to run it. Can you really go on like this for that long? You'll wear yourself out – work yourself into an early grave. And for what? But if I was to buy it . . .'

For long moments, Carina was frozen, motionless as if she

were carved out of a block of stone. But her thoughts were racing, churning, as Grandpa Luke's voice seemed to come to her from beyond the grave.

There's something fishy going on with Melbrook . . . he's been a bit too friendly since our Robert died. And: *The Melbrooks have never liked that we got the freehold of this place . . . Good land, better than most, and slap bang in the middle of the estate. I know for a fact they'd have it back if they could . . .*

Grandpa had warned her. Grandpa had been suspicious of Cal worming his way in, as he'd put it. *Be careful, my girl*, he'd said.

And had she taken heed of his warnings? No! She'd succumbed to Cal's charm, to his apparent kindness, and never stopped for a moment to think he might have an ulterior motive.

Oh, but he was clever! Giving her work when she needed it, going out of his way to drive her home when she was caught in the rain, being supportive at the time of the fire, cultivating her children even. And the master stroke – agreeing to become a trustee of Grandpa Luke's bequest to Mattie. She'd been grateful to him – actually grateful – when all the time it was this that he'd had in mind. Reclaiming the farm for the Dunderwick estate. And what could she do about it? Nothing! Nothing! If Arthur Clarence, the other trustee, agreed that it was in Mattie's best interests – and she couldn't imagine he would do otherwise when it was Lord Melbrook who suggested it – then Cal would set things in motion and take over Meadow Farm for what would no doubt be a paltry sum. Their home! Everything Robert, and Grandpa Luke in his day, had worked for! Mattie's inheritance!

Cal had woven a pretty, shining web, and she had walked right into it.

'You bastard!' She jerked her hand away from his, pushed

herself to her feet, pointed towards the door with a trembling finger. 'Just go, will you? Get out of my house!'

'Carina . . .'

'I wondered why you were being so kind to me,' she spat at him. 'Well, now I know! But you won't have it all your own way. I'll fight you, Cal. I'll fight you every step of the way. You'll never have what is rightfully Mattie's if I can find a way to stop you.'

Cal was on his feet too, his hands spread helplessly.

'Carina – I don't want to rob Mattie . . .'

'No? Oh, I think you do! Meadow Farm belongs to your estate – that's what you think. And you'd sell your soul to get it back. Well, it's not going to be that easy. I'm not quite the fool you take me for. Now get out! Get out, and don't you dare come back!'

Quite suddenly Cal was angry too.

'If that's what you want.' He strode to the door, turned with his hand on the latch. 'I can see there's no point arguing with you. If you want to work yourself into an early grave, or finish up in the poorhouse, I can't stop you.' Without another word, he opened the door and left.

Carina stood staring at the closed door for a moment, shaking from head to foot. And then the tears came again, tears of anger, tears of self-recrimination, tears of despair. She'd felt so safe with him, so cared for. And all the time . . .

Had he come here tonight, pretending sympathy, because he knew Mattie was desperately ill and wanted to make his move in case the little boy died and he no longer had the power that came from being his trustee? Bastard! Bastard! How could he seem so charming and supportive when in reality he was cold, calculating, callous?

She was still holding his handkerchief, bunched in her balled fist. Furious with herself and with him, she crossed to the range, opened the door and threw the linen square on to the glowing embers. There was something satisfying in seeing it scorch, crumble, glow and disintegrate. But at the same time it was like watching her half-acknowledged dreams burn and die, and the pain in her heart was so sharp she could scarcely breathe.

How could she have been such a fool? But she had, she had. And the shame of it was overwhelming.

She sank to the floor, her back sliding down the wall until her head reached her knees. Then, with her arms wrapped around herself, she wept as if her heart would break.

It was there that Sally, who had heard the raised voices, found her.

'Carina – whatever is wrong?'

'Don't ask,' Carina grated through her tears.

Sally dropped to the floor beside her, putting her arms round the shaking body of her sister-in-law and holding her tight. They stayed there for a very long time.

The loud rapping at the door startled them both. Sally scrambled to her feet, ready to go and answer it, but Carina pushed past her, her heart hammering in her chest.

A young girl in nurse's uniform stood on the doorstep, the same girl she had met on the first day she had visited Mattie in hospital. She was called Ivy, and she lived in Dunderwick, Carina now knew.

Her heart plummeted. She could think of only one reason why Ivy should be here at this time of night.

'Mattie . . .' she whispered, clinging to the doorpost for support.

'It's all right, Mrs Talbot. He's fine.'

For a moment she couldn't take in what the young nurse had said.

'We think he's turned the corner,' Ivy said. 'His fever has broken and he's taking fluids. And asking for you! I've just come off duty, and knowing how worried you've been, I thought I'd call in on my way home and let you know.'

'Really? Really?' She still couldn't believe it.

'Really. After what he's been through, he won't be back to his usual self for some time yet, but when you visit tomorrow, I think you'll find he's on the road to recovery.'

'Oh thank you! Thank you!'

When the nurse had gone, riding her bicycle across the farmyard to the accompaniment of Cymru's staccato barks, Carina and Sally collapsed into one another's arms again. But this time the tears they shed were tears of joy.

Mattie was going to be all right! All Carina's prayers had been answered! Nothing else in the world was of the slightest importance. Certainly not a conniving rat like Calvert Melbrook.

Chapter Twenty-Six

Frank was in the foulest of moods. He stood in the doorway of one of the sheds, smoking a Woodbine – it was raining this morning, just to make things even more depressing – and when Cymru approached, sniffing at his legs, he aimed a kick at him. The dog backed away with a yelp, looking hurt and bemused; he wasn't used to being treated with anything but kindness.

'Get out of it!' Frank snarled.

The news that had greeted him when he'd gone in for breakfast had been the last thing he'd wanted to hear. That little blighter Mattie had turned the corner, it seemed. He was going to make it, or so they thought. Carina and Sally were both so relieved and delighted they couldn't stop smiling, and their celebratory mood had enraged Frank even more. He had been so sure the little bugger was going to die and leave the coast clear for Sally to inherit the farm without any further intervention on his part, but it didn't look as if that was going to happen. It was going to be down to him – again. He didn't suppose there was any great hurry; Mattie was still only a kid, and in any case he'd be wise to wait a bit after his failed attempt to let him drown. The last thing he wanted was for Carina, and more importantly Sally, to get suspicious. And his feet were well and truly under the table. If he had got Sally pregnant as she seemed to think he had, she'd want him on the scene.

Truth to tell, though it had been part of his plan, he wasn't all that happy about that either. The thought of being tied down to a wife and a screaming nipper made him knot up inside. But if that was what it took . . .

At least the farm would be his in all but name. The cloak of respectability he needed. And he knew all about farming, even if he didn't like it much. He couldn't suppress a grin as he thought of Sally teaching him the rudiments of what to do while he pretended the ignorance of a city boy born and bred. Talk about teaching your grandmother to suck eggs!

He dropped the butt end of his Woodbine and ground it out with his heel. He'd just go back for one more cup of tea and then he'd better start work. For the moment, he had to keep them sweet. Later . . . well, there were plenty of better ways to live than working your fingers to the bone in all winds and weathers.

Turning his collar up against the drizzly rain, he headed back towards the house.

Sally and Meg went to the hospital with Carina that morning. Sally was as anxious as she was to visit Mattie; until they'd seen for themselves that he was better, they were almost afraid to believe it. And Meg couldn't wait to see her little brother. Carina hoped she'd be allowed in for a short while, although children weren't usually welcome as visitors.

It was the Welsh sister on duty. They met her in the corridor outside Mattie's ward – since she had become such a regular here, Carina now went straight in.

'Good news,' she greeted them. 'Or did you already know? Nurse Miller said when she went off duty last night that she'd try to call on you on her way home.'

'She did,' Carina said. 'What a kind thing to do. I had the

best night's sleep last night that I've had for a week. Is he really better?'

'Better, certainly. Doctor thinks he's turned the corner, but of course he's not out of the woods yet. It's going to be a while before he's anywhere near fit. He's been through a lot, and it will take careful nursing to get him well again.'

'He will recover eventually, though? Get back to his usual self?'

'Hopefully, yes. But it's too early to say whether there will be any lasting effects. Doctor will want to talk you through it all before you take him home.'

'Take him home?' Carina's heart leapt. 'You mean . . . ?'

The sister smoothed her crisp white apron.

'Not today, if that's what you're thinking. And probably not tomorrow either. We need to keep an eye on him for a day or two at least to make sure there's no recurrence.'

'Oh.' Carina's heart plummeted again. 'A recurrence?'

'There's no reason to think there will be. It's just that we have to be sure.'

Meg was getting impatient, fidgeting and tugging at Carina's skirt.

'Where's Mattie?'

'In there. We'll go and see him in a minute. I'm just talking to the nurse.'

'So when did you begin to see an improvement?' Sally asked.

'Quite soon after Mrs Talbot left. Once the fever had broken, the change was quite miraculous. It's often the way.'

Carina became suddenly aware Meg was no longer tugging at her skirt. She looked around; there was no sign of her.

'Meg?'

The sister smiled. 'I don't think she could wait any longer to see her little brother.'

'Oh no! She hasn't . . . ?'

'I think you'll find she has.'

Worried as to what Meg might be up to, Carina hurried to the door to Mattie's ward, which was open. She went in, ready to chastise her daughter, but stopped short, her heart melting at the scene that met her eyes.

Meg was standing beside the cot, her plump little hands thrust through the bars. Mattie had rolled over to face her, and his hands were reaching for hers. As Carina watched, he managed it with a good deal of wriggling, and a wide smile transformed his wan little face.

Sally was behind her, one arm around her waist.

'I think he's going to be all right, Carina.' Her voice was choked.

'I think they both are,' Carina said.

Isobel Luckington wiggled her toes luxuriously.

'Mm . . . more . . .'

The young man massaging her feet obliged.

He couldn't have been more than half her age. A lick of blond hair fell into his eyes as he worked, but he didn't dare stop to brush it aside. He was too much in awe of Isobel, and too anxious to keep on her right side. At the moment, he was her favourite, but he knew that if he displeased her, she wouldn't hesitate to bestow her favours elsewhere.

And her favours were well worth having. Visits to the theatre, always in a private box overlooking the stage, dinners at the finest hotels in Bath, presents of more or less anything that took his fancy but couldn't afford on the allowance he got from his father. That was paltry compared to Isobel's largesse. No, he was more than prepared to do her bidding if it meant he could enjoy the finer things in life without having to work for them.

Presently, of course, there would be other duties expected of him, but he enjoyed those too. Isobel was still a very attractive woman, sophisticated and worldly too, ready to teach him all she had learned of the art of lovemaking. She was far more exciting than the silly prissy girls in his social circle, or the hearty horsey types he met when he and his family holidayed on their country estate. Altogether it was an arrangement that suited him admirably.

A tap at the door interrupted the now-familiar ritual.

'Come!' Isobel called languidly without bothering to remove her foot from Marcus Frobisher-White's lap.

A uniformed maid entered the room, her nervousness at what she might find evident.

'I'm sorry to disturb you, Mrs Luckington, but . . .'

'Yes?'

'You have a visitor.'

Isobel glanced at the ornately carved clock on the mantelshelf.

'At this hour?'

'Yes, mum.'

'Well – who is it?'

'It's Lord Melbrook, mum.'

'Really?' Now Isobel did remove her foot from the young man's lap, sitting up, straightening her skirts and slipping her feet into her soft kid shoes.

'Show him up, if you please, Maria. Don't leave him waiting in the hallway.' She turned to the young man. 'I think perhaps, Marcus, it is time to say goodnight.'

Marcus rose, put out but not daring to show it.

'Off with you then! And don't forget you are to accompany me to the recital in the Pump Room on Friday.'

'As if I would!'

He collected his jacket, draped casually across the back of a chair, and left.

On the stairs he passed Lord Melbrook, who nodded at him curtly, and experienced a stab of dislike. How come he was being dismissed like a tiresome child so that this old man could come waltzing in? He'd like to give him a poke on the nose. Arrogant bastard.

But Marcus Frobisher-White knew his place. And he was well aware on which side his bread was buttered.

As the front door of the grand house closed after him, he turned his collar up against the drizzle that was falling and began whistling tunelessly as he strode out, hoping to catch a passing cab to save him from having to walk all the way home.

Isobel greeted Cal with a kiss on both cheeks.

'This is an unexpected pleasure!'

'Unexpected, certainly,' Cal said with a wry smile. 'I'm sorry if I've spoiled your evening's entertainment.'

'Oh pooh! You know I much prefer your company to that of any of my gauche young friends.'

It was no more or less than the truth and had been for as long as Isobel could remember. As children, running wild in the fields and woods on their families' respective estates, she'd wanted for no other company, even though she was three years older than him. He was the only playmate whose daring matched hers. As they grew older and Isobel discovered the pleasures of kissing – and more – she used her feminine wiles to initiate Cal with the experience she had gained from adventures with other, older boys. But not one of them matched Cal. For a while she even thought she was in love with him, dreaming about him by day and by night, wanting nothing, no one but him. But close as they were, she never let on to him the way she was feeling. She was too afraid of spoiling their very special relationship.

And then he had met and fallen in love with Alice, and for a while everything had changed. Racked with jealousy, Isobel had wondered what in the world he saw in the girl. Yes, she was pretty – prettier than Isobel would ever be. But she didn't have an adventurous bone in her body. She'd bore him in no time. Then he'd be sorry and come running back to her.

Just to show him, she deliberately kept her distance, tossed her head, spoke to him curtly if their paths crossed. The young men who flocked around her were balm to her wounded pride and broken heart, but nothing more than that. They were her lackeys; she couldn't respect them, much less fall in love with them, though it seemed Cal was becoming more and more involved with Alice, not less as she had hoped.

Percy Luckington was different from any of those fawning young men. Though he was thirty years her senior, he was still handsome. His jaw was firm, he hadn't developed ugly jowls, his hair, iron grey, made him look not old but distinguished and he stood tall and straight with no hint of the pot belly that marred the physique of so many older gentlemen. Added to this, he was a highly respected surgeon with a home in the elegant Royal Crescent and inherited wealth besides his not inconsiderable earned income. And of course there was no question of her being able to play him as she played her younger admirers. That in itself made him attractive to her.

If she couldn't have Cal, she might as well settle for Percy Luckington and the life he could offer her, she decided.

It was Alice dying so tragically that brought Isobel and Cal together again. She was never quite sure why she went to see him when she heard of it, whether she was hoping deep down that there might now be a chance for her, or whether, as she liked to think, it was simply because she wanted to offer her condolences to a very old friend. If she had entertained a hope of taking Alice's place, it was quickly dashed. Cal was plainly devastated.

He had cried in her arms, Cal, the strong, the proud, the invincible. Afterwards he had apologised and she'd told him no, he needed to let go, to let out all that terrible grief. That there was no need to pretend with her, who knew him so well. She would be there for him, whenever he needed her. And she'd done it not in the hope of replacing Alice in his affections but because she was filled with tenderness and a quite different sort of love.

She'd comforted him, and the bond that had always been there between them had been renewed and strengthened. And so it had continued, though she was married to Percy and Cal had joined the army and gone overseas. Nowadays she loved him like the brother she had never had. And tonight, as he came into her sitting room, she knew instantly that something was wrong.

'I can see you need a drink,' she said, fetching the decanter even as she spoke. 'Neat? Or would you like some water with it?'

'You know me, Isobel. I like my drinks just the way I like everything else. Straight.'

She poured two fingers of whisky into a tumbler and handed it to him.

'In that case, perhaps you'll tell me what's up with you without me having to ask too many questions.'

'Nothing's up with me, as you put it. I was in Bath and decided to call on my oldest friend.'

But he took a deep drink, emptying the glass in one go, and threw himself down on the chaise longue.

'Don't give me that, Cal.' Without asking, she took the glass from him and refilled it. 'I know you too well. Something is very wrong. Is it the estate? Are you about to have to break it up or face ruin?'

Cal laughed shortly and without humour.

'It hasn't quite come to that yet, though if Stafford had lived it probably would have done.'

'Then it's a woman. Your little seamstress, if I might hazard a guess.'

'What gives you that idea?'

It was Isobel's turn to laugh.

'Oh Cal, it's as plain as the nose on your face. I think you've fallen in love with her.'

'Don't let my mother hear you say that. She'd have forty fits.'

'And since when have you ever cared about what your mother thought? I agree with her, of course. A farmer's widow would hardly be a suitable candidate for the title of Lady Melbrook. But that's the way things are headed if I'm not much mistaken.'

She sat down opposite him on one of the elegant spindle-leg chairs and gave him a straight look. He took another, more judicious, sip of his whisky, and sighed.

'You're right of course. As always.'

'You've come to the conclusion that it would be most inappropriate to have a relationship with her?'

'No, dammit. As you yourself pointed out, I don't believe in taking notice of what people think. The hell with that!'

'So what's gone wrong? She doesn't reciprocate your feelings?'

'Huh!' He took another drink. 'I think that's putting it mildly. She hates my guts. Threw me out of her house.'

'Oh Cal! You didn't make some ham-fisted attempt at seducing her?'

'No, nothing like that. I've just buggered it up. She thinks I'm after her land. That I've been cultivating her to get my hands on it.'

'Why would she think that?'

'It's a long story.'

'And I have all the time in the world to listen to it.'

'The crux of the matter is that when the old man died, he left the farm to his great-grandson, who is still an infant. I agreed to take on the role of trustee until he comes of age.'

'And how does that make you the villain of the piece?'

'Carina is struggling, badly. I offered to buy the farm and she has somehow got it into her head that I am abusing my position. And she seems to think that everything I've done to try and help was in order to worm my way in with her.'

'Oh dear. And is there any truth in that?'

Cal grimaced. 'That's the irony of it. In the beginning, I did have my eye on getting Meadow Farm back. As you know, the freehold was given to the Green family by my great-grandfather in gratitude for the then tenant saving the life of one of his children. A generous, if understandable, gesture. It's prime land, bordered on all sides by farms that belong to the estate, so it would make sense if it came back under the same banner. And properly run, it could contribute considerably to the profitability of our holdings. Or at least that was my thinking. Except that somewhere along the line . . .'

'You fell in love with the woman,' Isobel finished for him.

He shrugged helplessly.

'I suppose that's the top and bottom of it.'

'Oh Cal.' Isobel sighed. 'You don't seem to have much luck in matters of the heart. All these years mourning Alice, and then you have to fall in love with the most unsuitable of women. Did you ever tell her what I told you about her husband's father?'

Cal shook his head.

'I couldn't see the point. She's had enough to contend with without me adding to it. She lost her husband in a tragic accident, then old Luke in a fire that also cost her half their winter hay. And on top of it all, her son has been in hospital for the best part of a week fighting for his life.'

'Oh my goodness – that's dreadful! Is he going to be all right?'

'I have no idea. I don't think anyone does. Carina is distraught, of course; she accused me of trying to get my hands on the farm quickly, in case the boy died and I no longer had any control over what happened to it.'

'Oh Cal . . . no wonder you're so upset. Being accused of something so callous would be dreadful under any circumstances, but coming from her . . . Let me get you another drink.'

'I think I've had enough. I have to drive home, and I can't do that if I'm paralytic.'

'Then stay the night here. You know the guest room is always kept made up. And if you go home, you'll only spend half the night brooding alone.'

'Perhaps you're right. In that case, I will have another drink.'

Instead of refilling his glass, she set the decanter on the table beside him.

'Help yourself. To as much as you need.'

He smiled faintly. 'I can always rely on you, can't I, Isobel?'

'I should hope so. Now, tell me, what is wrong with the little boy?'

'Apparently he has contracted some disease carried by rats. At least that's what the doctors think. Carina allowed their farmhand to take the children out for a walk; he managed to lose Mattie, and when Carina found him, he was ankle deep in mud in the river. With all the dry weather we've had, they think the water was probably polluted.'

'How on earth did the farmhand come to lose him?'

'God knows. It's all open fields. But actually that man is another reason I'm concerned about Carina. It seems he turned up out of the blue claiming to be a childhood friend of Robert's and offering his services, which Carina was in no position to refuse. But from what she's said, she doesn't like or trust him, and there's been talk in the village that he might very well be the one responsible for the burglaries that have been happening lately in and around Dunderwick, and even the robbery with violence at the bookmaker's in Hillsbridge on the day of Robert's funeral.'

'And he's living at the farm?'

'Yes, and involved with Sally, from what I can gather. I'm not happy about him, Isobel. From what I've seen of him, it wouldn't surprise me if the rumours didn't turn out to be true. It's one of the reasons I made the offer to buy the farm – I'd like Carina to be shot of him. But instead of improving matters, I just seem to have made them ten times worse.'

'You really do care about her very much, don't you?' Isobel said gently.

'Yes,' he said. 'I do.'

'Then why don't you go and see her again – try and explain . . .'

'I don't think so. She made her feelings very plain.'

'Oh, you and your pride.'

'It would do no good.' He put down his empty glass and pushed the decanter to the back of the table. 'Thanks for your kind offer, but I really think I should go home. I have meetings arranged for the morning.'

'If you're sure.'

'Yes.' He stood up, rubbing his leg, which always seemed to pain him more when he let his feelings get the better of him. 'Thanks for listening, Isobel.'

'Hopefully talking about it has helped.'

'It hasn't changed anything, though, has it?'

'I suppose not.'

She went with him to the door, kissed him on both cheeks, then watched him walk to his Benz, parked at the kerb. His limp was more pronounced tonight, she thought. And her heart went out to the man she had loved, one way or another, for almost the whole of her life.

The idea came to Isobel quite suddenly, and she wondered why it hadn't occurred to her before.

After Cal had left, she'd returned to her drawing room, poured herself a whisky in the glass he had used – though there were plenty of clean ones, she liked the feeling of intimacy with him that it gave her – and made herself comfortable on the chaise, pondering the whole sorry story.

She felt protective of him now in just the same way she had when Alice had died. There was something dreadfully poignant when a man as strong as Cal let down his defences. With him, the hurt would run far deeper than in many people whose emotions were closer to the surface.

Of course, what he should do was what she had suggested – go and see Carina, lay himself bare, as he had to her, and try to put things right. But he wouldn't do that. His pride would never allow it.

Well . . . if he wouldn't do it himself, then she would do it for him.

She might be unsuccessful, of course. She had the impression this Carina was a strong-willed woman, the very antithesis of that milksop Alice. It made Isobel warm to her. Someone who could stand their ground was the right person for Cal, even if she was only a farmer's widow.

Certainly, with her husband dead only a few months, it was far too soon to be suggesting any such thing to her, but at least she could try to explain that Cal had no intention of robbing her son of his inheritance, that he only had Carina's welfare at heart, and mend some bridges so that the way would be open for him when the time was right.

Cal, of course, would never sanction her interference. If he knew what she planned to do, he would forbid it. But he wouldn't know, at least not until after the event, and perhaps not even then if Carina gave Isobel the same short shrift she'd given Cal.

But her shoulders were broad. She'd do this for him. Even if it did mean her chances with him were scotched for ever.

Isobel poured herself another drink and sat long into the night planning her strategy.

Chapter Twenty-Seven

Sally had decided it was high time something was done about the wreckage of the burned-out barn. Since the firemen had finished hosing down the smouldering remains that terrible day, it had remained untouched, a constant reminder of the awful thing that had happened.

That morning, the rain had stopped and the sun had come out, though it was but a pale echo of the blazing globe it had been during the summer months. The leaves had begun drifting down from the trees too and were lying in drifts of brown, ochre and yellow. Soon they would be bare for winter. The barn would look even more desolate then.

Amongst the debris were large pieces of charred timber. If she sawed them up into chunks, they would provide firewood for the cold months ahead. The masses of burned hay would have to be forked up and loaded on to a trailer. Then they could get Captain to pull it to somewhere where it would at least be out of sight.

Carina had gone off as usual to the hospital, taking Meg with her. Now that Mattie was so much better, the sister had said it would be all right for the little girl to visit him. Frank was somewhere out in the fields, and Sally was alone. She wasn't feeling well; she was nauseous every morning now, though she hadn't actually been sick, thank goodness, and she decided that making a start on clearing the barn would take her mind off it.

Pulling on her boots, she crossed the farmyard and stood for a moment contemplating the massive task ahead of her. Then she rolled up her sleeves and made a start, rescuing the timbers that could be used as firewood and stacking them in a corner of the farmyard. She fetched a shovel and a broom, clearing the debris from underfoot as she went deeper into the ruins of the barn.

As she swept and shovelled, something suddenly caught her eye. Something that glinted dully in the sunlight. Puzzled, she bent down and picked it up.

A button. Brown and shiny when she had wiped the patina of grime off it. A button that was exactly the same as the one she had found in Captain's stable after Robert had been killed, if she remembered correctly. Though at the time she had wondered if it might have belonged to the intruder they'd surprised the night before, she hadn't given it much thought lately. The very idea that it might have been torn off in a struggle, and that Captain might not have been responsible for Robert's death at all, had seemed like fantasy.

But now, to find another, not in the stable but here in the barn, defied all logic. The hired hands who had been helping with the harvest had been in here, of course, as well as in Captain's stable, but the likelihood that one of them should have lost two buttons in different places seemed an unbelievable coincidence. Besides, if she remembered rightly, the first one had still had thread attached, and a fragment of fabric, as if it had been torn off in a struggle.

Sally threw down her broom, went into the house and up to her room. She'd kept the first button; now she retrieved it from the small oddments drawer in her dressing table and compared the two. They were identical, no doubt about it.

Pushing them both into the pocket of her trousers, she went back to the burned-out barn, grabbed her shovel and began shifting debris in the spot where she had spied the second button. And there, under a heap of charred hay, sodden from yesterday's rain, she found it.

It was only a remnant, scorched and singed. Much of it had been completely destroyed. But unmistakably it had once been part of a jacket. A jacket with three buttons identical to the ones in her pocket still attached. Perhaps the one she had just found had been on a cuff, and the sleeve had burned completely away. How the rest of it had survived she had no idea, unless a fireman's hose had been trained on the exact spot where it lay.

Quite suddenly Sally felt not only nauseous but horribly sick. She bent double, retching violently into a heap of sodden, fire-blackened straw.

Oh, she must be wrong! She must be! She wouldn't believe it! She wouldn't!

But for all her denials, she could think of no other explanation but the one that was making her dizzy and ill. And if she was right, she didn't know what in the world she was going to do about it.

She had cleared a small section of debris, piling it into the cart, when Frank came swaggering into the farmyard. Her heart leapt into her throat. As she'd worked, she'd thought of nothing but what she'd found, going over and over possible explanations. But none of them could dispel the awful thought that the jacket with the brown shiny buttons might belong to Frank. And if it did, why had the first one she'd found been in Captain's stable? She was sure she had found it on the day of Robert's funeral.

That was before Frank had arrived on the scene, so it made no sense, unless . . .

Unless the intruder she had always suspected of being responsible for Robert's death was, in fact, Frank.

She didn't want to believe it, didn't want to think it for even a moment.

Why would Frank have been creeping around that night when she and Robert had both been so sure there was someone out there in the darkness? The theory she'd had that the intruder had spent the night in the stable and been surprised by Robert next morning didn't hold water either. Frank was nervous of Captain. He'd never have bedded down so close to the big old horse. And if he and Robert were old friends, why would they fight if Robert had found him there? His most likely reaction would have been to invite him into the house for a cup of tea and a good cooked breakfast, not to try to throw him out. No, there was some other explanation. There had to be!

But still the suspicion that the jacket belonged to Frank refused to go away. Still it nagged away at the corners of her mind, no matter how she tried to tell herself it couldn't be so.

She'd have to talk to him about it so as to set her mind at rest.

But now, as she saw him walking towards her, her stomach tied itself in knots and her mouth went dry, so afraid was she of what his answer would be.

'What you doing?' he asked, strolling over to her and thrusting his hands in his trouser pockets.

'What does it look like? Trying to clear up some of this mess.'

'You've got your work cut out there.'

'Don't I know it. It's got to be done sometime, though. I thought it might as well be now.'

'Leave it and come and have a cup of tea. My throat's like the bottom of a parrot's cage.'

There was no avoiding it any longer. Sally leaned over and picked up the charred remnant of fabric, which she had put down on top of one of the heaps of debris yet to be cleared.

'Was this a jacket belonging to you?'

'What?'

'Did you lose a jacket like this in the fire?'

The intense look on Sally's face made him uneasy.

'I don't know what you're on about, Sal. You know I lost pretty well everything in the fire.'

'But this . . .' She gave the remnant a wave. 'Was this yours? Or did it get left behind by one of the casual labourers? It's important, Frank.'

Though he didn't know why Sally was so insistent on having her question answered, all Frank's antennae were flagging up a warning now. He shrugged, attempting nonchalance.

'Never seen it before. Why? What does it matter anyway? It won't be much good to anybody now, will it? Get rid of it, for goodness' sake, and come and have that cup of tea.'

Sally tossed the piece of charred fabric back on to the heap of debris.

She should have felt relief. She hadn't given away the reason she was interested in the burned jacket and Frank had denied being the owner. But somehow the awful suspicion refused to go away.

Much as she wanted to, Sally was not sure she believed him.

It was early afternoon when Carina and Meg arrived home. Sally had returned to her self-appointed task of clearing the ruined barn, but she was still fretting, and when the Rover turned into the farmyard much earlier than expected, her heart came into her mouth. In her present state of mind, her first thought was that something bad had happened. Had Mattie had a relapse? Even, God forbid, died?

She threw down her spade and rushed out. But one glimpse of Carina's face told her she was wrong. Her sister-in-law was wreathed in smiles, and Meg was hopping up and down in her seat, impatient to be lifted down.

'Oh Sally, you'll never believe it! They say we can bring Mattie home tomorrow!'

'Oh, that is good news! When I saw you home early . . .' She broke off, not wanting to articulate what she had thought.

'We had to leave; there's another child been brought in, poor little mite. Screaming the place down. Something wrong with her ear, I think, a mastoid maybe. Anyway, they put her in the other cot in Mattie's room, so of course we had to go. But never mind! We can go back and get him tomorrow. Imagine it, Sally! Mattie's coming home!'

'That's wonderful.'

The dark clouds that had engulfed Sally all day since her discovery lifted a little. She had been wondering if she should share her suspicions with Carina; now she told herself she couldn't spoil Carina's happy relief with what was, after all, nothing more than stupid conjecture.

She was in love with Frank. She was going to have his baby. To think that he had been responsible for Robert's death, and heaven only knew what besides, was beyond ridiculous.

In the event, even if Sally had wanted a private conversation with Carina, it would have had to wait. She and Meg hadn't been home long when they had a visitor.

Hester Dallimore.

When she came knocking on the door, Carina felt guilty at

the way her heart sank. Hester was, after all, her aunt, and she'd come a long way to visit.

'I hear our Mattie has been taken bad,' she said without preamble the minute she was through the door.

'Yes, he's been very ill in hospital,' Carina said. 'But he's much better now, thank goodness, and—'

'He's coming home tomorrow,' she had been going to say, but Hester cut across her. 'You should have let me know.' Her tone was indignant.

It crossed Carina's mind to wonder how she *did* know. Perhaps one of the nurses had said something, or another patient or their relative had seen her visiting day after day and the bush telegraph had done the rest. Hester would have been mightily upset that others knew something she did not, especially since it concerned her own family. That would be the reason she was here now, so that she could take whatever news there was back to Fairley Terrace and be the one in the know, as she would put it.

'I'm sorry, but my first concern has been Mattie,' Carina said. 'I'm afraid I haven't had time for anything else.'

'Not even for letting your mother know?'

'I didn't want to worry her.' Carina really didn't want to have this conversation. 'Have you walked all the way over?'

'I have. That's what families are for.'

'You must be dying for a cup of tea.'

'Well, yes, I am. But only if you're making one. I wouldn't want to take up any more of your precious time,' Hester added pointedly.

'The kettle's on the hob,' Carina said. 'It's no trouble.'

When the tea was made, she sat down and filled Hester in on what had happened. Hester listened avidly, somewhat mollified by knowing she now had plenty of detail to flesh out the story that was going around, and would even be able to refute some of the more colourful suppositions that had embellished it as it was passed from one to another.

While they were talking, Frank came in, closely followed by Meg. Instantly Hester's interest was aroused, especially as Frank took one look, realised they had company and walked straight out again.

Meg was about to follow him, but Carina was too quick for her.

'Meg! Come and say hello to your Auntie Hester.'

A mutinous look crossed Meg's pretty little face, but she stopped and came back, albeit reluctantly.

'Hello, Auntie Hester.'

'Hello, Meg. My, how you've grown! And who was that?' she asked Carina, her beady eyes eager for yet more gossip.

'That's Frank, our hired hand.'

'Really? Well I can't say I cared for the look of him!'

'He's nice.' Meg jumped to Frank's defence.

'Well, he looked shifty to me. Who is he? Where did he spring from? He's not local, is he?'

'He was a friend of Robert's when he lived in Bristol. He's helping us out.'

'And he's nice,' Meg said again.

'Well I hope you know what you're doing, Carina. You can't be too careful. You and the children, here all by yourselves with no man about the place . . . I worry about you, you know. They still haven't caught that varmint that robbed Ticker Bendle, and in broad daylight too . . .'

'I'm sure any friend of Robert's is perfectly safe to be around,' Carina said tartly. She didn't like Frank, didn't trust him, but she wasn't going to admit that to Aunt Hester.

'He plays with us,' Meg interjected.

'Was he the one looking after Mattie when he got lost?' Hester persisted, ignoring Meg, who was becoming more and more impatient to be heard.

'Mammy's other friend is nice too,' she said loudly. 'And he's got a dog and puppies. We're going to see them again when Mattie's well. And he lives in a really big house, and he has *oranges* growing in—'

'Meg, will you please go and play in your room,' Carina said sharply. But her intervention came way too late. Hester was all agog.

'Who's this then?'

Carina sighed. 'I've been doing some work for Lord Melbrook, sewing curtains. The children came to the house with me.'

'Lord Melbrook!' Hester exclaimed, for once almost speechless.

'Yes. But he's not a friend,' Carina said. 'And I don't suppose you'll be seeing him or his puppies again, Meg. So put it right out of your head.'

'But Mammy . . .'

'Will you do as you're told and go to your room. And Aunt Hester, don't you think it's time you were going? You've got a very long walk back . . .'

'I suppose I have.' To Carina's surprise and relief, she gathered her things together and stood up. 'Just keep me in the know about what's happening, will you? I am your aunt, after all. And your mother's sister.'

'Yes, Aunt Hester,' Carina said.

It wasn't a promise she thought she would keep.

What was wrong with her? Carina wondered. She should be happy. She *was* happy. Overjoyed. Mattie was coming home.

Yes, she was worried at the thought of the responsibility of having him in her care. Though the worst of the illness seemed to be over, he was still far from recovered. While he was in hospital, there were trained nurses keeping an eye on him twenty-four hours a day, and a doctor on call. Should he suffer any kind of a relapse here at home, it would be up to her to decide whether it was serious enough to warrant calling the doctor or taking him back to hospital. She could well imagine she would be anxious, constantly feeling his forehead to check his temperature hadn't risen again, and think the worst if he refused food or became restless and grizzly or listless and sleepy. All things that might very well be perfectly normal and mean nothing at all. And she couldn't watch him round the clock. Oh, she'd have him downstairs with her during the day, and probably put a mattress on the floor in his room so she could be near him at night. But all her usual jobs had been piling up while she'd been spending so much time at the hospital; there were things that would take her out of the house. Besides which she'd have to get some sleep at night or she'd be good for nothing.

It wasn't going to be a picnic, but it would be worth it just to have him back where he belonged. And somehow she didn't think it was her anxiety about looking after Mattie that was casting this vague but persistent shadow. The ache deep inside that prodded at her now and again. It was Cal.

How could she allow what he had done to mar her joy and relief? she asked herself. Grandpa Luke had been right. He was a cad. A scheming cad who had used his standing in the community – and his charm – to worm his way in and attempt to reclaim the farm that he no doubt believed was rightfully his. Why should she care?

But she did.

She was worried, too, that he might take advantage of his position as trustee to force through a sale of the farm whether she wanted it or not. Could he do that? She supposed he would need Arthur Clarence's agreement, but she couldn't see the solicitor arguing with Lord Melbrook. She'd go and see Clarence, tell him she wanted Cal removed as a trustee, but she wasn't sure she would have any say in the matter, and in any case it might well be too late. She couldn't do anything about it until Mattie was well again, and by then the whole thing might be signed, sealed and settled.

After all, what she had said to Cal before throwing him out might well prod him into pushing the sale through quickly while she was otherwise occupied.

The whole thing was a terrible mess. She blamed Cal for his duplicity and herself for being naive enough to be taken in. And she cringed inwardly as she remembered the feelings she'd had for him.

And perhaps still did. Was that the reason for this hollow feeling deep inside that refused to go away?

Much as she wanted to deny it, Carina rather thought that was the case.

Chapter Twenty-Eight

Next morning, Sally went to the hospital with Carina and Meg to fetch Mattie home so that she could nurse him while Carina drove. In the event, she ended up sitting in the rear seat with Mattie on her lap and Meg alongside her because Meg refused to be parted from her brother.

Carina had brought his very best clothes and also a blanket, as there was an autumnal bite in the wind today. His little face peeked out of the folds, still pale and noticeably thinner, but his eyes were bright and alert. He seemed to be taking an interest in everything, as if he had never seen it before. But he was very quiet, which was unlike him, and he made no effort to wriggle and squirm in Sally's arms.

At home, Carina settled him on the sofa with his comfort bottle and his soft toy, and Meg immediately fetched her favourite doll and laid her against a cushion at the opposite end of the sofa to Mattie.

'I'm the nurse,' she announced. 'You're my patient, Mattie, and so is Elsie.'

She dragged a stool to the dresser, climbed up on it and took a teaspoon from the cutlery drawer.

'What are you doing?' Carina asked.

'This is my fermometer. I have to take their tempters.'

'Temperatures,' Carina corrected her. 'You can take Elsie's if you like, but leave Mattie alone.'

'I have to take *his* tempter.' Meg bustled over to him.

'You'll do nothing of the sort. He's to be kept quiet. And if you don't do as you're told, you'll be playing in your room.'

Meg pouted. 'I need an apron. Nurses have aprons.'

'Put on your pinafore, then.'

'No, it's got to be white.'

Carina sighed. 'All right, I'll find something.'

She got out a clean tea cloth and tied it round Meg's waist. 'Will that do?'

'And a cap?'

Carina found a lace doily and fixed it in Meg's curls.

'Now please play nicely. I've got a lot to do.'

She checked on Mattie. He seemed to have fallen asleep, exhausted, no doubt, by the excitement of the car ride home. But his breathing was normal. The bottle he had been sucking on had fallen out of his mouth and was lying on his chest. She took it from him and stood for a moment looking down at him, her heart filled with love.

Mattie was home. He was going to be all right. Nothing else in the world was of the slightest importance.

Mid-afternoon. Mattie was asleep again, having his usual after-dinner nap, but still Carina kept stopping in the middle of catching up with her chores to check on him. Sally had taken Meg out with her so that the little girl wouldn't disturb him.

Carina took the flat iron off the hob and picked up the pile of clean sheets. With one last look at Mattie, she ran up the stairs. Meg's bed needed changing; if she was quick, she'd get it done and be back downstairs before he woke up.

She'd stripped the bed and was just unfolding a clean sheet

when she heard a knock at the back door. Huffing with annoyance because it might well have woken Mattie, she gathered up the dirty bedding and hurried down. She couldn't imagine who could be calling, and hoped it wasn't Cal.

She opened the door, all ready to tell him she had nothing more to say to him, and got the surprise of her life.

Isobel Luckington! And drawn up in the farmyard, a motor with a uniformed driver at the wheel.

'Oh!' she said, otherwise speechless.

'Mrs Talbot.' Isobel smiled, that arch smile that set Carina's teeth on edge. 'I'm sorry to call unannounced, but I really wanted to speak to you. May I come in?'

Flustered, Carina stood aside and Isobel swept into the kitchen, annoying Carina still further. Who did the woman think she was?

'Ma-ma!' Mattie had woken up. He had pushed aside the blanket she'd covered him with and was holding out his arms, begging for attention.

Carina turned her back on Isobel, going instinctively to pick him up. Then she changed her mind. She didn't want to transfer her agitation to him. Children were so quick to pick up on something like that. She sat him up against the cushions and gave him his bottle, which was lying on the floor beside the sofa.

'Here you are, Mattie. Just stay there for a minute, there's a good boy.'

'What a beautiful child!' Isobel had followed her across the kitchen. 'He's been ill, I understand, and in hospital. But he's better now, I assume?'

So Cal must have been talking to Isobel. How else would she know Mattie had been ill? Well, if she was here to plead Cal's case, she'd get short shrift.

'We brought him home this morning,' Carina said shortly.

'But he still needs a lot of attention. So if you wouldn't mind telling me why you're here, I can get on with what I need to be doing. Cal sent you, I suppose.'

Isobel smiled again, that same supercilious smile.

'No one *sends* me anywhere, my dear. And Cal doesn't know I'm here. If he'd had any idea I was coming to see you, he'd have expressly forbidden it. But I know that you and he have had some kind of misunderstanding, and how much it has upset him, so I decided to do something about it.'

'Misunderstanding?' Carina repeated. 'I think it was a little more than that. And if you think you can change my mind about selling him our farm, then I'm afraid you've had a wasted journey.'

'That's not why I'm here at all. Couldn't we sit down to talk about this?'

Carina's mouth set in a firm line.

'I don't think so. I'm sorry if I seem rude, Mrs Luckington, but really, there's nothing to talk about.'

'Oh my dear, I know you've been through a dreadful time. I do understand, but—'

'How could you possibly understand?' Carina flared.

Isobel touched her lips with a gloved finger, as if she could take back the words.

'I can't, I suppose. But I do know Cal has been worried about you, and done all he can to help.'

'So that he could get his hands on our farm!' The bit was between Carina's teeth now. 'He wormed his way in, even agreed to be a trustee for Mattie's inheritance, and all so he could steal it.'

'Cal would never steal—'

'As good as. He might call it a sale, but it would be for a paltry price.'

'How little you know Cal.'

'Well enough to see him now for what he is. I must admit, he took me in to begin with—'

'Carina, stop and think. Would he really have done all the things he's done for you in order to get his hands on a few more acres of land? Oh, he might have buttered you up, yes. But turn out in the middle of the night when your barn was on fire? Stay with you to help sort out the dreadful consequences? Ask you to choose the fabric for drapes for his home? Of course not! And when he suggested buying the farm, he was thinking only of your good. He's worried that you will make yourself ill trying to run it with only that awful man, about whom you know nothing, to help you.'

'Why *then*?' Carina spat out. 'Why when Mattie was at death's door, if not because he thought he'd lose his chance if Mattie died?'

'Because, as I understand it, you appeared to have reached the limits of your endurance.' She raised her eyes, meeting Carina's directly. 'It's not the farm he wants, my dear. It's you.'

Her words startled Carina.

'But I thought that you and he . . .'

'We're just old friends. We'll never be more.' Isobel smiled faintly. 'I can't pretend that I haven't wished it were otherwise. I've lost him twice in my life. Once to his first love, Alice, and now to you.'

Carina was speechless now. Isobel picked up her handbag, which she had put down on the kitchen table.

'Really, there is nothing more that I can say, but please think about it, Carina. And be kind to him. He's a strong man, and as with all strong men, he hides his feelings. But let me assure you, they run very deep. He's far more vulnerable than you might imagine. And he does love you so.'

With that she turned for the door, and left without another word.

As she crossed the farmyard to the motor she had hired to make the drive from Bath to Dunderwick, Isobel realised she was trembling.

It hadn't been easy, saying what she had said. In a way she thought that she herself was not unlike the Cal she had just described to Carina. She didn't often let her true feelings show either. But they certainly ran deep. All she could hope for was that it hadn't been in vain. Really, all she wanted was Cal's happiness.

The uniformed chauffeur climbed down from the motor as he saw her approaching, ready to help her up.

A man turned the corner, carrying a pitchfork. The hired hand, presumably. As he came nearer, Isobel, now on the running board of the motor, turned to look at him.

And froze as she recognised him.

Francis Turnbull. She'd have known that swagger anywhere.

She glanced towards the house. Carina was standing in the doorway, Mattie in her arms. Isobel sat down quickly in her seat, shading her face with her hands.

Had he seen her, and recognised her? She didn't know.

'Back to Bath, ma'am?' the chauffeur enquired.

'No. Dunderwick House,' she said.

And prayed she would find Cal there.

Frank stood staring after the car, horrified.

Mrs Luckington. Bloody Isobel Luckington, the patronising, stuck-up bitch. Mrs Luckington, prison visitor. What the hell was she doing here?

Of all the bloody bad luck! And just when things were going so well.

Had she seen him? She could hardly have failed to.

Recognised him? Maybe she hadn't. But if she had, the game was up, good and proper. He couldn't take the chance. He'd have to cut his losses, get away from here, and fast. Otherwise he was going to end up back inside – for a very long time.

Frank was heading for the house, and Sally would be in soon for a cup of tea before going to get the cows in for milking.

Carina didn't want to see them, or anyone, at the moment. Didn't want to have to talk. She wanted to be alone to go over in her mind what Isobel had said, and sort out her racing thoughts. She bundled Mattie into his pushchair, strapped him in and covered him with a blanket. Some fresh air would do him good too, perhaps put some colour into his cheeks.

'Can you get your own tea, Frank?' she said. 'I'm going to take Mattie out for a bit.'

'Yeah. You go on,' Frank said abruptly, not wanting her to know it suited his purposes very well to have her out of the way.

Carina set off across the yard and up the track. Sally and Meg were nowhere to be seen. But they wouldn't be far away, and Frank would tell them she'd gone out for a walk when they did put in an appearance.

She walked briskly at first, then slowed her pace, and stopped when she reached the gate leading into the field, leaning against it and pulling the pushchair up alongside her.

Unbelievably, Mattie had fallen asleep yet again, but she supposed he needed it to help his little body recuperate from what it had been through. And at least it gave her a bit of peace to think about what Isobel had said.

He does love you so. The words rang in her ears, echoing and re-echoing.

It couldn't be true, of course. It was beyond belief that

someone of Cal's class should love someone like her. Yet Isobel had been so insistent that it was the case. Why? Why would she say something like that? Was it just another attempt to get Carina on side so that she would agree to sell him the farm?

A tiny shard of treacherous longing tugged at her, and to her dismay Carina realised that deep down she wanted Isobel to have been telling her the truth. She didn't want to think that Cal had been manipulating her all along, pulling the right strings to make her dance to his tune. The thought that there was an ulterior motive behind everything that had passed between them hurt dreadfully, and not just because she was ashamed for being so gullible. She had had feelings for him, and still did, no matter that she had told herself she hated him. He had stirred her senses in a way no one else – not even Robert – ever had. She had wanted him in a way she had never wanted anyone before. It was him she had turned to when she had been desperate and afraid. And he had been there for her.

Isobel had posed a question for her to think about, too. Would he have turned out in the middle of the night when the barn had burned down and stayed to support her through the dreadful consequences if he had merely been buttering her up, as she had put it? That might account for his other kindnesses – going out of his way to give her a lift home when she was caught in the rain, putting work her way when she had needed it, even buying back her precious ring from the pawnbroker and inviting the children to his home to see the puppies. Any of those things could have been part of his plan to win her trust. But as regards the fire, Isobel was right. What Cal had done that night and the following day was surely above and beyond that.

Was it possible – was it really possible – that he had feelings for her too?

Something like hope, or even joy, warmed Carina through

and through, marred only by the twinges of guilt she couldn't quite get away from.

Was it wrong to feel this way just months after the loss of her husband? She had loved Robert. Married him and borne his children. Mourned him – and still did. No one could ever take the place he held in her heart.

But this was different. Cal was different. Without detracting from the love she had for Robert, there was room for him too.

Carina began to walk again, and the cool breeze was like a kiss on her cheeks, and the soft patter of falling leaves music to her soul.

Never had a relatively short journey seemed to take so long, Isobel thought as the chauffeur drove from Meadow Farm to Dunderwick House. It was imperative she see Cal, tell him what she had discovered, and quickly. If Francis Turnbull had recognised her, as she felt sure he must have, then he would be a desperate man. And that could mean only one thing. That Carina, her children and her sister-in-law could be in mortal danger.

'Hurry, can't you?' she urged the chauffeur.

'I'll do my best, ma'am.' The chauffeur, though puzzled by the sudden urgency, was trained to remain respectful to clients no matter what.

But the motor proceeded at the same sedate speed, and Isobel could do nothing but wring her hands and try to remain calm.

She could only hope Cal was not away on business, or out visiting one of the farms on the estate. If he was, she didn't know what she was going to do.

Sally and Meg had finished putting out feed for the hens and collecting the eggs. A couple of the hens had escaped from their pen, so the wire netting had had to be repaired, the wandering birds shooed back inside and the search for eggs widened to include the surrounding hedges. But now they were headed back to the house, Meg carefully carrying some of the eggs in her little basket while Sally took care of the rest.

The door to the kitchen was ajar. Sally pushed it fully open to let Meg go first, then as she stepped inside herself, her eyes widened.

'What are you doing?'

Frank was beside the kitchen table, the biscuit barrel where Carina had used to keep her little stash of cash in his hand. An assortment of odds and ends were scattered on the table in front of him, as if he'd just tipped them out. He swung round, guilt written all over his face.

'What are you doing?' Sally asked again.

'I've got to go.'

'Go where?'

'Anywhere away from here.'

'Frank, you can't go!' Sally was horrified, the fact that he was turning out the biscuit barrel forgotten for the moment. 'I'm going to have your baby!'

'Sod that. I gotta go, I tell you. And I'm not going empty-handed. Where's the money?'

'What?'

'The bloody money. I thought Carina kept it in here.'

Sally could hardly get her head round what was happening.

'She used to. She's put it somewhere safe. Frank . . . you can't do this!'

'Where is it?' His voice was hard, a snarl almost.

'I don't know!'

He crossed to her in a couple of quick strides, grabbed her by the arms.

'You'd better tell me, and quick.'

'I don't know!'

He shook her. An egg rolled out of the basket on her arm and smashed on the slab stone floor.

'Where is the bloody money?'

'How many more times? I don't know where Carina has hidden it and I wouldn't tell you if I did!'

'Bitch!' He yanked her forward and gave her a push backwards so that she landed in Grandpa Luke's chair, the basket of eggs flying across the kitchen floor. 'We'll just have to wait till she gets back, then. But she'd better not be too long. On second thoughts, I'll have a look for it myself. But you're coming with me. I don't want you running off the minute my back is turned.'

He yanked her up again, pushed her towards the stairs.

Sally cast a quick glance over her shoulder at Meg, cowering in a corner. She only hoped the little girl didn't follow. Frank had gone mad, he must have done. The safest place for Meg was down here, out of his way. And if Carina returned, she might be able to warn her so she could go for help.

At the top of the first flight of stairs, Frank gave her another couple of pushes into Carina's bedroom and down on to the bed. Then he began pulling out the drawers of the dressing table, emptying the contents on to the floor and swearing as he did so. The change in him was terrifying. From the lover who had wooed her, he had become a wild animal, feral and dangerous.

Now he kicked out at an upturned drawer, swearing again.

'Just my luck. After all I've done . . .'

In that instant, with those few spoken words, Sally knew the truth. She'd been right to suspect that the remnant of charred jacket was his, a fool to believe him when he had denied it.

Frank *had* been in the stable, long before he'd turned up on their doorstep. It was him, not Captain, who had killed Robert. She still didn't understand, but she knew without a shadow of doubt that she was right.

Anger coursed through her, driving out fear. She launched herself at him, beating at him with her fists.

'You bastard! You murdered Robert, didn't you? You murdered my brother!'

Frank parried her blows easily, caught her hands and twisted them behind her back.

'And what are you going to do about it?' he sneered.

'I'll see you answer for it if it's the last thing I do!'

He laughed then, a harsh and horrible sound.

'Oh yeah? Well let me tell you, there's the old man too. Might as well be hanged for a sheep as a lamb, as they say.'

Sally's eyes widened in horror, and he went on: 'He was getting in the way, the silly old bugger. Thought he could threaten me. Well I showed him, good and proper.'

He smirked now as he thought of it. He'd returned from one of his night-time forays, breaking into houses to steal whatever he could lay hands on, and there was the old man waiting for him. Telling him, Francis Turnbull, to pack his bags and go or he'd have the law on him. Well, he wasn't having any of that. A doddery old fool like Luke Green wouldn't take much doing for. It had been easy. Much easier than getting Robert Talbot out of the way. And then he'd started the fire, left the old man in the barn and made sure it was well alight before he raised the alarm. The perfect crime. He was still proud of it.

'You killed Grandpa too?' For a moment Sally stopped struggling, shocked to the core.

'Yeah,' he sneered. 'And good riddance.'

That was when Sally did the unthinkable. With her hands

still twisted behind her back, she lifted her head and spat, catching him full in the face.

'You bitch!' He was angry again, but also excited by her display of spirit.

There was time enough yet to make his escape. By the time Isobel Luckington got back to Bath, or Bristol, or wherever it was she lived, and raised the alarm, he would be well away.

Still pinioning Sally with one big hand, he raised the other and wiped the glob of spittle from his face with his rolled-up shirtsleeve. Then he pushed her back again towards the bed, forced her down on to it and began to unbuckle his trousers.

At last – at last! – the hired motor was descending the tree-lined drive that led to Dunderwick House.

'Wait here!'

Isobel had the door of the motor open and jumped down, not waiting for the chauffeur to help her.

A gardener was tending the flower beds.

'Is Lord Melbrook at home?' she demanded.

The gardener straightened up, a handful of weeds in one hand, hoe in the other.

'He's somewhere about.'

'But where?'

'You got me there.'

With an impatient shake of her head she went to the door of the orangery, rang the big brass bell on the wall outside, then walked straight in. A maid met her as she reached the passage beyond.

'I need to see Lord Melbrook, urgently. Is he in?'

'I think he's in the library. I'll tell him you're here.'

'Don't bother.' Isobel swept past her and threw open the library door.

Cal looked up from a ledger he was working on.

'Isobel? What are you doing here?'

'I've just come from Meadow Farm.' Seeing his surprised look, she waved an impatient hand. 'There's no time to explain now. I'll tell you later. Cal, I'm dreadfully worried. I happened to see that hired hand of theirs, and I recognised him. He's an escaped prisoner – and a dangerous one. We need to alert the police immediately.'

'Isobel, slow down! What are you talking about?'

'The man working at Meadow Farm is an escaped convict. I know him from my prison visiting. He was inside for committing robberies, some with dreadful violence. He shared a cell with Joel Talbot for a while, I believe, but he escaped a couple of months ago. And he's here, now, in Dunderwick. How much clearer can I make myself?'

Cal slapped his pen down on the desk; ink splattered across it and on to the pages of the open ledger.

'Dear God! I warned Carina . . .' He grabbed his jacket, hanging over the back of his chair, and pushed past Isobel into the passageway, calling for Biddy Thomas.

'Whatever is the matter, sir?' As always, Biddy looked disgruntled, as if she had been interrupted in the middle of some very important task.

'Ring the police, Biddy. Tell them there is a dangerous escaped convict at Meadow Farm.'

'Can't you do it, sir? You know I don't like using that contraption.'

'Just do it!' Cal snapped. 'I'm going over there.'

'I have a hired motor waiting outside,' Isobel offered.

'No, I'll drive myself.'

'Then I'll come with you.'

'Better not. If he sees you, he'll know the game is up.'

'I think it's a little late for that,' Isobel said. 'I'm coming with you, Cal. If there's any trouble, I might be able to calm him down.'

Cal didn't want to waste time arguing. While Isobel dismissed her hired car, he got the Benz going. Isobel clambered up beside him and Cal roared off as if all the hounds of hell were after him.

Chapter Twenty-Nine

Sally was barely conscious. In the struggle before he'd raped her, he'd put his hand around her throat to restrain her, and he supposed he must have pressed too hard. Well, too bad.

She'd put up a fight, he'd give her that. She'd got a lot of her old man in her. He'd shared a prison cell with Joel Talbot and knew him for a tough character. Killed his own wife and should have hanged for it, in Frank's opinion. But for some reason they'd charged him with manslaughter, not murder, and he'd ended up just getting life. And that had been to Frank's advantage. If he hadn't shared a cell with Joel, he'd never have got to hear about the farm where his son and daughter had gone to live with their grandparents.

Frank had grown up on a farm. He knew how isolated they were. How out of touch with the wider world were the folk who lived in the nearby villages. Back in the day, he couldn't wait to get away from the muck and the mess and the bloody hard work, day in, day out, the cold dark mornings when your fingers froze, the nights when you were too tired to do anything but fall into bed and sleep until cockcrow. But when he was planning his escape from prison, he knew there would be no better place to lie low for a bit.

He'd had to get rid of Robert, of course. He'd never have

been taken on as a hired hand while he was around. And he couldn't have used the convenient smokescreen of being a city boy from Bristol. His original plan was to move on when the hue and cry had died down, but then he'd seen the possibilities. A pretty girl who was going to inherit now that her brother was dead – if he could worm his way in there, he'd be made. And when he tired of the farm, as he knew he would, he could sell up and walk away with the proceeds. By then, nobody would be looking for Francis Turnbull.

It had been something of a shock to discover that Luke had made Mattie his heir, not Sally, and he'd realised he'd have to make sure Mattie was out of the picture if the farm was to be hers. It had been a setback that the boy had recovered from whatever illness he had picked up from the river water, but there would be other opportunities to get rid of him, Frank had thought. All he had to do was bide his time.

As for Sally thinking her father was dead, that was an added bonus. Robert must have known different, of course – he would have been old enough to be aware of all the details – and the old man, too, would have known. Another reason why it was best he was out of the way. Frank had wondered if Luke Green had suspected he might have met Joel in prison.

No, everything had been going his way. Until bloody Isobel Luckington had come on the scene and ruined it all. He had to get away – fast – before she had a chance to tell the rozzers. There was no way he was going back inside, and he'd do whatever he had to to make sure he didn't.

With barely a glance at Sally, spread-eagled on the bed, he went back to tipping out drawers, looking for anything of value. There wasn't much, apart from the ring Carina had made so much fuss about. Burgling this house wouldn't be worth anybody's while. He pocketed the ring, leaving the box on the dressing table, then took one last look around in the hope that he might yet discover where she had hidden the money. A carved wooden box on the windowsill, half hidden by the curtains, caught his eye, but it was locked and he couldn't waste time looking for the key. He'd have to take it as it was and prise it open later.

Anxious now to be on his way, he hurried downstairs. There was no sign of Meg – she'd probably run off somewhere. He went out to the yard, to where the Rover was parked up against the wall. If he could take that, it would help his escape. He'd never driven in his life, but if Carina could do it, it couldn't be that difficult. Once he was well away from the farm, he'd probably abandon it somewhere it was unlikely to be found in a hurry and head off on foot. In the motor he would be far too visible. But at least it would give him a head start.

Just as long as he could get it going. Sweating now from a rush of adrenalin, he cranked the handle. Alleluia! The engine spluttered into life. Now all he had to do was collect his few belongings and enough food to last him a day or two and he could make his escape.

Leaving the motor running, he went back to the house. In his room – the room that had once been Grandpa Luke's – he hastily threw clothes and the wooden box that he felt sure was Carina's money box into a holdall he'd found at the back of a cupboard. He dumped it just inside the back door, then went to the pantry. There he grabbed a loaf of bread, a hunk of cheese, the remains of a joint of roast pork and a slab of fruit cake. He found a couple of brown paper bags and stuffed it all inside.

Time to go.

He emerged from the pantry and stopped short.

Carina was in the doorway with Mattie in the pushchair,

staring in horror at the egg-splattered floor, the overturned chair, the oddments scattered over the kitchen table.

He'd left it too late to make his escape unnoticed. Now he was going to have to deal with Carina as well.

Though she had been enjoying her walk, relishing the peace and the chance to organise her thoughts, Carina had decided that Mattie had been out for long enough. The afternoon air had grown cool and a thickening cloud base was threatening an early dusk. She didn't want him to catch a chill that would set back his recovery. So reluctantly she had turned for home.

As she entered the farmyard, she was startled to hear the rattle and low drone of the Rover engine. Who on earth had started it up – and why? Surely Sally wasn't planning on trying to drive it herself without anyone to instruct her? Carina quickened her pace.

The kitchen door was open, as it might be on a summer's day. But the weather was no longer good enough for that. The last week or so it had remained closed to keep in the warmth. She began to manoeuvre Mattie's pushchair inside. The front wheels caught on something, and she looked down to see what was blocking the way. To her surprise she saw it was their old holdall, bulging now. And sticking out of the top was what looked like the wooden box where she had been putting any spare cash for safe keeping.

'What . . . ?'

As she looked up from the bag, she suddenly became aware of the disarray in the kitchen. Broken eggs, the shattered shells sitting in glutinous, yellow-streaked pools, the large basket Sally used to collect them upturned beside Grandpa Luke's chair, Meg's smaller one on the floor beside the table, which was covered with scattered odds and ends. One of the dining chairs overturned.

And all the glasses and bottles from the chiffonier lying in an untidy heap in front of it, though the doors appeared to be closed.

Alarm coursed through Carina's veins. What in heaven's name had happened? And where were Sally and Meg?

'Meg?' she called.

But it was Frank who appeared in the doorway to the pantry, although almost simultaneously the chiffonier doors opened and a terrified, tearful Meg emerged from the hiding place she had retreated to when Frank had forced Sally upstairs. Now she scooted carelessly over the broken china and glass to reach Carina's side and grab hold of her legs.

'Mammy! Mammy!'

Carina put a protective arm round her shoulders, drawing her close, and faced Frank furiously.

'What in the world is going on here?'

Frank didn't answer her. He strode across the kitchen, grabbing the holdall.

'Get out of my way!'

Outraged, Carina stood her ground.

'What do you think you're doing? What's all this mess?'

'Carina!'

Sally had appeared at the top of the stairs, clinging to the banister. She was dishevelled, her legs bare beneath her shirt. Blood was streaming down them.

'Sally!' Carina cried, shocked.

'Let him go, Carina! He's dangerous! He killed Robert and Grandpa! He'll kill you too!'

In that first startled moment, Carina simply couldn't comprehend what she was hearing. It was too much to take in. But from the state of Sally, there was no mistaking what had happened here. Frank had raped her, and now he was trying to make his escape.

Beyond caring about the possible danger, Carina rammed the pushchair into his legs.

'You're going nowhere!'

'Just try and stop me!'

Frank tried to push his way past the pushchair, failed, and grabbed Carina by the front of her coat, yanking her forward. Meg fell to the ground, screaming in terror, and Frank practically trod on her as he attempted to force his way through.

'He murdered Robert and Grandpa!' Sally's voice was hoarse, rasping painfully in her throat.

This time Carina half grasped her meaning.

'He what? Oh my God!' The strength seemed to drain out of her so that her legs almost gave way beneath her. And in that moment, Frank took his chance.

Somehow in the struggle the pushchair had turned around so it was now facing the door, and to Carina's dazed horror she realised that Frank was attempting to lift Mattie out. He meant to take her baby as a hostage! She flew at him, tripped and stumbled, falling headlong on the flagged floor.

Desperately she lunged for Frank's ankles. But he had realised Mattie was strapped in and it would take him precious moments to release the harness. Instead he turned and snatched up Meg, who was cowering in the doorway, sobbing.

'Just try to set the rozzers on me now and she'll get it!' he snarled.

He yanked the pushchair out of his way, almost toppling it over, and ran out of the door. Mattie had begun to scream, but for once he was not Carina's priority. She staggered to her feet, not even aware of the pain in her shoulder and hip, which had taken the brunt of her heavy fall on to the flagstones, nor the deep cut in her hand from contact with a fragment of broken china.

But she had also twisted her ankle badly, and as she tried to run after Frank, it almost gave way beneath her. Pain as sharp as razors shot up her leg. Somehow she managed to hobble to the doorway and out into the yard, but she had no hope of catching Frank, who was now halfway across the yard and making for the Rover with Meg squirming and screaming in his arms.

'Oh dear God!' Panic was welling and she managed a few more stumbling steps. But by now Frank had reached the motor, thrown Meg into the back seat and was making for the driver's door.

The sudden loud crack from right behind her almost made her jump out of her skin. She saw Frank jerk violently, twist and almost fall, then grab his left arm. She spun round.

Sally was in the doorway, one of Grandpa Luke's old guns braced against her shoulder. Even as Carina registered what she was doing, she aimed and pulled the trigger again. The second shot went wide, and Sally swore. Frank, now turned sideways on to her, was presenting less of a target, and in any case she was still groggy from his attack on her. She'd winged him, but that wasn't good enough. He had got the car door open and was climbing into the driver's seat now. She needed to be closer if she was to have any hope of stopping him in his tracks.

Somehow she forced her shaking legs to carry her out into the farmyard, taking aim again. But just as she did so, Meg bobbed up, and she realised that in trying to hit Frank, she risked hitting her little niece.

'Carina, I'm sorry . . .' She lowered the gun. The adrenalin that had roused her, propelled her down the stairs when she heard the commotion below and driven her to grab the gun from its cabinet was spent. She swayed, and Carina only just managed to catch and support her.

411

The Rover was moving off now at a reckless speed, scattering two or three hens that, for all Sally's efforts, had managed to escape again and almost hitting Cymru, who was barking at the end of his leash.

And Carina and Sally could do nothing but watch it go.

'If he's cornered, he'll be dangerous,' Isobel warned.

Cal didn't reply. The only thought in his head was that Carina, Sally and the children were alone with an escaped convict. He was driving as fast as he dared, while Isobel clung on for dear life.

'I think we should wait for the police,' she went on, bracing herself as the Benz jolted over a bump in the road. 'Goodness only knows what he might do. Take one of them as a hostage, perhaps.'

They rounded a bend at the top of the hill and Cal was all ready to put his foot down on the long straight ahead. But to his dismay, the road was blocked by a herd of cows that David Perkins was driving in for milking.

'Get out of my way!' Cal yelled as he came to an enforced halt.

'Sorry, m'lord, but they go at their own pace.' David looked anxious. He didn't like crossing swords with the lord of the manor, but what could he do?'

'If you won't move them, I will!'

Cal edged forward, nudging the cows with the bonnet of the Benz. Some lumbered slowly to one side, pushing others as they went; a few took off and started to canter down the road. As he inched his way through the herd, Isobel tucked herself well into her seat. Though she was country born and bred, she wasn't keen on the big smelly bodies pressing against the side of the car.

As they cleared the last of them, a motor appeared in the

distance, heading towards them, then turned off abruptly into a lane that led at right angles off the main road.

Cal frowned. 'That looked like Carina's car.'

'How could you tell from this far away?'

'There aren't many motors hereabouts, and in any case, I know it well. But where's she going? There's nothing down that lane but another farm and a few cottages.'

'Doesn't it come out on another main road? The one that eventually runs between Dunderwick House and my old home?'

'Yes, but why would she go the long way round to get anywhere?'

'I have no idea. But if it was Carina, at least she's safe.'

'Let's hope so.'

'And I think you should slow down before you kill us both.'

Cal ignored her warning, increasing his speed again. Until he knew for certain that Carina and the children were safe, until that rogue Francis Turnbull was back behind bars where he belonged, his own safety and even that of Isobel was the least of his concerns.

When Frank saw a motor coming in the opposite direction, his first instinct was to get off the road as quickly as possible. He didn't want anyone to see what direction he was taking. Even if the other driver didn't take any notice of him right now, when the hue and cry was raised, they'd likely remember passing him.

Just ahead, he saw a lane leading off to his left; he swung into it, grazing the bank and almost jolting the steering wheel out of his hand. Trouble was, he could use only one. His arm was hurting like hell, and blood was gushing everywhere. He'd have to stop, try to bind it up. He stamped on what he thought was the brake and the car shot forward. Shit! He found the right pedal, pressed down hard, and the motor slewed and skidded to a stop at an angle across the narrow lane. Frank swore again. Meg, in the back seat, was still screaming. He jerked round, glaring at her.

'Bloody shut up!'

She flinched, drawing back into the corner of the seat, but at least the screaming stopped. She was only whimpering now. He fished in his pocket for the piece of rag he used as a handkerchief and attempted to tie it around the wound, but he couldn't do it one-handed. He did manage to hold it in place while he pulled his shirtsleeve down over it, buttoning the cuff to hold it there. That would have to do for now. The most important thing was to put some distance between himself and Meadow Farm.

But the engine had cut out.

This was turning into a fucking disaster. Frank was used to thinking on his feet, but just now it wasn't only his arm that was out of action; his brain wasn't working as it should either. For a start, he could hardly believe Sally had shot him. He'd thought he had her exactly where he wanted her. She'd *shot* him, the bloody bitch. He was lucky, he supposed, that her aim wasn't up to much. But he didn't feel lucky. He felt nauseous, and he couldn't think straight for the pain.

'Stay bloody there!' he barked at Meg, who simply stared back at him with wide, horrified tear-filled eyes and shrank even further back into the seat.

He got the door open, climbed out with the starting handle and went around to the front of the Rover. This time it took a while to get the engine going, and by the time it spluttered into life, he was feeling quite ill. Blood from the wound had seeped through the makeshift bandage and pooled on the ground, running in little scarlet rivulets towards the bank. He straightened up and the world swam around him. He leaned against the bonnet of the car, fighting the blackness that was threatening to close in on him, and after a few minutes it receded to the periphery of his vision. He stumbled back to the driver's seat, wondering if he dared rest for a bit before going on. Scarcely anyone used this lane, he felt fairly sure. But it would be just his luck that someone did today. He'd head for Frome and out over the county border into Wiltshire. Further ahead than that he couldn't plan. All he knew was that he had Meg as a bargaining chip if things turned ugly.

She'd begun crying again noisily and he began to wish he hadn't abducted her. If the little brat didn't shut up, she was going to drive him crazy. One way or another he'd put a stop to her bawling.

Gritting his teeth against the pain, he managed to get the car straight and set off again.

'Carina – listen!'

The sound of a motor engine coming closer carried across the farmyard.

'Is he coming back?'

Wild, impossible hope flared briefly; died. That wasn't how the Rover sounded. But she knew that throaty roar.

'It's the Benz,' she said, and almost simultaneously it turned in to the farmyard, came to an abrupt stop.

'Carina?' Cal had taken in at a glance that something was terribly wrong. 'What's happened?'

In that moment, all the differences between them were forgotten. Carina only knew that Cal was here, that she was no longer alone in this nightmare.

'Frank's got Meg!' she cried, almost hysterical. 'He's taken her in my motor!'

Cal swore. 'Why didn't I follow it? I knew something was up . . .' He was turning the Benz as he spoke. 'You stay here, Isobel. I'm going after him.'

Carina didn't know what was going on or what he was talking about. She only knew he was her best hope of finding Meg, and dealing with Frank.

'Wait!' She limped to the Benz. 'I'm coming with you.'

Cal didn't argue. Though he didn't want Carina in danger, he knew there was no way he would be able to persuade her otherwise, and in any case, when – if – he caught up with Frank, Meg would be in desperate need of her mother.

The moment Isobel had vacated her seat, Carina climbed up into it. Cal was already racing the engine.

'Look after Mattie!' she just had time to say before he let in the clutch and pulled away.

'I will. Just go,' Isobel called over the roar of the engine.

'How do you know which way he went?' Carina asked, her voice shaking with emotion, as they bumped along the rough track.

'I saw your car.'

'But—'

'Just be quiet and let me drive. I'll tell you later.'

It was Carina's turn to hang on for dear life as Cal swung out on to the road, throwing the Benz around bends as if he were on a race track. It was, of course, much faster than the Rover, but Frank had a good start. And who knew what chances he would take, desperate as he was.

'He's never driven the Rover before.' Carina was in too much of a state to stay silent. 'And Sally shot him. In the arm. He might not be able to use it.'

It was as if Cal hadn't heard her. For the moment, his concentration was solely on keeping the car on the road while

416

travelling as fast as possible. He was, though, cursing himself for not having followed the Rover when he'd spotted it turning down the lane that led to practically nowhere. Now all he could do was hope to catch it before it reached the main road. If he couldn't, he would have no idea which direction it had taken.

'We'll find them, Carina,' he muttered.

And prayed it was a promise he could keep.

Back at the farm, Isobel had taken charge. She helped a still groggy Sally inside, righted the pushchair and released Mattie, who only screamed more loudly as she lifted him out. He didn't know her, of course, and she had no experience in dealing with a terrified child.

'Give him to me,' Sally said.

Isobel hesitated. Sally didn't look to be in any state to cope with him either. Besides the streaks of blood that had run down her legs, there was an ugly bruise around her throat, her voice was hoarse and she was deathly pale.

'Mattie, darling, it's all right!' Sally said.

The little boy jerked his head round at the sound of the familiar voice, hoarse or not, and struggled violently in Isobel's arms. She set him down and he toddled rapidly across to where Sally was seated in Grandpa Luke's chair and launched himself at her.

'Shh, Mattie, it's all right. There's no need to cry.'

She took the antimacassar from the back of the chair and laid it across her bare legs, then lifted him on to her lap, rocking him gently.

As his sobs quietened, Isobel gave a sigh of relief.

'I'll put the kettle on,' she said.

In all her pampered life, she had hardly ever had to do such a thing.

'Oh Cal, what have you got me into?' she whispered, shaking her head.

But if she was going to be of any help here, she was just going to have to do the things the servants usually did. Compared to the ordeal Sally and Carina had endured – were still enduring – it was a very small thing.

The lane had begun to slope steeply downhill between thick hedges and drifts of leaves along the grass verges. Frank's vision was odd now; sparkling dots seemed to be dancing before his eyes like the pieces in a kaleidoscope. There was a bend coming up, but it didn't look too sharp. He reckoned he could get round it without slowing.

He yanked on the steering wheel, and then it seemed everything happened at once. Fast, so fast, and yet at the same time in slow motion. He hit the bank, the motor veered across the road and back again, the wheels mounted the bank, the world turned upside down. And the darkness closed in on him again, this time so quickly and surely that he was quite unable to fight it.

The Rover lay overturned against the bank. As they rounded a bend in the lane and saw it there, Carina's heart seemed to stop beating and the blood left her head in a rush.

'Oh my God! Oh my God!'

Cal slammed on the brakes and the Benz skidded to a halt. He was out in an instant, running down the hill. Carina jumped down too, following him on legs that seemed not to belong to her.

There was no sound or movement from the crashed motor but the hiss of water on hot metal. She stopped short, covering her mouth with her hands, repeating and repeating the same words like a mantra.

'Oh my God! Oh my God!'

If Meg was dead . . . oh, she couldn't even contemplate it, yet it was there in her head and her heart, pulsing in her veins, an indescribable white-hot terror.

Cal was clambering up the bank, leaning into the back of the Rover so far that only the lower part of his body and his legs were visible. Somehow, shaking from head to toe, Carina forced herself to go closer.

Cal was straightening now, emerging carefully as his booted feet scrabbled to get some purchase on the steep bank. Lifting Meg clear of the wreckage. A silent, still Meg. Carina gasped, choking on wordless sobs.

And heard the most wonderful, most welcome sound she had ever heard in her life.

A wail. Tearful, trembling, but still wonderful.

'Mammy!'

She was alive. Meg was alive! Carina ran the last few feet towards them, took her daughter from Cal's arms, hugged her close.

'Oh my darling! You're safe. Mammy's here . . . Mammy's here . . .'

'Take her back to the Benz,' Cal instructed. 'Make sure she's not hurt.'

Carina did as he said. With Meg on her lap, she managed to prise the little girl's arms from around her neck.

'Just let Mammy look at you . . . Does anything hurt?'

Meg nodded, pointing to her mouth. Sure enough, her lip was bleeding from where her sharp little teeth must have bitten into it on impact. There was a lump on her forehead too, which would be an ugly bruise tomorrow, but apart from that she seemed remarkably unscathed. She'd been thrown into the well of the car – perhaps she had already been cowering there – and in the confined space she had been protected from the worst of the crash.

But what of Frank? Not that Carina cared a jot for his welfare; he deserved everything he got, and more. But she wanted him alive. Wanted him to face justice for the terrible things he had done.

Cal had been up on the bank again, leaning into the front of the Rover. Now he scrambled down and walked back up the hill to the Benz.

Carina questioned him with her eyes, not wanting to say anything to upset Meg more than she already was. He shook his head.

'He looks to be in a bad way. Certainly unconscious. I don't know if he's alive or dead; I can't reach him. There's nothing more I can do. But you can be sure of one thing: he won't be going far.' His voice was hard. Carina was still looking at him uncertainly, and he went on: 'Don't worry, I'll call the police and the ambulance – probably the fire brigade too. But for the moment, the most important thing is getting you and this little one home.'

'Oh Cal, how can I ever thank you?'

She'd said something similar once before, and he responded now in much the same way. A grin. A sparkle in his eyes. A long teasing look.

'I expect I'll be able to think of something.'

Chapter Thirty

Sally was distraught.

It was late evening and already dark now that the nights were drawing in. Cal had left with Isobel to take her back to Bath. Sergeant Love had been and gone again after taking statements, though he had warned that they should be prepared for a visit from a senior officer from Bath, especially if Frank died, which was entirely possible since he had been in a very bad way when he had eventually been pulled from the car. Carina had stripped her bed and put the coverlet to soak in cold water in the big stone sink, then tidied her room. She'd realised at once that her ring was missing, but somehow, important to her though it was, this time its loss didn't matter nearly as much. It was, after all, only a ring. What she had so nearly lost today was totally irreplaceable. In any case, it might well be found on Frank when the nurses at the hospital emptied his pockets.

With the necessary chores done, she put the children to bed. Mattie had fallen asleep at once, but Meg had taken a long time to go off. She was still dreadfully upset by her ordeal, and Carina had lain down beside her on her bed, cradling her in her arms and singing softly to her until at last exhaustion overcame her. She wouldn't be surprised, though, if the little girl woke again later, disturbed by nightmares. Carina only hoped her experience didn't leave a permanent scar, but children could be surprisingly resilient.

At last, satisfied, she tiptoed from the room and went downstairs.

Sally was once more sitting in Grandpa Luke's chair, her face buried in her hands and muffled sobs racking her body.

Carina went to her. 'Oh Sally, darling, don't,' she begged, kneeling down beside the chair. 'You'll make yourself ill. It's been terrible, but it's over now. We've just got to try and put it behind us.'

'It's all right for you.' Tears squeezed out from between Sally's fingers and ran down her bruised neck. 'It's over for you.'

Carina didn't know what to say to that. It wasn't over for her and never really would be. Frank had killed Robert. She had been taken in by him, and if she'd listened to her intuition and sent him on his way, Grandpa Luke might still be alive. Sally would never have got involved with a monster. Meg would have been spared an ordeal that might have scarred her for life. Mattie might not have contracted whatever disease it was that had almost killed him. Carina was convinced now that Frank had lost him deliberately. Mattie had stood between him and the farm that he wanted for himself. The man was pure evil, she knew that now. The sickening thing was that in her heart, she had known it all along.

But her heart bled for Sally. Used, betrayed, raped. And on top of everything else, she had lost the baby she had been carrying. Even if the father was a monster, it was still her baby and she would be mourning its loss.

'Sally . . .' she began in an effort to comfort her, 'I can't begin to imagine what you're going through . . .'

Sally's head jerked up. Her face was puffy, her eyes red from crying.

'I killed him, Carina!'

'No you didn't. He's not dead yet.'

'As good as. I've killed him. And I loved him so . . .'

'Don't think about that now. Look at it this way. What you did was really brave. You saved Meg. He still took her, I know. But you were the reason he didn't get very far. She's safe in bed now, and asleep, and that is all thanks to you.'

'He wouldn't have hurt her.'

'Oh, I think he would. He's evil, Sally, and I'm sorry, but he didn't love you. Look what he did to you today. He'd never have done that if he loved you.'

'I made him angry . . .'

'Because you found out that he killed Robert and Grandpa Luke. Have you forgotten that? He murdered your brother and your grandfather.'

Sally pressed her hands to her face. Above them her eyes were clouded, slowly filling with horror. It was as if in her grief she *had* forgotten. The events that had followed the realisation had blotted out what had gone before. She crumpled, and began crying again.

'After they'd gone, he was all I had.'

'You've still got us. Me and Meg and Mattie. I know we can't ever make up for losing your real family. But we love you. We're here for you, and always will be.'

'Oh Carina!' Sally threw her arms round her sister-in-law. 'How can you be so kind to me after all the trouble I've brought to your door?'

'You're not to blame,' Carina said, rubbing Sally's shoulder gently. 'He killed Robert before you even met him. And how were you to know what he'd done, or would do?'

'But I did know. Oh – not until it was too late to save Grandpa. I knew the buttons and the piece of charred cloth I

423

found in the stable and in the barn belonged to him . . .'

'Buttons? And charred cloth?' Carina remembered that Sally had found a button in the stable and raised her suspicions about it. But more? And in the barn?

Sally explained haltingly. 'I even asked him if they were his and he denied it,' she finished. 'I believed him because I wanted to believe him. I was in love with him. I was having his baby. And now I've lost that too . . .'

More tears spilled down her face and Carina knew this was not the moment to suggest that that was for the best. Not only would Sally have been disgraced, with a baby she would have to bring up alone, but it would have been the child of a murderer, rapist and thief. Suppose it had taken after its father? She shuddered at the thought.

'I am so sorry, Carina,' Sally was going on. 'I couldn't bear to think that Frank had done such terrible things. I closed my eyes to what was staring me in the face. I should have told you. Then at least Meg and Mattie would have been spared . . .'

'Well it's too late now to wish you had,' Carina said, though privately she agreed with Sally. 'And as I said before, what you did this afternoon saved Meg. If you hadn't shot Frank, he could have been clean away by now, and goodness only knows what he would have done to her when he no longer had any use for her. Just hang on to that.'

Sally nodded, still tearful but calmer.

'And now,' Carina said, 'I think we could both do with a glass of brandy.'

The knock at the door startled them. Between them they had finished the brandy, though thankfully it had only been a quarter-bottle to start with, and not full at that. But unused to strong drink as they were, they were both somewhat flushed, though it had certainly helped to restore their equilibrium, and the nightmarish events of the day, and of the preceding months, seemed a little more distant.

'I'll see who it is. You stay there.'

Carina got up and went to open the door, fully expecting to find either Sergeant Love or some other policeman there. But it wasn't a policeman at all.

'David!' she said in surprise.

He stood on the doorstep, twisting his cap between his hands, looking awkward.

'I've heard about the trouble,' he said awkwardly. 'I just came to see if there was anything I could do . . .'

'That's kind of you, but no. We're fine now. Meg is safe in her bed and we're just sitting quietly.'

'Oh, good . . .' He hesitated, summoning up the courage to ask the question he had really come to ask.

'Is Sally all right?'

There. He'd said it. He'd made up his mind the day he'd ridden his bike to Hillsbridge to fetch the doctor for Mattie that he was going to fight to get Sally back. But with the little boy so ill in hospital, it hadn't seemed the right time. He'd have to wait until things were back to normal at Meadow Farm. This evening, though, when he'd gone down to the Dunderwick Arms for a half-pint before going to bed and heard the story that was the talk of the pub, he'd known he wouldn't rest until he was sure Sally was all right. It might be wildly exaggerated, of course, stories always were when they were passed along from mouth to mouth, but there was bound to be some truth in it. Perhaps it was the reason Lord Melbrook had pushed his way through the herd of cows when he'd been bringing them in for milking. He had certainly been in a rush to get somewhere fast. Whatever, David was convinced something very bad had happened, and he

425

could think of nothing but Sally, caught up in the middle of it all. Nervous of her reaction as he was, he just had to see her.

'She's all right,' Carina replied, blocking the doorway.

'Could you tell her I'm here?'

'I don't think she's up to seeing you or anyone just now,' Carina said firmly.

'Is that David, Carina?' Sally called. Her voice was still hoarse, and probably would be for days.

'Yes,' Carina said over her shoulder.

'Let him come in.'

Carina frowned. 'Sally, you're in no fit state . . .'

'But I'd like to see him.'

She'd treated him badly, she knew. She'd thrown him over with no thought for his feelings. And all for a murderer. A rapist. God knew what else. Suddenly she very much wanted to be in the presence of a good man, a man who would do anything for anyone, who wouldn't harm a fly. It seemed very necessary to her somehow, as if just by being here for a while he could expunge the taint of evil that Frank had left behind.

'Are you sure?' Carina was still doubtful.

'Quite sure.'

Carina stood aside, letting David into the kitchen. Then she went upstairs. Best to leave them to it, and she wasn't far away if Sally became upset again. But she was actually quite pleased that David was here. It gave her the chance to be with her children, which was really all she wanted.

Mattie was fast asleep, his favourite soft toy resting under his chin. She smoothed his hair away from his face and dropped a kiss on his head. Then she went to Meg's bed.

Thankfully, she was asleep too; the bad dreams hadn't come yet to disturb her. But Carina settled down on the floor beside her bed anyway. In the soft glow of the lamp she had left burning in case Meg woke, frightened, her daughter looked very young again, almost a baby, her soft skin peachy, lips pursed and slightly parted like the unfurling petals of a tiny rosebud. Carina's heart filled with love. Too often she favoured Mattie over Meg, she knew, and it was very wrong of her. Meg was her baby too; just because she was older than Mattie and more of a problem sometimes didn't mean she should be relegated to second place. And when the chips were down, Carina had realised she loved both of them equally. To have lost Meg would have been every bit as terrible as losing Mattie. She vowed that in future she would make more time for Meg, be less impatient with her.

They were safe now, both of them, and the gratitude she felt for that was overwhelming.

She glanced towards the window. From here, all she could see was the sky, clear now, with a myriad of stars tiny pinpoints of brightness against the velvety blackness. And one star, bigger, shining more brightly than all the rest. Carina felt her eyes drawn to it, and at the same time she was overwhelmed by the same feeling of peace and wonder that she had felt that day in the churchyard, kneeling beside Robert's grave. It was as if the star was a sign from him.

'You look after the children,' she said wonderingly. 'You look after all of us.'

At that moment, she felt his presence as surely as she ever had done during his life.

How long Carina sat there, she didn't know. She must have dozed, because when she came to, she could no longer hear the murmur of voices downstairs. She got to her feet, stumbling slightly, partly because her ankle was still troubling her and partly because her feet had gone to sleep and now felt like pincushions at the end of her legs. She wriggled them to bring them back to life and went down, holding tightly to the banister.

Sally was alone, still sitting in Grandpa Luke's chair, but no longer crying.

'Has David gone?' Carina asked unnecessarily.

'Yes. But he's coming back tomorrow to give us a hand with the farm work. He is such a nice boy, Carina. I don't know how he could be so nice to me when I've treated him so badly.'

'Because he thinks the world of you, Sally.' Carina collected the glasses they had used for the brandy and stacked them on the cupboard beside the sink. She wasn't going to bother with washing up tonight. 'Would you like a cup of warm milk?'

'No thanks. I think I'll just go to bed.'

'Warm milk would help you sleep. You go on and I'll bring some up to you.'

'Perhaps you're right. Thanks.'

Carina watched anxiously as Sally climbed the stairs, but she managed them on her own. She set a pan of milk to warm, got out two cups. She'd make a warm milk for herself, too. Though she couldn't help wishing they hadn't finished the brandy . . .

Just as well, she chided herself. What would Robert say? And for some reason, the thought made her smile.

She took the milk up to Sally, who was propped up against her pillows waiting for it.

'Try to get some sleep,' she said, putting the cup down on the table beside Sally's bed. 'Nothing will seem quite so bad in the morning.'

Sally didn't reply.

Carina went back downstairs and settled in Grandpa's chair with her own cup of milk, but she soon realised just how edgy she was, jumping at the slightest imagined sound. She'd thought sitting with the children had calmed her; now she wasn't so sure. There's nothing to be afraid of, she told herself, but it didn't seem to help. A branch tapping against the window, the creak of a timber as the old house settled, the rustle of the rising wind in the chimney, all perfectly normal everyday sounds, set her nerves on edge. But for all that, the warm milk and the brandy she'd had earlier were making her drowsy, exhaustion creeping up on her once more, and eventually she dozed, her head tucked into the comfortable wing of the old chair.

A rap at the door, swiftly followed by the click of the latch, brought her wide awake and trembling. She half started to her feet, but before she could reach the door, it was opening and the figure of a man was silhouetted against the fitful moonlight. Carina froze. In that split second, her only thought was that somehow Frank had escaped again and was coming to get them.

'Carina?'

Not Frank. It was Cal.

'Oh – you frightened me!' she gasped. Her heart was still beating too fast and she wanted to cry with relief.

'I'm sorry. But I knocked several times and you didn't answer. Really, though, you shouldn't leave the door unlocked.'

'I wouldn't have if I'd known. I thought Sally would have locked it after David left . . .' In the light of the nervousness she'd been feeling, she couldn't understand why she hadn't checked. But there it was. She hadn't. And now, although it was only Cal who had come in uninvited, she was upset all over again.

'I didn't expect you to come back,' she said, feeling foolish and trying to hide it.

'I was worried about you. I didn't like to think of you here alone after the day you've had.'

'I'm all right.'

'You don't look it. I think what you could do with is a drop more of that brandy.'

She gave a small apologetic laugh.

'It's all gone, I'm afraid. Sally and I finished it earlier.'

Cal raised an eyebrow.

'In that case it's a good thing I came prepared.' He pulled a small silver hip flask out of his pocket.

'Oh Cal, I mustn't. I've had too much already.'

'A drop more won't hurt you. Where is it you keep the glasses? In the sideboard if I'm not mistaken.' He crossed to the chiffonier as he spoke, opened it and pulled out a liqueur glass. 'This won't hold more than a couple of sips.'

He poured some amber liquid from the hip flask into it and handed it to her.

'Now sit down before you fall down.'

Carina did as she was told, taking one of the dining chairs, sniffing her glass and taking a tiny sip. Then she wrinkled her nose.

'This tastes different. Nicer.' She sipped again.

'That's because it's not brandy, it's whisky. Which is why I've only given you a snifter. If you mix your drinks, you're liable to have a sore head in the morning.'

'Oh, I can't have that . . .'

'After all you've been through today, I think a bit of a headache is a risk worth taking.'

He emptied the hip flask into another glass and sat down just around the corner of the table from her.

'Is there any news of Frank?' she asked, taking another small sip.

'I couldn't say. I took Isobel home and came straight back here.'

'Sally's worried that she's killed him.'

'If she has, it's no more than he deserved.'

'No, but . . .'

'I know. It's not a good feeling to have ended someone's life, even if they are the enemy.' There was something in his tone that made Carina glance at him sharply, and the look in his eyes told her that momentarily he was in another time, another place. His days fighting in the Boer War, she guessed. What was it Isobel had said? *He's a strong man, and as with all strong men, he hides his feelings. But let me assure you, they run very deep. He's far more vulnerable than you might imagine.* She had been talking about his feelings for Carina, of course, but it didn't stop there. Concealed beneath his seemingly impregnable shell, Cal hid other emotions too.

His reverie lasted only a moment, however.

'Carina, there's something I have to tell you. Something I should have told you a long time ago.'

She gazed at him, puzzled and somewhat apprehensive, and he went on:

'I expect you've been wondering why Frank killed your husband if they had been boyhood friends.'

'Because he knew Robert would never harbour an escaped convict, I assume.'

'The fact of the matter is that he and Robert didn't know one another at all.'

'But . . . You've known that all along?'

'No, no. That part I've only learned since Isobel recognised Frank as Francis Turnbull. It's something she told me some time ago that I should have shared with you. And Sally. Though I think you should be the one to break it to her.'

'What?' Carina was now totally confused.

'Her father isn't dead, as she always believed. He is serving life imprisonment for killing her mother while in a drunken rage. How he escaped the hangman's noose, I don't know, but he did. He and Frank shared a cell – that's how Frank came to know about the farm, why he turned up here when he escaped from prison. Joel Talbot is still alive, and not more than twenty miles from here.'

To begin with, Carina could scarcely comprehend what Cal was telling her. Scarcely believe that Grandpa Luke had kept something like this a secret all these years. And Robert was just as bad. Though Sally had been just a little girl, Robert would have been old enough to know the truth about what had happened, but he had kept up the pretence that both his parents were dead. How could he have lived with a secret like that?

And yet the more she thought about it, the more sense it made. It explained his violent aversion to strong drink, and Grandpa Luke's reaction when Robert lost his temper. It explained why Robert would never talk about what had happened to his parents. Perhaps if it hadn't been for Sally, he would have confided in her, but he had been intent on keeping the truth from his sister. He'd wanted to protect her, she supposed, and in a way Carina could understand that. But he should have told her, all the same, helped her to come to terms with it. Now it would come as a devastating shock. Just something else to shake Sally's world to its foundations.

'That's just awful,' she said in a small voice.

'Isobel says that Joel isn't a bad man,' he said, as if it would somehow soften the blow. 'He lost his temper, it seems, when the drink was in him. Since he's been in prison, he's a reformed character. In fact, she had been thinking about recommending him to the parole board for release. She doesn't believe he's a danger to anyone any more.'

'Well that's something, I suppose . . .' Carina took another sip of the whisky, feeling guilty now that she knew that alcohol had been behind all the problems and tragedies of the Talbot family. 'I don't think Sally is in a fit state at the moment, but when she is, I'll break it to her.'

'I was hoping you'd say that. It would come much better from you, I think.'

'Oh Cal . . .' She set down her glass and covered her face with her hands. 'When is all this going to end?'

'Right now. It's a fresh start from tomorrow onwards.'

He reached across, covering her hands with his.

'Carina . . . am I forgiven?'

'Oh, don't be so silly!' She laughed, lowering her hands, but he did not release them. 'Cal, I am so sorry for the awful things I said to you the other day. I don't know what got into me.'

'Forget it. As long as you aren't still thinking that all I wanted was to get my hands on your farm . . . Mattie's farm.'

'Of course not. After what you did today . . .'

'Would you think it again if I asked you to marry me?'

'Oh!' Carina was completely taken aback. 'Why would you do that?'

'Because you need taking care of. Because . . . well, because I love you, I suppose.'

'Oh!' she said again. Anything else was beyond her.

'I know it's probably far too soon. You're still mourning Robert. I understand that. But I'd like to think that one day . . .'

Really, it was not something that needed any thought at all.

'Of course I'll marry you, Cal.'

'Good.' His eyes met hers, not teasing now, but full of love. 'You know, after Alice, I never thought I'd feel this way again about anyone. You've given me something I thought was lost for ever. I hope I can do the same for you.'

'You already have.' A thought struck her. 'But what will everyone say? What about your mother? I'm no lady . . .'

'I couldn't give a damn what anyone says. And you are a lady. Don't ever think you're not. Come here.'

He got up, pulled her into his embrace and kissed her. As their lips met, the now familiar thrill ran through Carina. She could scarcely believe this was happening. That she could be so lucky.

'Do you want me to stay with you tonight?' he asked.

Carina thought of how scared she had been down here alone with the boards creaking and the branches tapping the windows.

She nodded.

'I'd like that, but . . .'

'Don't worry. I'll sleep down here in the chair. It won't be the first time. And if anyone tries to break in, they'll have me to reckon with.'

He kissed her again, and Carina melted into his arms. She felt so safe, so happy . . .

'Thank you, Cal – for everything,' she murmured against his mouth.

'Carina,' he replied, 'the pleasure is all mine.'

Chapter Thirty-One

Carina must have been exhausted; she dropped off the moment her head touched the pillow. But long before dawn she was awake again, her thoughts spinning, and she knew further sleep would be impossible. For a long while she lay turning over everything that had happened the previous momentous day, both the terrible and the wonderful. She trembled at how close she had come to losing Meg; she went cold with horror to think of what Sally had been through; she glowed with warmth at the thought of Cal sleeping downstairs to keep them all safe.

He loved her. Unbelievable as it was, he loved her. Had even asked her to marry him. That thought set off another torrent of conflicting emotions, the joy tempered by a guilt that still niggled at her – that she was betraying Robert. How could she feel this way about someone else so soon? Would people think she hadn't loved him? And would it ever be any different? However many years passed, would she still feel that she was denigrating his memory by falling in love with – marrying! – someone else?

And then there were the countless dilemmas. When and how to tell Sally that her father was not dead as she had been led to believe, but alive and in jail? What would happen to the farm – Mattie's inheritance – if she married Cal? How would Sally manage if she was no longer there? And more questions. Had Frank survived? Would she ever get back the ring he had stolen from her?

In all the confusion, she seemed unable to make a decision about the most ordinary things, torn between longing to get up, go downstairs and be with Cal again, and feeling she shouldn't disturb him so early.

In the end, she could resist the impulse no longer. She got up and dressed, shivering in the sharp cold of the autumn morning, but still too shy to let him see her in her dressing gown. Then she crept down the stairs as quietly as she could in case he was still asleep. Pale pearly light had crept into the kitchen; by it she could see his blanket-covered form folded into Grandpa's chair, his leg propped up on a stool, and a tide of warmth and tenderness filled her.

She was about to tiptoe away again when he spoke.

'Carina?'

'Sorry. Did I disturb you?'

'No. I think I was already awake.' He patted the blanket. 'Come here.'

He took her hand, pulling her down onto his lap and kissing her. The morning smell of him was erotic – warmth and sleep – and his mouth tasted faintly of whisky. The feeling of desire that was now beginning to feel familiar to her tickled deep inside. She wanted to remain here for ever, safe in his embrace, with all the problems that troubled her a distant bad dream. But she had reckoned without Meg.

'Mammy?' She was standing in the doorway, her thumb tucked into her mouth, one of her rag dolls under her arm. 'What are you doing?'

Embarrassed, Carina began struggling to her feet. Cal, as usual, was unfazed.

'We're saying good morning. Do you want to come and say good morning too?'

Meg ran to them, trying to climb onto Cal's other knee, and he pulled her up into a bear hug that included all of them. After a few moments she wriggled, and Carina set her down on the floor and got up herself.

'Time for breakfast, I think.'

'Mattie was awake just now, but he's gone back to sleep,' Meg said.

'We'll leave him for a bit, then.'

Carina busied herself making enough porridge for both children, all the while keeping a sharp ear out for anything that would indicate Mattie was awake again. She didn't want him coming down the stairs on his own.

'I expect you'd like a cup of tea,' she said to Cal, who had folded the blanket and was washing his face at the kitchen sink.

'I would, but then I have to go.'

'So soon?'

''Fraid so. Duty calls.'

Carina bit her lip. There were so many things she wanted to talk to him about.

As if reading her mind, he said: 'I'll come back later. We can talk then.'

Carina heard signs of life from upstairs; she wasn't sure if it was Sally or Mattie – she'd have expected Sally to need to sleep late after her ordeal. But it was her sister-in-law who appeared, fully dressed.

'You should be resting,' Carina chided her.

'The cows have to be milked,' Sally said. 'Don't fuss, Carina, I'm fine.'

She didn't look fine; she was still very pale and a bit shaky, but Carina knew it was useless to argue.

As soon as he'd finished his cup of tea, Cal kissed her and left. He had made no mention of his proposal, and Carina wondered if he'd thought better of it. Logically, it would only be sensible, but the thought made an empty space yawn inside her all the same.

And then she heard Mattie gurgling and a thud as he climbed out of his cot, and she ran upstairs to fetch him. The day had begun and there was no more time for fretting and wondering.

Sally was still out in the milking shed when David arrived, his face flushed from the bitter wind that had sprung up, his eyes anxious.

'She shouldn't be working today,' he said when Carina told him.

'I said exactly the same,' Carina agreed. 'But she wouldn't listen to me. Perhaps you can make her see sense.'

'I can try,' David said doubtfully.

He must have had more success than either of them expected, for a few minutes later Sally came in.

'David's finishing up for me,' she said.

She was deathly pale, and went to sit down in Grandpa Luke's chair, her arms wrapped around herself, and occasionally rubbing her stomach.

'I think we ought to get the doctor to have a look at you,' Carina said anxiously as she poured her a cup of hot sweet tea.

But Sally would have none of it.

'We can't afford doctor's bills. I'll be fine.'

'Just sit and rest, then. If you so much as move from that chair, I'm sending for the doctor, and no arguments.'

'I don't suppose there's any news about Frank?' Sally asked, pulling the rug Cal had used over her knees and up to her waist.

'No. Cal said he'd come back later, so we might learn something then.'

'He's been a knight in shining armour, hasn't he?' Sally said. 'Who'd have thought it?' Her lips twisted into a small, bitter smile. 'I have to say, your taste in men is far better than mine.'

Carina hesitated, unsure how to respond. In some ways it was an ideal opportunity to tell Sally that he had asked her to marry him, but really she didn't think it was the right moment. It would only emphasise the fact that Sally's own dreams were in tatters, and raise the questions about her future that were worrying Carina. Besides which, she wasn't at all sure that Cal hadn't had second thoughts, and might have decided he'd spoken too hastily.

'I don't know what would have happened if it hadn't been for him,' she said. 'But Sally, if Frank should die, you mustn't think it's your fault. You were only trying to protect Meg when you shot him. And it's not as if you put a bullet in his heart. It was only in the arm. If he hadn't taken the Rover, we could have got medical attention for him. He has no one but himself to blame.'

Sally nodded. 'You're right, I know. I should never have allowed myself to be taken in by him. But as I said before, I couldn't think ill of him. He was all I had . . .'

Again Carina hesitated. Was Sally in a fit state to learn what Cal had told her last night? Perhaps it would go some way to easing her pain and loneliness if she knew the truth . . .

She pulled up one of the dining chairs, sat in it and took her sister-in-law's hand.

'There's something I have to tell you, Sally. Something I've only just found out myself. You're not alone.'

'I know. I have you and the children . . .'

'Not just us. Sally . . .' She chewed her lip, almost afraid to

439

speak the words. 'You remember how you said you wished Robert had told you what had happened to your parents?'

'Yes.' Sally seemed to be holding her breath.

'Well, I can tell you now.'

'But . . .' Sally looked confused. 'You said Robert had never told you either.'

'He didn't.'

'Then how . . . ?'

'I'll explain. But let me do this in my own way. You already know most of what happened – you worked it out for yourself. Your mother did die as a result of a terrible fight when your father came home drunk one night. But he didn't kill himself afterwards when he realised what he'd done, and certainly Robert didn't kill him either. Sally . . .' She leaned forward, looking directly into her sister-in-law's troubled eyes. 'Your father isn't dead. He's in prison, serving a life sentence for manslaughter.'

Sally stared at her, stunned. Then as Carina's words sank in, she shook her head.

'No. That can't be true. Why would they say he was dead if he wasn't? Not only Grandpa Luke and Robert, but Grandma too . . .'

'I can't answer that,' Carina said. 'Perhaps it was because they were ashamed. Certainly Grandpa Luke hated him for what he'd done to his daughter. And I expect they were trying to protect you.'

'But . . . where did you get this from. Is it just gossip? You know what folk round here are like . . . They get hold of half a story and twist it . . .'

'No, nothing like that. It came from Mrs Luckington. Isobel. She's a prison visitor – one of the good works she took on after her husband died. She realised that the Joel Talbot she knew was my father-in-law, and told Cal.'

'You mean . . . you've known this and kept it from me?'

'I've only just found out myself.' Carina was uncertain whether she should go on and tell Sally the whole story. But she decided she must. Better to have it all out in the open. 'Isobel also recognised Frank as an escaped prisoner who used to share a cell with Joel. And that, I'm afraid, is why he tried to make a run for it. When he saw her, he must have realised the game was up.'

'You mean it was because of Daddy that he came here? Killed Robert?' Sally asked, horrified.

'It wasn't your father's fault,' Carina reassured her with more certainty than she was feeling. 'I think it's some time since he and Frank shared a cell. But when they did, he must have talked about the farm – and you and Robert. Which only goes to show he still cares about you. And incidentally, Isobel says that he is a reformed character these days. It was the drink that caused him to behave the way he did. Now . . . well, I don't suppose he's had any for years.'

'I just can't take this in . . .' Sally pulled the blanket more tightly around her, staring into space over Carina's shoulder. 'Daddy is alive. He's been alive all this time . . .'

'I'm sorry to give you such a shock,' Carina said. 'But I thought . . .'

'It is a shock, yes, but . . . it's a miracle, Carina. My daddy is alive!' She said it wonderingly. Her eyes fastened suddenly on Carina's, bright and sparkling now. 'Will I be able to go and see him?'

'Oh Sally, I don't know . . . Aren't you rather putting the cart before the horse?'

'But if Mrs Luckington can see him, surely I can. His own daughter!'

'I expect you could. But are you sure that would be wise?' Carina said, feeling terribly out of her depth.

441

'Well of course I want to see him!' Sally retorted. 'Wouldn't you want to if it was your daddy. I loved him, Carina. Oh, he might have done a bad thing, but I'm sure he never meant for it to happen. He must have suffered dreadfully all these years. And not one of his family ever visiting him.'

'I suppose that's true,' Carina said doubtfully. Sally's reaction had taken her completely by surprise. And yet was it really so surprising? Sally had long ago worked out that her father had been responsible for her mother's death, and must have worked through her feelings for him too. Somewhere along the line she had come to terms with it and chosen to forgive him. Now the only thing that mattered was that he had been miraculously returned to her, her own flesh and blood, the father who had never been anything but kind and loving towards her.

'Would you come with me?' Sally asked, gripping Carina's hand tightly.

'Well, yes . . . I suppose so. If that's what you want . . .'

'It is. I can't believe it. I really can't . . .'

A knock at the back door. Carina got up and went to answer it. It was David, standing there awkwardly, twisting his cap between his hands.

'Right. I've finished with the cows. Is there anything else I can do?'

'Oh David . . . if you can spare the time . . . But don't stand there on the doorstep. Come in and have a cup of tea. The pot's keeping warm on the hob.'

'Yes, come in, David!' Sally called. Her voice was bright and excited.

'You seem better,' David said, coming into the kitchen.

'I am. I've just had news that's better than any tonic. You'll never believe it . . .'

The words were tumbling out now, one on the other, as she related what Carina had told her.

'I want to go and see him as soon as I can,' she finished. 'I can hardly wait!'

David, who had been looking bemused, frowned, his reaction to the suggestion much as Carina's had been.

'In prison, you mean. They're blooming hellholes. No place for a girl.'

'I don't care. We'll find out from Mrs Luckington what I have to do. And then I'm going. So don't either of you try to stop me.'

'Well . . . if your mind's made up . . . But I'll go with you, Sal – if you want me to, that is. I wouldn't want to think of you in a place like that without somebody to look after you.'

Carina was half expecting Sally to say it was all right, that Carina was going to accompany her. But to her surprise, she did not.

'All right,' she said. 'I'd like that.'

Busying herself with the chores, Carina couldn't help smiling to herself. Perhaps at long last Sally was beginning to appreciate David. As long as his father could spare him, there were all kinds of things that needed to be done on the farm. With Frank gone and Sally out of action, she could find plenty that would keep him around for a while yet. And with any luck, it would bring him and Sally closer together.

Carina hoped with all her heart that that would be the case.

Evening. The children were in bed and Sally had gone to her room too, needing to rest after her traumatic experiences of yesterday and the excitement that today had brought. But Cal had not returned, and Carina was beginning to think he wasn't going to when she heard the sound of a motor engine – unmistakably the roar of the Benz – in the yard outside. Her heart leapt and her pulse raced as she hurried to open the door.

'I thought you weren't coming.'

'It's been a busy day.' He kissed her, a quick, light kiss that left her yearning for more. 'How have things been here?'

'Oh, you know . . . Sally seems a lot better, thank goodness. She's been very anxious to find out how Frank is . . . Do you know?'

'There was no change when I was at the hospital this morning. He was still unconscious and he's lost a lot of blood.'

'You think he may still die?'

'Very possibly.'

'Well, I hope I've convinced Sally that it won't be her fault if he does. And I've told her about her father. I was afraid it might upset her, but quite the opposite. She's happy and excited, and . . . For goodness' sake, sit down. Would you like something to drink?'

He reached into his pocket for the hip flask, giving her a sideways smile.

'I came prepared. I don't suppose you've had a chance to restock.'

'No, and I won't be. I don't want to get a taste for it. You can have your whisky if that's what you want, but I'm sticking to a cup of tea.'

'Don't worry, Carina, I won't try to tempt you into bad habits unless I think you need it.'

'You shouldn't drink so much either.' She couldn't believe she'd said that.

'Perhaps I won't need to now.' He smiled again, this time directly into her eyes, and her heart gave another flip. Could he possibly mean *now that I've got you*? She longed to ask, but did not dare.

'So. Finish telling me about Sally,' he said, sitting down on one of the dining chairs, the hip flask untouched on the table in front of him.

Carina did so, taking a chair across the corner of the table from him.

'She wants to visit him in prison,' she finished. 'We wondered if Mrs Luckington might be able to tell us how we can arrange that.'

'She could, I'm sure. But wait until Sally's recovered properly from her ordeal. It won't be a pleasant experience.'

'I told her that. But at least she won't be going alone. David Perkins has offered to go with her. He's turning out to be a real trump. He's been here all day working on the farm, and he's promised to come back tomorrow.'

'Has he now.' Cal fingered the flask thoughtfully. 'I presume at the moment that's just a neighbourly arrangement?' Carina nodded. 'Would he be interested in a permanent position, do you think?'

'Oh, I don't know . . .'

'If he was, he could well be the answer to all your problems,' Cal said. 'I've been very impressed by the way High Combe is run, and young David will have learned well from his father. As a trustee of the estate, I could arrange for him to be paid a proper wage, and later he could be installed as manager.'

Later. Again that oblique reference to the future. A future when she might no longer be living at Meadow Farm . . .

'I'll speak to him,' Cal went on. 'Find out how the land lies. And of course you must discuss it with Sally. I'm presuming she would want to continue living here.'

'Where else would she live? But she and David were good

445

friends before Frank came on the scene, and I'm pretty sure she'd be happy with that.'

'Good. Right. So do you want to know what I've been doing today?' He raised a teasing eyebrow.

'Well . . . yes . . .'

'To begin with, I've been trying to sort out your Rover. It's in pretty bad shape, I'm afraid. In fact I doubt whether it can be repaired. So I've taken the liberty of looking for a replacement for you. I've found a nice little Austin for sale in Bath and put down a deposit. I've asked them to keep it until I can take you to see it. Which should probably be as soon as possible, since you will be pretty stuck out here with no transport.'

'I suppose I would be, yes,' Carina agreed. Somehow, with all the other problems chasing around in her head, she hadn't stopped to wonder how she was going to manage if the Rover was damaged beyond repair. 'But I don't know how I'm going to be able to afford—'

'Let me worry about that,' Cal said. 'And now to more important things.'

He stood up, pulled her to her feet so that she was facing him, and took something from his pocket.

'Your ring. It was found on Frank when he was admitted to hospital.'

'Oh – I thought I'd never see it again . . .'

'Where have I heard that before? I'm beginning to wonder just how many times I'm going to have to rescue it for you. You'd better put it on before it gets lost yet again.'

'Thank you, Cal.' She took it and slipped it onto her ring finger, and Cal's hand closed over hers.

'Just wait a minute, Carina.'

He delved into his pocket again, this time producing a small padded box.

'Is there room for this one too?'

He flipped the box open. Inside, on a bed of velvet, a huge sapphire surrounded by tiny diamonds winked and sparkled in the light of the oil lamp.

'Oh!' Carina was speechless.

'You did agree to marry me, didn't you?' Cal said. 'If not, this will have to go back to the shop.'

'Oh Cal!' Carina couldn't tear her eyes away from the ring. It had probably cost more than the sum total of all her worldly possessions, more than she had ever dreamed of. But it wasn't the monetary value that was important. It was the fact that Cal had chosen it for her. The fact that he really had been serious when he had asked her to marry him.

Tears sparkled in her eyes, rivalling the sparkle of the diamonds.

Cal was holding the ring poised over her finger. But suddenly Carina knew what she had to do. Slowly, with the tears spilling now onto her cheeks, she slipped Robert's ring back over her knuckle. Perhaps Cal's sapphire would have fitted above the slim row of tiny diamonds. But that didn't feel right. She would treasure that ring for ever, just as she would always love Robert. But this was a time for new beginnings. Carefully, deliberately, she placed Robert's ring on the third finger of her right hand. The left now belonged to Cal.

'Carina . . . you don't have to . . .'

'Yes, Cal, I do,' she said.

'Then you haven't changed your mind about marrying me?'

'No, though I thought you'd changed yours about asking.'

'No chance of that.'

His arms went around her, pulling her close, and his mouth sought hers. This time his kiss was all she could have wished for and more, deep, searching, setting her on fire with the longing that had sparked the very first time his hand had touched hers and which was now flaring into a blazing inferno. Her left hand lay against his shoulder, the sapphire still catching the light; the sight of it there on her finger only intensified the desire that was consuming her. She was his. She wanted to be his more than anything in the world.

Instinctively she pressed her hips to his, delighting in the feel of the lean maleness, the hard strength of him, lost in the pleasurable sensations that shivered inside her like a bow playing on taut violin strings. Unnoticed, her shawl slipped from her shoulders to the floor as they kissed, one long shadow now against the whitewashed kitchen wall instead of two. Her hair was coming loose from its combs; with a swift tug he pulled them out so that it flowed down her back in a shining curtain, and the moment's sharp pain as he did so somehow only intensified the intoxicating pleasure she was experiencing.

All the guilt that had plagued her was forgotten now; all worries and fear and stress melted away. She was conscious of nothing but his nearness and the magic they made together.

One hand moved to her small, firm bottom, holding her close, while the other was on her breast, squeezing, exploring, feeling for the buttons of her dress. She arched her back, throwing back her head, and felt his mouth moist on her throat, pressing against the tender skin, biting gently.

'Oh Cal,' she moaned, 'I want you so!'

He drew back, and a sudden sense of loss panicked her. But he held her still, looking down into her face, his eyes mirroring her desire, but his expression intense and serious.

'Are you sure, Carina?'

For reply, she nodded, slipping her hands around his hard muscled back and pressing close to him again.

'I'm sure.'

It was all he was waiting for. Before she knew it, his hands had gone behind her knees, lifting her off her feet and carrying her to the rag rug in front of the fire. He set her down carefully, kneeling beside her. By the glow of the dying embers, she caught sight of another scar as he undressed, this one running from shoulder blade to breast bone, and it stirred tenderness in her alongside the raging desire.

And then she was in his arms again, skin to skin, and there was no more time for thinking.

Afterwards, as they lay in one another's arms, partially covered by her shawl, which Cal had reached for, Carina thought she had never known such bliss. This was what she had instinctively known was missing from her lovemaking with Robert, these heights that she had never before climbed, this valley of complete contentment, this tide of love, satisfied, replete. All she wanted was to make the moment last forever. But of course she couldn't.

She stirred lazily as reality began to creep back in. Suppose Sally or one of the children should wake, come downstairs and find them here?

'I think we'd better . . .'

Cal raised himself on one elbow.

'You're worried we might be discovered?'

'Well . . . yes.'

'But you're not sorry?'

'No. No. I'm glad. But . . .'

'I know.' He got up, pulled her to her feet, kissed her as she buttoned her dress, tangled his fingers briefly in the fall of her hair.

'Leave it loose, Carina. It's beautiful like that.'

'It would get in the way dreadfully.'

'Not when we're in bed.'

The excitement shivered inside her again, not urgent now, but a thrill of anticipation.

'Do you want me to stay?' Cal asked.

'Better not,' she said regretfully.

'I could always sleep down here as I did before.'

'It wasn't very comfortable, was it? And I don't want Sally wondering . . . I want to tell her in my own time.'

'All right, my love.'

When he left, Carina watched the light from the headlamps of the Benz arc around the farmyard and run a narrow tunnel of light up the track. Then she went back inside, cleared up, and made herself a cup of warm milk. She drank it by the dying embers of the fire, reliving every wonderful moment of the last hours and relishing the warm glow that still seemed to suffuse her whole body.

Then, taking the small oil lamp, she went upstairs. First she looked in on Sally; she was sleeping soundly. Then up to the children's room. They too were both fast asleep, Meg cuddling one of her rag dolls, Mattie with a thumb thrust into his mouth. She smoothed the covers over them, very gently, so as not to disturb them, tiptoed out and went to her own room.

As she slipped between the sheets and lay back against the pillows, Carina thought that for the first time in a very long while it felt as if all was right with the world.

Epilogue

Eight months later

The churchyard was bathed in early morning sunshine. It glinted on the lettering of the newly erected gravestone before which Carina knelt, and sparkled in the droplets of water spilled on the granite kerb as she had filled the matching vase with wild flowers gathered this morning – cornflowers and poppies, corn marigolds and meadow sweet. It warmed the dew-wet grass so that the air was fragrant with an evocative fresh perfume and cast a long shadow from the tower of the centuries-old church.

She had come early so as not to have to rush this special pilgrimage. Later, the day would be filled with bustle and excitement; she needed this quiet time with Robert before the preparations began.

Her wedding day. Today she would marry Cal in the church in whose shadow Robert's grave lay. Today she would promise to love and to cherish until death did them part, just as she had promised Robert. The memory of her first wedding was as clear in her memory as it had ever been, and just as sweet. But death *had* parted them and now she was to move on to another chapter in her life. It was, she knew, what he would have wanted for her. But for all that, she had needed to let him know he was not forgotten, and never would be. That his memory was cherished by both her and the children.

'Is Cal going to be our new daddy?' Meg had asked when she had told her what they were planning.

And Carina had replied: 'He'll be there to love you and care for you. And I think he would like it if you called him Papa. But your daddy will always be the one who had to go to heaven with the angels. Nothing will ever change that.'

Meg had nodded solemnly before becoming excited again about the prospect of spending more time with 'her' puppy, Cinders, and living in a house where oranges grew on trees. And if she did but know it, she would soon have a baby brother or sister to play with too – Carina had decided not to tell the children yet.

Since Cal's proposal, the months had sped by, as momentous as the ones that had gone before, but happily in a good way.

David was now working regularly at Meadow Farm and Cal had installed him as manager. He and Sally seemed to be growing closer by the day, and he had accompanied her several times to see her father in prison. These occasions had, of course, been very emotional ones for her, but with David's help she had coped with them very well, and was hoping that now that Joel was a reformed character, the day would soon come when he would be released on parole. Carina was concerned by the prospect of the new problems this might throw up, but Cal had told her that if it did happen, they would deal with it, and she was content to put her trust in him. Besides, she didn't want anything to cast a shadow over her new-found happiness. Life had thrown so much at her in the past year, it was good to be able to take a breather from all the stress.

As for her misgivings about being suited to being the wife of the lord of the manor, they had, to a great extent, been allayed. Isobel Luckington had proved to be a wonderful friend, helping her to prepare for her new life. Though Carina still felt apprehensive as to whether she would live up to the role, it was no longer quite so daunting. She'd learned which cutlery to use at a meal, what words and terms were acceptable and what would be frowned upon as common, and even how to curtsey should the occasion arise. It would take a while for her to feel confident in the company of the gentry, but Cal merely smiled at her fears. 'All you have to do is be yourself, Carina, and everyone will love you just as I do,' he had said.

She only hoped he was right.

Her relatives were going to be out of their depth at the wedding, she knew, and it was the one thing she regretted. It was the reason Harry, her brother, had declined the invitation, she guessed, but Mam and Dad would be there. Isobel had promised to look after them, but she knew from experience that Isobel could be very daunting, and they would probably escape as soon as they reasonably could.

Aunt Hester was another matter entirely. Carina could imagine her fawning and simpering and staying on until the last possible moment, anxious to make the most of the opportunity to hobnob, as she would put it. Certainly she would want to have plenty of tales to take back to her neighbours in Fairley Terrace, and Carina hoped she wouldn't make a nuisance of herself.

'Don't worry!' Cal had said. 'It's not a big society wedding. Just my close family and a few friends. They are all glad to see me happily settled at last. And you need to relax and enjoy your day.'

'I will.'

Certainly she intended to enjoy it, but relaxing wasn't quite so easy. It had been strange last night knowing that this was the last time she would sleep in this room, in this bed, and sleep had not come easily. It was only when she decided that she would get up early in the morning and visit Robert's grave that she finally dropped off, and when she had woken, the resolve was as firm as ever.

She'd left a note for Sally on the kitchen table and walked to Dunderwick, gathering the dew-fresh flowers on the way. Filled the stone vase with water from the standpipe in the corner of the churchyard and arranged them. Knelt in the grass, though it soaked her skirt through at the knees, and talked to Robert.

I've done my best to keep my promise to you, my love, and it's made me very happy.

But please don't think I'll forget you. I won't, ever. I love you still. I'm starting a new chapter in my life, that's all . . .

She remembered suddenly the last time she had been here, the wonderful feeling of a burden lifted when she had talked to Robert, and how only minutes later, when she was walking home, Cal had come along and given her that first ride in his Benz. It was, she thought, almost as if Robert had had a hand in it. As if he was still taking care of her in the only way he now could. Helping her to keep her promise . . .

'Thank you, my darling,' she said aloud.

One of the cornflowers was at an angle, perhaps with its stem not properly in the water. Carina bent forward and rearranged it; she didn't want it wilting in the heat of the day.

Then she got to her feet, blew a lingering kiss to the name on the headstone, and turned, not away from Robert, but towards a new future.

The Widow's Promise

Bonus Material

Jennie Felton reveals her favourite . . .

Book . . . *Gone With the Wind* by Margaret Mitchell.

Film . . . *Crocodile Dundee*. A real feel-good film I can watch time and again.

Food . . . Roast beef and Yorkshire pudding!

Drink . . . Prosecco. I can always find a reason for celebrating!

Place . . . In this country, I have many happy memories of holidays spent with Terry and our two daughters at Mullion Cove, Cornwall. Abroad, I fell in love with Hong Kong when Terry and I went there to research for my Janet Tanner book *Oriental Hotel*. The Star Ferry, Victoria Peak, Stanley Market . . . loved every minute, especially visiting the War Cemetery – very moving.

Season . . . Spring. I love April, May and June, when everything is bursting back to life.

TV Programme . . . I like good police/courtroom dramas.

Song . . . 'The Last Night of the World' from *Miss Saigon* – which is also my favourite musical. I've seen it about four times, and would go again tomorrow, and the next night, and the next . . .

Possession . . . A Carnegie Hero Fund Award certificate presented to my father for saving the life of a fourteen-year-old boy who was drowning in strong currents. Sadly two men died in the attempt and one was forced back to shore, but my father – who had no life-saving training – brought the boy in by his hair.

Item of Clothing . . . A soft cream linen hat that has seen better days. I lost it once in Paris, got on a bus only to realise it had been on my lap while we waited, and forgotten. We got off the bus at the next stop, raced back along what seemed like miles of pavements, and there it was, where I had dropped it! Whew!

Colour . . . Green. I was never allowed it as a child as my mother was superstitious. When I proved that was nonsense by being forced to wear a green gown to visit my baby daughter seriously ill with meningitis, I made up for lost time, having as much green as I could.

Flower . . . Sweet peas. So pretty and delicate and the scent is gorgeous!

Perfume . . . For glam nights out – Lancôme's Trésor. For summer – Happy by Clinique.

Way to spend the day . . . With my children and grandchildren. Perhaps at Longleat, always a favourite. But when driving through the safari park we give the monkeys a miss since many years ago they tried ripping the beading off the window frames of our brand new Saab. Had to physically restrain Terry from getting out to try to chase them off!

Introducing the Families of Fairley Terrace...

The Withers at No. 10

Gilby and Florrie Withers are devastated to lose their beloved son Jack in the mining disaster. Luckily their other son Josh wasn't working at Shepton Fields. But will they be able to keep him close by when his feelings for his late brother's fiancée become too strong to ignore?

The Donovans at No. 6

When the hudge goes down, the Donovans lose their patriarch Paddy. With her elder brothers Ewart and Walter working away, it's up to daughter Maggie to help her mother Rose keep the roof over their heads and look after younger son Billy, whilst dealing with the loss of her fiancé Jack Withers too.

The Buttons at No. 5

Carina Button grew up at No. 5 Fairley Terrace with her parents Daisy and George and brother, Harry. But after the mining disaster, they move away to Wales, fearing the Fairley pits to be unsafe. Carina only returns to visit her mother's sister, Hester Dallimore, who lives at No. 9, as a young woman, but finds love with Robert Talbot which changes the course of her life completely . . .

The Days at No. 4

Twenty-eight-year-old Annie Day loses her loving husband John, leaving her two little girls, Kitty and Lucy, without their beloved father. Surely it's only a matter of time before they are turned out of Fairley Terrace – how will they survive?

The Oglethorpes at No. 3

Dolly and Ollie Oglethorpe are well known in the community, with Dolly serving as midwife for the Ten Houses. They are one of the lucky families as both Ollie and their son Charlie escape the disaster.

The Rogers at No. 2

Queenie and Harry are not so fortunate – they lose their young son Frank in the accident and things are never the same for them again.

The Coopers at No. 1

Edie Cooper and her family are blessed not to lose anyone in the mining disaster, but the repercussions of that day are to have a greater impact on Edie's future than she can imagine. A whole new world opens up to her when she takes a job at Fairley Hall, where she discovers both friends and foes amongst the staff and the Fairley family.

To find out more about the fates of the Families of Fairley Terrace, look out for all the other titles in Jennie Felton's enthralling series.

Keep reading for a sneak preview of the next book in Jennie's captivating Families of Fairley Terrace series

The Sister's Secret

Coming soon from Headline.

April, 1901

Rowan Sykes didn't know whether it was the loud knocking at the back door immediately below her bedroom window that woke her, or the raised voices. Or even if she'd been asleep at all. She'd lain awake feeling sorry for herself for so long after she'd said her prayers, and Mammy had tucked her in, drawn the curtains to shut out what remained of the daylight, and left the room, pulling the door almost closed behind her, that she really couldn't be sure. Everything seemed to have merged into one, sleeping, waking, a sort of muddled dream.

What she did know was that the day she'd been looking forward to for weeks was over, and nothing had gone the way she'd hoped. In fact, everything that could have gone wrong had done so. And it would be another whole year before it was time for South Compton Fair again.

The fair was very special, her teacher, Miss Yard, had told the class. Centuries ago, in 1249, King Henry III had granted the town a special charter to allow it to be held in the street. In those days it had been a livestock fair, when cows, sheep and even horses had been bought and sold, and a bit of that still went on early in the day. But in recent years, much to the delight of the local children, the afternoon and evening had been given over to things that were much more fun. There were sideshows and rides – shooting galleries, roundabouts and swings, and

465

stalls selling toffee apples, sugary sweets and cockles in twists of greaseproof paper. Rowan didn't care much for the cockles. Daddy always had a plate of them for tea on a Saturday when he came home from watching the football match, if South Compton had been playing at home, and they tasted mainly of the vinegar he sprinkled liberally on them. But she loved toffee apples – they were the best thing in the whole world.

Besides the smaller rides, there was also a switchback called the Noah's Ark that was set up in the town square. Rowan had never ridden on it – Mammy said she wasn't big enough. But she'd been hoping that this year she'd be allowed. After all, she was six now, and would be seven in November. At the thought, she had thrilled with anticipation and excitement.

This morning, however, to her utter dismay, she had woken to rain falling from a leaden sky.

'Not much like Fair weather,' Daddy had said, brushing the moisture from his shoulders when he came in from a trip to the privy on the opposite side of the track that ran along the back of Fairley Terrace.

'No, you can't go in this.' Mammy's lips were pinched into the tight line that was her usual expression. Mammy was not a smiley person, but Rowan thought nothing of it as she had never known her any different. 'Nobody with any sense would even think of it.'

'Oh, but . . .' Rowan wailed.

'It's early yet. It might brighten up later on.' Daddy winked at her, a conspiratorial wink. 'You know what they say – rain before seven, clear before eleven.'

'Old wives' tale,' Mammy muttered under her breath.

'Well, let's hope not. I want to get my runner beans in today. The trench is all dug and ready.' Daddy always planted the runner beans on South Compton Fair day.

'A couple of days won't make much difference. Come and eat your breakfast, Rowan, before it gets cold.'

When she'd finished her bacon, egg and fried potato, Rowan retuned to the window. It had misted up in the heat from the kitchen fire. She rubbed it clear with her sleeve. Nothing had changed; it was still raining, running in rivulets down the pane and making puddles on the track. She drew patterns with her finger in what remained of the steam and pretended she was casting a magic spell.

'Rain, rain, go away. Come again another day.'

By mid morning, she was hopeful the spell was working. The sky had lightened and the rain no longer pattered against the window.

'Mammy! It's stopping!'

'For goodness' sake, Rowan, come away from that window and find something to do!' Mammy snapped. 'You're not going to the fair if there's any chance it's going to start again. I've got enough washing to dry without adding your clothes to it.'

Mammy took in washing to help make ends meet, and when the weather was bad it had to hang on a line strung across the kitchen until there was room on the airer in front of the fire. A wet Monday was the worst. But Dr Blackmore's wife had had visitors and had sent a pile of bedlinen and towels when they had left yesterday.

Tears of disappointment pricked Rowan's eyes, but obedient as usual, she went up to her room and fetched a drawing book and pencils.

It wasn't fair! she thought as she spread everything out on the kitchen table. Unless the rain stopped completely, Mammy would never let her go. Daddy might say it would be all right, that they could dodge the showers, but in the end Mammy would have her way. She always did. Just to rub salt into the wound, she knew that Earl, her brother, would go this evening with his mates – Earl was seventeen and did as he pleased.

If Laurel was here, she'd find a way to take Rowan, whatever the weather. Laurel was her older sister, older even than Earl, and she had a way of twisting Mammy round her little finger. Rowan could never understand how she managed it, but was glad of it all the same. Laurel was her ally, standing up for her, telling her she was beautiful, even though the children in her class at school called her fat and ugly and laughed at the white ribbons Mammy tied in her hair. Laurel could make everything – well, almost everything – right, or at least a hundred times better. She would know how much Rowan wanted to go to the fair, and would have defied Mammy and taken her.

But Laurel wasn't here. She worked in Bath and had lodgings there, only coming home on her days off. Rowan missed her dreadfully.

Sometimes, just sometimes, she wondered about her other brother, Samuel, who was older than Earl but younger than Laurel. What would it be like if he lived nearby? Would he take her part as Laurel did? But really she scarcely knew Samuel. When the family had moved to Somerset, into number 5 Fairley Terrace, recently vacated by people who had gone off to South Wales, Rowan had been just a baby, while Samuel, at thirteen, was already working in the pits back in Yorkshire. He'd come with them initially, but he hadn't stayed long. The only job open to him was as a carting boy – on his hands and knees for pretty much the whole of his working day, dragging a putt of coal by a rope that ran around his waist and between his legs from the coal face to the passageways where the roof was high enough for ponies to take over the job. His skin had chafed until it bled, the dialect of the other boys and the colliers was unintelligible to him – as was his to them – and he missed his pals and the good times they had shared. Just a month he'd lasted. Then he'd gone back to Yorkshire, lodging with the family of one of his old friends. He didn't often visit, but when he did, Rowan swelled with pride at how handsome he was, and how big and strong, with eyes that twinkled just like Daddy's.

Miraculously, by dinner time the rain had stopped completely and there was enough blue in the sky to make a pair of sailor's trousers, as the saying went. Enough for Mammy to agree that Daddy and Rowan could go to the fair, though she herself would be staying at home trying to get Mrs Blackmore's sheets dried and ironed. The sun even showed itself as they headed along the road to town, Rowan holding Daddy's hand and skipping along beside him.

The fair spread out over all the roads leading to the square. They stopped at a roll-the-penny stall, where Rowan first won tuppence, then lost it along with the other threepence Daddy gave her. Daddy hustled her past a tent proclaiming 'Fivepence to see the Bearded Lady', but stopped to buy her a toffee apple and a twist of cockles for himself.

She was loving every moment, but still it was the switchback ride in the town square that attracted her most of all.

'Please, Daddy, can we go on it?' she begged.

They were on the opposite side of the street, heading for the children's roundabout, but Rowan was hanging back, tugging on Daddy's arm.

'Please! I really, really want to ride on that one.'

'The switchback? I don't know about that . . .'

But smiling at her enthusiasm, he let her lead him back to the edge of the small crowd gathered around the ride.

Cars shaped like animals with bars across the front of the seats and attached to a central spindle were whirling round an undulating track; music blared from a hurdy-gurdy but it couldn't quite muffle the screams of the laughing passengers. Quite a lot of the cars were empty; tonight, when the youth of the town – Earl included – came to the fair, there would be a scramble for places, perhaps even a fight when the pushing and shoving began.

Rowan tugged on her father's arm.

'Please! I could sit on your lap . . .'

'We'll see. Just let me eat these cockles. And you'd better finish your toffee apple. If you drop it down yourself your mam will have something to say about it.'

The ride was slowing. A swarthy young man with a mop of dark curls emerged from what she supposed was the control hub at the centre of the switchback, stepping on to the still-moving platform and swinging himself with easy grace between the occupied cars ready to release the bars and let the occupants out. Rowan stared, fascinated. He looked like a character from a storybook. The hero, of course . . . She only wished she could be so daring! She was even afraid to turn somersaults over the bar of the big iron roller that was used to flatten the football pitch. She wanted to do it – oh, how she wanted to! – but when she reached the head of the queue of children she absolutely couldn't. Launching herself off the metal drum was quite beyond her, and she'd be forced to give up, climb down again and slink away with the jeers and jibes of the others echoing in her ears.

'Scaredy cat!'

'Don't want us to see her bloomers.'

'Nor her fat arse.'

'Fatso scaredy cat!'

But she wouldn't be afraid to ride on the switchback. Not if she was on Daddy's lap, with his arms round her waist, holding her tight. Or tucked in beside him, her head against his chest. It would be so exciting.

Author photograph © Will Nicol

Jennie Felton grew up in Somerset, and now lives in Bristol. She has written numerous short stories for magazines as well as a number of novels under a pseudonym. Her Families of Fairley Terrace Sagas is her new series about the lives and loves of the residents of a Somerset village, beginning in the late nineteenth century, which started with *All The Dark Secrets*.

Stay in touch with Jennie!

Visit her on Facebook at
www.facebook.com/JennieFeltonAuthor
for her latest news.

Or follow her on Twitter @Jennie_Felton,
and join the #FamiliesofFairleyTerrace conversation!